He was going
to drown her!

"Please, I swear I won't fight you ever again!" she cried desperately.

Her words were drowned as he lunged into the next wave, taking her with him. She came up sputtering.

"Promise again," he gasped as he slicked his hair back from his brown forehead with a shove of one big hand. "It may keep me from beating you within an inch of your life."

"Promise?"

"To never fight me again—and add to that, 'No matter what you do to me, my absolute lord and master.'"

"You vile, wretched bas—" she gasped before he pulled her hard against him in the next glittering surge of emerald-and-diamond water.

"Say it!" he ordered, but his voice trembled with his own emotion. He kissed her hard just as the next wave hit.

Dear Reader:

Harlequin offers you historical romances with a difference: novels with all the passion and excitement of a five-hundred-page historical in three hundred pages, stories that focus on people—a hero and heroine you really care about, who take you back and make you part of their time.

This summer we'll be publishing books by some of your favorite authors. We have a new book by Bronwyn Williams entitled *Dandelion*. It continues the story of Kinnahauk and Bridget and their grandson, Cabel. Brooke Hastings makes her historical debut with *So Sweet a Sin*, a gripping story of passion and treachery in the years leading up to the American Revolution. *Seize the Fire* is an exciting new Western by Patricia Potter. Caryn Cameron's latest, *Silver Swords*, is an adventurous tale of piracy set in Florida in the early 1800s. You won't want to miss these or any of the other exciting selections coming soon from Harlequin Historicals.

We appreciate your comments and suggestions. Our goal is to publish the kinds of books you want to read. So please keep your letters coming. You can write to us at the address below.

Karen Solem
Editorial Director
Harlequin Historicals
P.O. Box 7372
Grand Central Station
New York, New York 10017

Silver Swords
Caryn Cameron

Harlequin Books

TORONTO • NEW YORK • LONDON
AMSTERDAM • PARIS • SYDNEY • HAMBURG
STOCKHOLM • ATHENS • TOKYO • MILAN

Harlequin Historical first edition August 1989

ISBN 0-373-28627-9

CARYN CAMERON

is a former high school and college English teacher who now writes full-time and is the author of best-selling historical romances under another name. She is a lifelong Ohioan who, with her husband, enjoys traveling and family genealogy. She also plays the piano and keeps in shape with Scottish Highland dancing.

Chapter One

Off the coast of Florida
May 9, 1821

Do not worry, my friend," Melanie said, as if by giving an assurance of safety she could comfort herself. She patted Jasmine's arm. "That ship is probably not even chasing us. It just seems that way because it's right behind us, that's all."

"Bah! It had better not be one of those pirate ships they're all buzzing about in New York, Miz Lanie. Not seeing as how I promised your parents I'd get you back home to New Orleans all safe and sound." Jasmine made a gesture of dismissal and thrust the stiff-ribbed parasol she had just fetched from their cabin at her mistress. "And that means covering your skin 'gainst this sun."

The wind yanked at the opened parasol so that Melanie had trouble controlling it, but together she and Jasmine steadied it against the buffeting. Silver-blond Melanie McVey and dusky-skinned Jasmine Bouchet, mistress and maidservant, so different in appearance they seemed like sunstruck day and exotic night, stood shoulder to shoulder at the stern rail of the merchantman *Bonne Femme*. The heavily laden vessel plowed through whitecapped water where the cobalt Atlantic merged with the azure, gilded Gulf of Mexico at the southern tip of the new state of Florida.

Behind them on deck all was hubbub. There were cries of "Lash cargo! Secure decks! Unidentified vessel off the stern!" and the sailors ran back and forth in response to orders.

As if to defy encroaching danger, Melanie tossed her curls in the cool whip of wind. Only moments before she had felt regret that her great travel adventure was almost over. She found herself half dreading returning home to her fiancé's arms and the looming gala wedding she had once desired. Ten weeks in New York City without her parents, although she had been well chaperoned by her aunt and the hovering Jasmine, had filled her with a heady sense of independence. Despite a handsome, wealthy and intriguing fiancé awaiting her in New Orleans, she was not certain she wanted to surrender that independence to anyone again—ever. And so she shook her head at Jasmine's suggestion that they go below.

"Bah!" Jasmine repeated. "Bad enough you all been getting your complexion all toasted up here with only that flapping bonnet brim 'tween you and that broiling sun. No self-respecting, well-born young lady, 'specially not one from a fine New Orleans sugar-cane plantation, going to let herself look like a lobster! But, *certainment*, that—" here Jasmine pointed a slender, stiff arm and accusing finger at the closing ship in their wide white wake "—might be a pirate ship, and you giving that no more heed than you do to keeping the pink off your nose! Your mama would fall into the declines if she heard all this."

"What mama doesn't know I hope will not hurt her—or you or me, *Beignet*," Lanie insisted pointedly, with a little squeeze of Jasmine's arm to punctuate the use of her pet name for her friend. *Beignets* were New Orleans sugared puffy confections, though Lanie was the only one who knew Jasmine had a tough, tart streak in her that hardly made that sobriquet suitable. "I just think it is rather stimulating to see a race between two ships," Lanie added, in another attempt at reassurance. "I'm sure they won't catch us. Besides, this ship of Justin's is much bigger if it comes to a little scuffle." But Lanie turned away again to squint in fascination at the sleek vessel, which seemed to lunge closer each moment.

"Then you come below to the cabin with me and right now," Jasmine protested in her most imperious voice, although she only dared to pluck at Lanie's sleeve. "Anyhow, this new gown from your nice trousseau's getting all damp with salt spray up here!"

But Jasmine knew better than to continue to plead when Lanie did not budge. They had been around and around a number of topics in their seven years as mistress and servant and best friends—although it was only Lanie's firm decision to marry Justin Lyon that had caused Jasmine real pain. Both were twenty-four years of age, though their early lives, like their looks, seemed miles apart. But Jasmine put great hope in the fact that she had witnessed a change in her Miss Lanie during this jaunt to New York.

Maybe, Jasmine thought, it had been because Miss Lanie had for the first time been away from her mama's helping hand and watchful eye. Maybe it had been the bracing sea air and sense of freedom out here on God's great open ocean—a freedom that even a slave girl could sense. More likely it was that the sheltered heiress had met liberal-thinking New Yorkers at banquets and balls. Jasmine had seen her choose her own friends and listen to new ideas on things like equality of all men that had swept the original New England colonies years ago and later America's great ally France in a bloody revolution. Why, Miss Lanie had even listened to folks talk about abolition of slavery itself.

True, Miss Lanie had always possessed the defiant streak that had culminated in her choosing her fiancé, Justin Lyon, over her father's wishes, and that decision had actually caused a rift between the wealthy New Orleans planter and his beloved only child. But still it seemed that Miss Lanie's strong, willful personality had just begun to bloom to full potential during the trip to New York.

Now Jasmine Bouchet could only hope and pray for one thing—that her Miss Lanie's new maturity would cause her to see her rich, powerful fiancé, who owned people's very souls just the way he owned this ship, for what he really was.

And then maybe she would wake up before it was too late to save herself. Because otherwise Jasmine had no hope for Miss Lanie's future, or her own.

"Captain Tambourd!" Melanie interrupted Jasmine's fervent thoughts and waved at the wiry man standing by the aft wheelhouse. "That's probably just another ship bound for New Orleans and in a hurry with perishable cargo, don't you think?"

Though the wind tugged her words away, the captain hurried to join the ladies at the rail and lifted his spyglass again. Everyone aboard the *Bonne Femme* nervously fulfilled Mademoiselle's McVey's every whim. Her fiancé might have stayed behind in New Orleans, but he owned this ship. It did no good to take chances with Justin Lyon's hair-trigger temper or delicate sense of honor, Captain Tambourd reminded himself, even if Mademoiselle McVey had turned out to be charming and delightful—if slightly forward in her desire to know how everything worked. He enjoyed talking with her, even if her perpetual presence on deck, and that of the stunning slave girl who trailed her, had distracted his crew entirely too much.

"Unfortunately, we seem not to be outrunning her," the captain admitted with a shake of his grizzled head. "Perhaps they desire our cargo of massive French furniture meant for the spacious, tall-ceilinged drawing rooms and bedrooms of New Orleans in their cramped, little cabins, eh," he tried to joke, but then sobered instantly. "After ten weeks in New York City, you have heard all the talk of stamping out American piracy, no doubt. I do not wish to alarm you, *mademoiselle*, but the five navy vessels President Madison and his government assigned to this area are quite, quite inadequate. *Oui*, twenty-seven vessels lost last year in these southern sea lanes alone, and the northern insurance companies clamoring for revenge." He almost told her he'd heard the record for the last few years was at three thousand atrocities of various kinds, but he had never yet granted any woman the right to know as much as he did.

"But Congress just passed the death penalty for piracy!" Melanie protested. "Everyone knows that in New

York they have been hanging men convicted of high seas piracy!"

"Everyone in New York knows, perhaps, but do they know or care out here?" He punctuated that bit of wisdom with a shrug at the frowning woman. "These pirates," he said with a sniff, "though they call themselves gentlemen of fortune, they know no bounds. But do not be unduly alarmed, *mademoiselle*," he said, still addressing only Miss McVey, as if her slave girl were not even there. "She could be just a fast schooner out of Boston or a packet set for New Orleans, eh. Still, since she gains on us like this, I shall have to order preparations and request you to go below—with your maidservant, of course."

The young woman did not answer but stared again as if mesmerized at the bloom of sail behind them. Ah, but Melanie McVey was an exquisite creature! thought Captain Tambourd. He shuddered to think of her fate if that was a pirate vessel—or of his own fate at the hands of Justin Lyon if he did not protect her fully. The pirates would think her quite a prize.

Melanie McVey was slender, but in the most important places her curves were truly luscious. Even the proper neckline with ruffled collar of white lawn chemisette peeking out, her short, dark blue spencer jacket and full robin's egg blue skirts with petticoats and bustle could not hide that. Her skin blushed like camellia petals, her hair shimmered with the pale silver-gold of moonlight, and her sharp, sea-green eyes fringed with thick brown lashes seemed to pierce the captain—all men, no doubt—with her directness whenever she asked a question.

She was a classic sort of beauty despite her young years. Her nose seemed almost sculpted, its regal tip set perfectly between high slices of cheekbones. Only her slightly full lower lip with its alluring hint of a pout gave away her tendency to want and get her own way. Both a pity and a wonder, Captain Tambourd mused, that a roué like Justin Lyon, rich as he was, could win the hand of such a woman. The captain had heard that, for many reasons, Mademoiselle Melanie McVey was the most sought-after but selective young woman among the aristocratic families of the tall grass plantations surrounding Queen New Orleans.

He noted with another slanted glance that Mademoiselle McVey had now perched one hand defiantly on her hip as if she dared the other ship to be a pirate vessel—or with that fascinated look, perhaps it was just the opposite.

"I declare," she said in her lively way, "I suppose we cannot expect all Jolly Roger captains to be as gentlemanly and patriotic as New Orleans' Jean Lafitte."

Captain Tambourd just raised his thick eyebrows at that. The less the fine ladies of New Orleans, especially this one, knew about the real Jean Lafitte and his underhand dealings with so-called upstanding leaders in the community the better. "Mademoiselle McVey," he said and fought to keep his eyes from the way the wind molded her skirts to her fine form, "I regret to say that ship does present a probable rather than a possible danger. And so, now I must order my crew to battle stations and you to go below—and your maidservant of course also."

"But it is so far back yet. We will just stay out of the way and go below as soon as we really know what is happening," she promised and took the black girl's hand to pull her away from the rail.

Captain Tambourd thoroughly eyed the servant for once. She saw it, and defiance flickered in each pool-dark eye before she properly dropped her gaze. It had always annoyed him that the two women should carry on like best of friends instead of mistress and slave. They were so different, and yet something he could not name made them very close. The maid's hair was wavy jet black, like darkest night next to her mistress's curled pale blond hair. The maid's heart-shaped face, the skin the hue of sugared café au lait, contrasted with her mistress's oval face and creamy, almost iridescent complexion.

Captain Tambourd realized Miss McVey's heritage of rich Irish father and aristocratic Creole mother stamped her features with a controlled, calm beauty despite her impetuous, lively personality. It seemed to him her sensual allure seethed beneath the surface. But the mulatto maid flaunted her sensuality more openly, a heritage of some rich white father and his exotically seductive quadroon mistress, no doubt.

With a stiff bow the captain scurried to his men, shouting orders, which his first mate conveyed to the crew through the brass speaking trumpet. The bosun beat the call to battle stations on the drum. He'd give the women just a few more minutes and then insist they go below the water mark where cannon balls could not harm them. If it were a pirate ship, he had no choice but to fight, Captain Tambourd thought regretfully. He'd heard all sorts of chilling tales of what could happen to women on board if they were taken, and he wasn't certain which Justin Lyon would have his head for first—losing his precious imported Empire furniture or losing his beautiful, wealthy fiancé.

The hunters were closing in for the kill. It obviously *was* a hunt now as the smaller ship made no attempt to give the *Bonne Femme* a berth, but plunged after it. Lanie and Jasmine stood together near the top of the companionway, peering at the action on deck, holding hands. They had always been close in times of trial—except when Jasmine had sided with Lanie's papa when it came to the uproar over Lanie's betrothal to Justin Lyon.

Since they had argued over that, things had been slightly touchy between them. Lanie still coiffed Jasmine's hair as often as Jasmine did hers, and they laughed and chatted and shared all things—except the topic of Justin Lyon. Jasmine realized it did look odd she was not all for Lanie's marriage since Lanie's papa, Michael McVey, had promised to free Jasmine on Lanie's wedding day. But Lanie had no idea there were actually two things Jasmine wanted more than her freedom—to live with one man and to kill another.

"Just a few minutes more, *Beignet*," Lanie said. "You know I cannot abide that little cabin for long." Jasmine nodded understandingly. Anyone who knew Lanie well was aware of her fear of being closed in or locked up—a remnant of a childhood misfortune, when her visiting cousins had jokingly rolled her up in a carpet the slaves had been beating to clean it. She had nearly suffocated before they could roll her out onto the grass.

But the others aboard, even the hardiest sailors, would have liked to hide out below decks, even in a tiny cabin, when they realized what they were in for up on deck. Everyone on board the *Bonne Femme* could see their pursuer was a two-masted, narrow-hulled schooner of shallow draft. She had to be making nearly eleven knots in this stiff breeze, for she was closing the gap between them. She flew the Spanish flag, but the women had heard Captain Tambourd tell his men not to trust that.

The New Orleans crew raced to sling out nets to repel boarders, and to pump water into the longboats in case of fires. The sandbags that had cushioned the satiny finishes of Justin's furniture in the hold were hauled up and piled against the bulwarks while matting was laid over the rails to halt flying splinters.

"That sand they're spreading all over the deck, is it to make footing better?" Jasmine whispered to Lanie as if the other ship could hear.

Lanie only nodded. No need to elaborate that she knew it was to soak up the blood that could make the men slip if they had to fight at close range.

She had tried to get Jasmine to go below without her, but her friend would not leave her. It had always been like that, Lanie thought, and put her arm around Jasmine's narrow waist. They had been almost inseparable since that day she had defiantly rescued Jasmine from Justin's beating when the girls were both seventeen. That was the first day Justin Lyon had noticed Lanie. He had given her Jasmine as a gift, but told her she must someday repay him for the favor. And so, in wedding him, no doubt she would, Lanie thought.

"Bah!" Jasmine interrupted her thoughts. "That smells awful, like stale eggs!" They watched the gunners place their slow-smoldering sulfur matches in wooden tubs. At least the pursuers had a real surprise in store if they tried to come abreast of their heavily laden prey. The *Bonne Femme*'s deckhouse was made to swivel so two more deck guns could join the fray. Lanie only wished that handsome naval cap-

tain at a New York soiree whose name she could not recall
had not told her that if you fought a pirate ship, there was
no mercy or quarter given if they took you.

At that thought, the fluttering in her stomach, which had
been like delicate butterflies, began to beat like a bird's
wings. For one of the few times in her life, she admitted fear
to herself. Not the slow, strangling fear she had felt during
those two terrible years the levee broke and flooded the
fields and she thought they would actually lose Magnolia
Hill, but a sharper, more tangible kind of fear, which was
like the jab of a dagger.

"Let's go down below and say a prayer for Justin's men,"
she told Jasmine suddenly.

Even though the prayer would help something Justin
Lyon valued, Jasmine breathed a sigh of relief and nodded
her agreement. Behind them, Captain Tambourd's shrill
cries of "Crack on more canvas!" and "Stand to your
guns!" hurried them down the steps.

Twenty minutes later, over Jasmine's frenzied protests,
Lanie insisted on creeping up to the companionway just to
peek. The ship still vaulted forward, but there were no
blasts, and the single porthole in their cabin looked the
wrong way to see anything but distant, desolate, sandy
shoreline. Lanie peered carefully up the steps until her head
barely showed. Another step up, and she saw the crew of the
Bonne Femme frozen in expectant poses, just waiting. She
edged up farther. No one glanced her way. Yet another step
up.

In that instant, the masts and rigging of the other ship
leaped into view. It rode lower in the water than the *Bonne
Femme*, so she could not see the deck, but she did see, clear
in the blazing sun, musketeers thick in the rigging and a
black flag with skull and crossed swords whipping wildly in
the wind.

Her shocked stare locked with the dark eyes of one tall,
sable-haired man dangling from the pirate ship's rigging
with glinting silver sword already drawn. She gave a stifled
cry. The man was naked to the waist and bronzed like the
Indian she had glimpsed on the New York docks. She had

seen few bare chests but those of slaves; this man's rippled with clearly defined muscles even down where his flat belly plunged into his wide belt stuck with pistols and another sword. Raven hair flecked his chest and, even at this distance, she felt as if his eyes raked her and his hard hand reached out for her.

She dived to elbows and knees on the steps as the enemy ship shot a cannonball as a warning across the *Bonne Femme*'s prow. An unearthly shriek tore from the throats of the demons on the pirate vessel. Musket barrels and cutlasses glinted in the sharp sun. The ship shuddered under Lanie as the rudder fought the force of wind against sail as the bigger vessel tried desperately to veer away from her pursuer. She wondered desperately why the *Bonne Femme* didn't fire her guns, but perhaps the pirates were already too close.

"Stop and be boarded by Gasparilla's crew, or be skewered to the last man!" The coarse cry in English pierced her ears. The first smothered bellow of cannon fire from the *Bonne Femme* drowned heathen whoops and a pelting rain of musket balls. Lanie turned and scrambled down the steps.

Silver Swords held fast in the rigging as the two ships neared in the plunging seas. His muscles tensed with expectation and alarm. He knew he must fight well today to impress their leader, Gasparilla, and to convince him that he was worthy of his trust. So he'd downed only one of the three rum cups of "liquid courage" his portion called for before battle. This brazen, lumbering merchantman thirty feet off their starboard bow was doomed, he knew, for the "J. L. Ships" painted on its hull with bold gilt paint meant Gasparilla would show the vessel no mercy. Not even to that beautiful woman whom he had seen huddling in the companionway just before she fled.

At the signal he shouted again with the rest of the brigands he'd joined barely a year ago. The merchantman's first cannon shot had splintered the pirate ship's mainmast, but there was no time or range for other deadly fire from their guns. Gasparilla had followed exactly in his prey's wake until the final lunge around to crash into the vessel. Already, beneath his precarious perch, Sil could see the grappling men heave their big, three-pointed hooks. Stinkpots with their sulfurous fumes and grenades made from case bottles filled with gun powder and scrap iron careened upward onto the larger ship's deck. With a huge crunch and grating crash, the schooner *Fortune* rammed the *Bonne Femme* in her waist.

Though the rigging cushioned Sil, the blow almost jarred his grip and his teeth loose. Yardarms cracked and locked and swayed; grapnels and rigging fouled. It was time to swing down for hand-to-hand combat, yet he hesitated one moment as so many thoughts screamed through his brain. But to face any crisis, he told himself, "The readiness is all." And with his other comrades, weapon in hand, the man they called Silver Swords swung himself aboard the other ship.

Pirates ran along the bowsprit like tightrope walkers to board. Some climbed the stern chains to the taffrail. Sil jumped and clung to the shrouds and shinnied down to the deck. All was chaos: smoke drifted, metal clanged, men went down, blood flowed. Unlike most of his mates who wielded their big cutlasses like scythes in a bloody cut-and-slash advance, Sil used the sword with which he'd earned his reputation and nickname among them.

Keep moving, he urged himself, but he scarcely needed the admonition, for his fleet, natural motions were at their peak for a man in his twenty-eighth year. Withdraw, advance, sideward lunge. He sliced one man's arm open, then pushed him over the rail; perhaps the wretch would make it to shore. He had to show Gasparilla he could fight with the best—or worst—of them. He couldn't help the poor bastards who had evidently chosen to defy certain capture and turn a mere looting into a bloody massacre he was helpless to stem. Yet he wanted—needed to save the woman. He knew well enough what could lie in store for a beautiful female in the midst of such raw brutality and the drunken, brazen lust for conquest and riches.

He fought right behind the bloodthirsty Gasparilla. The man seemed invincibly young despite the years he'd been doing this. He reveled in the chase and battle as much as in the loot and the harem of captured women who awaited his every whim back on Gasparilla Island.

But then a man rushed at Gasparilla with a pistol. He raised his arm to fire; Gasparilla saw he was doomed the same moment Sil did. Quick as lightning, Sil lunged. His sword caught the man's arm, and the pistol discharged into the deck at Gasparilla's feet. Before Gasparilla could kill his attacker, Sil had lifted the bleeding man and heaved him over the rail. Without a word, Gasparilla clasped his shoulder briefly and they both plunged into the fray.

The pirates greatly outnumbered the merchant sailors; it was soon over. When the New Orleans crew pleaded for quarter, Gasparilla only laughed and spat derisively at their captain.

"Quarter? Quarter! You bastards dared lift a hand against the renowned Gasparilla when he ordered you to submit!" he roared. "*Vaya al diablo!* I'll have every man jack of you sliced up and tossed to the sharks!"

"They've already met the sharks!" the pirate called Specs yelled, and the jubilant buccaneers roared a relieved laugh. It was always like that after a capture, Sil marveled. One minute they'd be killing and dying and the next celebrating raucously.

"*Basta!*" Gasparilla silenced their joke. He wiped his bloody cutlass edge threateningly on the tattered shirt of the ship's captain while the man tried not to cower at the proximity of the ten-inch blade to his throat and heart. "Let other gentlemen of fortune bow before the might of my rival Jean Lafitte and his lackey Justin Lyon!" Gasparilla roared. "Gasparilla alone sends all J. L. Ships to the bottom with the corpses of their crews!"

At that, Sil saw his chance. "But that's just why the crew should not be slain—at least this once," he put in quickly at Gasparilla's shoulder. His deep voice was hoarse from shouting. "When you loot and scuttle a piece of your vilest enemies' fortune, someone's got to be left to tell those pompous New Orleans sons of bitches who deserves the credit.''

Sil watched as José Gaspar, the man the authorities knew only as Gasparilla, pondered this. Fortunately, Gasparilla never fought drunk or he'd have been likely to split the skull of anyone who mouthed policy he alone prided himself on making. Gasparilla was slim, bearded, with salt-and-pepper hair; the black eyes were still as sharp in their own way as the pointed chin and nose. He'd been the terror of the Gulf of Mexico for more than a decade and before that had spent years preying on ships in the Spanish Main, but it was as impossible to guess his age as it was to predict his next move.

"Damn my eyes! No wonder I say you're my smartest man, Sil!" Gasparilla bellowed and clapped him on the shoulder. "And anyone else who claims a stranger who has only been with us a year is not to be trusted, I tell you, *vaya al diablo*! Cast these J.L. lackeys adrift in a longboat, and the rest of you search below. Everything onto the *Fortune* she'll hold, and we'll burn Señor Justin Lyon's grand ship to the waterline!"

The New Orleans captain spoke up at last in his halting English. "Monsieur Gasparilla, I beg your mercy at least for the two women on board. One is only a slave, but the other is the daughter of wealthy parents. They will surely pay a fine ransom for her safe delivery to her home in New Orleans!"

Gasparilla's dark eyes sparkled as he swung to face Sil again. "Today, when you saved my life, I saw you are the man I can trust, Silver Swords. See that the women are locked up in one piece, and then we shall see what to do with them, hmm. Ransom or the auction block or a little fiesta right here on the deck, eh?"

A frenzied cheer ripped from the pirate throats as Sil shoved his way through them toward the companionway where he had seen the blond woman earlier.

Lanie and Jasmine stood, holding hands, not speaking, waiting. They heard each door in the corridor being opened. They heard a man's booted footsteps and the clank of metal blades coming closer. Lanie had stuffed a tiny dagger in her bosom, but besides that they had only the small, double-shot dueling pistol, which she held trained on the door with a trembling hand. They could tell from the shouts and cries and then the scuff of feet carting heavy furniture on the deck overhead exactly what had happened. When the door latch rattled, Lanie thrust the shuddering Jasmine behind her. They had bolted their door, and had already decided they would not open it even if ordered to. But there was no need for such bravado.

"Ladies, I'm coming in," the rough, deep voice called through the door. "This ship's been taken, and if you intend to stay in one piece, there had better not be a knife or gun in your hands when I enter."

"He's bluffing," Lanie whispered through trembling lips. Yet, for some reason, she could not shake the certainty that such a commanding tone must belong to the overwhelming man she had seen clinging to the rigging earlier. As if in answer, the door slammed inward with a terrific crash, ripping the iron bolt from the wood. A man lunged in, surveyed the room in a flash of dark eyes, then rose warily to his full height.

He and Lanie stared at each other as if there was nobody else in the room or on the ship. Or in the world. His gaze slid up, then down her to fix at last on the gun. Her finger on the trigger shook at the distinct feeling he could see right through her clothing. At this intimate range he looked so big he dwarfed the room. Brows as dark as storm clouds obscured his eyes as he frowned in the dimness. His curly chest hair and dark, heavy mustache were dusted with silver. Over his left eye a slash of silver through his collar-length black hair looked like the brand of the sword he held. He was square-jawed but lean-faced, and he breathed heavily through slightly parted, taut lips. His skin gleamed with a sheen of sweat, and blood stained the brown trousers stuffed into knee-high black boots. All this stunned her in the second before he spoke in that deliberate, rough voice.

"Hand me the gun, butt first, ma'am, or I can't promise the next men down here will treat you half as well as I."

It was that "ma'am" and the proper diction that calmed her. And it suddenly seemed ludicrous that two little bullets could ever stop a man as big and calmly commanding as this one. Yet in that same instant, she hated him for his inherent mastery over her. It was as if he embodied all her hatred for what had happened to Justin's men and ship and her own freedom today. And she hated and feared him for making her think he was a devastatingly handsome man in the same instant he acted like a barbarian.

Seeing no way out, she did as he said. When their fingers touched, lightning crackled through her arm and she jumped back.

He acted as if he had not noticed. "I'm going to put each of you in separate cabins down the way," he informed them in that maddeningly calm, rational voice. "The men will be looting this cabin, and I don't want you here or hatching silly plots that would never work."

"No," Lanie retorted. "We want to stay together. I demand you talk to your Captain Gasparilla or whatever he calls himself about our freedom!"

"You demand nothing!" he spat out. He stood slightly over six feet, Lanie noted, only six inches taller than she, but he seemed a giant. "It will be decided later. I tell you, ladies, you will do as you are told as soon as you're told or suffer dire consequences. Now you will both come with me, or I shall have to demonstrate that fact."

Jasmine, who had much more practice in taking orders from masters, gave Lanie a tiny push forward. He stepped aside to let them pass. The man, Jasmine thought, despite the blatant fact he was their captor, had called her a lady, too. He had looked Miss Lanie over toes to head, but Jasmine who was used to being ogled as if she were up for sale, noted that he had kept his eyes strictly to her face. She appreciated that; it was not very common.

"May I not take several things from my cabin—a shawl at least?" Lanie asked, but her voice shook as much as she did.

The pirate did not answer as he put Jasmine in the first small cabin and bolted the door. When he took Lanie's elbow, quite properly as a gentleman might, she flinched away.

"Damnation! Don't you dare to touch me!" she exploded.

"Such language. And, I assure you, that's the very least of your worries." He pulled her against his side with a quick arm around her as he smacked open the door to the next small room with his sword hilt. The dimness, the tight, crushing size of the first mate's cabin smothered her at once. She had not thought they would do this. She could not bear to be closed up like this.

"No!" she cried and tried to yank away.

He half carried, half pulled her in. Instantly, she found herself turned to face the wall. He sheathed his sword and lifted her hands until she was forced to lean her palms on the wall, higher than her head. He kicked her legs slightly apart and wrapped an iron band of arm around her waist to pull her tight against him. She tried to scream, but he clamped a big hand over her mouth.

"Listen to me and carefully, woman!" his voice hissed so close to her ear it burned her there. "You will do as you are told! There is every possibility you will be protected and ransomed eventually *if* you comply. And, I assure you, I will do whatever I have to do to have you obey me!"

He cursed her silently as she froze in his grasp. He could feel her frenzied fear, yet her boldness stung him even through his power over her. She infuriated him with her blend of cool defiance and hot panic. It had been years since he had felt the need to protect a woman—or this instant, rampant desire for one that sapped his strength so suddenly, and he didn't like or need that one bit. He had his duty, and he had no intention of having anything get in his way.

But she was shivering in his hold, and he realized suddenly that she must think he meant to rape her.

"Quiet now," he soothed, his voice hushed and raspy. "I mean only to do my job and not harm you. But so far you've defied me at every turn, and I've taken one weapon away already. Do you have another? I can't afford to have you harm yourself or anyone else.''

He recalled the tragedy of the beautiful captive who had taken her own life after her capture last month. Specs had told him that while she was waiting in her cabin she'd slit her wrists with a dagger she'd had hidden in her garter. He thought of his own mother's probable fate, though he tried to stem the rage it always evoked in him. Slowly, he loosened his hold on the woman to allow her to move away.

"I have no other weapon, and I am certain it would get me nowhere if I did," she lied while she brushed furiously at her sleeves and the waistline of her expensive blue gown as if his touch had dirtied her. Fear stiffened her lovely features, but he noted her distracted glances were at the small, dim room as much as at him.

"Tell me your name," he said to calm her.

Her eyes locked with his. "Mademoiselle Melanie McVey."

"Of?"

"Magnolia Hill Plantation just east of New Orleans."

"The captain says your father is rich."

"You are disgusting and greedy and hardly to be trusted with any such information! I will speak only to Gasparilla!"

"Then if we're back to that already, I must search you for weapons, Miss McVey. I'm afraid you're hardly to be trusted, either."

His polite use of her name and his cultured voice contrasted with his curt, brusque orders in a way that unsettled her even more. But she recognized him for the filthy, depraved pirate he was. And if he found the dagger she had hidden in a small embroidered sheath between the swell of her breasts, who knew what he would do?

"If you so much as touch me again, I shall scream the ship down! I shall tell your—your commander you attacked me!"

"And after what he has done today you still think he would honor that?" he goaded. She felt that simple reply like a slap across the face. This was a new world, she warned herself. Perhaps she had to play by their rules. Damnation, but she hated this smug, nasty brute!

"Surely, even pirates must protect those they will ransom!" she said angrily.

"And so I shall." He loosed his heavy weapons belt and dropped it in the corner of the tiny room where the first mate had slept. His hips looked narrow and his thighs rock hard without the dangling weapons to obscure them.

She stared saucer-eyed at him. Did he mean to keep his things out of her grasp while he searched her or— Her thoughts slammed to a panicked halt. Her heart thundered in her breast, and she felt her nipples point and tingle against her chemisette and bodice. If this man so much as touched her with those big, bloodied hands, she was not certain what she would do. And that terrified her more than anything yet. She read some undefinable anger at her challenge on his stony face. Palms raised toward him, she backed into the corner of the tiny room. She fought to keep herself from screaming simply at his overpowering presence in the smallness of this place.

He took one long stride toward her to pin her completely without touching her. "Gasparilla has ways of testing for virginity, so you're safe with me," he declared outrageously. "You see, he trusts me more than I do you. I don't have a weapon right now, and you're not going to, either. Now lift your skirt and petticoats for me so I can check your garters, Miss McVey, or I'll gladly do it for myself."

Chapter Two

When Lanie raked her nails toward the pirate's face, he lunged. He pushed her away before she could do any damage, then pulled her against his hard chest. His iron arm clamped her arms to her sides. When she tried to kick, he lifted her off the floor until she quieted and gasped for breath as well as self-control. Panic at being closed in this room with this dangerous stranger had given her a burst of power. Now, panting and near sobs, her strength evaporated to leave her limp in his arms.

She was not certain whether it was her own anger or this man's touch that made her go all wild and shaky. Justin had been an aggressive, intriguing suitor in a way others had never dared, and it was partly the hint of dark seductive power he emanated that had made her select him, but the sweeping emotions this man's mere touch evoked in her were something altogether new.

One big hand moved under her heavy skirt and outer petticoat to skim and pat at her legs, especially the tops of her silk stockings and garter ribbons. His touch was sure and warm even through the innermost percale petticoat, which was the only barrier between her bare skin and his. Her curls tumbled loose in his face. Her head fell against his shoulder as he shifted his weight to slide his hand along her hips and buttocks.

Then he set her down. Her skirts cascaded to the floor while his hand marauded to pat along her waist through her garments, then quickly cupped and lifted each breast. She bit her lower lip to keep from cursing him or crying out. His fingers touched her breastbone and moved between her breasts while she held her breath. This bloody brigand's touch sent sharp shivers along every nerve. Then his fingers thumped the hidden sheath, and she was caught.

"I thought you'd have a dagger somewhere. Unloose this jacket so I don't have to tear it."

She knew only too well he meant it. The dagger would do her no good. Even if she could overpower him, there were many others to face before she reached freedom. And she had no intention of not living through this and getting herself and Jasmine out intact somehow!

"All right. Take your hands off, then," she acquiesced.

He stepped away only to turn her to him when he saw she meant to unhook her puff-sleeved spencer with her back turned. For the first time in this day of ruin and danger, she felt herself blush hot as she merely undid the braided frogs of the jacket, although she was fully clothed beneath. Slowly, so he would not touch her again, she slipped her fingers into her oval-cut bodice and pulled out the case with its slender dagger. She could feel his eyes on her, studying her every move—every lift and fall of her breasts beneath the percale damp from her exertions and terror. She handed him the dagger with a slanted narrow look.

He shoved the sheath in his waistband, against his bare brown skin. "You seem to be as clever and bold as you are beautiful, Miss McVey," he said with a stare so piercing she lowered her lashes. "But you'd best remember I'm your only protection now and act accordingly."

She was struck again at how properly he spoke even when grunting orders, though his Yankee accent grated her nerves raw. Of course, all pirates did not have to come from the dregs of society, she supposed. Jean Lafitte and his brother Pierre hardly did. But this man actually dared to snap her a sharp, almost military bow and click his booted heels before he gathered his things and opened the door to leave her. He turned, and his blue eyes studied her astounded face again.

"Silver Swords at your service, Miss McVey," he said and closed and bolted the door behind him.

Three hours later, Silver Swords transferred Lanie and Jasmine to the deck of the pirate vessel, *Fortune*. Grappled together, the ships rolled like a single huge log with each swell of sea. The sleek *Fortune* sported an unencumbered deck for ease of fighting and high bulwarks for protection and storage. Men were working hard to mount the doomed *Bonne Femme*'s mainmast on the pirate ship to replace the one that had been shot apart. Heaps of Justin Lyon's precious French Empire furniture littered the deck as the women glanced nervously around in the late afternoon sun. To Lanie's dismay, Silver Swords sent Jasmine with the short, pirate called Gunner Joe to be locked up below while he pulled her briskly forward along the deck.

"Save your defiance and bravado for the likes of me," he ordered gruffly out of the corner of his mouth without breaking stride. "Gasparilla's moods change like quicksilver. Any theatrical displays, especially if he's been drinking, may get you pitched over the side or worse." He gave her arm a jerk to emphasize his warning as she found herself facing Gasparilla.

"Ah, *señorita*," said the wiry pirate chief as he ran his sharp black eyes thoroughly over her. He sat in a huge, highbacked mahogany armchair once destined for a plantation veranda or city drawing room as if it were his throne among his tattered, motley subjects. She expected any moment to be forced to her knees to do obeisance at his booted feet, and that infuriated her. She was no one's menial or slave!

But she stood erect, hands clasped before her, fighting to bridle both fear and fury. She could feel the eyes of the others on her, especially Sil's boring into her back as Gasparilla leered. Her stomach churned at the sight of the numerous raised, zig-zag scars on his face and arms.

"Melanie McVey, our guest from a New Orleans sugar plantation with a wealthy papa," Gasparilla announced grandly to his barbaric courtiers. His Spanish-accented speech was ponderous. "And that papa would like her back in one pretty piece and still a virgin, no? As if such a pretty woman could be yet a virgin, yes, *hombres*!''

The men roared their agreement with that jest. Lanie kept her chin up and fixed her stare on a bloody blotch on Gasparilla's shirt front; she wondered which of Justin's officers or crew had sadly decorated it for him. When the noise subsided, she said quietly, ''Yes, I am a virgin, betrothed to be wed. And my father will pay for my safe delivery in that same condition.''

''And a rich fiancé, too, no doubt,'' Gasparilla gloated. He rubbed his hands together at the thought. ''Perhaps a double ransom then! Such a pity, eh, Sil, this one will not be put up to auction like her pretty slave girl, hmm.''

''The slave—my maidservant—is very dear to me,'' Lanie dared to interrupt despite the fact she distinctly heard Silver Swords clear his throat behind her in warning. ''My father will ransom her, too. We need to stay together. Please, she's not to be auctioned here and—''

''A tongue as sharp as your sword, eh, Sil?'' Gasparilla roared. ''I know I would spend my treasures to buy this one for a slave in my bed and tame her,'' he continued with a wave of his beringed hand while he licked his thin lips. Lanie tried to defy his stare, but Gasparilla was darting glances around the deck while the ruby stud in his left ear winked bloodily at her.

He must be drunk or demented, she thought, as his gestures became more grandiose and his voice rose. ''I hear the slave's a pretty mulatto with skin like toffee and breasts big as pillows!'' he shouted, and he gestured obscenely to his crew. ''Where is she, *hombre*?'' he asked Sil. ''This one we will save for ransom, but Gasparilla, king of the American pirates, he deserves a taste of toffee before his own auction!''

Lanie took a step back at his words and the roar of the crew's laughter. Even someone as brutal as Silver Swords wouldn't drag Jasmine up here for such defilement! The smell of pitch and sulfur from the *Bonne Femme*'s decks sickened her. She looked pleadingly at Silver Swords.

"The girl *is* toffee skinned," Sil agreed with a stiff grin, "but green at the gills and ready to puke from the roll of the ships together. I'll let you know when her stomach settles, Gasparilla. Right now, you'd have her dinner all over you instead of what you're more interested in!"

Lanie breathed again even though the crew hooted and howled at that reply. She knew Jasmine had a stomach forged from steel, and she silently blessed Silver Swords for Jasmine's temporary rescue. Everyone guffawed, Gasparilla most of all as he slouched on his throne and slapped his knee. Then he sobered and sat upright; his eyes glittered like polished obsidian.

"Too bad a rich papa," he said morosely. He leered at Lanie again as he leaned forward, elbows pinned to knees. "Terrible, hmm, Sil, a ravishing beauty like this one just asking to be ravished."

"I am only asking, sir," Lanie put in carefully amidst the snickers before Sil could answer, "to have my father or my fiancé informed so they can send the money for me and for my maidservant. They will pay handsomely for both of us if we are untouched. Perhaps my fiancé will know first, since this chair you use and the ship you burn are his, and he—"

"*Merde!*" Gasparilla shrieked, and stood. "You can't mean Justin Lyon!"

She blinked in surprise. "You have heard of him? Yes, I—"

"She might be lying," Sil cut in and stepped forward to seize her arm. She yanked back, but his grip only tightened until she actually felt her arm go numb.

"Justin Lyon's bride here—his virgin—waiting in my hands!" Gasparilla crowed and threw his hands up as if to heaven. "Fortune, it is truly mine this day!"

Lanie gaped at his antics. She could not even begin to fathom what he was thinking. She let Sil pull her along the deck away from the raucous scene.

"Please make it very clear to that monster that my father will pay for my maidservant, too," she told Sil as he hurried her along. "And I thank you for keeping her out of their clutches back there."

His stony face did not soften one bit. "She'll have to stand for auction on shore," he informed her curtly. "And perhaps I just spoke up because I fancied her for myself. She seems one hell of a lot more obedient and bright than you!"

She faced him at the door he hurried to unlock. "You wretch! I'm the one who's sick—of your insults! And I'm telling you to inform that madman that Jasmine's life and safety are worth money to them, too. I intend to save her, so—"

"You really don't know what you just did back there, do you?" he interrupted. "Hell, but you've got a lot to learn to even save yourself!"

"What do you mean? Did what back there?"

"I told you to save your defiance and demands for me and not rile Gasparilla, so of course, you did just the opposite! The man's damned dangerous!"

"And you're not, I suppose? Look, I'm not afraid of you, but I—"

"Now you look, lady! I'm not only tired of your lies—that you don't have a weapon hidden, all this bravado that you're not afraid—but I'm telling you these lies are going to get you in trouble around here just as they do in the world outside."

"In the civilized world, people don't capture and hold ladies against their will!" she retorted, and tried to pry his grip from her wrist.

"Is that right?" He threw the words at her as he pulled her into the cabin. "Why don't you just ask your little slave girl about her freedom out there in your precious civilization?"

Exhausted, frightened and furious because he had bested and insulted her, she smacked a fist into his hard shoulder. In return, he slammed the door and pressed her against it. He grasped her chin in his big hand to still her and tipped her head until she almost seemed to offer him her mouth. Her breasts pushed against his chest; his powerful thighs held her hips and stomach against the unyielding wood.

"Now listen and listen well, Miss Melanie McVey!" he rasped out. "I'm your lord and master from now until your freedom's bought, if you're that lucky with that quick, bossy mouth of yours!" His sky-blue eyes lowered to her mouth, and she noted they softened rather than hardened before he went on in a much quieter voice. "It's for your own safety and your maid's, too. I'll do what I can to see neither of you is mistreated, but you can't go around like you're queen of some rich sugar-cane kingdom here. So you learn to keep that mouth shut unless I give you permission, or so help me, I'll—"

A frown crumpled his brow. His lips, bare inches from hers, narrowed, tightened. The look scared her. He seemed to want to blot her from his sight, and yet there was something else there she could not quite read. He took a step back, and as he did so their eyes locked. She drew in a sudden breath, not of fear but almost of anticipation. He did not remove his hand from her chin, but his thumb stroked her throat, then slowly down to her mother's cameo necklace, which she wore. Neither of them seemed to breathe.

She stood as if mesmerized. His other hand moved from the wall next to her head to tangle in her wind-snarled hair. So close, they traded breaths in unison. She scented rum on his breath; salty sea air seemed to sweep the room around him. And then, the moment she felt herself almost sway into him, he jumped back.

"You stupid woman! You'll be the death of me and everything yet!" Sil shook his head to clear it. He felt furious with himself—with her! He had almost caressed her, almost lowered his lips to take hers. This jumble of feelings, longings he had buried years ago and which could now get him killed, was the last thing he needed. He needed to concentrate only on the things he must. Duty. Revenge. Safety. Not some demanding, seductive spitfire Gasparilla expected him to protect from everyone else, when she made him forget his own missions, for which he'd already invested years of his life.

And then there was his loyalty to Rebecca. He took another step. This woman had crashed into his life today to threaten that, and he wanted her only to obey him and cause him no trouble. Not to defy him so she drew attention to herself. Not to look at him like that so he wanted to comfort and crush her to him. Damn Miss Melanie McVey! He preferred her sullen contempt and icy hatred as long as she didn't make waves for him!

He pushed her to the single cot in the tiny room and sat her down hard. Before she realized what he was doing, he had her locket off and hidden in his big fist.

"You—you dirty, vile, bloody thief!" she sobbed out for lack of a better insult. But his touch, both rough and gentle, left both of them shaken, and they knew it. Their eyes did not meet again. With great difficulty, she sat where she was so he had no excuse to touch her again. Still, she screamed every degrading epithet in French she could think of while he stormed out and slammed and locked the door.

She took deep breaths to calm herself, but her churning emotions only racked her further. Through tears she sat staring hopelessly at her knees for long minutes until she noticed with surprise that her bonnet, her fringed white shawl and her only sturdy pair of leather walking shoes were laid out neatly on the cot beside her.

After he cursed then calmed himself for not keeping a tighter rein on himself with that snappish, spoiled woman, Sil unbolted the crowded storage room down the hall where the slave girl was locked in. He went in so swiftly and silently he caught her standing on a box marked Limoges Porcelain, and staring out through a crack in the hull at the burning *Bonne Femme*. But instead of mourning the destruction of the vessel that would have taken her home, she was cursing it with a raised fist. He stood amazed a moment, just listening to the tirade. The French he'd learned on a voyage to France some thirteen years ago was not fluent, but it gave him the drift of her jubilation at the ship's destruction, and her hatred of its owner.

"Damn your black, murdering soul, Monsieur Lyon! Defiler of women, deceiver, son of a bitch! You deserve to lose every ship, every stick of furniture, every last dollar! I

hope you roast in hell, impaled on the devil's pitchfork and
tormented as you do others for all eternity!''

She whirled and gasped when he closed the door behind
him. "Oh, sir, I did not mean that of you. And I was not
trying to escape!" She reverted quickly to English, so perhaps, he thought, it was best neither she nor her volatile
mistress knew he spoke French at all.

He extended a hand to help her down from the box. He
fought to keep a hint of a grin from his face. This woman's
strategy with him was all honey while her mistress only
flaunted her sharp stinger.

"I didn't think a woman shaped like you would get far
through a little crack in the boards like that," he said.

Jasmine Bouchet dimpled beautifully at his rejoinder. Her
hand lingered on his arm before he stepped away, but her
sweet mask shattered when he asked abruptly, "Why is it
you hate Justin Lyon if he's to wed your mistress? It is his
name I heard, I believe, though I hardly caught all you
said."

The smile froze on the lovely, full lips. Her great velvet
brown eyes framed by sable lashes met his, then slid away.
"He owned me once—my mother and brothers, too. He did
not let us be together. He sold me away. I ran off and he
wanted to beat me. *Voilà*," she lied smoothly, without a
tinge of the guilt she felt when she lied to Melanie McVey
about it, "that's all."

"He *wanted* to beat or he did beat you?" Sil pursued.

She shrugged, and he could tell she wished to say no
more. "Miz Lanie, she saved me," she said simply, her pert,
well-cultivated French accent suddenly buried in slave dialect.

Lanie. He repeated the nickname silently to himself. It
suited her, at least when she wasn't flashing anger and defiance. Her parents must have called her that when she was
a child. But then his thoughts skipped to his own parents,
and he jerked himself back to reality. He had promised
vengeance, even if it was not yet time to act. He could not
be distracted by a woman—perhaps two of them—who
would only get in the way of his bloody justice when it came.

He clipped out his orders to the girl in a harsh voice he
hadn't intended, informing her she would stay locked in and
have her food delivered until they went into port. Though
she was less deserving of his anger than her mistress, he
slammed the door, then shot the bolt with all his might.

The morning of the third day after their capture, the
Fortune nosed through Gasparilla Pass and rounded the tip
of Gasparilla Island into Charlotte Harbor. The guns on the
tip of the island that guarded it from entry by naval or other
pirate vessels banged off the usual salute and, once again,
Gasparilla's personal black flag of piracy waved proudly
from the stern. Two ships were anchored just offshore; another was careened on its side on the stretch of beach while
men crawled along it to scrape barnacles and worms from
its hull. Boca Grande, the little town and home base of the
pirate band, came alive to greet them as they anchored just
offshore.

Lanie's eyes skimmed the jumble of buildings as she and
Jasmine were rowed ashore with the other booty. They
passed a crude wooden jetty with two small sloops tethered
to it. The buildings consisted of about twenty log and
thatched huts or open-sided enclosures of various shapes
and sizes and one finer looking house set amidst slash pines
and coconut palms. She later learned that was Gasparilla's
"palace." Here he kept his harem of women until they
bored or displeased him; then he put them up for auction or
just helped them disappear. An irregular central square was
cluttered with a raised wooden platform, several large
cooking fires, a collection of cheering women and young-
sters and a fence holding in a few scrawny pigs and cows.
Dogs darted here and there barking madly. And beyond the
swarming village scene, huge wooden-roofed warehouses
now receiving the pirates' plunder sprawled into the green
darkness of palmetto thickets.

Silver Swords half escorted, half dragged Lanie and Jasmine from the longboat and hurried them down the crowded
beach. Lanie refused to return the curious, harsh stares of
the various women and half naked children. She looked

straight ahead until one screaming banshee of a woman snatched and ran off with the silk boots she carried. But Sil only pulled her on with a terse, "Those are no good to you here anyway. No captives are allowed anything but the clothes on their backs. Just don't lose those stout shoes, or the only dress you'll have to your name for months."

Months! Her spirits fell even further. "I hate you," she told him in the panic of despair.

"I don't give a damn how you feel as long as you've learned that my word is law for you," he cracked back.

Despite the heat of the sand, she kept her shawl tight around her so as not to lose that. He hurried them out of the crowd, through a cluster of chickens, which scattered at the approach of two fighting dogs, and toward a hut at the far end of the village.

A slender young girl waited at the door, her waist-length black hair so dark and sleek it glinted bluish in the sun. She wore a bright paisley skirt to just above her shapely knees and a wisp of a sleeveless white cotton blouse off her shoulders through which her large nipples clearly showed. She was olive skinned with huge rabbit eyes, which lit with blatant happiness at Silver Sword's return. Her hand covered her mouth as if she did not want them to see her wide smile.

"This is Serafina, my much valued cook and housekeeper," he told them with a smile meant for Serafina alone. Lanie had not seen him smile; its blinding whiteness in his bronze face dazzled her. She saw him wink at the girl and briefly touch her shoulder. "Serafina is from Havana, and she will feed you some of that delicious fish stew I smell, right, *señorita*?"

When Serafina nodded at the big man, Lanie saw why she hid her mouth and why her huge eyes bespoke pain as well as passion. Serafina's upper lip was split by a disfiguring cleft palate that made her voice echo strangely when she and Sil conferred.

"Two guests for a very brief time," Sil said in a low voice. "Specs will be right outside if they don't behave, and I'll be back shortly." He patted the girl's shoulder again before she led them into the shade of the thatched log house. Lanie saw

Serafina's eyes follow Sil longingly before she turned to them. With her free hand, the one that did not cover her mouth, she indicated they should sit on the woven floor mats to eat.

Silver Swords came back all too soon after they ate and spoke in Spanish to Serafina; she nodded and went out. The pirate called Specs—presumably because he wore spectacles—appeared at the door. His thatch of hair was sun-bleached like straw. He looked the part of the erudite scholar with his squinty eyes magnified behind thick lenses, but his sharp tone and the equally sharp edge of his cutlass spoke the truth about him.

"Miss McVey will stay here with Specs," Sil told them. "Jasmine, you'll have to come with me for the auction. And I don't want any protests from either of you because there's nothing I can do about it!"

Lanie leaped to her feet, but Specs pushed her instantly down on her mat. "Heed his words, girl," Specs warned in a low voice. "Protestations of any form are wasted here."

"No, please! I can't let her go! We're friends, too, and I can't—"

"You can and will!" Sil cut her off and turned to block her view of the distraught Jasmine in the corner of the hut. He spoke in a low voice to the girl; Lanie saw her nod and take a short skirt, which Sil had removed from a chest along the wall.

But when Jasmine began to undress Lanie could not keep quiet.

"No!" she cried again. "You can't take her out that way, you crude barbarian!"

"Miz Lanie, there's nothing to be done!" Jasmine's shaky voice cut her off. "He explained to me on the ship. You can't help this—never really could. It all just bubbles in the air, the way we carried on together. You the master's daughter and I'm—"

Her voice broke. Lanie froze at how easily Jasmine slipped back into slave intonations instead of using the cultured voice she was so used to. Sil turned and blocked

Specs's view while Jasmine pulled the skirt over her head and wriggled out of her garments, then dropped them to the palmetto-thatched floor. Then, naked to her waist, Jasmine Bouchet followed Sil out the door into the blazing sun.

Lanie sat with her guard's owlish eyes alternately on her and on the spectacle outside. She heard the crowd gather for the auction, which would sell Jasmine like a chattel to one of these beasts. But then a thought hit her that stopped her tears. Although importing slaves had been outlawed in the United States since 1808, many Louisiana plantation owners still bought domestic slaves or ones imported through the illicit influx of the pirate Jean Lafitte's smuggling.

So what these pirates did blatantly here in Gasparilla's stronghold was only what the proper gentlemen of New Orleans still did privately, wasn't it? Hadn't Silver Swords said just that to her the other day when he derided her idea of civilization? Maybe that was why she had seen Jasmine's eyes flare in anger as well as fear when she took her last look at Lanie. But Lanie's father often freed trustworthy workers, and had told Jasmine she'd be free on Lanie's wedding day. Jasmine would have had her freedom in just a few months!

"Please, Specs, may I just look out?" she asked. "I promise I won't move from the door. Please."

He shrugged. His magnified blue eyes were deceptively tolerant. She joined him at the door to peer out. She could see Jasmine standing stolidly on the wooden platform in the square, head held high. The tall Scottish pirate they called Red Legs, who wore a plaid skirt, stood just beyond to act as auctioneer. Lanie crossed her arms over her breasts as if in self-protection while she watched. She could not pick out either Sil or Gasparilla from the crowd. Red Legs's distinctive Scottish burr floated to her across the blinding white sand between the hut and the square.

"A real bonny lass with sweet jibs both fore and aft, lads! Old Emma's took a look and says the little thing's been wi' a man or two, but that makes her all the more knowin' aboot what a real man likes! An' we'll jus' start the bidding, lads, at twenty dollars!"

Lanie's stomach churned. But for the fact she had two rich men to ransom her, she would be standing there before them all half stripped in the blazing sun with her legs and naked breasts on display. One of these vile, bloody men would take her to his hut and plunder her all night anyway he wanted. As was going to happen to Jasmine. Suddenly, it was as if she was there with Jasmine—was Jasmine. The impact of how that must feel weakened her knees and almost made her retch. It was wrong, dead wrong. Pirates or New Orleans slave owners—was it so very different? Tears crowded her eyes. Without realizing it, she bit her lower lip so hard she tasted blood.

How she ached to help Jasmine. She could not bear to let this happen to her friend. Could the slaves at home feel hateful and angry toward their masters? She knew well enough how she felt toward her pirate captors. She was a slave now, just like Jasmine. But her agonized thoughts crashed to a halt as she heard Sil's distinctive voice in the rapid flow of bids call out, "One hundred dollars!"

"Sold to Silver Swords!" Red Legs soon called out, and everyone cheered.

He had meant it, Lanie thought, that he fancied Jasmine! Lanie felt sickened with anger and hopelessness. She turned her back on the scene outside and slumped down in a corner of the hut with her face to the wall while Specs watched alone.

As darkness fell that first night ashore, Lanie had never felt more afraid. Serafina, like a loyal, liquid-eyed puppy, waited hand and foot on Sil at the evening meal. Lanie hadn't been allowed a chance to talk to Jasmine and, shattered by the thoughts that still tormented her, she hadn't really tried. Today had made everything she had always cherished—the plantation and the mansion at Magnolia Hill, even Mama and Papa—seem dirtied somehow because it all rested on slavery. She had already suffered agonies of fear, now she felt the strangest murmurings of confusion and betrayal.

It staggered Lanie that she felt so alienated from Jasmine, too. Lanie had always thought they had shared their deepest feelings, had really been friends. Now she realized that there were things about Jasmine she had never known. When had Jasmine slept with a man, she wondered, and why had she never told her friend? Lanie was starting to realize that Jasmine had never truly seen her as a friend, that she had always seen herself as a slave on the far side of a wide gulf between them. How easily she'd called her "Miz Lanie" in that slave dialect today. No, their friendship, just like her southern pride and ideals of Magnolia Hill, had shattered just as her whole life in this imprisoning pirate village had.

Lanie refused the flat bread, turtle soup and rum. She sat on the mat in the corner, her hands clasped around her bent knees where she rested her chin, unmoving, agonizing. She scooted even farther back, wrapping her skirts tightly around her legs, when Sil came over to hunker down beside her with a bowl of soup.

"You're not going to starve yourself, Miss McVey. I'm here to see you don't become damaged goods."

"But you intend to damage my maidservant to your heart's content!" she shot back so no one else could hear.

"Do I?" he challenged. "Of course, I should have known better than to expect a bit of gratitude from you. I spent my hard-earned money to keep her away from the group of six men who were bidding together. They'd have her used and left her half-dead on the sand already!"

"Oh, I didn't know. I thought—" she murmured half to herself.

"Just eat this before I feed you myself. Hell, yes, times are tough here for a delicate lady like yourself." His voice was mocking. "But I don't need your stubborn fussing tonight. I'm going to have enough to worry about keeping the randy celebrants away from your and Jasmine's sweet flesh once they get into their grog tubs and bumboo."

"Bumboo? What's that?" she asked, curious despite her disdain.

"It's a virulent punch of rum, sugar, water and nutmeg I'll see you get to try some other moonlit night," he said.

Damnation, she thought. She could never tell if he was teasing or not, so she just glared at him.

"It's just a question of my holding them off until they pass out from the stuff," he concluded, as if she had asked.

"And drinking it is beneath you, I take it," she countered archly.

It annoyed him she forever threw his protection and hospitality, such as it was, right back in his face. And she kept her warm jacket on and held the white shawl he'd gotten for her for chill evenings across her middle as if he had lechery in mind. But his eyes dropped to her bosom, and the words spilled out before he could stop them.

"You'd better say your prayers it's beneath me, Miss McVey, as it would probably make me crazier than you already do. And you're sleeping tied to me tonight until I can deliver you to the women's stockade on Captiva Island tomorrow. Now eat this or I'll hold you down and spoon it into that smart little mouth of yours myself."

Sputtering with fury because he'd bested her again, she snatched the pewter bowl from him and began to eat.

There was a tense silence among the three women as the howls outside rose and fell later that night. A shrill, wavering voice shouted a song about pirate's justice and drowned bones. Others took up a distant, bawdy song that kept coming back to, "Between her thighs, her beauty lies!" which made Lanie blush even in the dimness of the single oil lantern. Others pounded pans and bayed at the full moon like dogs. Her eyes kept meeting Jasmine's nervous glance, then they would both look elsewhere.

"You not be afraid." Serafina's muffled voice came from behind her hand. "Sil, he always mean what he say. They know to fight him mean to face his swords. He the best in the world with his swords," she assured them with a toss of gold-hooped earrings. Lanie had not noted them before in the loose bounty of her raven hair. "And some of the women," Serafina went on, "they like men all wild and rough that way. They chase those kind, not come here."

Lanie shuddered inwardly. She wished she could block out the pictures those sounds suggested, of men chasing writhing women and carrying them off down the sand. It was not her imagination that some of the hoots and shrieks came closer. Then she heard Sil's loud voice outside. It calmed her, yet made little shivers race along her back, from tailbone to nape of her neck. Her nipples pointed to hard nubs and her stomach flopped over. Then two shots rent the air.

Jasmine jumped, then whispered to Lanie, "If he's going to leave me here, and deliver you to that other island tomorrow, what's going to happen to me, Miz Lanie? Bah, this is real bad here. Bad as most anything I been through."

"I am so sorry—sorry about everything, Jasmine," Lanie managed. She reached out for Jasmine's hands and clasped them tightly. Tears blurred her eyes. "I am sorry, *Beignet*," she said again. "When we get out of here—I swear I will get you out safely, too—we will still be friends at home. We will both be free there, so—"

"So you think back at home even a freed slave and the mistress of two of the largest plantations on the river gonna be friends?" Jasmine demanded. "It's hard enough to know you own me, but if you gonna be Justin Lyon's wife, too!" Jasmine insisted. Her voice had turned so venomous at the mention of Justin's name that Lanie jerked her hands back as if Jasmine had burned her.

"I regret that you feel that way," she said in shock. "But we have a lot of other things to worry about, Jasmine. And I say no matter what, we are friends for good!" Lanie insisted, her voice strangely desperate.

"Well, if'n the mistress say so, that's it for sure!" Jasmine retorted before she could keep the buried bitterness or overdone slave accent from her words. She shook her head. It wasn't Miss Lanie's fault she'd been raised that way any more than it was her own fault she'd been born a slave. Miss Lanie meant well, and Jasmine loved her a lot. But still, it hurt real bad, 'specially when one was facing a new scary life without the protection Miss Lanie had afforded these past seven years.

"Sil, he take care of us all," Serafina said in the awkward silence between the other two women, but her eyes were sad as she surveyed the beautiful women her beloved Sil had brought home this morning. There was heat lightning like the kind that crackled on dark summer nights over the gulf between him and this moonlight-haired woman. Serafina mourned any wild hope she had ever cherished that he would look on her that way someday.

Doing everything Sil asked was the only way she had found so far to stay near him. He was her entire life since she'd discovered him half drowned on the north beach a year ago. He had had a broken leg, and the drowned body of his friend had been beside him. Since then he'd protected her from those vultu es who used to brutalize and laugh at her all at once. And so, anything Sil wanted was the way it must be for Serafina.

Sil came in late at night to relieve Specs and Red Legs, who had taken turns guarding the door until everything quieted. Lanie jumped as his big form blocked the lantern light, then she lay still as he bent down to blow out the sputtering light. Serafina was gently snoring on her mat in the far corner while Jasmine huddled, sound asleep, on the mat at right angles to where Lanie had finally stretched out in utter exhaustion. Lanie held her breath as Sil's body, silhouetted in the moonlit doorway, leaned over Jasmine. Lanie went hot all over and prickles tormented her lower belly. Surely with two other women here, he wouldn't dare assert his rights to his new property now! If he tried, she'd scream. She fight him for Jasmine!

But he stood and stretched, then dragged a mat from the other side of the room and placed it beside her to block her in against the wall. Quickly, she sat up to let him know she was awake.

"Lie down," he whispered sleepily. "I'm beat, and if you don't behave, you're going to be, too."

"So clever with your threats," she hissed sarcastically.

"Facts, not threats. Lie down or I'll have to tie you to be sure you don't do something entirely foolish. I'll be no good tomorrow if I don't get some sleep."

She lay down, wedged against the wall in an effort to move as far from him as she could. She heard him yawn.

"Not even going to say I'll never be good even if I get some sleep?" he goaded, his voice maddeningly low and lazy. "Here I am a bloody pirate with my helpless victim and too tired to treat her the way she fears—maybe even expects."

"You bastard!" She made the mistake of slapping out at his face, but he moved first. She only got a handful of sopping wet hair. He'd been swimming! His big hands manacled her slender wrists over her head. His hands felt cool; he smelled so clean as he shoved her down. He rolled onto his side next to her to blot out the rectangle of moonlight at the door of the hut. She felt trapped and closed in again, but that was not what panicked her now.

They both froze. She realized her foolish mistake. Every time she defied him, he had the excuse to touch her. He silently cursed himself. He knew he had goaded her into fighting him, just so he could put his hands on her, rough or not.

He loosed her wrists; she could feel his eyes pierce the darkness between them. "Good night, Miz Spitfire," he whispered and flopped on his own mat. He lay still, and she heard his breathing quiet into a steady rhythm.

Her stomach tied in knots, Lanie lay tensely until her muscles cramped from pressing her legs so tightly together. Tears stung her eyes, or she dreamed they did, as her exhaustion pulled her into restless, rolling sleep.

She drifted in the arms of the silver sea, calling out to her father, riding her plunging horse next to his through the rolling sea of big cane grass that was the McVey fortune. She was the only child; someday it would all be hers. But the levee waters rolled in to bring Justin Lyon. Now Justin was pulling her this way and that, just like papa used to. He kept telling her what to do, trying to lock her up in his plantation house when she wanted to swim in the waves.

But the waves smothered her until she was certain she was going to drown. Then a tall, black-haired pirate with a silver streak of hair, like the swing of his sword, over his stern eyes was touching her, holding her up, caressing her.

She hated him. She feared him. He took her freedom, too. Where was Jasmine? She had to save Jasmine! But she dreamed she melded perfectly against the pirate in the strong, crashing waves. She swam with him, to him. She wanted to fight him with the big sugarcane machete she had learned to use when papa wasn't looking. The pirate lifted her; he pressed against her and she responded with open arms and heart and legs. No. No, wasn't she supposed to be sleeping next to Justin in his big bed? But then she sank again, and he slipped away in the reaches of the black and silver sea of her tears.

She sat bolt upright, drenched with perspiration. Her face was glazed with tears. She gasped a silent "Oh!" when she realized it was, blessedly, all a dream. She was not lying next to Justin Lyon in their marriage bed on his plantation—but in its own way, that suddenly seemed just as frightening as this.

The pirate lay with long limbs sprawled next to her, breathing heavily. One big arm lay crooked above his upturned, rugged face while dawn pearled the doorway beyond. He was not sleekly handsome as Justin, but he was— ruggedly disturbing. Reality crashed over her in a big, cold wave. Unstrung to her very soul, she lay down, grateful she had not disturbed him. And yet there lay heavy on her heart so many strange confusions she could not shake as she drifted off again in troubled sleep.

Chapter Three

Lanie sat in the prow of the small sloop Silver Swords handled as if he had been born to it, thinking of her wrenching goodbye with Jasmine. Despite the recent bitterness between them, the women had hugged each other. It had been a brave, stoic embrace at first, but when Lanie had vowed in a voice choked with emotion she would take Jasmine home with her when her ransom arrived, they had both trembled with tears. Gasparilla had ordered Serafina to go with them to Captiva Island as cook and housekeeper, so Jasmine had been left in the charge of a fat old pirate called Gunner Joe and his Mexican woman. This time, Lanie had known better than to plead with the stony-faced Sil when he said it was time to go. She had waved and waved at Jasmine on the shore until she became a speck lost on the blinding horizon.

The sloop tacked south into Pine Island Sound, past tiny mangrove islands hemmed with bone-colored beaches. Spindly-legged blue heron waded in the shallows, and gold-crested pelicans swooped and crashed into the azure waters for fish. Two sleek dolphins arched and played through waves just off the ship's bow. The sun was warm, the breeze balmy under the cloud-puffed sky, but the beauty of the day hardly softened Lanie's grief and worry. Besides, Serafina and a bald pirate named Tortuga were ever watchful of any move she made, even to shift on her narrow seat. And whenever the alluring, seductive setting tempted her to relax, she would feel Sil's eyes fixed on her.

Not only was she being delivered to a stockaded fort as a captive, but her captor there was to be Silver Swords. She'd gained much other possibly useful knowledge by eavesdropping since she had been captured. Increased naval raids and threatened attacks from other pirate bands encroaching on Gasparilla's prime hunting grounds had forced him to make new plans for his prisoners. Soon the compound on Captiva Island—named for the female captives kept there—would be abandoned for a more defensible site at Turtle Bay. Over the years only old men who would not compromise the women's chastity had guarded Captiva. But several weeks ago, with the new threats, Gasparilla had put the wily, stern Sil in charge, since he trusted him. Another reason, Lanie thought, for her never to trust the man.

With a bravado she hardly felt, she leaned back under his narrowed gaze with her elbows on the low bulwarks as if she hadn't a care in the world. She tilted her face up to let the sun creep under her wide bonnet brim. Jasmine would have scolded at that, Lanie thought, and a tiny smile tilted the corners of her stiff lips. "Indelicate, my dear," her mama would say of her brash posture and her courting the sun. "Indelicate, my dear," Mama said with one arched eyebrow at so many things Lanie loved to do. From not crossing her ankles when she sat to daring to repeat papa's favorite oath, "damnation!" Mama had tried to stem the tide of her daughter's independent nature. Tears rose to Lanie's eyes as she thought of her gentle mama's pain when she heard of Lanie's capture. And what would Mama say if she ever heard of her sleeping next to a pirate whose eyes always undressed her? Or of one who touched her so familiarly if she hesitated to do anything he asked? Suddenly, Lanie grinned. "Indelicate, my dear," of course. And so it was, indeed, to be in that man's clutches on some wild, tropic island, Lanie told herself with a twinge of mingled dread and defiance.

"I allowed you to keep that bonnet to protect your fair skin out here," the deep voice slashed through her reverie. Lanie jerked upright. Tortuga had the tiller now, while Sil loomed over her. "You'll have no imported French creams to soothe a skin burn on Captiva, Miss McVey," he mocked with one booted foot propped on the planked seat so that it almost touched her skirts.

She shrugged her shoulders and did not answer. She had decided to show her utter contempt for his brutish ways by ignoring him. Rising to his taunts only meant catastrophe. She stared insolently at his big hands, hooked in the broad black leather belt, which emphasized his narrow hips and flat belly and which held his pistols and two swords. She marveled that his hands were always clean, even the fingernails. The narrow gold band he wore glinted at her from the little finger of his left hand. Suddenly, her vow of silence was too much to bear no matter how indelicate her mama would say she was.

"I declare, you stole that wedding band from some other helpless female," she accused, "just like you took my locket!"

He lifted his left hand to stare, almost as if surprised, at the slender ring. His jaw clenched hard. He jerked his hand down to rest on a sword hilt.

"I'm glad to hear you admit you're a helpless female at least. It makes my job so much easier," he clipped out. "You're just lucky to be allowed that bonnet, shoes and shawl so far. But all that can easily change on Captiva. Gasparilla's given me full sway there, though he's decreed the punishments I administer if anyone fails to toe the mark. I look forward to the inevitability you will not."

Sil stalked to his seat and took the tiller from Tortuga with a brusque nod. The woman had done it again! She intrigued him, taunted him, then threw everything in his face when he so much as made conversation. And how dare she mention Rebecca's ring, let alone accuse him of stealing it! It was his special talisman, which had guided him through all the tough times. That wedding ring was the mark of his vow to be true to her memory—and the child's. It was as dear and sacred to him as his dangerous duty to the navy and his personal oath to avenge his parents' loss. He'd be damned before he'd let this strong-willed woman get in the way of his dedication to all he'd lived for. He'd have to watch that she didn't incite the other prisoners in the stockade, or word might get back to Gasparilla and ruin things. And he wouldn't let her get him all riled again. The next time she stepped out of line, he was going to control her without losing control of himself!

He shot a narrow, frowning glance at her. She was turned away, facing toward the flow of tiny islands he deftly took the ship around. He looked pointedly away, too, but for the next few hours his eyes kept drifting to her, and his thoughts did, too.

Lanie stood with Sil in the hot noon sun in the stockaded compound on Captiva. It was across a sandy stretch of beach from the water, hidden in a grove of coconut palms on the narrow barrier island between Pine Island Sound and the broad Gulf of Mexico. The compound was oval-shaped with a hard-packed dirt floor. Five small palmetto thatch-roofed huts in which the prisoners lived stood in a semicircle facing a central driftwood fire with pots and a big kettle. Across from the huts stood an open-sided, roofed kitchen, rain cisterns and tubs, and a large, raised-floored hut with open sides for Sil and the guards. Two thatch-roofed wooden guard towers, each sporting Gasparilla's black, skulled flag, glared down on the crowded area.

Even in the heat, Lanie began to shiver. The closed huts were so tiny. She would never be able to sleep in one of them! The other buildings were open, but there would be no privacy from Sil's and the two guards' prying eyes. She had on far too much clothing for the heat and stifled breeze here. And, as the women captives stepped forward at the clanging of Sil's iron bar on a gong, she noted their eyes seemed either frightened or hard.

"Ladies, I have the distinct honor," Sil began, and she shot him a sideward glare at the sarcastic edge to his voice, "of introducing a new Captiva resident. I present Miss Melanie McVey from a sugarcane plantation outside New Orleans."

He introduced each woman to Lanie in turn. The seven, all with varying degrees of tattered gowns and straggling hair, were a conglomeration of nationalities, looks and languages. Doña Inez with her long nose, swarthy complexion and harsh glare was a Cuban importer's wife. Doña Maria de Madrid was indeed from Madrid; she seemed distant and aloof. Augusta, Lady Wyndham from London was frizzle-haired, blue-eyed and betrothed to a duke. She reminded Lanie of a nervous, frightened marsh rabbit. Lanie was relieved to hear three French women's names, as she could speak to them in French and Sil would never know what she said: Celeste Beaupré, a bayou planter's wife; Nanine de la Rouen, the oldest of the women; and Honorée Clemenceau, pretty and petite like a china doll. The one called Miss Pamela Ramsay from an indigo plantation in the West Indies slitted her eyes at Lanie instead of Sil, as if she were the enemy. Pamela was voluptuous, with chestnut hair and green eyes, but looked almost horsey, with large features crowding her long face. Each time she glanced at Sil or tried to catch his eyes, hers lit as if with green sulfur fires within.

"Miss McVey will be taking your place, Nanine, in Honorée's hut," Sil concluded with a smile at Nanine, an elderly, white-haired woman. She clasped her hands together in anticipation. "Your son's ransom has arrived in Havana and you'll be dropped there next ship out," he told her.

Lanie watched while petite Honorée and Celeste hugged Nanine; the sour Doña Inez whispered to the Spaniard, and Pamela Ramsay raked her hair back with splayed fingers and wet her thick lips with a quick lick of her pink tongue. Then she plopped her hands on curved hips and, smoothing her tawdry gold gown, swished over to Sil.

"Put the new fish in with me, and I'll keep a good eye on her for you, Sil," she purred. Her sharp green eyes met Lanie's in some unspoken challenge. "I can't abide the way the Lady Wyndham is always chattering her prayers in my hut at night. Always afraid she'll be ravished, when I know you'd never give a rap for the puking likes of her," she said with a twitch of skirts and a tilt-eyed, wide-mouthed, smile up at Sil.

"If I have to tell you again not to scare Augusta Wyndham with your own fantasies, Pamela, you'll be visiting the

Little Hut," Sil retorted and ignored her sputtering out-
rage.

He ordered the women back to whatever they were doing
and took Lanie to the open kitchen where Serafina was already busy chopping eggplant and garlic from the small
garden Lanie had seen outside. "You'll spend at least two
hours a day helping Serafina prepare meals," Sil informed
Lanie curtly. "And if you know what's good for you, you'll
keep clear of Doña Inez and Pamela Ramsay," he added
with a little squeeze of her upper arm.

She tugged away from him. "And clear of you! Then I'll
be just as happy as can be in this paradise you pirates pro-
vide for your hapless victims," she shot out so loud that
everyone turned to stare. Serafina looked sad as Lanie and
Sil glared hotly at each other. Some were shocked, some
amused. The man named Watchman, because of the array
of pocket watches he'd looted over the years, dared to bellow a laugh. But behind Sil and Lanie, Pamela Ramsay
raised a fist before she yanked it back into the folds of her
skirts and spit hard into the dirt at her feet.

Ten days later, Lanie sat on a three-legged stool in the
roofed, sideless kitchen of the compound where she and
Serafina were weaving broad-brimmed palmetto bonnets for
the other captives. Lanie's first night here, Pamela Ramsay
had stolen her Paris bonnet and ripped it to shreds when
she'd demanded it back. Her cheeks had soon gone pink and
peeled in the sun until Sil asked Serafina to make Lanie a
palmetto bonnet. Lanie had not only thanked Serafina for
it, but helped her cook. Lanie had found it best to keep busy
to make the time go and keep the ten-foot logged walls from
closing in on her. She couldn't accept how hopelessness and
boredom drugged the women here to dragging lethargy or
even bitter disputes when they should all be working together to survive their dire situation—and their dictatorial
captors.

But when she had tried to arrange an evening's entertainment among the women, two had shyly refused, two had
just stared, and Pamela and Doña Inez had laughed. Still,

she had tried to befriend the women who would let her, especially Honorée and Augusta. She missed Jasmine terribly and prayed she was safe and well, but reaching out to others helped some.

Lanie had also endeavored to keep spirits up by persuading the other women to clean their pitiful huts and decorate them with the fresh palmetto branches and shells Serafina brought to the compound from beach walks. Lanie had encouraged Honorée and Augusta to enjoy conversation over more leisurely meals, despite the wretched surroundings. As a result, the three of them often talked through the long evenings before the torches went out, sharing stories about their distant homes. Lanie even got Serafina to sit down with them, though she was hesitant to say much.

The other captives ignored Serafina because they thought of her only as a servant or because they found her speech hard to understand and her appearance embarrassing. Pamela Ramsay took out her bitterness on the girl when Sil wasn't in earshot. Although it annoyed Lanie that poor Serafina adored a brute like Sil, Lanie went out of her way to spend time with the girl. Serafina had become a sort of challenge, as she had obviously detested Lanie in the beginning for some reason, and Lanie was only slowing winning her over.

Today in Serafina's gentle company, Lanie was humming under her breath, the first time she, who loved to sing, had done so since her capture. "You're so clever with your hands, Serafina," she told the girl as she tried to emulate her dexterity with the palm fronds.

Serafina was so pleased that for once she forgot to cover her mouth when she smiled. "Now, what did you say were some of those wild vegetables you put in that delicious salmagundi salad last night?" Lanie asked.

Serafina explained about the different herbs and edible wild food she gleaned from the native vegetation. The usually reticent girl talked and talked. But, as Lanie listened and her hands worked on, her eyes drifted to the guards in their towers again. They, at least, had a breeze. Old Watchman with his grandfatherly face and crinkly blue eyes was actually the most trigger-tempered of all, she had decided. He always kept his pistols primed and his cutlass blades whetted, though he never seemed to need them. Even from here she could see his ten-inch, curve-bladed cutlass stuck through his belt, from which also dangled his numerous pocket watches.

How she would love to get her hands on that cutlass the next time Sil ordered her to obey! When she was sixteen she had coerced her father's overseer, André Delacroix, to teach her how to handle the big sugarcane-cutting machete. Cane machetes looked a great deal like these pirate cutlasses. Her thoughts drifted away from Serafina's chatter like the cigarro smoke that wafted down from Parrot, the other guard in his tower, so she did not notice that Pamela had sauntered up until her shadow fell across their feet.

"At least that's one thing you're good at, McVey," Pamela said and fanned her flushed face with her spiky palmetto fan. "Domestic work with Sil's little dago drudge. Must have done all your own cooking on Papa's plantation, I take it," she taunted Lanie with a nasal snicker.

Though Serafina's nimble fingers halted, Lanie plunged on bending and weaving the green fronds into a hat brim. "I will thank you not to vent your spleen on Serafina," she shot back without looking up. "And, in case you haven't noticed, Your Majesty, Queen Pamela, this is not anyone's papa's plantation here."

Pamela's thick lips pursed into a pout, and her stabbing green eyes darted around the compound to make certain Sil was still across the way speaking with the others. "I've noticed all right, you mouthy little twit. I've been in this hellhole for seven months just waiting for that maddening stud to bring me news of my freedom—or do something exciting!" She laughed through her nose, then jabbed her fan toward Serafina. "Listen, girl, if you tell him a thing I've said, I swear I'll tear that clacking tongue out of your useless, ugly mouth."

Serafina flinched and said nothing. Lanie started to rise, then decided against drawing the guards' or Sil's attention.

But she covered Serafina's trembling hand with hers and tilted her face up to Pamela's at last.

"And I'm telling you, Miss Ramsay, if you ever insult Serafina again, *I* will tell him. And you can just leave Honorée and poor frightened Augusta alone, too. I declare, I've known bullies before, but they were all loudmouthed, repulsive men. Damnation, but you have proved the sexes equal in at least that."

"Don't you think I'm on to your game?" Pamela hissed.

"My game," Lanie brazened with her voice rising, "is to survive this place—and to get some of you cowed or bitter women to admit we need each other while we're here!"

Pamela snorted. "Your little evening entertainment, you mean."

"It would help to pass the time. I can sing, and Serafina tells me she knows a dance called the fandango, so—"

"Your game is to seduce Sil with your dramatics, out of bed and then in!" The woman swung toward Serafina. "You did know that, didn't you, little mouse Serafina? This slut's hoping to take your adored god from you, to turn our stony-faced jailer into the stallion stud he has every potential of being if he wasn't so pious and dedicated to heaven knows what!"

It was Serafina's scream that stopped Lanie from launching herself at the woman's distorted, poisonous face to shut her up. She had leaped to her feet and shoved Pamela by the time Sil tore across the clearing to yank them apart.

"Your new little bitch McVey is a rabble-rousing rebel, Sil, and I—" Pamela got out before Sil shoved her into Parrot's arms as he ran up.

"You two have been circling each other for days," Sil scolded as he pulled Lanie back. "Now listen, both of you! There are no leaders here besides me! Parrot, put Miss Ramsay in her hut until tomorrow morning until she can find a more civil attitude and tongue! Miss McVey shows so much ambition here to organize things I'll just take her along to Turtle Bay and put her to work organizing a broom on dirt floors for the afternoon."

He gave Lanie no chance to react or protest. But Pamela screamed out that it wasn't fair and he should take her, too. The last thing Lanie saw as he hustled her out of the stockade was Serafina's woeful wave before the wooden door thumped shut behind them.

She was so excited to be out of the stockade, she almost thanked him. But Sil practically tossed her into the sloop, and she dared not speak until they had sailed a good way north. When they crossed the broad mouth of the harbor past Boca Grande, she wondered how Jasmine was doing in the midst of all those barbarian pirates. And how were her parents reacting? By now they must have heard of her capture. As for Justin Lyon, no real feelings would come as she expected them to. Her emotions, even her memories seemed mired in mental mud. Perhaps he wouldn't even want her after this defiling experience, anyway. At least he and Papa might have the authorities out looking for her. The navy had a small base at New Orleans.

Sil was glaring at her, just as he had been doing for days. He seemed to be daring her to cross him. At the thought of being alone with him, taking his curt orders, being under those sharp eyes, her stomach rose and fell just like the boat did through the waves. But she had no intention for one moment of letting him think he had cowed or controlled her as he had the others. At last, desperate to escape the perusal of his stern, steady gaze, she spoke.

"Sooner or later, the United Stated Navy will clear all of you out like foul bilge from a ship, you know," she said and swept her arm toward Boca Grande.

He looked startled, then guilty. "The navy. Will they?" he said after a moment's silence.

"They cleared the Lafitte brothers out of Barataria Bay near New Orleans, you know, and forced them to move to Galveston Bay. Texas may not be a state yet, but the navy will eventually get him there, too. And Jean Lafitte has fine manners and was an American hero in the War of 1812, which is more than I can say for most of the low scum around here."

"My, my, but your sweeping knowledge of naval history boggles a limited mind like mine," he retorted. "And what does the American Navy think of your fiancé's little deals with Lafitte?"

She whirled to face him so fast her hair whipped in her face and some of it swept in her mouth when she answered. "What are you talking about? Of course, some plantation owners have dealt with Lafitte for slaves in the past. That would be bad enough. But Lafitte has nothing to do with Monsieur Lyon's shipping or importing business!"

"No? Then I can only say I must admire the job Lyon's done keeping his underhanded dealings secret from someone he's no doubt been—well, intimate with."

He ignored her protests as he cut the sloop in toward shore. He felt great relief that she evidently knew nothing about Lyon's alleged undercover dealing with Lafitte. But Gasparilla believed it, and other evidence pointed to it. It was something he and the navy would certainly pursue when he got out of here. Sil regretted he had even tipped her off about it, but he had to know that she was innocent of any suspicion.

These past ten days, he had grudgingly come to admire her spunk. She'd greatly bolstered the attitudes of some of the more morose and weak women in the compound. The more he watched her alluring beauty and grace under pressure, the more he'd longed to get her alone. He'd told himself time and again it was just to be certain she was not really privy to Lyon's dirty dealings. It was not that she heated his blood or that he found her appealing and wanted desperately to protect her in his weaker moments. After all, her fate must be no concern of his in the grander scheme of things he was committed to. The United States Navy had sent him on this deadly covert mission to penetrate Gasparilla's stronghold at any cost, any sacrifice. He was to discover all Gasparilla's contacts before he sent for help to destroy the pirates' lair from without and within, and this woman would only get in the way of that.

"I was just fishing for information," he told her in the awkward silence. "It's just that Gasparilla would give his

ruby ear stud to have a man in New Orleans to legally un-
load goods such as the ones we took off the *Bonne Femme*,
and I've heard rumors Lafitte has someone like that.''

"Well, it is certainly not Justin Lyon!" she reiterated.
"And I'd thank you to go fishing with someone else's reputation, though of course a man like you has not the slightest understanding of that!''

"A man's reputation? It's of great importance here in our
little civilization," he told her. "Here a man's reputation
depends on the most loot, the most kills, the most wom-
en—''

She returned to icy silence. Damnation, she fumed, she
was not going to discuss her fiancé with a low-bred cutthroat! Still, it started her wondering about the way Justin's ships were so seldom stopped, and pirates seemed to
take only other shippers' vessels—before Gasparilla, that is.
And then, too, there was the way Justin treated his slaves.
Of late she had started to bother over matters like that.

Turtle Bay was a deep blue cove, with a stockade much
like the one on Captiva except its walls were only half built.
The huts looked completed except for their roofs. Like the
hateful tyrant he was, Sil drove Lanie all afternoon right
along with the men who were already there. She swept the
dirt floors and holystoned the new tabletop in his hut until
it shone. She even helped one of the pirate women thatch the
new kitchen roof, carrying fresh-cut fronds up a shaky ladder to her. Finally, however, she just gave in to the heat and
Sil's earlier suggestion to rip her velour inner sleeves from
the puffy over sleeves that covered her shoulders. Her gown
was already a mess, torn and dirty. Reduced to this from the
haute couture trousseau she had purchased in civilized New
York but a few weeks ago! She would have loved to go
barefooted like the other workers, but feared someone
would take her shoes.

She glared at Sil whenever she could, but he stayed busy
barking orders at the crude carpenters when he wasn't crit-
icizing her. She ignored everyone as best she could, especially the skinny boy with bovine eyes who was cutting fresh

palmetto fronds for the thatch. And she was dying of thirst. Even some of that rum bumboo punch the pirates all got roaring drunk on would be welcomed now. Was the brute trying to kill her? Did he want to break her down? To make her beg? Determinedly, despite cut fingers, aching legs and a sore back, she worked on. Slowly, as the hours dribbled away, the workers began to drift off. It was then Lanie spotted the cutlass the boy had left among the fronds while he'd gone to talk to Sil.

Daring thoughts bombarded her. If she was careful, maybe she could smuggle the cutlass to Captiva hidden in her skirts. No, too ridiculous, too dangerous, but she could hide it nearby to retrieve when the women were transferred here. First, however, she had to take it. It galled her to ask Sil's permission for anything, but she sauntered over and said meekly, "I need to have a moment alone in the bushes. You understand." He only nodded and turned away.

She tried not to walk too fast. She darted one glance at Sil. He was pointing upward and staring at a new watch-tower. Quick as lightning, she stooped to grab the weapon and the bouquet of palm fronds it lay in. She strolled around a corner in the path, then darted off it with her armful.

She looked desperately for somewhere clearly marked to bury it. Though the idea of trying to get it back with Sil in the boat was ludicrous, she wished she could surprise him with it to make him jump over the side of the boat and into the harbor. She didn't know the first thing about sailing, but she was certain the wind would take the sloop far enough toward land so she could escape. And he'd be left behind treading water—if he could swim.

Her eyes lit on a leafy gumbo-limbo tree with peeling reddish bark. It was the tallest tree around. She fell to her knees and began to dig with the blade to bury it in the sandy soil.

"I usually trust ladies to take care of nature's necessities alone," the voice behind her said, "but you've always been the exception."

She gasped, turned, was on her feet to face an angry Sil.
He stood, fists on lean hips, with his booted feet spread. It
was then she realized she held the cutlass in both hands facing him as if she meant to fight. She knew she should throw
it down and take whatever punishment he was planning to
mete out, but everything suddenly churned wild inside her:
the taking of the ship, the blood on the deck, selling and
buying Jasmine, her forced captivity and this man's claim
about her fiancé. She knew how to wield a machete to chop
the heavy cane. He might take her but she could at least
fight him first.

"Another surprise from little Lanie," he goaded as if he
had read her thoughts. He drew one of the two silver swords
she'd heard had made his reputation among the pirates.
He'd fought four of them off at once to earn their admiration, Serafina had said.

She yanked her mind back to this unreal reality. The devil
actually grinned at her. His smug, superior, avid look—that
did it! She darted forward once and clanged his weapon
soundly before retreating. He lifted his dark brows in surprise, then began to circle her, shuffling carefully through
the loose sand on the path. She knew she was not as sure
footed. These shoes had raised blisters on her heels. She had
taken the bustle from her gown, and the once fashionable,
ankle-length skirts now dragged in back.

"This is your worst mistake yet, Lanie," he said, using
Jasmine's name for her as if to throw her more off guard
than she already was. He darted, tapped her blade twice as
if to play with her, then retreated in a half crouch. To her
dismay the clang of metal brought the straggling workers on
the run.

"Slice her skirts off, Sil! Get her good!"

"Aye, use your other sharp sword between those powerful thighs on her, eh, Sil?" someone shouted and roared
more bawdy encouragement.

She broke out in a sheen of sweat that made the hilt slippery in her grip. She knew things had gone too far and she
could not win. Yet something in her urged her on. When he
stepped forward again and gave her a quick smack on her

bottom with his blade, she lunged. She took him unawares. With a whack and a clang, the heavy blade of her cutlass smacked his sword from his hand.

He looked both surprised and angry. Swiftly, he drew his other sword and advanced. She parried his light blows first to the right, then left, right, left. He was playing with her again, she was certain. Her arms began to ache and tremble from the weight of the cutlass. Her wide eyes were riveted to each move of his big hands and the flashing silver blade. For the first time since she'd blindly begun to fight, she was distinctly afraid.

"I'm tiring of this," he told her. He was breathing heavily now, too, but perhaps from anger rather than exertion. "Have you been acquainted with pirates before or did dear Justin teach you to use a cutlass?" he taunted.

Her panicked brain caught none of his words until he finally declared, "*En garde*, then, Miss McVey. And to the victor belongs the vanquished!"

He darted. His sword blocked her panicked half swing. They stood, blades locked, stiff-armed, close together, shoulder to shoulder. She made the mistake of glancing up from the union of their weapons to his eyes. When she tried to step back, he shoved. She sprawled on her backside at his booted feet while the cutlass went flying out of reach. She sat there dismayed while everyone cheered and Sil sheathed his swords and scolded the boy named Johnny whose weapon she had taken. And then, just as she moved to get up to brush herself off, he pulled her to her feet. In one swift movement, she found herself thrown over his shoulder like a sack of cotton before he strode quickly toward the shore.

"Put me down! Please!" The words jostled out of her as she kicked and squirmed helplessly. He only cracked a hand hard on her already bruised bottom to still her.

"Too late for politeness between us. You've been a thorn in my side from the beginning!" he roared.

He strode down the beach far away from the others. He walked around a jumble of rocks, into another cove, splashing surf into her face with his long strides. She stopped her futile struggling. How good and safe the sight of the stockade on Captiva would seem now! Sil's booted feet were crunching ribbons of shells tossed up by the tides. He dropped his sword belt and pistols. He splashed out into the surf boot deep, deeper! He was going to drown her! She pushed both hands on his back to lift her upper body away from him. "Please, I swear I won't fight you ever again!" she cried desperately.

Her words were drowned as he lunged into the next wave, taking her with him. The impact of the cool wall of water stunned her. She came up sputtering. His hands were on her waist, lifting her as he had in her dream, not shoving her down. Her skirts clung to her legs; her soaked hair blanketed her face. She shoved it back and gasped for air just as the next wave hit. But he held her still and they rode up and over it together.

"Promise again," he gasped, as he slicked his hair off his brown forehead with the shove of one big hand. "It may keep me from beating you within an inch of your life."

"Promise?"

"To never fight me again—and add to that, 'No matter what you do to me, my absolute lord and master.'"

"You vile, wretched bas—" she had sputtered before he pulled her hard against him in the next glittering surge of emerald and diamond water. One hand was fastened hard in her hair to hold her head still while his other arm grappled her slender form against his own hard one. The pull and sway of tide blossomed her skirts up around her waist so her bare legs touched taut material stretched over his powerful thighs and the slick leather of his boots.

"Say it!" he ordered, but his voice trembled with his own emotion. He didn't want to order her around, he wanted to lure her, to please her. She had held him prisoner these past ten days in a way he hoped she'd never know. He could not resist watching and touching this amazing woman. He had tried and he had failed. He kissed her hard just as the next wave hit. Cool and clean, they rode it together.

Her hands clung to the soaked front of his slash-necked shirt. It pulled free from his belt like her floating skirts so that her fingers wove through his mat of thick chest hair to caress bare flesh. His mustache, cool and wet, tickled under her nose.

She felt suddenly detached from the real world, from all she had ever been. The kiss, both sweet and salty, deepened and, like a madwoman, she did not resist. His tongue plundered the warm, wet cove of her mouth. She challenged the sleek plunge of it in a new kind of duel, tongue tip to tongue tip. He nibbled at her lower lip; she bit him lightly and licked the drips from his mustache. He moaned and pressed her more fiercely to him.

"You're as hard to break as a rapier blade—and as dangerous," he muttered. "But I can't help it that—"

They nearly lost their rise-and-fall footing in the next roll of water. His hands plunged under the bloom of her skirts. She gasped when he cupped both bare buttocks under the short linen garment the French called panties. He molded her to his hands, slid lower to stroke the backs of her thighs. His legs intruded to separate hers so she almost rode him in the surf. Her bent knees bobbed easily along his hips and then his ribs as he tipped her back to kiss and nip her pointed breasts through her stretched, wet bodice.

Then he crushed her in his arms until her stiff budded nipples flattened against his chest. Through his soaked trousers, she felt the taut thrust of him that was somehow only exciting and not alarming. For the first time in her life, she was somehow swept up beyond herself and all caution.

He was drunk with passion. The tumult of the fight had lowered all his barriers, until his mind was flooded with the luscious sensuality of her willing body.

But then he felt the press of the thin ring on his small finger as he grasped her sweet flesh. Another woman's face, wan, floating, swam through his brain. It had never been like this with Becky. Not this mind-wrenching, body-yearning desire to possess a woman! But her memory sobered him, slapped him to himself like the next white-capped wave. This stunning, flesh-and-blood woman could mean the ruin of his revenge, his mission, his loyalty to Becky—and his very death. With one glance of her sea-green eyes, she had made him forget and forsake all his vows!

"Damn you! Damn, damn!" Lanie heard him mutter, as he lifted her away and began to haul her toward the shore like so much booty again.

Dazed by what had happened, she floundered to find her feet in the sand as they staggered ashore. At first she had only been grateful he hadn't hurt or killed her. And then! She couldn't face him when she realized the wanton way she had acted, and with a cutthroat pirate at that. And he'd been the one to stop, not she. It was that taboo on the female captives to be ransomed that had halted him, she thought, and was suddenly grateful for one of Gasparilla's rules.

While he turned his back and strapped on his sword belt, she crumpled in the sand with her face in her hands. She was so ashamed, so confused, so exhausted. And yet it had all been so exhilarating, wild, and free! She was his captive, and yet she soared beyond all bonds when he touched her like that and she responded!

He pulled her to her feet and hurried her, unspeaking, toward their boat in the sand. She blessed the fact he could not tell her tears from the water than ran down from her glazed hair.

It was after dark when Lanie finished washing the sticky salt from her hair in rainwater from the compound cistern. She had washed and hung her gown to dry in her and Honorée's tiny hut. She dared not leave it in the open, lest Pamela or Doña Inez steal or ruin it. She would put it on damp and let it dry on her in the sun tomorrow.

She felt exhausted and yet she could not sleep. She was sore where that demon had smacked her bottom with the sword and bruised in several other unmentionable places where he had held her to him in the water. She told herself she had escaped unscathed but for that. After all, he had only warned her to tell no one on Captiva what had happened. And he had threatened that the next time she disobeyed him she could expect to find herself spending time in the dreaded little prison outside the stockade walls they called the Little Hut. But deep down she knew she had not escaped unscathed at all.

In her wildest dreams she had never imagined that a man touching a woman could be like that. Especially since it was all so improper, so indelicate, so—rough. And with a foul brigand who lived by abduction, theft and murder! The dark, stubborn streak and hint of sensuality that Justin had evoked in her had never even come close to the plunging passion Silver Swords ripped from her. It was deadly dangerous, terrifying, uncivilized—and so overwhelmingly alluring!

She froze when she heard men's voices in the distant dark: Sil's and old Watchman's. She squinted to see them hunched together over the single lantern in their open-sided hut. Once again, the mere sound of Sil's voice in the night shattered her senses. Quickly, before they saw her in her petticoat and chemise, she darted into the shelter of her hut.

"By ginger, Sil, you gotta see the prettiest watch I bought off a bloke on the north beach today," Watchman said. "Now don't fuss none. He was alone and only looking for turtles, and I knowed who he was. Used to work for Gasparilla years ago but went off by hisself. I says to him, cast off if he values his hide, and paid him real fair for this watch. Must be getting old, Sil. Should a kilt him for it and not paid a farthing. See, it's got a real nice miniature painting of a pretty lady inside. The initials on it is J.B. Real fine work, see?"

Sil froze, and the hair along the back of his neck prickled. After all these years of wondering? After all his careful, restrained questioning about what had become of them—it had to be!

"Can I see it, Watchman?"

His hands shook as he snapped open the engraved gold top to display the familiar watch face his father had proudly taught him to tell time with, and opposite it the miniature enamel of his mother's sweet face his father had always carried in his inside waistcoat pocket—next to his heart.

"Like it, Sil?"

"I know you value your watches, Watchman," Sil said, his voice ragged, "but I'd give a lot to have this one. Real pretty. The woman—she looks like someone I knew once."

"Not the one you been pining for what gave you that little ring you wear?"

"No, not her," he managed.

"You know me and my watches, Sil. Just don't know 'bout selling it, by ginger."

"The man you got it from," Sil asked, his voice now deadly cold, "what direction did he cast off to?"

"Due south. Right toward Sanibel."

Sil's heart flopped over. Probably one of Scarface Jack's men from Sanibel Island on a scout here to plan a raid. Scarface Jack's pirate crews had been nosing in this territory just a bit too much, but Gasparilla's perverted moral code balked at pirate civil war. The sooner they moved the women from here, the better, by next week at least, Sil told himself. But right now, duty and danger aside, he just had to chance looking on Scarface Jack's Sanibel for the man who'd had this watch. He couldn't help if it he risked his other task—he'd waited ten years for this revenge. He'd let Watchman keep the watch safe for him and set out alone at dawn in the sloop as if he was going back to Turtle Bay. And he'd have to replace the sword Lanie had dented today with that swift swing of her cutlass. He had no doubt, if he met with danger on Sanibel, even his skill at swordplay might not be enough to save him.

"What's the man's name who had this pretty trinket, Watchman?" he asked. "I like to know who's come calling on my island, that's all."

"Your island," Watchman grunted with a chuckle. "That's a good'n, Sil. Little Caesar, we used to call him. You know, like that Roman emperor what had it all and then got hisself stabbed to death."

Sil only nodded. The old man's rambling next words didn't even sink in as he began to polish his silver swords.

Chapter Four

By noon Sil located the man Watchman had spoken of. Gasparilla had evidently named Little Caesar when he was dead drunk, for the ugly brute, broad-shouldered and black-bearded, stood more than six and a half feet tall. But Sil didn't waver from his plan. He told the man he'd come to fetch him because Watchman wanted more information about the tiny map they'd found hidden behind the picture of the woman in the watch. The man's beady black eyes flamed at the hint of a map. Rumors about buried treasure were always rampant in these parts.

It amazed and worried Sil how smoothly lies came to his lips lately. He'd hated himself the day he'd lectured Lanie on not telling lies when his whole life was one massive lie. But it was all for a good cause, he told himself—actually more than one. Still, he'd played too long by pirate rules, he thought as he led the man to the northern tip of Sanibel Island where he'd anchored the sloop. His mother's face— real, not painted on enamel—flashed through his brain again as if to urge him on. How wonderful their hours to-gether had been during his boyhood in New York, even the long months his father was away at sea.

His mother had taught him, encouraged him—had him reciting Shakespeare scenes with her until he knew so many by heart. "It's life, real life in these plays!" she'd told him more than once. But he hadn't believed her until he'd grown up and lost and suffered. And now, like her favorite char-

acter, Hamlet, he faced the probable murderer of his father
and told lies while he bided his time for bloody revenge.

He halted next to the beached boat he'd rowed in and
turned to face the giant of a man. "You've had the watch
for years, you say?" he asked. "Watchman wants to know
if you got a real good claim to it."

The story spilled from the greedy bastard's mouth. "So,
that wily old Gasparilla, see," he rattled on, "he got drunk
that day after we took the ship—the day I got the watch.
Gasparilla, he made shark meat outta the captain of the
Seaward Bound for trying to defend his wife he had on
board."

Tattered heartbeats tore Sil's chest. The *Seaward
Bound*—his father's merchant schooner! Gasparilla had
murdered his father before his mother's eyes!

"See, the captain's wife was the woman in the painting, I
swear it," Little Caesar plunged on with a nod of his shaggy
head as he propped one filthy bare foot on the prow of the
boat. "An' on one of Gasparilla's drunken whims, he let the
crew cast lots for her, 'stead a standin' to auction. She was
a-cryin' and a-beggin' to be kilt with her husband. Judas
Priest, after that she never did look much like that happy
painting in the watch," he said and shook his head at the
memory.

Sil's fists clenched so hard his arm muscles cramped and
knotted. He fought to keep his face merely interested, but
he longed to explode ten years of agony at this monster.

"But I won her fair an' square an' took her back to Boca
Grande," Little Caesar continued. "Had the watch hidden
in her skirts, so it was mine, too. Gave herself airs like a fine
lady, but I took that outta her." His obscene voice droned
on while the horrible scenes he described played through
Sil's mind.

"But, Judas, the stupid bitch drowned herself in the bay
one day," Little Caesar muttered. "So Gasparilla, he sold
me one of his castoffs from the harem. I swear, the map's
mine and I just forgot I put it in the watch!"

"There is no map," Sil said, his voice deadly cold.

"No map? What the hell's all this about then?"

"This, you foul bastard, is about justice for the captain of the *Seaward Bound* you helped kill and—"

"Now, lookee here! That was Gasparilla's say-so!"

"And the woman you killed as surely as if you'd held her under the water was my mother!" Sil drew his sword so fast it barely grazed the sheath. He could have cut the monster down where he stood with his mouth gaping air like a fish, but his stomach turned at outright slaughter. "If you would care to defend yourself," he said, giving the proper challenge to a duel in a voice he could barely contain.

The giant backed away several long strides on the hard-packed sand. But when he had his leeway, he yanked neither his sword nor his cutlass from his belt. He drew a pistol from inside his slash-necked shirt. Sil ducked as he fired, but felt the bullet tear through his left arm. He hadn't even seen that gun! He lifted his sword and charged the man.

Little Caesar cocked his gun to fire again, but before he could pull the trigger Sil's sword had connected with his chest. The force of Sil's rush carried him past his opponent, but when he spun around, sword still held at the ready, he saw that Little Caesar lay still on the damp sand, face up, eyes wide, a huge red flower blossoming on his shirt front.

Sil didn't wait to see if he was dead. His arm was going icy numb. The shot might bring others. Jack Scarfield's men wouldn't think a thing of torturing a captive to tell them why he was here. They'd happily kill someone who'd killed one of their own!

He rowed for the sloop with his one good arm as if the oar were a paddle in a canoe. He heard shouts behind him but did not look back. He clambered up the rope ladder over the bulwarks, abandoning the rowboat. He sliced through the anchor rope, then threw his sword to the narrow deck. He looked back then: four men on the shore shouting at him, brandishing cutlasses. The giant of a man sprawled in the surf had not moved.

Pain chattered at him as he unfurled the mainsail. His sleeve had gone shiny crimson but at least it was his left arm. His first taste of revenge had turned bitter in his heart. One job done and another, he told himself, far greater yet to do.

But when that was done, if he lived through it, whom would he seek redress against for Becky's death birthing the baby? He was the only one at fault in that.

Funny, how Becky's face was harder to recall since Lanie McVey had catapulted into his life... He knew his thoughts were plunging like this sloop... Father had taught him to sail... He had gone on two voyages with him on the *Seaward Bound*, one to England, one to France... But then he'd been in school when they sailed the Florida passage together for their twentieth anniversary. It was a regular business trip for Father, and the only time Mother had gone with him... She had said her son's studies were more important, or he would have gone with them and be dead now, too... He didn't want to die... Didn't want to faint... Had never fainted but that time Tortuga set his broken leg in Serafina's hut...

One-handed, he tried to tack toward Captiva in the next burst of breeze, but his head slumped on his chest and he crumpled to the deck.

By the time one of Gasparilla's crews found him, the little sloop had taken him north past Captiva off Boca Grande. They'd sponged his bullet hole—a double one as the lead had gone clear through. Since he'd lost so much blood, Old Emma, the meddling hunchbacked crone who was Gasparilla's answer to any ailment, had decided not to bleed him with leeches. He'd been delivered to his hut on the beach where Tortuga's Mexican woman and Jasmine had tended him, though all he did was sleep and eat for two days.

He finally told Gasparilla that Jack Scarfield's man Little Caesar had been spying on Captiva and that he'd had to kill him. He asked for ten more guards for the stockade there, but pickings were good in the gulf and Gasparilla insisted he could only spare Specs and Red Legs.

On the third night Sil was almost back to normal strength, so everyone left him alone with Jasmine. After all, he recalled with an embarrassed grimace, people would expect him to want his money's worth since he'd paid good coin for her. He wondered what poor Jasmine herself felt, a slave who had been sold into this second slavery.

Now that the others were gone, it surprised him how servilely Jasmine acted. She fussed over him worse than even Serafina did, and she was nervous and jumpy. Maybe this perpetual-motion slave-girl routine was her method for survival here, and he could understand that. Deep down, she probably hated him as much as Lanie did. He supposed Lanie would rejoice when she heard he'd been shot.

"I'm real fine at rubbing a sore neck or back," Jasmine told him in her rich, soft voice when she padded in, barefooted with the supper dishes she'd scraped clean with sand.

"Thanks, but no," he answered. "One more good night's sleep and I'll be heading back to Captiva. But I do appreciate all you've done for me these last few days."

At that, she sat across the small hut from him and leaned her back against the wall. She stretched out her sleek legs, then nervously smoothed her ruffled skirt over her knees. Gasparilla had auctioned off Lanie's extensive trousseau, and most of the women of Boca Grande now paraded around in elegant Parisian garments, like this jade-green taffeta petticoat and chemise Jasmine wore for a gown.

Finally, she spoke again. "I was pleased to help. You one of the few kind ones here, and Miz Lanie needs your protection more'n I do, even."

He wasn't quite certain how to follow that up, since he didn't want to drop his facade of ruthless pirate with her. He had the urge to calm and comfort her but could not let that get in the way of his duty any more than he could allow the way he felt about Lanie to affect him.

"When I had the fever, I could always tell without opening my eyes when you came into the hut to sponge my face off," he told her. "That outfit rustles." He couldn't help picturing how alluring Lanie would look in it, but he thrust that from his mind. "How does it feel wearing something Lanie bought for her wedding to your admired friend Justin Lyon?"

He watched a frown crumple her fine brow. He squinted to see her face in the dimness of the hut. She crossed her arms over her full breasts. "Bah! Decent clothes real scarce here, though why I worry about looking decent 'round this place is a laugh."

He noted she had skimmed right by his probe about Lyon, but at least she was back to that same old defiant streak she shared with Lanie. But he found himself wondering if Jasmine actually knew something dire about Lyon she'd withheld from her mistress. Lanie evidently adored the slippery bastard. How he'd love to have more on Lyon than he already did! With a start, he realized he was actually envious of Lanie's feelings for a man he'd never met.

"And did you worry about looking decent back on—what's its name—Magnolia Hill Plantation?" he inquired.

Jasmine's dark eyes slammed into his at that turn of talk. "According to the fine folk of New Orleans, slaves never really decent, one way or t'other, even decked out in Miz Lanie's best. 'Course, she thinks she been real good to me, but there's only one human being I'd want to belong to—" She let the words slip before she bit her lip and looked away.

"Some lucky man you belong to body and soul?" he asked, though he realized too late he should not have worded it that way.

"Not what you think, 'cepting if you're counting yourself as my master here," she answered warily.

He lowered his voice. "No, Jasmine, I'm not, though I don't want anyone else here knowing that. I bought you because you didn't deserve to be treated like a piece of merchandise that day—or ever."

Her mouth dropped open and her teeth gleamed white before she closed it. "Then I can't ever thank you enough. Miz Lanie's real lucky to have a man like you guarding her safety over there on Captiva. And thank you for being a gentleman and not making all sorts of demands on me."

He shifted his weight to sit cross-legged. The girl was clever, but how clever? Did she sense, as he knew Serafina did, how drawn he was to her mistress? Had he given it away that he had been born more gentleman than pirate and this rough, crude facade was the act of his life? The last thing he needed was any of these women guessing he was not what he said he was.

"Maybe I don't make all sorts of demands because I don't favor tart-tongued women who don't know their place in a man's world!" he threw at her. Insults always worked with Lanie. "Or maybe I don't like dark-skinned girls, however pretty," he added to be certain she'd back off.

"Bah! I've seen the worst of it between white men and dark-skinned women," she blurted as if he'd pulled some plug in her bottled-up emotions. "My mama belonged to a white man once who kept her for a fancy mistress. But she made the big mistake thinking she as good as white 'cause he was kind and a gentleman to her. He gave her a fine house of her own on the rue des Ramparts in New Orleans—at least till he got tired of her and the babies she bred him with their dark skin." Her voice dripped acid, seemed not her own, but she finally got hold of herself and stopped the tirade. "*Voilà*, I got only this fine house," she said more quietly, and threw a graceful bare arm out to encompass the crude hut.

He shook his head so she wouldn't feel the need to say more. He wanted to tell her she was safe with him, that he hadn't touched any of the women here at Boca Grande, even the ones who'd thrown themselves at him. And not just because he didn't want to fight their men for them. Since Becky had died bearing the stillborn child and he had come home too late, he hadn't been able to face touching another woman that way, maybe planting a child in her—until Lanie. It had only been since Lanie had crashed into his well-laid plans that he'd even cared about possessing a woman's body again, about making hot love to her and her alone—

"Jasmine, this fine house is all yours tonight," he told her. He stood quickly. "And, when your Miss Lanie's ransomed, I'll do my best to see you go home with her." If I'm still alive and here then, he thought. He flexed his wounded arm and realized it didn't hurt him for the first time. "You'd better get some sleep," he added before either of them could reveal more.

He went outside under the black satin sky sprinkled with diamond pinpoint stars. He gazed across rippling obsidian water in the direction of Captiva and realized he missed Lanie. Tomorrow it was back to playing prisoner and captive, to living lies about who he was and what he wanted. But the thing that scared him most tonight was that he wanted Lanie McVey. If he could only possess her once, carefully to make certain not to make a child, he'd be free of the way she imprisoned his thoughts and feelings! To cool the hopeless lurch of lust he felt for Lanie—surely since he still loved Becky, that was all it was—he sprinted down to the beach and jumped into the cool water of the bay.

When the single oil lamp went out, Jasmine still lay in the lonely darkness of Silver Sword's hut, staring up at the low ceiling. She marveled at the fact she'd almost shared with him one of her two deep secrets, which even Miss Lanie didn't know. She'd almost told him about the man she loved and would always love—the man who wanted her and whom she would maybe never see again. And if she did she would turn away again, because there was something so big that must be done.

But it was not the deep shadows of this hut she saw as she stared and remembered. She envisioned again the dim, slanted ceiling under the livery stable eaves that day when she had found her heaven on earth.

It had been the one bright, warm time in those dark, cold days she had run away from the Bouchet Plantation to New Orleans to find her dying mama, Nola Bouchet. Mama, like many slaves, had taken the name of the plantation that had bred her. The stunning, elegant woman had been a mere housemaid in a shabby mansion near the rue Chartres in her last years. When she began to waste away for no apparent reason, the family that owned her had been going to sell her until she became too ill to move. One of the plantation carriage drivers who sometimes spent hours in town waiting for Monsieur Bouchet to go about his business had told Jasmine her mama was dying. Desperate, she'd walked clear into town without permission to see her. But when she heard he shocking things her mama had to say, she became more desperate yet.

After Nola Bouchet had sighed her life away, the seventeen-year-old girl had walked the streets of New Orleans endlessly. No mama; no papa. Her youngest brother had been sold far away. Her brother Sam, two years behind her, was a fieldhand on the Bouchet Plantation. But she was a house servant and seldom saw Sam.

Step after weary, desolate step through the streets and squares, past the shops of the Queen City, Jasmine knew the hue and cry for a runaway slave could have started already. If she went back it could mean whipping or branding at the least, but she felt too numb with grief to fear that now. Then, too, the Bouchets had said they were going to take Monsieur Justin Lyon's price for her at last so he could give her as a mistress to some bosom friend. She'd wanted to kill herself when she thought of belonging to Lyon or any friend of his.

She walked along the curve of the Mississippi and gazed into the murky depths and thought about drowning herself—of joining Mama at the pearly gates. But she saw a bargeman haul up a fish on a line and slice off its head while it was still wriggling. Then she knew she would devote herself not to her own death, but to someone else's.

Jasmine saw it now again in her mind's eye, felt the warm Louisiana sun on her back as she walked away from the steamy river where she'd gone to drown herself. Hawkers chanted in singsong voices to sell their chicory coffee, sweet *beignets* and redfish stew. People so busy and dressed so elegantly bustled by on the streets with their slaves behind them loaded down with packages, but her thoughts were all her own. She had to find a way to make her plan reality. Perhaps she should be glad Justin Lyon wanted to buy her.

Then her bleary gaze snagged on one particular shop window and her nose twitched with the sweet mingling of floral fragrances emanating from the open door. For the first time in hours, her aching feet halted. Tears stung her eyes. A sachet shop with the sweet jasmine odor for which she'd been named reminded her of Mama again—a happy

Mama, beautifully gowned, her laughter all silvery so long ago. Then she saw Mama's face ashen gray with hovering death and sickroom smells just as she had been that morning when she spoke of the happy times.

"'Member when we used to gather all the gardenia and jasmine blooms behind the town house he bought for me, honey lamb? We'd dry them for potpourri and sachet. All my gowns smelled like summer—and the satin sheets, too, even on your little bed. And the ribbons I tied in your hair—"

"Don't talk anymore, Mama," Jasmine had pleaded. "Sure I remember that, but I was so young when I had to leave you—"

"You was almost five, honey lamb. And little Sam not even three. So glad, so glad you and Sam together at least at Bouchets'. Like to think of both of you being together and 'membering the old days when it was all of us together and happy—"

Weak from crushing emotion and hunger, Jasmine leaned her shoulder on the painted frame of the shop window. Her bedraggled reflection stared back at her in the shiny glass. And beyond that, a rainbow hue of silks and lace-edged satins and ribboned velvets on display with the petite wicker baskets holding the dried potpourri that tinged the air. And then, beside her, that other mirrored image she would never forget.

"You feeling all right, gal?" the wiry Negro man with milk-chocolate skin asked.

She jumped. Did Negroes ever chase escaped slaves? "Fine, just fine," she managed and started away before his gentle grip pulled her back by one tattered sleeve.

"Well, now, don't look fine to Desso Ross. That's me. I owns a livery stable of my own down by the docks. You not waiting for your mistress inside?" he asked and squinted through the glass window of the sachet shop.

"No," she told him quickly, panicked at his questions, whether he was a freed Negro or not. "Just on my own today and strolling here and there and looking."

She dared enough of a glance at Desso Ross to see he was one handsome-looking man in his late twenties. Clean-shaven with curly, cropped raven hair and bright brown eyes. His teeth were even and white and he was dressed real clean.

"If you looking for a friend, you got you one," he announced with a firm nod. And the next few days had been paradise.

Desso Ross was real understanding when he heard the parts of her story she wanted to share—bah, she wasn't telling anyone what she'd vowed to herself down by the river. He'd taken her to his place in a real fancy wagon he'd been on his way to pick up. In his three small rooms above his tiny livery stable wedged in near the docks, he'd fed her and listened—and looked.

"Well, now, you the finest-looking gal I ever seen," he'd said more than once that day. She'd fallen asleep on his bed when he'd gone downstairs to work, and horse smells mingled in her dreams with jumbled, fragrant memories of Mama and the sachet shop where she'd met Desso Ross. That first night he'd hidden her, he'd slept with his knees all pulled up on a lumpy old settee in the other room and not disturbed her a bit. The next day while she fixed him eggs and fish, he talked her into going back. He made up a real fancy story about how his wagon had hit her on the Bouchet Road and knocked her plumb out of her head so he didn't know who she was until now, and she didn't, either. It made it all so easy to pretend to herself she was someone else those two days with Desso Ross.

And he'd sworn that he'd take his meager savings and sell a few more horses and somehow buy her from the Bouchets for a wife even if some mighty white man who owned a rue Royale furniture store wanted her, too! It was then, even when Desso Ross had held her in his arms, that Jasmine Bouchet had known being with the tender, kind man was impossible. She had something else she'd vowed to do. She had her own fish to catch and kill, and no one and nothing could ever get in her way until that deed was done.

But still, she'd encouraged him to join her in his bed that second night. A trembling virgin, she'd reveled in his hot gaze and his sure hands. Desso Ross, thanks to Miz Lanie's protection later, was the only man she'd ever slept with—or loved. She'd snuck out of his bed before he woke the next morning and hightailed it back to the Bouchets with the story he'd given her. They'd believed her, but they had still sold her to Justin Lyon. That had been when Miz Lanie had rescued her. Sure, she'd seen Desso since then in town when she was chaperoning or shopping with Miz Lanie. She'd always looked away or avoided him, however much it hurt him and crushed her.

But that didn't mean she had forgotten the wonderful way his callused, clean hands had felt along her quaking flesh that first and only time she'd loved. It didn't mean she didn't dream at night sometimes of his lips in her hair or his mouth murmuring how he adored her along her soft throat. And no one, no danger or hardship would ever take the memory of her only, brief love away from her.

In Silver Swords' thatched hut in Boca Grande, seven years after Jasmine Bouchet had last been touched by Desso Ross, she sighed and swiped at the tears that coursed from the corners of her eyes. She pressed her thighs together and heaved a long, ragged sigh. And she kept staring up into the dark hundreds of miles from home and remembering that other dark, warm beautiful night of love.

Even though Silver Swords had been back at the Captiva compound for two days, Lanie was still cold to him. She'd seemed anxious to see him at first, but it was obviously only to hear whether Jasmine was all right. And they'd soon argued again.

Lanie was feeling more desperate and trapped every day, and now that Silver Swords had returned, she was racked by the same dangerous emotional confusion that had torn her before his departure. She dreamed of the day when her ransom would free her of him, and had even started to plot an escape. If only she could somehow think of a way to take

Jasmine with her, she thought, she would definitely try to run.

Needing something to keep her mind away from the turmoil that seethed inside her, she turned her attention to the entertainment she had organized. Sil had let her use the wide, shaded area of his hut for rehearsals, and everyone but Doña Inez and the waspish Pamela Ramsay, who sat sulking in the shade just down the steps, was helping with costumes. Lanie was delighted at the way a few of the women even hummed or laughed as they worked. It made them feel creative and optimistic, even for a few hours, and so lightened the sad drag of days in captivity.

Sil had allowed Serafina to gather shells and morning glory vines from the beach, and they were stringing shell necklaces. They'd made castanets from cockle shells for Serafina's fandango, and a sort of veil for the lower half of her face with flowers from the Spanish bayonet plant. Lanie planned to drape herself in Spanish moss and gold sea hibiscus for her songs. Augusta was reciting a Lord Byron poem about the ocean and Honorée was going to describe how she'd once seen Napoleon and his Josephine in Paris. And there would be a special meal of marsh rabbit, pompano with lime, mangos and guavas. Let Pamela just stew in her own bitterness if she would not join in, Lanie thought. She went back to assuring Serafina that everyone would adore her dance even as the disgruntled Pamela sauntered into the hut to watch more closely.

"And here I thought the fandango was a courtship dance," her shrill voice cut into the buzz of preparations. Everyone looked up. Honorée and Serafina shifted closer to Lanie. Out of the corner of her eye, Lanie saw the usually cowed Lady Augusta prop her fists on her hips. "Pointless for someone like our little mouse Serafina to be dancing a courtship dance, you must agree," Pamela goaded and snickered.

"I'm afraid we have no parts for witches, unless you'd like to try a little kindness for once, Miss Ramsay," Lanie told her. "And you're only invited if you can appreciate the efforts others make."

"This whole charade proves you're crazy, McVey!" Pamela challenged. "But then, I realize you love entertaining our stud stallion captor one way or the other!"

Lanie fought to keep from shoving the woman down the steps. "Just leave if you haven't come to help," she insisted and stepped closer to the tall woman. She had to look up slightly to her. She felt suddenly uneasy since her hands were full of the vine she'd been linking jingle shells on. She recalled only too well Sil's orders that she stay away from Pamela. And Lanie knew she'd been very brusque with him lately, so she didn't want to cross him in any way. But Pamela's continued sniping assaults on the meeker women infuriated Lanie.

"None of us is to blame if you're unhappy at your long stay here without word from your father or that Virginia planter fiancé you claim you're betrothed to!" Lanie said tartly, wishing a moment later that she could recall her words.

"She'll rot here with the rest of us!" Augusta blurted. "She's always telling me how all the pirates line up to ravish a captive when her ransom comes. Rubbish! She's the one who wants her ransom to arrive so she can whore for Sil and the rest of them!" Augusta exploded. "But her cad of a father and her fiancé don't think it's worth a farthing to fetch her back!"

Pamela shoved Lanie aside and lunged at Augusta, who darted away. Serafina screamed. Shells scattered. Pamela pounded the groveling Augusta's head and shoulders. When Lanie tried to pull Pamela off, the woman turned on her.

Pamela's fist smacked into Lanie's belly. She doubled over but struck out to protect herself from Pamela's onslaught. Lanie heard the men come running but it was too late now. She butted into Pamela to knock her down, then slapped her face once, twice before Sil's hard hands hauled her off.

Serafina pleaded and the others tried to explain, but Sil was furious. "Take your belt to that one, Parrot," he cracked out with a finger pointed at the shrieking Pamela. "I've promised this one the Little Hut."

"No, Sil, no, no!" Serafina's voice followed them out the door of the stockade as Sil pulled Lanie along by her wrist.

"I was just protecting Augusta!" Lanie argued. "That witch Pamela—"

"You're both being punished, but she's done her time in the Hut. Lanie, damn it, you've got to stop fighting my rules in front of them all when I let you get away with a lot already."

"Get away with a lot?" she mocked. "This entertainment is helping everyone, and you know it! We would all rot away forever in this hellhole if you had your way! If you had the least shred of decency, you would not allow women to be so degraded, so—"

"Keep your voice down!" he hissed.

She stopped her tirade abruptly when he hauled her up to the four-foot-square, four-foot-high hut, which stood in a little grove of pines outside the stockade. Holding her firmly, he unbolted the door to yank it open.

The hut had no real windows, only slits between the boards. Isolation from the likes of Pamela and this horrid man she welcomed, of course, but not here! Not here in such a little place! In the heat of the late afternoon sun it seemed so stuffy and hot—so small and closed and suffocating!

"No, I can't. You can't!" she cried before she grabbed hold of herself. No matter what, she had no intention of begging this ruffian for mercy.

"You've been warned," he insisted, but his voice wavered. "Maybe next time I give you an order you'll believe there are consequences for disobeying me. In, Lanie!"

"I won't!"

But she jumped into the hut as he grabbed for her. She had to half-crouch to miss the low ceiling, but she refused to feel cowed. All the moments she had thought she glimpsed a streak of kindness, of humanity in this man—she knew now she had been wrong. Yet she almost blurted out her fear of such places, nearly begged him not to leave her here. Pride and fury clogged those words in her throat.

"I hate you more than any of them—more than Gasparilla!" was all that came out in a breathless croak.

"We'll see, won't we?" he said harshly.

In response she only glowered. She did hate him, didn't she? She was terrified of being shut in here, and yet the way she somehow wanted his touch seared her even more. She dreamed of him at night—actually longed for the brute's caresses and kisses. Now she damned her weakness around him.

He glared at her. She thought he looked as confused as she felt, as if he could not decide whether to haul her roughly into his arms or shove her away. She backed another awkward step into the box and bumped her bottom into the wall. Her wide eyes darted around the dim interior. There was a woven mat to sit on, but nothing else inside except a tiny cracked chamberpot. She glared defiantly at him where he leaned to peer in as though he wanted to say something. She stared stubbornly past him, as if he did not exist, at the skinny shaft of sky silhouetting his broad shoulders. She crossed her arms over her breasts and, huddled awkwardly, turned her head away.

He cursed low, slammed the door and bolted it loudly enough for the whole stockade to hear.

As minutes crawled by, Lanie tried desperately to keep from screaming and pounding on the interior of the hut to be let out. A breeze slivered through the crude chinks between the boards, but her panic made her temperature soar. She sat cross-legged and fanned herself with one hand and then the other. To save her sanity, she pictured how cool her bedroom at Magnolia Hill would be with its flowing river breeze and wafting air from the hinged, bell-shaped punkah fan that went back and forth, back and forth. She tossed her head back and forth while her long hair stuck to the dampness of her neck and throat. She fought the terror, gasping for air, for life itself.

She sat now with her parents on the shaded veranda overlooking the terraced lawns and the distant purple-tinged cane fields. She heard the riverboat's shrill whistle at the family landing while the women drank cool *eau sucre* distilled from cane juice, and Papa had his punch fortified with whiskey. Now, she swam in the cool wash of waves with Sil's hands cradling her at Turtle Bay. She rode with him, she held to him—she wanted him.

But every time she opened her eyes in the dim box, fear stabbed her again and she slammed her matted eyelashes to her flushed cheeks to shut it out. She would die here, never see home again. It was worse than being rolled in the rug as a child, worse than being taken captive. She wondered dazedly if this was what slavery was like for her dear Jasmine—for all the slaves that felt so trapped in the great houses and fields of the humid south.

She twisted her body around until she could peer out the widest crack and gasp at air and freedom. Dusk shrouded the thick, strangling tropical foliage outside. Night was coming. Hadn't Serafina told her that women were left in the Little Hut for an entire day? She began to gasp and pant, though she knew she should be able to breathe better. She was not certain if it was tears or sweat that stung her eyes. Her parents. Magnolia Hill. Jasmine. It all seemed so shaky and distant now.

She would never be alive when her ransom came. And while she longed to hate the man who had done all this to her, she only wanted him to come back and take her in his arms!

Then she dreamed an ecstatic escape from the hut. She let herself go with it as Sil helped her out and lifted her in his arms. She held to him, buried her face against his naked chest in the darkness as he carried her away.

His voice, that very voice, so close. "Lanie. Lanie, are you all right? I had to leave you there until it was dark. Damn, I can't chance anyone telling Gasparilla I'm soft on you. It would be the end of both of us, but I swear, I didn't know it would do this to you!"

His words washed over her like cooling water. Her eyes slitted open. Beyond his worried face, pale in the moonlight, stars speckled the heavens. Sitting in the shallow water of a quiet cove, he held her in his lap, ladling water over her shoulders, tipping her hair into the coolness to wash her face so tenderly. Somehow, he had removed her wet gown.

She wore only her chemise and petticoats. She put a foot down to feel the sand.

"Is this real?" she managed, staring up at him. "I am so thirsty."

He lifted her out, dripping, and sat her on her gown on the sand. He held a flask of cool guava juice to her lips, and she drank greedily. "Slow, slow, sweetheart."

Startled, she sat while guava juice dribbled down her chin and throat to speckle the swell of her breasts. She had to be dreaming. She would never allow Sil to call her sweetheart and see her half naked like this. And then it all came back like a slap of icy water.

"Oh! Damnation! You put me in that hut! My clothes!"

"It's pitch dark, Lanie, and you've got enough on."

"Enough on for what? I can see you! I'm hardly in that horrible little hut anymore!"

"I didn't realize you wanted to stay in there longer. Why the hell didn't you tell me a place like that would make you delirious? And let's not argue this time. We need to talk."

She ruffled her gown up to hide as much as she could, and covered her breasts with spread hands. She was almost completely clothed by her chemise, but the material was taut and soaking wet, and she had glimpsed how her nipples peaked and strained against it.

"Talk?"

"I admire what you're trying to do at the compound, but I cannot appear to play favorites. You've got to learn to walk away from Pamela Ramsay's cruelty and stop defying me. Parrot and Watchman, possibly even some of the other women would eventually tell Gasparilla. And everyone here stays alive and well by his goodwill."

"His goodwill!" She spat the words at him.

"Such as it is. There is a chain of command even here, and it's to be obeyed. And you, Miz Lanie, are at the bottom of the chain, however much you've helped some of the women here and love to flaunt your contempt for me in the bargain."

His familiar use of Jasmine's name for her riled her even more. "Don't call me that! And don't you ever call me sweetheart again!"

"No? A man can't always hide his feelings, though I wish I could. It would be so much damn safer for both of us," he added, almost half to himself. He reached out to her to shackle one slim ankle with his big hand.

"Meaning?" she dared.

"Meaning, I'm weary to the bone of fighting not only you but myself," he admitted with a shake of his big head. His other hand took hers in a firm grasp. "Meaning I can't keep my thoughts—or my hands or mouth off you. Please, Lanie, let's not waste what little time we have—"

His smile dazzled even in the darkness. She gasped as he reached for her shoulders and slid her toward him in the sand. Where her petticoat scooted up, her bare flank grazed his sopping wet trousers, and she realized they were all he wore. He moved as quickly as a panther to press her onto the soft sand. Her damp cotton petticoat was suddenly all that lay between them again.

He lay full length beside her, gently holding her down. She wanted to fight, knew she should, but could not. Had he read her mind to know she wanted him touching her like this? He bent to kiss her and her arms lifted as if of their own accord to link around his strong neck. Her fingers entwined in his wet hair. The mere touch of him was staggering, exhilarating.

Their lips touched, tasted, drank. She moaned low in her throat as his mouth moved to bestow caresses on her eyelids and down her nose. Along the slant of cheeks, to her pouted mouth, down her throat to lick between her collar bones. She flicked her tongue across his earlobe and darted the tip in his ear. A sensation like butterflies fluttered down her belly and fanned gossamer caresses between her legs. Nothing had ever been like this for her. She felt swept away, whirling, soaring as she had that time in the waves with him. But all that was nothing compared to the deep plunge and pull of passion when he lowered his lips to her breasts through the soaking cloth.

She almost cried out at the sheer rapture of it. She arched her back. In the sudden tumble of his hands and hers, she helped him remove her chemise and skim down her sopping petticoat. He kissed her again and again, long and sweet and deep and demanding. His tongue traced warm paths that the night air chilled, down her throat, then around and over one nipple and then the other. He kissed, bathed each pert peak, then teased it back and forth endlessly before he sucked it. A big hand lifted to each breast, molded it, then slid down her fluted rib cage to caress her flat belly. Sensation shimmered everywhere in her. All thinking stopped when he slipped his fingers between the warmth of her thighs as she parted them mindlessly for him.

"Lanie, Lanie," he half whispered, half breathed against her breasts. "You're so beautiful and wild and free. You're made to be touched, to be loved and by me—"

She slid her hands down his corded back muscles to grip his waist as he pulled her under him. She heard him unbuckle his belt and felt him fumble with his trouser buttons. She had to stop him now, but she wanted it so desperately.

His powerful naked thighs, flecked with hair, separated her smooth ones. She stared up raptly into the deep, dark pools of his eyes as moonlight gilded the slash of silver hair over his left brow. He shoved a clinging wisp of her petticoat away and bent to kiss her hard again as he settled heavily, closer along her floating body to touch her everywhere. She actually thought he had pierced her hot flesh with his hardness when the gong first sounded.

"Damn!" he rasped. "I can't believe it!"

"What?"

"And after dark! That gong—it means Gasparilla's at the compound!"

She felt as shattered as the quiet of the night—and the union they had never quite achieved. As the gong sounded again and again, he sat up shakily and reached for his discarded trousers. "Your gown and shoes are under that bush," he said, his voice gone cold. "We'll tell them you got hysterical in the heat of the hut, and I got you out to sober you.''

Sober her—exactly. She sat dazed a moment before she mechanically began to pull on her clothing he tossed her. She was appalled by what had almost happened—by what she'd wanted terribly to happen. How could she ever face him after this? For once, she blessed Gasparilla for saving her from her own stupidity!

Her legs still trembling, Lanie stood in the line of captives outside Sil's open-sided hut in the stockade while Gasparilla summoned them up the steps one at a time. She had not had anything to eat or drink since noon but that guava juice, and she felt so dizzy. All this standing and waiting just after the rage of emotions she'd been through with Sil earlier. She prayed she would be sick or actually topple over before Gasparilla called her up.

Pamela Ramsay stood haughtily just ahead of her in line. She did not look much the worse for her earlier encounter with Parrot's belt. Blessedly, she ignored Lanie. Lady Augusta waited just behind Lanie, holding onto Lanie's skirts like a lost child.

Earlier, Sil had sat at Gasparilla's side, arguing vehemently about something, but now he had evidently been sent from the compound. As far as Lanie could tell, but for the big pirate called Gunner Joe who sat eating in the kitchen and one wrinkled woman called Emma who stood behind Gasparilla's chair, which they had hauled in for him, Gasparilla had come alone.

''He's drunk as a goat,'' Augusta whispered. ''When he's like that, I heard he might do anything. You poor dear. Taking on Ramsay, spending time in the Little Hut and facing Gasparilla all in one day.''

Lanie only nodded. At least no one but Sil knew the rest of it! But why was that old woman escorting each captive down the steps to her hut at the end of her interview with Gasparilla? ''What's she doing?'' Lanie mouthed over her shoulder to Augusta.

"I don't know, but I heard she's skilled with herbs, both curative and poison," Augusta hissed just before Gasparilla summoned Pamela up the steps.

Lanie kept praying Sil would return. She was so tired, so fuzzy-headed. She would feel much safer with him somewhere around. As the line inched slowly forward, she was realizing what a difference there was between Silver Swords and his captain. Gasparilla's comments boomed louder and bawdier in her ringing ears. Frequently, he upended the bottle he otherwise wedged between his legs.

Where was Sil? The minutes dragged as Gasparilla spoke with Pamela, even made her sit on his lap while he pawed at and nuzzled her. Lanie's stomach churned. But she and Augusta stared amazed as it actually seemed Pamela was whispering in the devil's ear. They strained to hear. Drunk as he was, the foul lecher had lowered his voice as if they were conspiring. Perhaps, Lanie thought suddenly, the nasty witch was a spy for him here; that could be the real reason her ransom was taking so long.

"What could the likes of her be telling the likes of him?" Augusta asked as if she had read Lanie's mind. But when Pamela was led off by old Emma, it was Lanie's turn all too soon. Augusta gave her a quick, reassuring pat before Lanie unsteadily mounted the two steps to the floor of the hut. Gasparilla squinted at her in the single lantern light.

"*Sí*, the golden-haired angel come to visit Gasparilla's hell," he roared. He guffawed at his own jest and swigged a gulp he almost choked on. "Justin Lyon's little bride. Has he had you?" he asked with a grand sweep of his bottle. "Can't say I'd wait a day past the engagement, rich papa or not. Ah, *sí*, I was once at the great court of Spanish King Charles with all the fine ladies. I'd have had you in my bed in a trice there!" He slipped into Spanish and raved on until he suddenly asked in English, "What's your name again, precious?"

Her voice came steadier than her legs. "Melanie McVey. I hope you've sent to New Orleans for my ransom for my maidservant Jasmine and me."

"Ha! Couldn't pay enough for you!" He leaned forward and licked his thin lips. His ruby ear stud glittered. "Emma!" he screeched, though the old woman had returned and stood nearby. "I want this one checked right here, right now!"

Old Emma took Lanie's hand and pulled her down the steps into the shadows. Lanie's head spun. "Please, check what?" she managed to ask the hunchbacked, wrinkled woman.

"He wants to be sure you unwed ones are still virgins," she said and cackled when Lanie gasped. "Gasparilla's wily as a fox. Don't even trust that handsome Silver Swords farther than he can throw him with all of you, 'specially not after tonight."

Tonight? Lanie thought. But Gasparilla couldn't know about what happened tonight! Had Pamela told him something? What could Pamela have told him?

"Hike up your skirts then," the old crone said and took a step forward as Lanie fainted at her feet.

"Lemme see her, jus' lemme see her. *Sí*, she's mine, no one else's!" a man's voice roared. Lanie slitted her eyes to see she lay on her own mat in her hut. Honorée was not there, but Old Emma knelt over her gently slapping each cheek. "Get out, you oaf!" Emma dared to order the pirate chief when he lurched inside. Lanie's stomach flopped over. Where was Sil? She kept her eyes shut, though she was sure the women knew she was bluffing.

"This one's still a virgin you say?" Gasparilla demanded. "You sure, you old hag?"

"Can't believe everything you hear, but I'm telling you, yes," Emma insisted. "That Ramsay woman I checked before, she's had a man or two, but not this one."

"Good," he said. "I want her untouched till the moment I strip her and take her before Lafitte's messenger with his precious ransom. I want the message returned to Lafitte and Lyon with all the details that I took their money but ruined their little virgin anyway. She'll be the prime piece in my harem till I break her." She heard him slop another drink. "And then, no care about slicing up Lyon's leavings. Lafitte and Lyon will both rue the day, damn their greedy souls, they took that ship from me last year!" he shrieked triumphantly.

Lanie wanted to scream and cry. To protest what she'd heard. Gasparilla obviously believed that Justin was somehow linked to Jean Lafitte. It was equally obvious that Gasparilla hated Lafitte. And she was to pay the price of her honor and her life for that! She knew the truth now. But why hadn't Sil warned her instead of just asking if Justin was in with Lyon? Her ransom would be received and ignored. She would be abused and killed.

Still, she forced herself to lie unmoving. She had no choice but to try an impossible escape from this compound or the one at Turtle Bay. But how much time was left before the ransom the other women longed for would mean not her freedom but her eternal captivity? She was on an island with hundreds of miles of tropical wilderness between her and home. Getting out of Sil's hands alone would be impossible. But he wanted her. How badly? Would he help her? Or had he known all along that her fate was to be different from the other captives'?

She lay very still, feigning unconsciousness until she heard Gasparilla stagger from the hut and yell for Gunner Joe to take him to the ship. She heard the old woman's bones creak and crack as she grunted to her feet beside her, then leaned down to pat her cheek. "Poor, pretty angel," she said, and was gone.

Chapter Five

Despite Gasparilla's disastrous visit, the women of Captiva presented their entertainment two nights later. The last notes of Lanie's sweet, bell-clear soprano voice hung in the humid night air as she finished her final song and curtsied pertly to the loud applause of the audience seated in a small semicircle on the floor of Sil's hut. Parrot whistled shrilly through his teeth, and Red Legs and Specs shouted their approval. Pamela Ramsay still sulked in the shadows, but she had wiped tears from her eyes as Lanie had sung of a lost homeland far away.

Lanie was relieved she had made it through the meal and the other performances tonight. Since she had heard Gasparilla's perverted plans for her, all she could think of was escape. And she realized her only chance for that was to ask Sil to help.

Still, she tried to act herself, even to smile as she hosted the entertainment. She would have to get Sil alone as soon as she could. Now, she held up her hands for quiet as the applause died away. "This evening, the ladies of this grand and luxurious establishment have sung and danced and recited their hearts out for you—you gentlemen," she announced. Red Legs chuckled at her word choice while Parrot snorted a laugh. Sil only shrugged his big shoulders and lifted his dark brows guiltily.

Lanie winked at Serafina, who had come to life during her dance this evening. The girl sat at Sil's side, still wearing her flowered face veil, but her eyes spoke her joy and pride.

Lanie gestured for Pamela, hoping to lure her from the
shadows. When she refused to budge, Lanie went on, "So,
all of us captives of Captiva would like to invite any of you
to perform who are bold enough to sing a song or tell a
tale—if it's proper for ladies' ears who live such a sheltered
life here."

Red Legs gladly took the challenge. He sang a nasal ren-
dition of "The Campbells Are Coming" while he danced a
Highland fling, then promised to bring his bagpipes next
time. Specs enlightened them with tales of his visit to the
island of Martinique, where the Empress Josephine was
born. Parrot ran to his guard tower to fetch his green bird,
for which he'd been named. For ten minutes, the yellow and
lime feathered chatterbox regaled them with every insult it
knew, unfortunately including, "Avast, mates! Up with
your main mast for the ladies!" From her seat on the floor,
Lanie blushed and shook her head. "Main mast" was pirate slang for the male's—well, member.

After that, Parrot relieved old Watchman in his tower
while Watchman displayed several of his best watches and
even passed them around. "Come on then, Sil," Watchman urged, "show them the one you bought off me. Paid
dear enough for it, and I wouldn't have sold it if you hadn't
got yourself all shot up over it."

Lanie's insides cartwheeled. Sil's wound was over a
watch? Everyone stared as he slowly drew a gold pocket
watch from inside his slash-necked shirt and unhooked its
chain from his belt. He snapped its top open and stared
down at its face for a moment. When he looked up, she
thought she saw his eyes glisten in the lantern light.

"Anyone drops this and it's the Little Hut for the rest of
the century," he said low as he begrudgingly passed it
around.

When it came to Lanie, she stared down with a start at the
lady's lovely painted portrait. This beautiful smiling
woman—somehow she looked familiar, and yet Lanie knew
she had never met her. Could this be a woman Sil had loved?
She seemed to have his high cheekbones, the same black hair
and piercing blue eyes. The scripted initials on the top of the

case said simply, "J.B." She stroked the ornate engraving with her finger for a moment. For the first time, she wondered what Sil's real name was; it seemed so natural now to think of all the pirates by their nicknames as if they had no other identities or pasts. Her eyes lifted and slammed into Sil's across the small space between them crowded with chattering people. Reluctantly, she passed the watch on.

"Come on then!" Red Legs shouted at Sil. "If the lassies liked old Red Legs flaunting his bony knees, they'll sit still for a tale or song from the likes of you!"

Sil had sat quietly all evening. Lanie had darted quick looks at him during her three songs; he seemed lost in thought even while he stared unblinkingly at her. But now he rose to still their raucous urgings and stood with easy grace before their crude curtain of stringed shells. "We *gentlemen*," he said mockingly so that everyone leaned forward in anticipation, "thank you ladies for your efforts tonight. And I agree with Red Legs that something a bit special is in order here."

Somehow tonight, with that watch of his father's held so close against his ribs, his thoughts had been on the two women he had loved. Becky, his childhood sweetheart, of course. He was deeply ashamed that he had let his passion for Lanie overcome him the other night. It was as if he was breaking not only his marriage vows to Becky but his promise to himself, the day he buried her and the child, that he would never deeply desire nor love another. And his mother's face even now floated before his eyes. She looked out so beautifully and perpetually calmly at him from the watch, and tonight it seemed to him she was urging him to use the gift she had given him in all the play scenes they had done together so long ago.

"Just a few lines from Shakespeare's tragedy *Hamlet*," he said. Watchman frowned and Red Legs looked so confused he wasn't even sure they knew what he meant. "He wrote plays and real fine poetry, for you blackguards who've never heard of him," he put in with a sheepish grin.

"Gasparilla says you're damned smart, Sil," Watchman interrupted. "Give it a go then!"

The women looked astounded, too. Lanie's lush lower lip dropped and Pamela swished out from the shadows to flop down at the front edge of the audience. A sudden hush descended but for the fitful breeze clattering the curtain of stringed shells and his deep voice. Not a rustle of a skirt, not a laugh or pirate belch or sound stirred from anyone.

"'Ere we were two days old at sea,'" Sil began slowly, "'a pirate of very warlike appointment gave us chase.'" He moved, he gestured as his voice resonated with the words. "'Finding ourselves too slow of sail, we put on a compelled valour, and in the grapple I boarded them. On the instant they got clear of our ship; so I alone became their prisoner. They have dealt with me like thieves of mercy; but they knew what they did: I am to do a good turn for them.' So, ladies," Silver Swords concluded to break the spell he'd cast where each woman recalled her own capture, "you are not the first to be imprisoned by pirates, nor to do a good turn for them with your efforts tonight."

Everyone clapped and called for more, but he suddenly realized how strange it looked for him to be reciting poetry before the likes of Gasparilla's motley band and their prisoners. After a year, this place was really getting to him! At least he'd finally discovered his parents' fates and partly avenged their cruel deaths. He had a lot of information for the navy, and he had to get away soon. But after insisting to his raucous, appreciative audience that he could not recall more Shakespeare, he did toss out one additional thing.

"Doubt thou the stars are fire;
Doubt that the sun doth move;
Doubt truth to be a liar;
But never doubt I love."

"Love, Sil?" Parrot shouted amidst the applause and cheers and whistles. "Not you, no sir! That's a good un!"

But Sil's gaze met Lanie's wide stare, and his heart leaped. He shoved away the thought he'd recited that for her. It had been one of his mother's favorites, that's all. But he couldn't help wondering what Lanie was thinking.

Lanie looked pointedly away from Sil as everyone stood. That little poem might have had the word "love" in it, but it also had the word "liar." But none of that mattered anymore, she told herself. What mattered was getting away from here. She wished she could think of a way to take Jasmine with her but that seemed impossible. When she made her way home, she would get a ship to rescue her. She was certain now that Silver Swords desired her. The first chance she got to speak to him alone, she would promise him what he wanted if he would only let her escape!

That night Lanie took down the shell curtain in Sil's hut while the other weary women drifted away. The men were either on guard duty or boiling some concoction in an iron kettle they had hauled over, and she smelled pungent nutmeg. Still basking in the glow of the camaraderie of the evening, she said to Parrot and Red Legs hunched over the pot, "Whatever is that sweet-smelling brew?"

"Bumboo, lass," Red Legs grunted without looking up from his stirring. "But the chief says we're not to make enough to get crazy on with guard duty coming. Damn Sil, we Highlanders always fight better on the stuff than off it!"

Parrot snickered, then said, "Since we got us one of our little slaves still up, let her stir it for a while and cool it. Like this, McVey," he said to Lanie and demonstrated spooning out a bit of it in a big ladle, then pouring it back and forth into an identical one to cool it. "Then you put it in cups and we drink it."

The sweet smell was enticing, and, curious to taste the amber brew, she obeyed. She was thirsty after her singing tonight. Besides, more than once at home she had taken swigs of Papa's whiskey punch on the sly and preferred it to the so-called ladies' drinks.

She was alternately stirring and cooling the cooked stuff—and taking an occasional nip, which was not bad—when Sil stepped from the darkness.

"'Double, double, toil, and trouble; fire burn and cauldron bubble,'" he said and laughed as he sat down on his bench to watch.

"More *Hamlet*?" she asked as she filled cups with the ladle.

"*Macbeth*," he said. "Witches, murders, revenge, seduction, passion, lust, the usual."

"No wonder you learn Shakespeare so easily," she taunted as she poured another cup and wished he were not here so she could take yet another sip of the deliciously rich liquor.

"Want to try the stuff?" he asked as he reached for a cup.

"Revenge and murder at least do sound very enticing to me lately," she countered, intentionally misunderstanding him. She realized this was her chance to ask him for help, but the drink was making her feel carefree and lighthearted despite all her worries.

He just grinned and took a hefty swig. Then he extended the cup to her. "The men made you fix it, you certainly ought to try a bit of it."

"They boasted it's only for men," she countered, but she reached for it. As soon as he had enough of it to make him tipsy—before he got all wild the way she remembered the pirates did that first night on Boca Grande—she would definitely ask him to help her escape. He might promise more easily if he were drinking this stuff, and then she would hold him to it in the morning. It was amazing how clearly she could think things out with this drink in her.

She took a big gulp. With him watching her so intently, it tasted different. It burned warmth clear down to her stomach; she felt it behind her cheeks and eyes and even way down along her thighs. But it was good. She took two more big swallows, then filled the cup and urged it back on him.

"Not too bad," she said, watching him out of the corner of her eye for signs he was maybe getting light-headed. "Both sweet and tart."

His eyes slid dangerously over her. "I like things that way," he said softly.

Her pulse pounded. Yes, he did want her. Perhaps she could somehow bribe him to get away from here. She began to feel warm all over. The liquor raced through her blood with her thoughts, tingled her skin, made her seem so light and floaty.

"You look dizzy," he observed. "Were you sneaking the stuff before?"

"Certainly not," she declared archly. "Maybe I am just not used to bugaboo. I mean bamboo."

"Bumboo," his voice came from far away. "Just too much on top of everything else you had tonight," he said and reached for her.

"No, I need to talk to you, I'm fine," she thought she told him as she tried to jump back. But he called for Parrot and picked her up in his arms. "No, wait. I wanna to talk," she insisted. "An' I wouldn't mind s'more."

He sighed and shook his head. "Hard enough to keep the amount of that stuff down so the guards won't get wild or sick," he groused to himself.

He was making her worse by carrying her. Was he whirling her around? The waves were rocking on the sea. But she wanted to ask him if he would let her escape because Gasparilla was going to kill her if this bugaboo didn't first. When Sil put her down at the door to her hut, she held to his strong arms.

"I'm sorry, Lanie. I shouldn't have urged you to drink it. I didn't think about a delicate stomach mixing a tiny bit of that with what you had earlier."

"I'm not del'cate. I can do for myself, even out'n the wilds!" she argued, but she was not sure where the thoughts and words were coming from now. "Damnation, I needjur help. Secretly!" she shouted.

"Tomorrow," he whispered. "Any other time. Keep your voice down."

"No!"

"Honorée," he called inside. "Lanie's tired and she's going to be sick."

"I'm sick of being here!" she heard herself insist. "Sick of taking your orders! We're not slaves here! I want you to bring Jasmine here, too. I'm going to free her. Free all the slaves—" She shook her head, but that made the waves pitch even steeper. That wasn't what she'd meant to say. She'd wanted to convince him to help her.

"Damn it, I even desire you when you're half lit, Lanie," she thought he whispered in her ear just before Honorée appeared and helped her to her sleeping mat. In the morning, though she could not remember a thing but being sick all night, she looked for her next chance to convince him again, this time without that vile pirate bumboo to ruin everything.

The next night Silver Swords surprised them all by insisting on what he called an attack drill. If the compound ever came under siege before they moved to Turtle Bay, Red Legs and Specs would take the women out through a hidden door he'd had Parrot cut in the back wall. And so, according to that plan, the captives' wrists were bound in back with the pliant beach morning glory vines Lanie had used to string shells. Sil warned them to keep silent, for any attackers would be interested in them for other things than ransom and safe return to their homes. Then they were tied in specific, separate spots in the surrounding grove and thickets while Parrot and Watchman pretended to fire guns at their mythical attackers and Sil oversaw the entire operation.

Hidden by herself in a thicket of guava and banana trees beside a white mound of crushed shells, Lanie cursed the fact she was securely tied to a tree trunk. But with her hands bound in back like this she'd never get far on the island if she bolted anyway. Besides, she had another escape plan, several of them. In the big brim of her woven palmetto sunbonnet in her hut she had hidden a kitchen knife she'd filched, and enough vine to build a raft from driftwood that littered the beach. Though private hoarding of food was forbidden, these last few days she had stored green bananas, figs, oranges and a hunk of bread to tide her over until she got far enough away to forage. She had hidden a fishhook and had learned enough from Serafina about living off the tropical foliage to survive. She was sure of it!

All she needed now was Sil's help to escape, and she was going to convince him even if she had to seduce him to do it. She had made a mess of it last night, but she was in full control of her wits today. She was desperate to get away before Gasparilla turned up again or her ransom arrived. Tugging fretfully at her bound wrists, she waited while she heard Sil taking other women back to the compound. She jerked and stamped and blew on her skin from time to time to discourage the monster mosquitoes.

Then, as if she had wished it, a sudden breeze sprang up to blow the bugs away. A favorable omen, she thought to buck herself up. But the foliage shifted and rattled repeatedly around her. The island itself seemed to moan and sigh. The moon shimmered spectral white to cast black shadows on her silver flesh. Every inch of her skin tingling from anticipation, she waited. And then she realized with a prickle of hair on the nape of her neck that Sil was deliberately leaving her until last. She heard his booted footsteps coming, but still jumped when his voice suddenly came close behind her to break the strange, shifting spell of the scene.

"I thought if anyone could keep the old Calusa ghosts off, it would be you," he told her with a hint of laughter in his voice. His knife glinted while he reached behind her to cut her free from the tree.

"Ghosts?" she asked, her opening plea momentarily forgotten.

"Of the Indian tribe that used to live here before the Spanish drove them off years ago. That's one of their shell burial mounds," he told her and gestured toward the big pile of shells with his dagger. "Word is that they used to sacrifice victims here to accompany their chiefs to the other world. Or," he said and leaned forward to encircle her warmly with his arms while he cut her wrists free, "maybe it was their beautiful, bold women captives that haunt this spot; I can't quite remember."

"I don't believe in ghosts," she insisted. "I declare, mosquitoes are the only things that haunt this spot!" She was trembling, but she knew it was not the ghosts. She always trembled when he stood so close. She rubbed her wrists where they had been tied. When he stared at her in the moonlight with glittering eyes, she went on quickly, "I really need your help, and I'd be willing to pay whatever you want.''

She cursed herself for that abrupt approach. But perhaps this would be easier than she had hoped. His big hands grasped her upper arms to turn her so he could see her face. The cool breeze billowed her loose, moon-gilded hair around her temples and lifted her skirts to caress her legs.

''Pamela Ramsay again?'' he asked. ''What's the matter now?''

''No, it's Gasparilla. I—I don't trust him to let me go when he gets the ransom.'' She hesitated to tell him all the horrid details Gasparilla had revealed unless she had to. She couldn't bear to admit he must have been right about Justin's being in collusion with Lafitte when she had not known the first thing about it. It made her wonder again how much she really did know about the esteemed Justin Lyon.

''I will give you anything you want,'' she plunged on, ''but I am asking you to allow me to escape.'' The words fell out of her so fast she could not stop them now. ''I will see my father makes you a rich man for just looking the other way here and not reporting my disappearance for a while. You're so different from the rest of them, Sil. I declare, surely you would like to give this sort of life up, and you could with a large sum of money. You could leave this horrible island and become an actor in New York or even Europe to start a whole new life!''

She could not read his stony expression, and that worried her.

''But life here suddenly has its benefits,'' he told her grimly. ''Like a gorgeous woman in the moonlight promising me anything I want to help her. I believe you're sober tonight, and I did hear that in the offer, didn't I?''

''Then you will?''

''You really believe your father or Justin Lyon or whoever would locate and pay some pirate off who'd let you slip away? They'd be more likely to bring the whole United States Navy you mentioned the other day to stretch my neck at the end of a rope once you're safe.''

She straightened her back and sucked in a breath until her stomach muscles hurt. She must get his promise quickly. They would be missed inside. She had even wondered if their being alone together at times wasn't what Pamela had whispered to Gasparilla the other night. She had to convince Sil.

"Besides the money later," she said, making her voice as silkily seductive as she could manage when she was so nervous, "you heard me right. I am entirely willing to offer you a—a payment before I go—of something that is very important to me." Gooseflesh skimmed her skin. She was hoping desperately that the mere promise of that would be enough. She could perhaps vow to meet him somewhere before she slipped away. For if she ever really let him touch her the way he had before, she feared she would never leave.

He tipped her even farther in his warm, strong grip so her lower torso tilted into his. She could feel the hard thrust of him as well as his sword hilt pressing into her softness.

"I've looked carefully, Lanie, and found no hidden fortune anywhere on you," he taunted. "Best stop playing games and tell me exactly what you're offering."

Damnation, the venal, greedy wretch was making this hard for her! Still, he had not said no; surely he would help her. "I mean myself—my willingness. I thought you wanted me."

"Oh, I do. But maybe you'd better convince me you mean it," he challenged.

She stared up at him for one trembling moment. His rugged, avid face was etched in shadowed planes and angles by the moonlight, which gilded his strong nose and mustache. Slowly, she slid her hands up to grasp his shoulders, then linked them behind his powerful neck. She pulled her upper body closer to his and rose on her tiptoes to reach his lips. Her breasts rubbed heavily along his chest. She fluttered kisses on his throat, nibbled an earlobe. Then she pulled his head down and kissed him full on the lips with brazen abandon.

He opened his mouth to her sweet assault as if to demand a deeper kiss. She darted her tongue to his, flicked it, slid it into his mouth just the way he'd taught her. She was startled at first as his hands dropped to her hips, then clasped the soft globes of her bottom through her skirt and petticoat to clamp her to him. She kissed him harder, pressed to him full length. Pleasure drowned her earlier panic. Her brain bombarded her with pictures of her luring him to the beach to lie with her, to crush her down with caresses like this. She rained fervent kisses down his neck again and raked her hands through his hair, which was black as the night.

But his raspy voice said so close by her ear his mustache tickled her, "What a pity it would be to have this lovely body gobbled up by alligators or panthers once you're away from the shelter of the compound on your own. Or drowned just trying to get off the island."

She gasped. Dazedly, she tried to pull back, but he held her to him. "Talk about these dead Calusa Indians," his voice rolled on with an even sharper edge to it. "There are marauding bands of Seminoles just north of here on the mainland hiding out from the Americans they detest. There may even be another Seminole war—you'd have to stroll right through on your little jaunt home. And you're still willing to pay the price of letting a vile pirate have his way with you just for the chance to have all that happen once you're out of my clutches?"

She felt doused in cold water. How dare he say all that when she had begun to—to what? To try to convince him the way he'd insisted on! she told herself firmly. She realized she had to tell him the rest about Gasparilla's horrid plans for her. She just hoped he didn't know all that already, or she was doomed. She cleared her throat. He was frowning; she could not see his eyes, dark in moonshadow, but she felt them on her. Why, why did he have to ruin the way things had been going?

She told him everything Gasparilla had said in his drunken rage the other night. He cursed low as he listened. His face so close looked shocked and furious. At least he had not known Gasparilla's plans for her all along. Her heart sang. Surely, she had him convinced now. She lifted her hands to the deep V-slash in his white shirt to gently rake her fingernails through his curly chest hair.

"I'm desperate for your help, Sil. You've seen I'm willing to prove it, however you say."

"However I say—what a pretty proposition. But since our delay's probably been noted inside, we need to go back. At least I assume you see the prospect of lying with me as a bit better than with Gasparilla. You're willing to sacrifice yourself to come to me later, after dark?" he asked. His voice sounded as if he were baiting her now. She tried to pull back but his grip was like stone. "You see no problem with a quick roll with a man you've been acting like you detest!"

"I didn't mean it like that. You're—you're hurting me!"

He didn't intend to be so hard on her, but what she told him had just complicated his already convoluted plans tremendously. He couldn't let harm come to her. But he couldn't just tell her that! He needed time to think without her alluring presence messing up his mind.

"Anything I want, you said," he went on. "Do you know what you're saying when you promise a dangerous man like me such a thing?" His voice cut like the edge of a sword. She tried to yank free again. "And you're ready to risk not passing Gasparilla's little maidenhood test next time he comes calling?" he added cruelly.

"I told you, next time he comes calling it might be the end of me!" she spit at him. "I think Pamela told him you have taken me off alone anyway!"

She could feel the tenseness in his hands and limbs, but she had no idea as to the extent to which her revelations had shocked him. Not only did it prove that Justin Lyon was in league with pirates in New Orleans, but it also proved that Gasparilla hated Lyon enough to abuse and murder an innocent woman he could get a small fortune for. And, if the bitter Pamela had babbled to Gasparilla, Lanie was not the only one in danger.

Worse, it infuriated him she'd offered herself like this, however much he desired her. Damn her, it wasn't only her lush body he craved, but her quick mind and defiant spirit.

She was ruining everything—Becky's memory, his plans here, his very safety! Once again, he built a painful wall to keep her from touching his most sacred vows and his very soul.

"You know, Lanie, I keep thinking that more than once I could have you writhing under me anyway without these little deals of yours. We're both rather good at seducing each other for our own selfish needs, don't you agree?"

Gasping at that final affront, she swung and slapped him hard on the left cheek. She waited for some retaliation, but there was nothing except his eyes gleaming in the moonlight. At last he spoke again.

"Regretfully, I'm taking you in now, Miss McVey, and turning down your tawdry little bribe."

Surely she had not heard him right! He could not mean he was actually totally refusing her! After he had led her on, now that he knew her fate? And when she had lowered herself to vow she would willingly lie with him!

"You cannot mean that," she stammered. "But my life's endangered—yours, too!"

"If I let you go, we're both dead. However badly I want you," he muttered, "I'm thinking alligators and sharks bite much harder than I do." He pulled her against him and kissed her with a hand tangled in her wild tresses, then lightly bit her lower lip.

The shock of his mocking refusal staggered her as much as his kiss. "You cruel, unfeeling bastard!" she spit out. "I take back everything good I ever said. I am the skillful actor here. I actually cannot stomach your touch any more than I could Gasparilla's. You sicken me." She went wild with mingled fear and fury in his arms, and swung at him and kicked at his booted shins.

He pulled her to him and clamped a big hand over her mouth. She flailed and clawed as he half dragged, half lifted her into the stockade. He nodded to Red Legs, who was inside the door, as though he merely carted a bunch of bananas and took her to her hut. He pressed her between him and the log wall.

"Listen to me, Lanie! Calm down!" he whispered. She stopped struggling at last but her green eyes spit fire at him even in the dark. He ached all over both to comfort her and to claim the prize she'd flaunted to get her way. Instead, he only clipped out, "By my orders and not Gasparilla's, we're moving to Turtle Bay at dawn tomorrow. You'll be safe there, I swear it."

He thrust her into the hut she shared with Honorée and stalked away. As soon as he got the women to Turtle Bay he'd better flee north to rendezvous with his naval contacts. But, hell, now he was going to have to drag a pampered, stubborn, damned distracting babe in the woods with him every step of the dangerous way!

The man they called Silver Swords could not sleep. His thoughts and emotions raged like a storm at sea. He'd been stuck on Captiva far too long, away from keeping a close eye on Gasparilla. Then, just when he thought at least Gasparilla trusted him to guard the women so he would be taken more into his confidence, the wily old bastard refused to listen to his advice. Sil had argued long and hard for moving the women early to the new Turtle Bay compound, though its stockade was not complete. But the night the pirate chief had pulled his surprise visit here, Gasparilla had turned down that request. And previously, when Sil asked for ten extra guards here, Gasparilla had allowed him only Red Legs and Specs. Sil wondered sometimes if Gasparilla really trusted anyone. Maybe that had been the secret of the pirate's brazen, bloody success all these years. Sil would be totally risking his position with Gasparilla when he moved the women on his own tomorrow. But then, he didn't plan to be in these parts long enough to feel Gasparilla's wrath or suffer his revenge.

Sil climbed the south tower steps to stand silently beside Watchman, and peered out into the blowing, fragrant darkness with him. Sil had the strangest feeling he was poised on the edge of a cliff just waiting for something to happen. It was as if the ghosts he had teased Lanie about really were out there haunting this island, just as his doubts haunted him tonight. Hard to believe that tomorrow night this place would be deserted, a memorial to the grief and desperation of many captive women.

He punched old Watchman affectionately on the shoulder, but they still didn't speak. Funny how he'd become fond of a few of these brigands; that didn't mix too well with his vow of revenge. He turned to stare into the heart of the stockade. The lanterns made lonely pools of wan light, one in the kitchen, one in his hut. He squinted as if he could see Lanie in the darkness of her distant little hut. He sighed. And then he heard the sound.

He turned to Watchman. "What was that?" he asked and mechanically drew his sword.

"A sneeze, I think," Watchman whispered. He, too, squinted as if his eyes could pierce the black night outside the walls. "Listen!"

They both heard a twig snap above the rustle of the shifting foliage. "Go down and tell Specs and Red Legs to undo the lock and get the women out the back way," Sil ordered. "And douse the lanterns. But leave the McVey woman tied by her hut, and I'll hide her myself. I don't want her to bolt."

Watchman hastened to obey, and Sil cocked a musket and pointed it over the wall to cover the main entrance. And then, distinctly, he heard a man's voice whisper from the darkness. When a form darted out, he fired. A scream testified he'd found his mark. Parrot opened fire from the north tower. And then the jungle beyond the walls blazed with gunfire. Sil threw himself to the floor of the guard tower as bullets whizzed and wood chips zinged down on him. He fumbled for another loaded musket. Damn, there were at least thirty hostile guns out there!

Crouching low, Sil got to his feet just as the raiders began a mad dash at the main gate. Eight men carried a log to act as a battering ram. Sil downed another man, but did not take time to reload. The battering ram boomed hollowly into the heavy wooden door under the guard towers. Damn, but he hadn't figured that. Holding both muskets, Sil tore down the steps and yelled to Parrot to come down and guard the door from inside. Jack Scarfield's men! It had to be! They might be after the women or they might be after the man who'd killed Little Caesar! At any rate, in those numbers and armed to the teeth, they were likely to get both. Curse Gasparilla for not giving him the men he'd wanted! He could hear the wild whoops of the raiders as they battered the door.

In the darkness inside the compound, Sil assessed the situation with one quick glance. Specs and Red Legs had most of the women out the back way; Parrot and Watchman stood their ground near the besieged gate ready to shoot the first men through. Across the little clearing, Lanie stood staring at him. She was fully dressed, as if she'd never been asleep. Her wrists were bound and tied to a crude bench near her hut. Sil tore toward her and cut her free from the bench with his drawn sword. He did not separate her wrist ties, in the hope she would see that disobeying him was fruitless. Instead, he grabbed her shoulders hard and shook her once.

"I have to trust you! Go outside, hide by the shell mound. Too many, coming too fast through the front. Don't run away from the mound unless they find the women!'' he shouted brokenly. He shoved her in the direction she should go and ran toward the gate just as it splintered and crashed inward with a roar as men vaulted through it.

Lanie turned to see Red Legs and Specs run into the compound through the back door. She jumped into the shadows of the wall behind her hut. Muskets cracked. Sil's men dropped the first several cutlass-wielding pirates. They shrieked and shouted threats, and Red Legs bellowed in his battle rage. Four men cornered him. He slipped, went down and disappeared in the melee. Swords and cutlasses glinted silver in the moonlight; metal clanged amidst the sporadic crack of gunfire. Lanie stood transfixed in the shadows. Her chance to run, and yet she could not bear to leave Sil there to be be overwhelmed and cut down like that!

She tore inside her hut for her escape supplies. Frantically, she seized the kitchen knife and sawed through her wrist bonds. She dashed outside again with all she had in this nightmare world clutched to her in a crude hat of palm fronds. The scene was crimson chaos, like a stained-glass window of hell she had seen in a church. Several of the attackers brandished torches. The roof of Sil's hut was already aflame. In hand-to-hand combat, men almost indistinguishable from each other shoved and fought and fell. Bodies littered the ground like lumpy sacks.

Run! Run, her inner voice screamed while her eyes darted around for Sil's tall form. She clutched her things to her breasts. That stranger sprawled nearest to her hut—she'd take his cutlass, and pistol, too! If there were really Indians and wild beasts out there she'd be protected.

Bending low, she darted out of the shadows for the weapons and picked them up. Two pistols, a bullet pouch, a heavy cutlass streaked with shiny blood that almost made her sick to touch it. She wiped it across the back of the fallen man's shirt and lifted her skirt to make a basket.

She began to cough and hack like the others in the thickening haze of smoke. Fire crackled skyward from the thatched roofs of the shacks. She saw Specs's corpse on the ground staring up as if into the stars, his spectacles askew on his contorted face like two tiny pools of dancing flames.

"The women?" a strange man's distant voice shouted in the hazy din. "Where the hell're the women Jack promised us?"

Lanie pressed herself to the wall behind her hut. And then she spotted Sil.

His sword a blur of motion, darting, lunging, side-stepping, hacking, he cut a path through the attackers. But one man exploded into him waist high from the back. He lost his second sword and went down, swinging, kicking, fighting. Nearby, the kitchen roof caught fire in one huge whoosh. The heat smacked Lanie even in the shadows of the wall. The fire's raw reds and vibrant oranges etched cavorting figures and gilded bodies on the ground.

She watched mesmerized as Sil staggered to his knees to get up. Another man behind him raised his cutlass and stepped forward to hack him down. Lanie dumped her booty on the ground at her feet and grabbed a pistol. Praying it was loaded, she ran out from the shadows, lifted it and fired. Sil's attacker sagged to his knees, but his heavy cutlass hilt gave Sil a glancing blow on the head before the attacker rolled lifeless to the ground.

"A back door! Hell, there's a back door, mates!" someone screamed and raiders streamed in the direction of the voice. "Out here! Out in back, come on mates!"

Sil stared around dazedly as if unsure where the voice had come from. Those who were still able lurched to their feet and lumbered off. Sil got up, swaying, as Lanie picked up her things and rushed to him. He looked shocked to see her, shaking his head as if he did not know where he was at first. She pulled him out of the carnage of corpses surrounding the shattered front door and shoved him ahead of her in the opposite direction to the one in which the marauders ran.

In the reflected crimson glare of fire, her new escape plan took shape. She led him out of the clearing, past the Little Hut, its roof now ablaze from windblown sparks.

"Got to help the men, the women," Sil stammered, his voice husky and panting. "Where are my swords?"

She hoped he was as dazed as he seemed from that blow to his head. "Just catch your breath here one second," she told him. He leaned, panting, his shoulder against a rough-woven palmetto trunk.

Quickly, she fumbled in her gathered skirt for a pistol and the vine she had brought to make a raft. She knelt to hack off a length of vine with her cutlass before Sil turned to stare, puzzled at her exertion. He rasped out, "That cutlass—give it to me."

She stood and pointed the pistol straight at him. "Turn around and put your hands behind your back! I mean it, Sil! I have got nothing to lose now, and I will shoot you!"

He gaped in disbelief. He shook his head to clear it. He almost told her he meant to take her with him when he left, but she'd believe none of that now.

But for the roar of flames, the forest seemed deathly silent as men beat the bushes behind the stockade. Boldly, Lanie poked the gun in Sil's ribs and then darted back a step. Their eyes met and held in the inferno, which threw their whole world into jumping shadows. She almost did not

believe her eyes when he spun away and thrust his hands
behind his back. A trick, she thought. Half conscious or
not, he was too dangerous for her unless she could out-
think the big brute.

She slapped the length of vine in his outstretched hands.
"Wrap it around your wrists yourself, and I will finish the
job," she said to take him unawares. Cursing low, he
obeyed. She pressed the gun muzzle against his back as she
completed the job one-handed. She reached out boldly to
unbuckle his empty sword belt under his hot, furious gaze.
Still holding the pistol on him, she moved to strap the belt's
length twice around her slender form and to shove the cutlass, kitchen knife and other gun through it. She bent to
stuff the food and the remaining coil of vine into her palmetto hat.

"Now move, prisoner," she clipped out. "Toward the
shore, but not the way they came. We have a lot to do before dawn. And I will give all the orders!"

She tingled with a strange, heady mix of fear and courage as she prodded the big, angry man in his ribs with the
gun barrel. "Move!" she repeated.

And he did.

Chapter Six

Lanie marched her prisoner through thick foliage, then along the shore toward the north end of the island at Redfish Pass. The day they had returned from Turtle Bay, Sil had pointed out a beach strewn with large, sun-bleached pieces of driftwood. The stockade's attackers had come from the south, so their boats and guards were nowhere in sight here. Behind them, the fire still spilled raw reds and oranges into the sky. Lanie was afraid it might draw Gasparilla's men from nine miles north, but she intended that she and Sil would be across Pine Island Sound on a raft before daylight.

"I have vines for binding driftwood together," she told him curtly. "You are going to build us a raft in a hurry. And if you disobey me or try anything, I swear I will shoot!"

She stared him down with a boldness she hardly felt. He glared back while waves swept nearly to their feet across the slick sand. His eyes seemed to reflect inner fires as well as the ones in the sky. It hit her then with stunning impact: she was actually planning to force this dangerous man to guide her across hundreds of miles. And his only payment would be that he obey her every wish. Suddenly, her legs turned to jelly. She felt her fingers cramp and her hand waver on the gun.

"Turn around while I cut you free to gather wood, and no tricks!" she ordered.

She held the gun on him, moving when he did, while he began to haul the straightest, flattest pieces of wood from the forest. She began to breathe a bit easier. Perhaps controlling him would be simpler than she imagined now that she held the upper hand—with a loaded gun in it. He worked diligently, quickly winding the vine to lash the pieces into a small, crude craft. It almost seemed that he really wanted to help her. Or was he afraid the raiders would find him and kill him, too?

"That looks good enough, doesn't it?" she asked him.

"It's evidently your decision, *master*," he clipped out. He stood erect for the first time in half an hour and flexed his back muscles. He propped both big fists on lean hips. "Or is a slave like me to address you as my *mistress*?" he taunted. "And, since we have no sail, am I to paddle us off this island with my splintered hands, *mistress*?"

"Stop it!" she said, furiously, for he had rattled her again. But she had not thought of what they would use for an oar. She steeled herself against feeling pity for him, not after what he had done to her and the others! Damnation, how she wished she could take Jasmine, Serafina, Augusta and Honorée with her! What would become of them? But then she heard on the breeze from somewhere down the beach a distant whooping and hollering. She turned her head toward the sounds as if to pierce the darkness. In that instant, Sil lunged at her, his quick feet flinging sand.

In her surprise, she gave a little scream and fired. The bullet pinged off the raft. She managed to dart back. He slid to a halt in the sand four feet from her. She jerked the gun at him chest high, wondering if there was another bullet in it. She was instantly grateful that the bullet had not hit him; she had not really meant to shoot him. But at least he backed off.

"Put that damn gun down," Sil said, his palms held toward her, white in the moonlight. It was the first time he had used his old calm, commanding voice since they had fled. Strangely, it comforted her. "I just don't want that gun on me when we're rocking our way across the sound and you're already so shaky," he explained hastily. "I'm obviously willing to help you, Lanie."

"And I'm supposed to believe that?" she demanded. "You're my prisoner now, so you'll help me all right, but not because you want to. I declare, I am hardly trusting the likes of you!"

He crossed his arms over his chest and stood with his booted feet spread in the sand. "Then let's just stand here and argue while they run to this beach to see who fired that shot!"

"I am telling you to stop trying to trick me. Go make an oar!" Her voice rose.

"Shall I carve you a real pretty one with my fingernails and decorate it with shells and beach flowers all fancy the way you like things?"

"Just do something, or so help me, I will tie you here for them to find!"

He grabbed a forked, long stick almost at his feet and lifted it. She thought for one moment he meant to throw it, but she only backed up one step before she realized his true intent. Yet he looked at that moment like a demon from hell with his smudged, furious face and raised pitchfork. The last flickers of distant firelight glittered in his eyes. Suddenly, she was more afraid than she had ever been. Not of her desperate plight or of the many dangers that lay between her and safety. Not even of his cleverness and strength if she took him with her. But of her own weakness for him— of the way she wanted to comfort and touch him and force him to do her will in her arms. She jumped at his next words.

"Take your petticoat off," he said. "We'll wrap this to make an oar and use the rest of the cotton for a sail. The wind's up and dawn's not far off. And keep that pistol aimed low in case you insist on shooting it again. Above my toes, there are parts of me we both might need."

She nodded gratefully before the full impact of his double-edged words hit her. But she kept the gun trained on him even while she wriggled out of her petticoat and threw it at him.

* * *

They were both soaked to the waist from waves lapping through the logs of their makeshift craft, but it floated. And the sail of ruffled petticoat took them away from the dark shores of Captiva. Her heart was lighter already; the thrill of being free from the stockade and the island was intense, though her captive could so easily become her captor again if she didn't watch him every moment.

She had draped Sil's belt around her neck to keep the powder and two pistols dry, and held her food supplies jealously to keep them from being snatched by the salty waves. She knew she looked ridiculous—worse than "indelicate," as Mama would say. And she realized that despite the gun she held shakily in Sil's direction she did have to trust him now. She did not know how to read the vast sprinkle of stars for directions. She did not know if he was taking them in circles or out of danger. The fires at the compound, which had given her her bearings, had gone out. As he tacked in what she hoped was the direction of the mainland, breezes and directions seemed to shift. She was grateful the weather was clear, the wind not too strong. But when dawn's rosy fingers crept over the eastern horizon, she knew they were on course.

When it was light, Sil steered straight toward the tiny row of barrier islands across Pine Island Sound. "We'll make for the Panther Keys," he told her, "and hide out there until dusk, in case Scarfield's men are foolish enough to probe farther north."

"You know the men who did all that?" she asked, newly amazed. She huddled on the other end of their small rectangle of bumpy wood. Their feet almost touched, though, and that was entirely too close. He looked nasty and forbidding this morning, and she could never forgive him his pirate past. Still, his eyes were clear and calm as he steered by shifting their crude sail on its two pine branches, which stretched it to catch the fitful morning breeze. The sky was cloudless and the sun already hot. Surprised to see her woven palmetto hat had not washed overboard in the dark, she put it on her head for shade.

They bumped into the sandy, mangrove-covered shore-line of small islands twice and once got stuck on a sandbar, but finally Sil got them into the shallows just off the sound and tied their raft in a tiny cove sheltered by sea-grape trees. Silent, suddenly exhausted, they slumped almost in unison. They stared at each other across their little space of raft as if sizing up each other anew.

"I hope you don't think I'm going to sleep tied up after that rescue you owe me for," he muttered. "All that sounds good to me right now is washing and eating some of that food you've got. But you did promise me anything I wanted if I helped you escape, and I intend to hold you to that."

"That was before!" she gasped. "And I'm the one who rescued you by shooting that brigand who was going to kill you! You are not giving me orders anymore! You are de-mented as well as—as totally lacking in morals!"

"I only know it's moral to keep promises," he said as he stepped into the shallow water and dragged the raft up on a ribbon of sand while she held onto a knob of driftwood for dear life. "But if you did save me back there when every-thing was so crazy, I'll certainly make it worth your while."

"I expect nothing in return but your cooperation," she assured him hastily, even as he turned and started up the sand away from her. "And don't you move another step without my permission!" she cracked out and lifted the gun toward him again.

He turned. "Then I'm to stand right here on the sand while you watch?" he asked. He shrugged dramatically and began to unbutton his trousers. She gaped when she real-ized what he intended. She, too, needed to relieve herself after all that time on all that water.

"No! All right, go on then, but not far," she added hast-ily, heaving a sigh of relief when he disappeared into the fo-liage on the tiny island. She took advantage of the time to see to her own needs and wash her face and hands. When he returned, looking as if he had had a swim, she had bananas and bread laid out for them on glossy green sea-grape leaves as big as dinner plates. The way his eyes raked her she almost wished he had swum off their beach-ringed, mangrove-covered island kingdom and escaped.

They sat, cross-legged, awkwardly facing each other across a four-foot gap. She kept one hand on the gun in her lap. Their eyes devouring each other, they ate.

Sated, drowsy and warm, she watched him through slitted lids as he pulled their raft farther up to hide it among the mangroves and keep it from drifting off with the encroaching tide. The late-morning sun filtered through leaves laced above their heads where they had moved into the shade. Bird calls filled the air, and the sky swam with soaring white storks and ibises. She knew they would both soon fall asleep, hidden safely away until dusk. She had to tie him up before they did. She watched him as he sat down much too close beside her. Pointing the gun at him again, she rose to her feet.

"Don't you think it's time you put that away?" he demanded. He glanced from her determined face to the pistol barrel, then back again. He almost explained to her that he would never risk going back any more than she, but he wasn't at all sure she would believe him. Besides, they could be recaptured, and she would be forced to talk. "We'll need that gun to shoot game to survive," he went on, his voice more quiet.

"I hope I don't have to shoot you to survive. But since you were always *so kind* to Jasmine and me," she said caustically, "I'll tie your hands in front of you so you can sleep."

"Lanie, I'm not going anywhere," he protested, fighting to hold his voice and temper in check.

"You might!"

Amazingly, he held his hands out silently. She stepped slightly closer and tossed a length of sturdy vine at him. "Wrap it firmly around one wrist, and I will finish the job."

"I'm starting to believe you must have made your fiancé propose this way," he goaded, even as he slowly obeyed. Her ties to Justin Lyon still ate at him. Nothing he'd heard of Lyon could make him believe Lyon was worthy of Lanie's love. "A woman who will do anything to get her way is not only spoiled, but damned dangerous," he went on. Suddenly, he could not resist goading her. "But I suppose Justin Lyon knows that by now."

"Just never mind! I hardly had to do much to get him to propose when I wanted him to!" she blurted before she regretted it.

"Poor man. And you had your pretty green eyes on what? The man himself? His New Orleans prestige, his ill-gained fortune, his land?"

She winced at that. She admitted to herself that Justin Lyon had evidently taken her for a fool. True, the man attended church and gave to charity. He owned a fine emporium with elegant imported Parisienne furniture in the best part of town, and everyone seemed impressed by him. Other eligible young women recognized him as a gentleman who was polite and spoke beautiful French and danced divinely and was sleekly handsome. But all of that was mere sham and show, and she had been taken in by it. It was her own fault; she should have trusted Jasmine more. Papa was against the marriage, too, but she had wanted to assert her independence, and in the wrong way.

The truth hurt and frightened her. Justin Lyon was evidently in league with Lafitte and into who knew what else? She had always rather seen Lafitte as a romantic figure, but she deeply resented that a man she had trusted—and thought she loved—had not told her the truth about himself. How could she love a man like that? When she was a girl, she had always vowed she would wed only for love. But so many things had gone wrong! And now she knew that the depth of sweeping emotion she had for Silver Swords made her feelings for Justin pale by comparison. And that realization was as terrible as it was wonderful.

"Do you plan to tie Justin up, too, when you're alone together?" Sil goaded further. "No doubt, you've promised him anything he wants, as you have me, but you'll go back on your word and tie him up one way or the other! Southern women and their slaves. Both inside marriage and out—"

"Damnation! Just keep your mouth closed!" she exploded. Furious at herself more than him, she whipped the remaining vine around his big wrists. This pirate did not have the right to lecture her about slaves, morals, marriage!

"Stretch out your feet, Sil. I'm going to tie them, too," she told him. "And if you can't keep a civil tongue in your head, I will gag you, as I don't have a little isolation hut to quiet you!"

Slowly, he stretched one leg toward her. She bent to reach for more vine, and the other leg struck out, smacking into her bottom to send her sprawling on her knees, gun and all. Before she could recover, he flung himself against her to knock the gun away. She cried out as he lifted his tied arms over her head to encircle her and pull her against him—face to face on the stretch of leaf-shaded sand.

She tried to kick, but he only rolled her over to pin her thrashing legs under one of his. When she realized she had kicked her skirt clear up above her knees, she quieted. On their sides, he held her to him with his tied hands at the small of her back. She could feel his precious gold watch nestled in the waistband of his trousers against her ribs.

"Now," he said, his lips inches from hers while she tried to hold herself stiffly away from the press of his big body against hers, "enough of this foolishness. Untie me!"

"I will not!"

"Fine. We've got hours, and I like our being this close. It leads to all kinds of interesting ways to pass the time. And you did promise me anything I wanted for helping you. Pirates always insist on being paid."

Her arms were doubled up against his chest. Her insides cartwheeled when he began to kiss her leisurely, expertly. She wriggled and squirmed at first, but he only shifted his legs and torso to mold himself more completely to her. He pressed her down to trace the outline of her lips wetly with his tongue. He kissed her again and again in gentle little forays that soon went wilder and deeper.

Somehow, she was kissing him back, matching lips, tongues, moans, inventing new caresses of her own. She had felt so hurt and confused and alone a moment ago. Now, everything seemed clear and certain. This had been creeping up on her so long, this strange, forbidden need for him. It was Sil she wanted, Sil she loved despite herself.

Breathing raggedly and yet in unison, they plundered each other's eager mouths. Her arms were somehow freed; she ran her hands over his back through his ragged shirt, then under it against his hard, warm flesh. He speckled kisses across her temples, wove them through her wild hair splayed on the sand, lavished them down her arched throat. Despite his bonds, he began to unhook her gown.

"Too hot for clothes," he muttered against the slant of her cheek. "Take that gown off. Help me."

She moved as if in a rushing dream. She shrugged off her loosened gown, tugged it from between them, then kicked it away while his simmering blue eyes scalded her everywhere. She unbuttoned his trousers when he told her to, and slipped them and his boots off, though she kept her eager eyes shyly averted. She trembled all over as he continued to clasp her to him under the cool green leaves.

His arms still possessively around her, he moved the entire length of her body, bestowing kisses, nibbles and maddening little circles with his tongue. Despite the cool shade and breeze, her flesh turned to flames that clung and curled against him. He pulled her under him and leaned on his elbows over her while his legs slowly, deliberately separated and spread hers. Poised there, he tasted her mouth again while she responded with urgent hands and lips.

"Lanie, Lanie," he breathed hot in her ear, "I was always your prisoner, too!"

She gasped and clung to him as he pushed slightly into her willing warmth, then paused. His mouth meandered from her lush breasts to her sweetly bruised mouth, then back again until she thought she would explode. There was nothing but beauty when this man hovered over her like a protective roof against the world. She wanted...she needed...she loved him as she had nothing else in this life!

"Yes, please, yes!" she heard a woman moan very close as he plunged swiftly, sleekly, completely into her.

The sword stab of pain passed as quickly as it came. He kissed her hard and moved his hands beneath her to cup and lift her. Tied—was he still tied, she thought dazedly as he began to rock in her. Shooting sparkles like fireworks in the sky careened through her as she met, then matched his rhythmic sway. Hot, sweet, deep, dizzy as if they rode the waves together again. She held to him, kissed him, then dissolved in a dazzle of sensation she had never before fathomed.

When the crash of passion ebbed, she dragged her heavy eyelids up to stare into his sky-blue eyes, which were studying her so close. "I never imagined—all that." She began an inadequate explanation as tears she could not stem flooded her eyes and spilled down.

"You're so beautiful, so special," he whispered. "But it's not over yet, my sweetheart. I wanted to be sure you felt it, too, and now—"

He said no more but set up a rocking rhythm against her. In her. Through her! Again she moved with him until she could not match his pace. She held to his big plunging shoulders hard, gripped his legs with hers. He groaned her name and settled harder against her as if he would drive her into the leaves and sand. Once again, she spiraled out of herself where there was only him to hold and to love. But just before he cried out her name and shuddered in his passion, he pulled slightly away and spilled his seed upon the sand.

He cradled her in his arms, kissing her again, gently now. The earth settled under her; she felt the breath of breeze brush her skin again. Sounds and colors returned. They had actually done it, she marveled—the marital act. Despite the dangers, she had never felt so happy or fulfilled.

She turned her back to him in his arms, and he let her. His hands were still tied behind her, but he did not insist she untie him now. He only pulled her, naked, against him as if she sat in his lap against the ground.

"Just sleep, sweetheart," he murmured. Slowly, he kissed her bare shoulder. His mustache grazed her, tickled her there. Her body still tingled everywhere he had touched her earlier, but his voice, his embrace comforted her.

She reached out and fumbled with the knotted vine to untie him. She was so tired she actually felt herself relaxing. She could stay like this forever and let the world float by. She rubbed the bronze skin of his freed wrists where the bonds had left deep imprints from his exertions. Her tousled head lay on his upper arm like a hard, warm pillow. She would trust him with her life after such passion mingled with tenderness. Sil would get her safely away from here. He knew the area and he knew how to sail.

Her thoughts merged, meandered. Yes, Sil knew the area—the area of her heart and soul—her once chaste body, her life, her future. She settled closer to his strength and warmth. But an errant shaft of sunlight through the leaves bounced off his ring and caught her eye. Half dazed, she reached out to touch it and felt him start.

"You don't have a wife somewhere?" she asked, suddenly aware what the ring might really mean.

His arm jerked slightly under her head. "No," he said. "Go to sleep or you'll be exhausted tonight."

"Did it belong to the woman in the painting in your watch?" she pursued.

"No," he said, his voice taking on a sharper edge. "The woman in the watch is—was—my mother. And the ring—she died," he added.

She heard the deep pain through his brusqueness, for his voice had shaken slightly. She tried to reason out the little he had told her. Despite her drowsiness, reality smacked her. This had been no marriage bed, no husband. He had not promised her a future. There was only this tiny tropic isle and a pirate who now held her as fully a prisoner again as he ever had.

She tried to shove those unsettling thoughts from her mind, but they danced back again and again to taunt her. She had let Sil seduce her; she had helped him. She had desired it and him. It had hardly been ravishment. She had betrayed Justin—Mama and Papa, too. And she had been acting as if she had fallen in love with this pirate. But he was still dangerous, and she had no intention of allowing this sort of scandalous thing to happen on a—a permanent basis now. This once—a slip on her part, but now she had paid her debts to him in full.

Again, she tried to plan ahead, but her thoughts kept slipping away. Her passions had exhausted her heart and her body. Soon she slept, sprawled in his arms.

They set sail just after sunset. They went northward again, at first hugging the barrier islands, thrown like pebbles along the west coast of Florida. When darkness descended, Sil steered by his own reckoning of the stars. North of Pine Island, off a tiny place he called Black Key, a fine breeze perked up, and he cut them out into the sound again. When she asked how his mother had died, he told her the story of his parents' disappearance with the family's ship and about how rumors said it had been pirates and not a storm. He'd eventually heard about Gasparilla's band and tracked them down. Hoping to find out what had happened, he'd joined forces with them for a while.

"To find a way to destroy him?"

"When I was sure what had happened," he admitted. "But I only got the proof recently and then all this—and you—came along to get in the way of my total revenge." He longed to tell her the whole story, but it was not his to tell, as this part had been. If they were captured, it was better that she not know. After all, to work their way north, they would have to sail or walk around huge Charlotte Harbor, where they could be spotted by Gasparilla's ships.

So he asked her about herself instead, and she told him all about the burden of being the only child—and a daughter—on one of the largest sugarcane plantations in Louisiana. About how she had learned to use a cane-cutting machete on the sly, and about the day she had raced her pony into the parquet hall of Magnolia Hill Mansion when her parents had forbidden her to come in where their adult guests were discussing horse racing.

"And I'll wager a guess Papa didn't spank his little girl as he should have, even if Mama might have scolded that it was—what was that she always said?" he asked as he shifted the flapping sail to catch the new breath of breeze.

"Indelicate. And that day, like most, I was far beyond indelicate," Lanie admitted with a little laugh. She amazed herself by talking to him so easily. She realized how deeply lonely she had been since she'd been separated from Jasmine. "No," she said, "Papa didn't punish me. As a matter of fact, after that, he always allowed me to mingle with the adults and speak my mind, too—if I did it delicately."

She was going to ask him what she had been building up to. She wanted to know his real name and how he had intended to do away with Gasparilla and all his men by himself. And she had to know about the dead woman who had owned that ring. But, after all, someone like him could lie about it all just to court her sympathies. But suddenly, her eyes were caught by a row of shore lights. They looked so close over the inky waters! Boca Grande! She had been trusting him, just listening and chattering away. She had been thoroughly seduced, that was for certain! He was sailing them right into Gasparilla's pirate's lair at Boca Grande!

"Turn this boat around at once!" she ordered. "I see where we are! I'm not so stupid as you think!"

"Keep your voice down! Sound carries on the water," he told her, his voice crashing to anger. "Sit down. We're sailing right by, and you're rocking the raft!"

She made the mistake of reaching for her pistol and trying to shove the crude pine boom of their makeshift sail at the same time. When he grabbed her, she kicked out and toppled over the side.

She fought her way to the surface, flailing, sputtering. She swept her sopped hair off her forehead, but there was no raft, no sail, no Sil. Surely he wouldn't leave her in this black night! Perhaps he would just as soon drown her as take her back to Gasparilla! Instinctively, she paddled in the cool, wet vastness to keep her head up; she'd never learned to swim. Her billowing skirts helped buoy her up at first, but then they sank sodden around her and weighed her down. The water was so wide, the sky so vast. Where was Sil and the patch of white sail?

She paddled harder, swung around. "Sil? Please, where are you?" She couldn't kick her feet with the shroud of skirts around them. She swallowed a great gulp of salt water. She heard nothing but rustling waves, saw nothing overhead but stars in the crushing cup of blackness. For a moment she felt the panic of closed places even under the heavens. Sil was sailing on. He was leaving her. Sharks he had told her once—sharks were in these waters! Had she been out here lost for hours already, or had this happened in an instant?

"Lanie?"

"Here! Where are you?"

A hump of wood swam at her from the dark line where sky met sea. He was in the water, too! He was straining to pull the raft toward her, holding out his hand to her. "Here! Grab on!"

"I didn't mean to—but I will not go to Boca Grande!" she gasped as he pulled her and she grabbed a knot of driftwood.

"I just had to cut across the bay somewhere," he gasped, "but now you've ruined that! Damn you, woman, you've ruined everything since we took your ship! Now keep your mouth shut while I try to hoist you up. And if you don't pull me up after you, I'll tip you over again and leave you on your own like you deserve!"

Panting and straining, with his hand hard on her bottom to boost her up, she clambered aboard. But there was no sail, and the raft was much more bumpy. She realized then, as she helped him up, that she had completely overturned them. Her guns, the gunpowder! The food, maybe the sail! If the wretch had only told her they were sailing by Boca Grande instead of staying inland! Why didn't he tell her the truth and trust her a bit? It was his fault as much as hers! Soon, tears mingled with the salt water on her cheeks.

"Catch your breath and stop crying," he ordered after he'd rested, sprawled out beside her, unspeaking, for a moment. "We'll never right this, out here. We're going to take turns hanging over the side and kicking in to shore, and hope to hell we're in before daybreak, when we'll be sitting ducks.''

"But not to Boca Grande! And what about sharks?"

"I'd put the odds on you if one of them tried to take you on!"

He was grateful he'd shoved his father's watch down his boot, though it would probably never work again after that dousing. He fished it out and thrust it in her hand. "Hold that. If it goes in, you might as well go with it."

He slid into the water and got a firm handhold on the raft. He could have strangled the spoiled, stubborn, demented woman. And yet all he could think about as he exhausted himself kicking the raft in the pull of waves was how he wanted her in his arms and between his legs again.

They lay exhausted, side by side, soaking wet in the sand on a little jut of land north of what Sil called Back Bay. Dawn had spilled pale orchid hues over the horizon just as they came ashore. But the blazing ball of sun was straight overhead when Sil finally tugged on her sandy, salt-speckled sleeve where he sat beside her.

"Wake up, Lanie. We've been asleep for hours. We need the shade or you'll burn. We've got to find food." Her eyes opened slowly, and she closed them again in the assault of sun. When she sat up, she saw clusters of little brown crabs staring at them with odd eyes and single claws raised in mock salute. But when Sil helped her to her feet, most of them skittered off sideways, giving the people a wide berth. Sandpipers and snipes darted here and there, pecking in the sand for coquina or grabbing the occasional stray crab.

She ached all over from swimming and kicking the raft to shore, though Sil had done most of the work. She had only gotten in under protest, to give him short rests. She got slowly to her feet while he wedged the battered raft in a mangrove thicket. He walked like an old person, too, tentatively, slowly.

"You're petticoat's gone," he told her when he came back. "At this rate, you'll be wearing my tattered shirt when we need that gown for the next sail." He actually dared a half grin, which she ignored.

"Absolutely not," she said, hands on hips. "I started out with an entire trousseau, and I'm not going to lose my last piece for any more of your makeshift sails!"

"This is all we salvaged," he said, evidently eager to change the subject. He held the cutlass he'd had the foresight to wedge between two driftwood limbs and the dagger he'd had, like his watch, jammed in a boot. He offered her neither weapon, but the idea of her keeping the man prisoner was hopeless and foolish anyway. The battle between them was now on far different ground, and she was more excited and alarmed than before.

They went back from the shore a bit to make a meager camp under a stand of slash pines and spike-leafed palmetto. Lanie would have loved to remove her gown to dry, the way he did his tattered shirt, which he had draped in the branches over her head to give her better shade. But she had no intention of their playing Adam and Eve completely unclothed in their little Eden.

They foraged for food and wolfed down tiny figs and the bland-tasting hearts of palm he harvested from the palmetto trees with the cutlass. When they finally found several coconuts on the ground that were not spoiled, they drank the milk, too. Neither of them could have climbed the eighty-foot trunks leaning at askew angles above their heads.

"I am still so hungry," she admitted. "Serafina taught me a lot about finding fruit and vegetables, but nothing about how to cook something like those crabs without a kettle or a fire. I can just taste crab gumbo right now."

His mussed head jerked up from the coconut meat he had been dicing on a length of pine branch. He shot her a dazzling smile that rocked her almost as hard as the sea had last night. "That's it," he said. "Go catch a few and we'll try to steam them."

"With what fire?" she challenged.

"Don't be a crab yourself," he countered, suddenly looking immensely pleased with himself. He dared to give her a light smack on her bottom as she got to her feet. "Just watch something Serafina taught me, bless her sweet little soul."

He dug a hold in the dry sand and lined it with green leaves. He filled that with tinder and topped it with dry pine needles. Then he took out his precious watch—which was no longer working—and with the tip of his dagger pried the glass dome off the face. He held it in the sun, rotating it until the beating rays were concentrated into a pinpoint of light on the pile in the hole. It smoked, smoldered and burst into flame.

"Now we cover the crabs above this with damp leaves and more sand and steam them!" he told her, as proud as a little boy who'd just lit his first sulfur match.

She clapped her hands like a child. "And Serafina taught you that?"

"Not using the glass this way, but how to cook them," he told her, his rugged face split with a huge, triumphant grin. He'd almost blurted out how he'd known a cook on his first navy ship during the War of 1812 who'd sworn by steamed crabs rather than boiled ones, but no need to spill any of that. Instead, he only prayed silently that Serafina had survived the attack on the compound and that he could rescue her eventually after he rendezvoused with the navy—if they made it all that way. He stood and smacked the soil from his hands.

"And where is the seafood to cook?" he demanded, to ward off her next question, which he saw coming. "Can't you follow orders? I suppose on Magnolia Hill you never had to turn a hand for your own victuals!" Hurt that he'd turned on her after the tiny triumph they had shared, she pouted, but he turned his back on her and strode off for the beach to gather crabs himself while she stared after him.

Their safe little haven was not safe for long. Lanie was bathing and washing her gown with sand and water in a small inland stream—where he'd told her to keep an eye out for floating logs, which might be alligators!—when he came crashing through the brush into the tiny clearing. Her hair still slicked to her head, she spun to face him and reached for her sodden gown to cover herself. He looked frenzied and carried his wadded shirt in one hand and the cutlass in the other.

"Sil, I told you I wanted some privacy here! And if you have come thinking—"

"That I have to have that sweet, willing body again," he interrupted breathlessly. "I do, but don't flatter yourself. I've spotted two of Gasparilla's ships, and they're in close!"

She gasped and struggled into her soaking gown. It stuck to her skin, and she left it gaping open in the back as she followed him. Near their little camp, they peered through dark green foliage at the sloop *Fortune*, the very ship that had captured Lanie's *Bonne Femme*, and another one, a square-rigger.

"That's the *Largesse* with the *Fortune*," Sil whispered. "They must be looking for us, because they know damn well Jack Scarfield's men are way south on Sanibel. If they send a boat in they'll find the raft or the camp, and we'll have to make a run for it."

Lanie began to tremble, but she found strange reassurance in the fact that Sil was adeptly fastening her gown while they watched the ships. Surely a man that thoughtful at a time like this was to be trusted! And he wasn't running out on the beach to summon his bloodthirsty mates, either. When he was done, she leaned lightly against him. He rested his hands on her shoulders while they watched together.

They could see men on deck and dangling from the rigging peering landward; they looked as big as toy soldiers. Sporadically a rough voice or curse would float to shore. Lanie's stomach churned at the thought of being in Gasparilla's foul hands again, though she feared all the miles through uncharted tropic wilderness to get to New Orleans, too. Blessedly, no boats put into shore, and the vessels edged on.

"But they're going the direction we want to go," she whispered.

"I know. And that derelict raft of ours is not going to last long. I think it will get us to the mainland, though. Our best bet is to wait until dark and then use your gown for a sail to cross the pass to the mainland. Then we'll hike north along the shore to be sure they won't spot us on the bay. And then—''

He paused. She craned her neck to look up at him over her shoulder. She realized anew this was deadly business. She would not falter now to give up her last garment for a sail to get out of here. Her heart thrilled to hear his confident plan. He was really on her side now, her protector, so he must care for her more than for his own reputation or revenge among the pirates.

"And then what?" she prompted, gazing earnestly into his frowning face.

"And then, if we're lucky," he told her grimly, "we'll be out of the reach of Gasparilla's pirates—but into marauding Seminole Indian country."

Tears prickled her eyelids, but she did not cry. She only nodded and let him pull her, trembling, into his strong arms for a comforting embrace. She encircled his waist with her arms and put her cheek on his bare shoulder. Pirates, Indians, alligators, sharks and Justin Lyon be damned. For one sweet moment, she was almost content.

Chapter Seven

Lanie and Sil left their derelict little raft hidden under a palmetto thicket on the mainland of Florida and hiked ten slow miles north under rainy skies. The foliage was thick and wet, the beaches sodden and shower-swept. The air was humid even for August. They forded five waist-deep rivers. Lanie wondered if she would ever feel dry again.

As the skies cleared, they made camp on the shore of a large freshwater lake a mile inland. Sil had been watching for signs of Seminoles and had seen none. But it was obvious this lake was a watering spot for the animals of the area, and once again they were cautious when they bathed. No need to face a panther or black bear or alligator. They surveyed the area and it seemed safe enough, so they put their camp in a thicket with a view of the lake.

It felt wonderful to drink and bathe in fresh, sweet water again. Lanie's eyes, too, drank in the beauty of the spot, the delicate floating lavender water hyacinths she was familiar with from the bayous of home, the splashes of red and yellow angel's trumpet on the banks.

She was pleased to see Sil shave his three-day-old brush of beard, even though he cut himself with the dagger twice without a mirror or soap. She watched him finger his face tenderly after that painful shave while he walked toward her up the gentle slope of lake bank.

"I could shave you if you are going to butcher yourself, I suppose," she observed as she prepared their evening food.

"Are we to the point I can trust you with a naked blade against my throat?" he countered.

"Of course. You have been a wonderful help. I am grateful to you for your expertise, you see," she admitted with a slanted look up at him through thick, sun-bleached lashes.

He sat down much too close to watch her finish mixing the salmagundi salad of sawgrass stems, cattail sprouts and Spanish bayonette flowers, all sprinkled with wild fennel, just the way Serafina had taught her. Their roasting duck eggs nestled in hot ashes at their feet.

"You're grateful for my expertise in what areas?" he prompted with a hint of teasing in his dark eyes.

"Hardly what you are implying," she declared archly, and quickly passed him his leaf piled with the salmagundi. "I am certainly not referring to the—well, the marital act."

He tilted his big, tousled head in surprise. His thick eyebrows shot up. "The marital act? Is that what they call it on the proper plantations outside New Orleans?"

"Yes," she replied testily and burned her hand reaching for a hot egg too quickly. She blew on her fingers. "I suppose you and your pirate friends have all sorts of crude names for it!"

He reached for her chin to turn her flaming face to his. How she got into such indelicate discussions all the time with this man she would never know! "With you, Lanie, I'd like to call it sharing love," he said, his voice a gentle rasp.

"Love! You didn't say—I never thought—"

"Never thought a pirate could feel love as well as lust for you?" He narrowed his eyes, and the little white crow's-feet that squinting into the sun had given him disappeared. He sighed for how he'd treated her and for his own broken vow to never care deeply for another woman. "Things were a little rough back there. I can see your point."

"It's so impossible, all of this," she stammered with an outflung hand, which she jerked into her lap. "I do not even know your real name!"

Like one mesmerized, she watched his nostrils flare and his lips move as he spoke. "Mademoiselle Melanie McVey, I would like you to meet Joshua Blair. Josh."

The watch, she thought, stunned at his sudden change in tactics to share his real self with her—the initials on it were J.B. His father's watch.

"Named for your father?"

"And proud of it. He was a brave, fine man."

And you, too, she almost said as he bent forward over their food to kiss her. She shivered with a deep, sensual, soul-struck delight. For one instant, she felt she knew the real Sil. The real Josh, she corrected herself. And she trusted and needed him so much . . . and loved him more than that.

Josh sat back again, loosing her chin but continuing to stare deeply into her sea-green eyes. He wondered what she was thinking, with that serious look on her lovely face, but nearly melted with surprise and pleasure at her response.

"I am pleased to make your acquaintance, Mr. Blair. Kiss me again, please—Josh."

That night, to keep mosquitoes off, they stretched her gown like a huge netting over them and huddled beneath it and a screen of leaves he'd made. They had not shared love since that first day they'd escaped, but she knew it would happen again tonight and she was not afraid. She did not protest when he removed his shirt from her and draped it over them, too. That other man in that other life had been wrong for her. She wondered in a flash of recognition if her insistence on her betrothal to Justin had been in childish rebellion against both Papa and her friend Jasmine, too. She had resented Jasmine's maturity, and had buried the knowledge that Jasmine, despite being born a slave, was just as worthy of opinions and stubbornness as she.

A mosquito buzzed around Lanie's face as the man she now knew as Josh settled close against her bare back and arranged their makeshift screen over them. "Our own little world," he murmured against the hollow of her spine between her shoulder blades as his strong arms encircled her.

"But it's still full of little demons," she muttered and slapped at the buzzing insect.

"Hmm," he said, "here comes another one." He nibbled at the satin skin of her shoulders, then the side of her throat. "And another, a big one hungry for your sweet, tasty flesh." He bit gently at her earlobe and flicked his free hand across her already pert nipples to stiffen them to aching nubs.

"I'll get rid of him," she said with a low chuckle at playing his game, then swatted at his tormenting hand. She could feel him hard and ready behind her, and she ached for his touch.

"If you smack at ones this hungry and eager, they just bite all the harder!" he told her. He could not resist her. His vow to never deeply desire another woman seemed as wispy as the wind. He tried to summon up Becky's face and voice, but it was impossible. Strange how he'd always been so true to her before. In a life lived for duty he'd never once tumbled another woman in distant ports where his mates went woman-hunting on shore leave. But now this woman needed and wanted him, and everything else that had once obsessed him seemed to shrink and waver.

Lanie knew she was lost in love. He had turned her to him and was nibbling at her lower lip while his big, callused hands traversed her back, her bottom, her thighs to clamp her to him. He pressed her on her back and flicked tiny bites down her breasts and across her flat, silky belly. She scattered teasing nibbles across him, too, and grew bolder as his skilled hands and mouth urged her on. Soon, breathing hard, she clung to him. Eagerly, she pulled him to her, into her. The only buzzing then was her blood rushing hard through her veins and her own cries of, "Please, Josh, yes! I love you so."

Just after daybreak the next morning, Lanie emerged from a screen of leaves to see him standing by the edge of the lake. She walked up quietly behind him, wondering what he saw. She watched as he lifted his hand to throw something in—a glint of gold—before he stopped with his arm in mid-arc. He shook his head. Then she saw him jam his gold ring back on his finger.

She froze when she realized what he had meant to do. He heard her, glanced her way, then looked out over the lake again.

"Josh, your ring. You don't have to throw it away. You said she's dead."

"No," he said. "I buried her and her—my—child two years ago. But I still can't throw away the memories and the guilt. In a way, she's not dead at all."

He felt so torn. To Lanie's credit, she did not ply him with questions or accusations. She took the truth of his agonized admission so well, he longed to tell her about his other vow to his naval duty, but he held back. There would be time for that later, when they got closer to their rendezvous spot with a navy ship. They were still caught between pirates and Indians, both of whom hated the navy with a vengeance. She'd be safer not knowing yet.

He held out his hand to Lanie and she stepped forward to take it. And then, looking into the distance, he told her calmly, almost without pausing, the story of his young wife's death in childbirth.

Rebecca Bailey had been his childhood sweetheart, and he'd gone to sea after only two months of marriage, not knowing he had left her with child. Her premature labor had been long and hard, and neither mother nor child had lived. He'd come home just hours too late, expecting to find her waiting for him at the door, but she was waiting, covered with a sheet, on their bed upstairs.

He blamed himself for both their deaths, he told Lanie. It had been his seed planted within Becky that had killed her, and he had left her to die alone. He had not even known that his tiny daughter, Susan, had existed until it was too late. All he had been able to do was bury them, and with them he had buried his heart and passions. Until recently.

Tears trembled on Lanie's lashes as she listened, but she stood still, holding his hand until he was done.

"Funny," he said at last, when his words slowed. "My parents, my wife and child, gone, and all I have of them are memories and pieces of jewelry they left behind, my own pirate's gold."

"But you are right to keep the ring," she urged gently. "I am not afraid of memories. I—I have some myself that need to be dealt with."

He turned to her. "You're not afraid of memories, but how should I feel about your very much alive Justin Lyon?"

"He is obviously the wrong man for me."

"Out here in the wilderness maybe, but back at Magnolia Hill, where marital acts are only that?" He dreaded eventually telling her he planned to have Lyon arrested, at the very least for questioning about collusion with the pirate Lafitte. There was so much standing between them, he thought, for them ever to be lovers in the real world. He shook his head and looked again over the lake.

She wished he was not so moody, so unpredictable, but perhaps that was part of his allure for her. She had the overwhelming urge to reach out to him as he had her. "About Justin," she said, "his pursuing me was exciting, I suppose. He was dashing, handsome, worldly. I met with some opposition about him and I was trying to assert my independence, I guess. Then, too, I was twenty-four when he proposed and a young girl becomes a spinster at only fifteen in bayou country, you know."

"Somehow, I can't imagine you worrying about what other people would say," he murmured, and they swung hands as they began to walk to their camp.

But instead of trying to explain, she sang, first in a wavering voice and then in her bell-clear, strong soprano:

Go to sleep, my little one
Until the years to fifteen run.
When the fifteen years have fled.
Then my *minette* will be wed.

"One of my Creole cradle songs," she explained, "so you see, there have been subtle pressures applied since birth to believe and accept certain things." She thought suddenly of Jasmine again—of slavery. How long she had accepted that, too, ignored it.

"Then, too," she went on, "Justin owned the next plantation to share the levee, and I just thought—" She let her voice trail off. Josh nodded as if he understood, and smiled. The sad mood was broken, and she felt better. They understood each other.

She let her thoughts drift to the future, when they would return to New Orleans. After they had somehow rescued Jasmine and Serafina, of course, she would explain to her parents that Josh had lived with the pirates only to avenge his parents. Surely they would accept him in time. After all, Mama's family had taken years to accept the wild Irishman she had dared to love!

Lanie hummed the Creole cradle tune again after he kissed her cheek and went up the bank to scuff out the remnants of their fire and to gather their meager belongings. She meandered along the marshy bank, past the cattails she had gathered last evening for food. Despite the possibility of pirates chasing them and the threat of looming Indians, she felt so safe and secure with this man.

She lifted her head as ducks and grebes flew in to settle on the pond with a flourish. She heard a high-pitched sound on the shore she could not place and wondered what sort of bird that was. She parted the cattails and saw a hidden mound of dry vegetation. Some sort of large bird nest? And something in the nest squeaked. It moved!

She bent forward just as a huge pink and white mouth lined with razor-sharp teeth lunged at her from a gray and white monster body hidden in the weeds.

She jumped, screamed, ran. The thing was a nine-foot-long, hissing alligator! She darted sideways and leaped for a low tree limb. She heard Josh's feet, his shout. The tree branch she clung to gave a loud crack and dumped her to the ground flat on her back.

She screamed and rolled, but Josh lunged past her to slash at the alligator with his cutlass. The beast barked once as the cutlass plunged between its eyes. It flopped, shuddered, thrashed, then lay still. Then Josh jerked Lanie to her feet and they ran.

Ten yards away, they threw themselves into each other's arms. "I didn't know—didn't see it," she gasped. She held tightly to him, but he was shaking, too. "It must have been guarding that nest. It was making sounds. And I was right near there last night picking cattails—and we were camped here—"

Her knees would no longer hold her, and she slumped to the ground. He hunkered down beside her with a comforting hand rubbing her back. He cleared his throat. "We're both novices at this—camping out with alligators, I mean. We've got to be even more on guard. Just rest here a minute. I've got to go back for something. Silver Swords or Josh Blair, I'm afraid I'm going to need that cutlass."

For the next two days they warily followed what must have been a deer path or a Seminole trail through miles of sawgrass that grabbed at them and cut any skin it touched. Amid the endless sea of tall, waving grasses, they spotted occasional islands of pine and cabbage palm trees.

Nearer the coastline, they camped beside the wide Peace River on an easily distinguishable jut of land Josh called Punta Gorda, fat point. There they slept, huddled together in exhaustion. The next day Josh began to gather wood for another raft to take them across the Peace River and up the Mayakka River northward and finally out of Gasparilla's reach.

Lanie rotated a duck on a spit over their little fire. They could only cook food on the days the sun shone through Josh's glass, and it had not shone for two days. The meat smelled delicious. Just imagine, she mused, camping along someplace called the Peace River with her life in such turmoil. But it sounded like a much safer place than the Mayakka, which Josh told her was a Seminole word.

She was not sure, however, that she would ever really be at peace with a man like Josh Blair in her life. Strangely, the thought was a delicious one. And as for sailing up the Mayakka in nothing more than Josh's tattered shirt so they could use her poor ruined gown for a sail— But she shuddered at the thought of Indians, for she knew they had been on the warpath for three years.

At home, she had cared no more about the Seminole Indian War than she had the plight of slaves—not until she'd had her life turned upside down had she cared. The Florida Indian tribes, Josh had explained to her, had once lived in Georgia but had been shoved southward by whites encroaching on their lands. The tribe had gladly sheltered runaway slaves from the south, and certain bold, vindictive Americans had used that as an excuse to raid Seminole villages.

Five years ago the United States Army and Navy had invaded Spanish Florida over the fugitive-slave issue. A bloody defeat of the Seminoles by Andrew Jackson, the first territorial governor of Florida, had followed. More than three hundred Seminole men, women and children had been slain, and the Indians had retaliated in kind.

For the past three years, renegade remnants of the tribe had been hiding in the Florida wilderness just biding their time to begin another war. This could happen very soon, as Florida had become a state this year, which meant more whites would be wanting to settle the land. The pirates traded with the Seminoles, but others knew to leave the Indians strictly alone until the armed forces could settle them down. Josh and Lanie had to either go by sea across the wide Gulf of Mexico or travel through the Seminole no-man's-land north to New Orleans.

"Lanie," Josh called, interrupting her frenzied musings as he emerged from the thicket, "look what I found!"

He carried what appeared to be a piece of dripping palmetto trunk. She squinted into the setting sun to see better. "I found some of this with Specs and Red Legs once and we devoured it," he explained, his rugged face beaming. "It's called palmetto honey, and it's as good as candy. My love," he declared grandly as he plopped the oozing bounty on the pile of leaves she had laid for a tablecloth, "sweets to the sweet."

"Oh, it's wonderful! Mmm," she said after she dipped a finger in and tasted it. "The best thing I've had since I left pralines in cane crystal behind at home!"

They oohed and aahed through a frenzy of eating the delicious stuff. Soon they were feeding each other. She ran her gooey finger between his lips, and he licked teasingly at her mouth. Some honey dribbled down her chin and he laved it off, then skimmed her fluted collarbones, above the tattered oval neckline of her faded blue gown. She flicked some honey off the corner of his lips.

Suddenly, they were removing each other's clothing. The duck on the unturned spit sizzled and burned until Josh swore and bent to lift it off. But then he reached for her again. Their eyes held as they came together in a cascade of kisses and caresses far sweeter than the honey.

Boldly, when she could not think, could only feel, she followed his lead. He could barely hold still as she pushed him determinedly down, the way he had her, until she could work her will. Her moon-gold hair trailed along his skin. She reveled in her power over him, the prolonged arousal of his strength and the desire she wanted to evoke so desperately.

"Witch!" he exploded. "Sweetheart, stop! I can't stand it."

"It is exactly what you do to me!" she insisted and kept on. He reached for her, turned her over, pressed her down. His face looked glazed with passion barely held in check. She was so ready for him, willing and waiting. Their perfect merging shook her to her core, shook the world. And they fell off the very rim of the golden, honey-sweet universe together.

Clothed only in Josh's tattered shirt, her shoes and palmetto hat, Lanie sat on the forward edge of the new, sturdier raft while they sailed up the Mayakka River. It was tough going against the current, and Josh paddled hard with a makeshift oar when the breeze softened. Her faded, well-worn gown, the last remnant of her once sumptuous trousseau, alternately bloomed or flapped in the fitful gusts. Despite a fairly cloudy day, Josh was dripping sweat already, and she insisted he give her a turn with the paddle again.

"You have been working too hard every day," she chided gently, but her eyes drank him in with pride as he begrudgingly handed her the paddle.

"Maybe it's our nights that are doing me in," he teased, and their eyes held. She felt their love leap between them again—that blend of growing need and trust seared by the lightning bolts of passion. And yet he had never mentioned any future for them, and she had been afraid to ask. She paddled hard, dipping the oar first right and then left to keep the raft toward the middle of the river in case anything lurked along the banks.

"You'll love Louisiana," she began tentatively, hoping she sounded merely conversational.

"Not if it's as warm as this," he muttered, but he suddenly wondered what else she would say. "But I've heard it's a lovely state."

"Oh, it is," she rushed on. "I've known some other northerners who have visited and never wanted to leave again. Except at harvest time, plantation living would be so restful and easy after the life you've led."

She did not dare face him as she went on. "I am sure you would love New Orleans, too. We could build a house back from the levee on land that will be mine when I marry, if you'd agree to stay. You could work with the barges and steamboats going to market, since you prefer a seafaring life," she said over her shoulder with a dramatic shrug in another attempt at nonchalance.

He frowned at her. His head hurt and he felt shaky. Besides, his guilt about Becky ravaged him when she dared suggest marriage. He'd been damn careful not to get Lanie pregnant, but in wedlock it would be a constant danger. "Ah, I can just picture it now." He knew his voice was caustic, but he couldn't help it. "Papa gives his only, treasured daughter a piece of land for a house where she can live with a reformed pirate. Meanwhile, Mama's agreeing with all new Orleans society that her daughter is not only acting insanely, but quite indelicately. And said reformed pirate is out on the levee bank with his silver swords fighting a duel to the death with Justin Lyon for your hand. Is that where all this is going?"

She paddled harder without looking at him. "I know it is not quite the time for permanent plans, but I for one do not see our relationship as a brief interlude just until we get out of here!"

"Let's be realistic, Lanie," he scolded as he scooted closer. "We won't get out of here if you put us in that bank with that wild, furious paddling. Let me have that oar."

"I'm doing fine!" she said sharply, holding the dripping piece of flat wood out of his way when he reached for it. "Just never mind all this right now. You're tired and you're hot!"

"It seems I spend my time either hot at you or for you. Why don't you just rest a minute, too, and look at me, damn it!"

She let the paddle drip across her knees while she turned to face him. She was embarrassed she had dared to broach the subject of their marriage. If a lady hinted such things, it was always with smiles behind a fluttering fan to a proper man with her mama just down the veranda, and never out with him alone, half naked in some desolate land! She felt her cheeks prickle pink, and not from the sun.

"I realize," he began, his voice low and rather shaky, "you're not the sort of woman to be toyed with and taken lightly. Nor, believe me, am I the sort of man who does that. I have never used women that way, not even those I could have, such as Jasmine or Serafina. I'm no saint, but I had a wonderful mother and wife. Believe it or not, this overseer of the women's compound on Captiva respects women—including and especially you—too much for that."

He took the oar from her and began to stroke slowly as he spoke. "But I won't mislead you by making commitments neither of us may be able to keep if—when, I mean—we get out of here. If that changes how you've been responding to me, I understand, though I won't like it very much and will probably be low enough to try to change your mind every night."

Suddenly, her eyes swam with tears that blurred his big bronze form into two wavering Joshes before she blinked. His blend of openness with moodiness, gentleness with ruthlessness rocked her to her very soul. She wanted him; she loved him.

"Thank you for your honesty," she managed, though she saw him grimace at her words. "So, we'll just have to wait and see."

"Wait and see," he repeated. He thought again about trying to explain his other commitments to her—commitments that still had to come first, but he was too hot and tired to try. He sighed, wondering why his head hurt so, and Lanie's heart went out to him. Carefully this time, so as not to tip the raft, she leaned forward on her knees to kiss his hot cheek.

Josh fell asleep in the shade as soon as they made camp, so she took his cutlass and went looking for food. Warily watching for alligators, she walked just a little way to harvest some tiny figs from the strangler vines she had seen and to look for bird eggs or crabs. It seemed dinner would be meager tonight, but she did not intend to go far without him. When she returned, he still slept heavily, drenched in sweat even in the shade. Her stomach cartwheeled with sudden fear. Could he be ill from something he had eaten?

She knelt to feel his damp forehead. He was burning with fever! His eyes slitted open at her touch.

"I feel funny," he mumbled. "Thirsty. So damned hot. I ache. Have you ever had yellow fever?"

She frowned. "No. But surely you can't! Where would you catch it? That's what people catch on crowded ships, isn't it?" He didn't answer.

Tattered heartbeats tore at her chest. He couldn't be really ill. Not this strong, brave man she needed so desperately. She ran to soak the hem of his shirt in river water and bathed his face until he opened his eyes again. They glittered with fever. Fear smothered her so completely for a moment she did not even catch his words at first.

"You've got to stay away from me, Lanie. You might catch it, too. You'll have to hide the raft. Don't build a fire. No smoke in the sky here. If anything happens to me, go on alone up the river and then walk west to the coast again to head north. Maybe there aren't any Seminoles around now, but keep your eyes open."

"I am not leaving you! Don't talk that way," she insisted, her voice breaking. "Just rest, and you'll be fine."

"If it's yellow fever," he muttered, "I've seen it take whole ships. Listen to me!" he cried and seized her wrist in an iron grip. "You've got to be careful. Don't even bury me if I die, but just go on!"

"Stop it!" she sobbed. "You are not going to die! I won't let you." But despite her raised voice and his grip on her arm, he slumped in sleep again.

For three frenzied days, she bathed him and waited, terrified for what he would do or say next. He fought her and raved deliriously between bouts of near unconsciousness. His bronze skin took on the yellow sheen that gave the malady its name, and he thrashed so hard she tied him down. She dripped water through his lips, she listened to his ravings, she feared, she prayed.

"Aye, aye, sir! To the foredeck," he muttered. It seemed he was always giving or taking orders. In her dazed, exhausted state, she had long ago given up trying to decipher the jumble of his words. "Frank, he's drowned," he went on. "I only got a broken leg but he's drowned. A rogue wave swamped us on the way in. Will they believe me? Now I'll have to do this all alone...Becky, she can't be dead. She can't be dead! My child! I killed her with my child!" he cried and sat straight up before Lanie pushed him down again.

"It's all right, Josh. I am here to take care of you!"

His eyes darted, looked beyond her before they focused on her distraught face. "Mother?"

Tears burned her eyelids. "No, it's Lanie. Your mother—she's not here, but everything is all right."

His agony, both physical and mental, pierced her heart. His dark eyes drifted here and there, but the fierce strength he'd had the first few days of the fever dissolved into limp resistance. And still his fever did not break! If she could only get it down! He was becoming weaker. He had said he might die—he must have known it was possible he would really die! And he had called for everyone but her! Even his mother. How Lanie wished she had her mother here, as Mama had overseen the nursing of anyone ill at Magnolia Hill.

And then the thought struck her: Mama always sweated fever, though they had never had yellow fever on the plantation. But all she had here to sweat Joshua with was one ruined shirt and her gown and no fire. He had warned her against making one and she knew it was for fear of the Seminoles. But she had to risk smoke in the sky. She could make certain it dispersed. If she could make a fire hot enough and cover him with leaves, perhaps she could have her own steambath out here. It would have to work! Without him, she would never make it anyway. And she had no intention of leaving the only man she had ever really loved alone in the wilds, dead or alive!

She scurried to dig two narrow pits for fire, one on each side of him. She made a tent by stretching her damp gown and his shirt across bent green branches. She strung big palmetto leaves on vines and draped those over, too. Then, trembling, she held his watch face above the dry tinder to set off the fires. The sun beating down on her little tent combined with the heat of the flames should surely be as good as Mama wrapping someone and skimming warming pans through the sheets.

Dripping wet herself, she fanned the smoke and fire with a big palmetto fan. Josh moaned and tossed, so she had to bind his hands to keep him from flopping his arms in the fire trenches. Waves of heat shimmered at her. He seemed to sleep, so still that she kept feeling the pulse in his neck to be certain it was still beating. Her head hurt, her eyes stung, she dripped sweat. She prayed it was just from exhaustion and worry and not the onslaught of the disease in her.

By sunset when she let the fire burn down, his skin felt somewhat drier. She smothered the fires, bathed him and dipped herself in the river before falling into a heavy sleep beside him.

When she woke, dawn grayed the sky through a heavy fog that silvered everything around. Slowly, as if in a dream, she reached out to feel his forehead.

Cool! Damp from the fog, but not hot. She had done it! She bent, trembling, and said a hasty prayer for deliverance. Then, joyous beyond words, she leaped to her feet. In radiant ecstasy at his deliverance and her victory, she splashed naked along the bank to clean herself and drink deeply. Fog drifted in patches like iridescent mothers-of-pearl skimming her skin and face. She lifted her hands in gratitude to the heavens, then shook her head to loose the long golden tresses she had tied back with a piece of vine. She had saved Josh! She had saved him, and she loved him, and as soon as he was stronger, they would get out of here! She spun and danced and glowed.

And then, through a scrim of moving mist, she saw on the opposite bank of the Mayakka River two bronze figures staring raptly at her!

Indians! An old man and a boy! She gasped and froze. They seemed to be bowing: a wisp of strange melodic chant floated to her ears, then faded. She darted into the fog and made her way through the bushes quickly to Josh.

When the fog cleared and she did not see the Indians anywhere, she helped the feeble Josh to the raft and moved their camp a little ways upriver. Perhaps the Indians had seen her smoke the previous day; perhaps their arrival had been pure chance. At any rate, she had not imagined them. They had not seemed unfriendly, however, but shocked, almost awed. It had seemed to her they bowed in some sort of greeting or obeisance. The snatch of song she'd heard had been eerie, but not warlike. What had they thought of seeing a naked white woman with gold hair streaming loose, cavorting like one demented in their Mayakka River?

Josh improved slowly the next day, but they needed more food. She carefully ventured out with the raised cutlass, held before her like a shield. She found hearts of palm and bay-berries. She discovered a precious papaya tree dripping its lumpy yellow fruit, but that was where she also found the snake.

She saw it before she heard it, coiled in an S shape as if to guard the precious tree. She jumped, as startled to see it as it was to see her, but she knew she was outside its strik-ing range. Yet she was frozen with fear and fascination. They stared at each other, mesmerized, just as she had yes-terday with the Indians. A thick, black, split tongue flashed from its mouth as if it would speak. The head swayed, and she heard the frenetic whine of thrumming rattles on the black tail with its diamond-shaped dun-colored markings. She smelled a strange musky odor like incense in church. The snake opened its jaw as if to strike, but then relaxed to slither down and away.

Lanie had seen snakes at home and was not usually afraid of them, though she knew they were to be respected. It was only when the rattlesnake disappeared that she began to tremble. She was not superstitious, but she took the fact that the snake had only warned her and backed off as a good sign. She carefully filled her skirt with papayas and hurried back.

"Josh," she called as she reached the tiny clearing, "you won't believe it but—"

He was not there.

She dumped the fruit and ran to the river, then searched the brush all around. She called his name quietly, desper-ately, and then, in a panic, searched everywhere again. But he wasn't anywhere! The camp was unharmed but for what was missing. The dagger, his watch and the raft were gone. Frenzied, she studied the riverbank up and down for a sign, a footprint. Nothing, as though he had just vanished into thin air. Surely, surely, he would never just—leave her here!

Suddenly, she was tired to death of being strong, of bearing up. She felt so bereft, so beaten. She had lost her home, her dear Jasmine, now Josh. With her back to a tree and the cutlass across her knees, she fell to the ground and sobbed.

Chapter Eight

Without Josh at her side, she spent an agonizing night. In her frenzied mind, each tiny sound became beast or Indian. Finally, she dozed from utter exhaustion sitting up with her back to a tree trunk, the cutlass in her hands. But she jerked awake more than once in the smothering darkness, overcome by haunted dreams and living terrors. Perhaps his fever had suddenly returned and he had taken the raft in his delirium. But he had still been so weak! Had Indians taken him? If she waited, would he come back? When the sun began to filter through the thick vegetation, Lanie stuffed the papayas in a crude basket made from palmetto leaves and set off westward.

She had to hack her way through the undergrowth at times. Her eyes soon ached from straining to see ahead in alternating mottled shade and stark pools of sun. She had no intention of allowing a wild animal or wilder Indian to see her first. She frequently squinted upward through the steamy foliage at the morning sun, using it to guide her approximately westward.

She had no idea how far the gulf coast was, or how long it would take her to get there. She only knew that, before the onslaught of his fever, Josh had said she should go west to the coast and then north to New Orleans. Surely, along the shore she could signal a ship to stop for her! Sometimes, in her fear and loss, she wondered if she could have dreamed the whole thing from the moment the pirates took her off

Justin's ship. Perhaps she would wake up at home and this entire terror would dissolve to half-remembered nightmare.

But she knew better. She would never forget Joshua Blair, her Silver Swords. His face, his voice, his touch—his love, if it had been that. Surely, he had been telling the truth to her if not to those pirates! He could not just have deserted her. Something terrible had happened to him.

When the sun stood straight overhead, she stopped by a little stream to eat and wash. Fear of the encroaching forest, of eyes she felt but could not see urged her to keep moving. Still holding the heavy, curved cutlass, she plunged westward, now chasing the sun. In midafternoon, she saw a narrow but definite path hacked and beaten through the heavy growth.

She halted. She looked both ways on the path and all around. She listened. Nothing but bird sounds and rising breeze rattling leaves and limbs. The path would save her time; it might even lead to some sort of pioneer settlement or the coast. She decided to take it west. But to her surprise it soon led to a clearing with a narrow, low hut topped with a palmetto-leaf roof.

She jumped off the path and hid in a thicket, but there were no sounds, no signs of life. Did the Seminoles have houses like that? Or could a white man have built it? And why was it so low and narrow? How she wished for the hundredth time that Josh was at her side! Then the scent of burning wood reached her nostrils. A camp fire? She moved closer, through the brush around the clearing, and saw twin fires smoldering from holes in the ground at each end of the hut. Her foot cracked a huge dry frond, yet nothing stirred. She tapped her cutlass against the trunk of a cabbage palm to see if that drew anyone. Nothing.

Holding her blade before her, she edged into the deserted clearing and shuffled stealthily around the corner of the hut. She jerked back, stared and gasped. Under the sheltering roof, on the base of logs, his rifle at his side, lay an Indian warrior!

She froze. He could have almost been asleep, but she realized he was dead. Relief flooded her, then fear crashed back. Dead and painted and all laid out with his face to the east. Surely he had died quite recently, for despite the heat there was no odor of death.

She stared aghast at the corpse, so awesome yet grotesque. One lean bronze cheek, his neck, throat and wrists were painted flaming red. He wore a tunic with a bright, multicolored sash and close-fitting deerskin leggings with thongs along the sides. Many bright handkerchiefs were knotted around his neck. His head was wrapped in an almost Oriental calico turban with white egret plumes. The face looked so still, so stern even in death. The two sunken fires wafted pine and bay smoke in the air like incense over the bizarre scene.

Lanie breathed again. She longed for the rifle, but she would never have disturbed him. Slowly, she backed away. When she saw a path leading out the other side of the burial site, she ran along it for a distance, then halted, panting.

Everything pushed in to panic her again: Gasparilla's perverted plans for her, Jasmine's fate, Josh's loss, how far she was from home. How afraid. Tears skimmed her cheeks. But then she heard a voice on the breeze. Hair prickled on the back of her neck. She heard other sounds. The sounds were hardly coming from the burial site, though they seemed sad and mournful. She sniffed hard, swiping at her face with her hand. Perhaps she was going mad in this heat, and her mind was playing tricks. It sounded like a Negro spiritual the slaves sang at home!

She followed the sound down the path. Another clearing, this one with a few sparse vines of pumpkin and squash twined around tall corn stalks, baking in the sun. And bent over a shell hoe with a little girl pulling weeds at her side was a black-skinned woman!

Lanie stared, open-mouthed. The woman sang a spiritual about crossing the River Jordan; Lanie knew the tune well. She spoke English! Indian child or not, there must be a white settlement nearby, and this woman was a slave tending this meager garden! But Josh had said the Seminoles harbored escaped slaves, too. This woman might have heard something about Josh.

Her heart thudding in her breast, Lanie decided to risk showing herself. The child, about four years old, spun and saw her the minute she stepped from the shadows. The child cried out and dropped to her knees with her head bowed, much as the man and boy on the Mayakka had done that foggy morning they had seen her. The woman turned and stared with eyes white in her coffee-hued face.

"Lawsy, so you the daughter of the sun old Allapa-taw been ravin' 'bout," the woman blurted in a low-pitched drawl. She was tall and big-boned with curly hair cropped close to her head and cheeks like the curve of a cutlass. She looked about thirty years old. Huge, bayou-dark eyes and a prominent mouth and nose crowded her face. She, too, wore bright colors, like the clothes Lanie had seen on the corpse; her bright skirt and long-sleeved, loose blouse looked like rows of ribbons.

"Get up, Wood-ko," the woman ordered, and nudged the girl's bottom with her bare foot. "This here just a yaller-haired white woman, and ain't no goddess like your grandpa said."

"I am so glad you speak English. You are working for the Seminoles, then?" Lanie asked tentatively while she tried to sort out what the woman said.

"Don't work for no one no how but my fambly and tribe since I been free down here," the woman declared. "This here *my* patch and this *my* child, and I won't have her grovelin' 'fore no white woman thinkin' she some heavenly daughter of the sun!"

"Of course not. I didn't realize—what exactly is that?" Lanie stammered, with a careful step forward. "I never meant to mislead anyone."

"My man's pa, the old medicine man Allapa-taw, he come back to the village and get everyone all riled over a sign from *In-li-Ke-ta*, that the Seminole word for heaven, see? He say he saw one a the heavenly race of Indians what live in the swamps and lakes in perfect happiness by the river, all bare-skinned and white-haired. 'Course he say she go poof into thin air when a human walk up. So the *micco* chief, as his last order 'fore he died, he send out a party of warriors to see. But they only brung a man back. He your man?''

Lanie ran toward the woman where she had held her ground behind the hoe. "Yes! Yes! They brought back a white man? He's all right? Please, tell me where he is!"

"Whoa, now!" the woman challenged and lifted her hoe while the child cowered behind her skirts. "Hold on there, and put that big knife down! Lawsy, you got this chile all riled again," the woman scolded.

That stopped Lanie despite her joy. Sheepishly, she lowered the cutlass she had not even realized she still held. No black person except for Jasmine had ever given her an order or scolded her, either.

Lanie grabbed control of her hovering hysteria. She had to be careful. Just because this woman spoke English, it did not mean she wouldn't be hostile, not to mention what her Indian tribe on the warpath would do.

"I declare, I did not mean to frighten her—your Wood-ko," Lanie apologized. "It is only that the man's been ill, and I did not know what happened to him. I—I thought I might have lost him."

Despite her stern look, the woman's eyes softened at that, and she put her hoe down to lean on. "I know all 'bout bein' all alone and wild and runnin' from something, like I bet you is. And you think your man's gonna be there to take care of it all and then he just gone. Gone 'cause someone want him dead or worse," she said, her voice bitter as she spit on the ground. The woman's high brow crumpled over her black eyes as she obviously recalled some tragedy of her own.

"Yes, that's the way I feel," Lanie admitted. "Please, if you could find it in your heart to help me, to take me to my man, I would be so grateful. I'm sorry if you lost your man when you had to run. I can really understand—"

"Lawsy, can you now?" The woman's strident voice cut in. "You talk fine and mighty like you at least the overseer's woman if not the masser's, too. And I not only talking 'bout myself losin' her man, not by a long shot. I brung Wood-ko out here 'way from the village 'cause I been livin'

on a certain Georgia cotton plantation all those years be-
longin' to a masser ain't got no heart. And after that, Zeena
got no stomach no how for their torturing and all that!''

"You don't mean they're torturing him!" Lanie cried and
seized the woman's wrist. "Please, tell me where he is? Not
Josh!''

At his name, the woman's slitted eyes widened in surprise. "That his name, your man?" she asked, astounded.
"Joshua, that the name o' my man, and the masser gonna
sell him 'way. We run and Joshua, he got kilt defendin' me,
but he say to go on south to Florida no matter what. My
Joshua shoulda been my little one's daddy, not a Seminole
warrior, no matter how brave he is. Joshua," she said
proudly, her chin held high, "he named for Moses' great
soldier in the Bible."

"Please help me then! Since you know the Bible, you
know it says to help others. Please, for your Joshua as much
as mine!''

The woman's eyes glittered as they met Lanie's desperate, demanding stare. Suddenly, guilt washed over Lanie to
be quoting the Bible to a black woman. After all, what sort
of love and compassion had her Louisiana churchgoing
friends extended to the slaves in their care?

"No white woman ever really *asked* Zeena for nothing
before," Zeena declared. "If'n you still want to play their
daughter of the sun, you might be able to make them back
off your man, but the tribe set great store in not tellin' lies.
Still, don't know no other way, as they just gonna make you
a slave or worse, I 'spose. Lawsy, Zeena don't wish that on
no one but heartless white folk, and I think you got a
heart."

"Please, then, Zeena," Lanie begged, trying to keep her
panic for Josh in check. "Please show me where to find
him. All Josh and I want is to be free, to go unharmed to the
coast and leave the Seminoles at peace! Tell me what to do!''

The woman named Zeena moved with slow, easy grace as
she dropped her hoe and gestured to Lanie to follow. Taking Wood-ko's hand, Zeena led Lanie to a spot, where they
hid the cutlass. Then they walked directly toward the Sem-

inole village, hidden from all sides by a crush of tropic wilderness.

Lanie spotted Josh the moment Zeena pointed out the village to her from the thick fringe of foliage. He was stretched on a rack of tree limbs almost as if he were dancing in their midst with arms and legs outspread. He still wore his tattered trousers, but his boots were gone. She almost ran to him at once, but Zeena's quick hand grabbed her.

"You crazy? And I swear, you ever hint Zeena give you this help, I tell Sho-caw all 'bout you myself," she hissed.

"Sho-caw?" Lanie whispered. "Is that your man?"

Zeena shook her head, and the bright glass beads around her neck rattled. "Sho-caw the new *micco* chief, now the old one dead. But Sho-caw, he want war right now when the other *micco* say try to live in peace. Sho-caw, he think old Allapa-taw crazy for his story 'bout you bein' a sign from heaven for peace. And you can't wear that white woman dress out there. Old Allapa-taw and Sho-caw's son what saw you out on the Mayakka say you stark naked with hair like the sun."

"But I cannot walk out there that way!"

"I'd a done more'n that for my Joshua!" Zeena said with a flash of eyes and a toss of the head. She walked to the edge of the clearing, pulling Wood-ko behind her. She turned toward Lanie, who was still hidden in the brush. "Can't help you no more no way without takin' a risk 'gainst the ones what took me in and never treat me like no slave. Zeena Seminole now, too. And don't be fool enough to try talkin' no English to them if you a daughter of the sun," she added with sleek eyebrows raised and a knife edge to her voice.

Lanie stood stunned as Zeena sauntered toward the village and sat on the floor of one of the open-sided, palm-thatched huts, talking earnestly to Wood-ko. Lanie scanned the scene; it reminded her of the pirate village of Boca Grande. About twenty small, open-sided houses and two larger enclosed buildings surrounded the open dirt square where Josh was tied. Most of the men were apparently assembling there. Communal cook fires in one house curled smoke into the sky where women gathered with their children.

But everything merged and blurred as she stared at Josh tied to that web of branches like something trapped in a spiderweb waiting to be devoured. The Indian men had a small fire burning near him, but surely it would not reach him. And then she heard the distant thud of drums begin.

Terrified, wanting only to run, she lifted her gown over her head with trembling hands. She removed her shoes and scuffed her clothing under a pile of dead leaves. She was naked, weaponless, defenseless, her earlier life jumped through her mind in jumbled scenes. She only knew, despite the danger, that she could not desert Josh. If she could not save him, at least she would be with him. But the way those Indians had bowed to her—perhaps, somehow, she could bring this off. At the last minute, she grabbed two dried palm fronds from the ground and held one before and one behind her. She stepped out and forced her feet toward the open square of the village.

The women and children saw her first. They stopped their chatter. Some pointed, a few bowed. She nodded without meeting their eyes and walked straight by. This was insanity; this was nightmare. She wanted to collapse and scream out her fear, but she marched on with shaking legs.

She thought that one old man, who was seated on the ground by a large hut, might be the one she had seen at the river. He spotted her and bowed. Tears filled his eyes and spilled down his wrinkled, leathery face. He managed to get to his feet and grab a bright patchwork, ribboned cloth from the high shelf of his house and run after her offering it. But Lanie did not look back.

The drums halted abruptly. The warriors saw her, as did Josh. His face showed shock mingled with joy and alarm. The tallest of these tall Seminoles, who had just joined the men, stepped toward her and said something harsh in their tongue to the old man, who was still at her side. They actually argued in terse but strangely melodic syllables while Lanie held her ground, staring at the tall man, who seemed to be in charge. Perhaps this was the one Zeena called their *micco* Sho-caw. When she realized Josh had not been harmed yet, she studied the man.

The discussion stopped abruptly. The old man spoke in his wavering, chanting voice to the assembled tribe. Was this Allapa-taw? Zeena had said he was her father-in-law and a medicine man. Still chanting, he offered her the patterned cloth again. She took it and wrapped it tightly around her body in a way that left both arms free. She cast the two dried palm fronds she carried in the fire, and saw that it had long splinters of wood laid all around it like wheel spokes. Boldly, she scuffed them into the flames, then turned to face the tall man again.

The idea came to her full-blown from the things Zeena had said. "Sho-caw *micco!*" she declared and pointed at their tall, stern leader.

Out of the corner of her eye, she saw several braves bow to her—or was it to Sho-caw? The women had followed her in a clump, and many of them were shaking rattles and chanting. Josh just stared. The old man, Allapa-taw, nodded and beamed at the evidence that his old mouth had spoken the truth of what he had seen on the Mayakka River. But the most startled one of all was Sho-caw.

He stood at least as tall as Josh, with sleek copper skin and jet-black eyes. He was graceful as a panther, lean-limbed yet muscular, with square shoulders tapering to a narrow belly and hips before the bulge of powerful thighs began, encased in thonged deerskin leggings. His hair was cut close under a wrapped turban such as she had seen on the dead chief, but he wore no plumes. His nose was straight and narrow, his lips taut with a cruel twist to the mouth under rock-hewn brows. He would have been a handsome man but for the hawklike glare that pinched his features. In the belt over his brightly colored shirt he carried a knife, a revolver and a pouch.

At last he nodded toward Lanie, and announced something to the villagers in a clear voice. In the flow of words she only picked out *micco* several times. Holding her wrap, she stepped bravely up to Josh and pulled at his rope bindings, as if she were angry. When Sho-caw's words stopped in surprise at her reckless daring, she turned to face him again. Her green eyes wavered at first under his flinty gaze, but she did not flinch.

He gave an order to his braves. Josh's hands and feet were freed. Lanie was escorted and Josh was walked on unsteady legs across the open square into one of the two closed buildings in the village. Sho-caw stepped in behind them and closed the bright calico flap. He drew his gun and pointed it directly at Josh, then indicated they should sit.

Lanie and Josh seated themselves on a mat. Sho-caw sat cross-legged near the door across from them and lowered his pistol barrel slightly. Silence followed. The chieftain stared at the matted floor, not at them. Josh seized Lanie's elbow as if to warn her not to speak. Finally, after what appeared to be a calming or respectful silence, which Sho-caw evidently thought was necessary, he began.

"Seminoles were men before the white men came," he said, slowly, almost quietly in choppy English.

"I regret all that has happened between our peoples," Josh told him as they stared eye to eye. Lanie could see Josh was still shaken, but his voice was calmly commanding. "All this woman and I want is to be left in peace and allowed to leave this land and your tribe alone."

"*Your* people do not leave us in peace. Not slave owners. Not your devil warriors." Sho-caw spat the words out bitterly and gestured with his hand. "And the *micco* Sho-caw does not think a daughter of the sun from *In-li-Ke-ta* walks the earth. Even if an old man for peace says so. The last *micco* spoke for peace. He is gone now," he added with an edge of triumph in his voice.

"I have heard your people trade for weapons and that some of you speak good English," Josh observed, refusing to rise to Sho-caw's taunts.

"*Halwuk,*" Sho-caw grunted. "Those of us who talk with white man's tongue do not think with his head. My people know the white man lies and steals."

"But I tell you the truth now. I know someone who will pay for our release if you will be bold enough to send a messenger," Josh said. Lanie whirled to face him. He had told her the Seminoles traded with pirates, but even the Indians could treat her no worse than Gasparilla would! Josh could not mean it!

"I make my own deals," the chief declared with a downward slash of hand. "But now this woman. I make Allapataw say she not a daughter of the sun. He say now she only sent by them for a sign we must go to war. She your woman?"

Sho-caw's sharp hawk eyes swept her, then examined her face as if he could read her mind. Lanie's belly muscles clenched with fear, but she returned his probing stare without a blink.

"Yes, my woman," Josh told the wily Seminole.

"Means your wife?"

"No," Josh faltered, his voice suddenly on edge. "This is one white man who will not lie to you."

Sho-caw rose swiftly to his feet as if the interview were over, so they jumped to their feet. "Like your woman was honest with Sho-caw's tribe?" the chief challenged, and his eyes slid over Lanie again.

"I claimed nothing of being a daughter of the sun, *micco* Sho-caw," Lanie said despite Josh's warning pinch through her skirt. Her voice wavered, but she went on, "But if I were, I would speak for American peace with the Seminoles."

"Halwuk!" he said again, and she wondered if he spoke a curse. "Peace is the biggest lie. You," he told Josh, pointing the pistol again. "I name you Ich-chaw. This woman, Ha-shay. You prisoners here but if you obey, you will move about the village. And keep clothes on your woman until you spread her under you in the marriage hut." He glared at Lanie again. "You will be wed tonight!"

Josh and Lanie sucked in quick breaths in unison. Her eyes big as dinner plates, met Josh's as the *micco* chief left the hut with no other words.

"Josh, I never expected—" she began.

"Thank God you came," he said in the same instant as he pulled her hard into his embrace. "They were preparing burning splinters to test my manhood before they killed me.

Revenge or good luck, I don't know. And I'd sure as hell rather test my manhood in some marriage hut with my daughter of the sun.''

His feeble jest did not lighten her heart. She trembled as they clung to each other, and tears of relief rolled down her cheeks. But at what Sho-caw had commanded, her legs dissolved to jelly, and she could barely stand. A Seminole Indian wedding ceremony and a forced one. And Josh—what did he really think?

They jumped hastily apart as an attractive young Indian woman came through the flap of the hut with the tall Zeena behind her. Lanie's eyes linked with Zeena's but neither gave a sign they had met. "Cho-fee, *ungah*, *micco* Sho-caw." The woman introduced herself with hand motions to indicate she was Sho-caw's wife and meant to feed them. "Zeena," she said and pointed to Lanie's secret friend with a string of other words. "Zeena English," Cho-fee told them shyly to announce Zeena would be their interpreter. Gratefully, Lanie sank onto the floor mat. When Cho-fee went to summon others to bring food, Zeena's quick wink buoyed her flagging spirits.

That evening, with only Zeena at her side, Lanie awaited her bridegroom in the marriage *chickee*, the building Sho-caw had brought them to. She and Josh had been separated just after they had eaten, with no talking allowed. Zeena had brought her water to wash and new clothing. She had explained the traditions of marriage could not all be followed that day, while the tribe was in mourning, so Sho-caw had arranged a hasty version. Zeena had the answers to all Lanie's questions except why Sho-caw had insisted his two captives be immediately wed.

"Still, this sure a sight better than just jumpin' over the broom back in Georgia," Zeena observed as she tried to secure the bounty of Lanie's hair in the traditional Seminole female style of a single knot on the top of the head. Lanie was clothed in Seminole dress—a brightly hued, floor-length skirt and a loose, long-sleeved blouse that gapped a good two inches from the skirt waist. She had also been given two strands of bright red glass beads, which did not compare to the massive piles of strands the women flaunted.

"These your marriage beads," Zeena explained. "Beads 'bout the most important thing to the women here. Other strings of beads tell how many little ones a woman birthed—two strands for each child. They wears other ones for fine deeds or skills. Now, Cho-fee, shy as she is even with that fierce man she got for a husband, she got herself forty-two strands. Lawsy, they almost weigh her down. When women get up in years, they takes a few strands off and pass them on down to daughters and others, like I will to Wood-ko. Finally, the women here buried just with one strand called the life beads, see. I gotta find you some life beads tomorrow fo' sure, or the way these people think, you good as dead."

Zeena also explained the Seminole marriage customs and ceremony. Ordinarily a brave courted a young girl until he was sure she favored him. He then killed a deer and left it at the *chickee* door of the girl's family. If she accepted the proposal, she made him stew and a shirt from the deer. Weddings were simply a ceremony where the tribe followed the man while he moved his earthly goods into his bride's family *chickee* and then went to the marriage hut, where the girl waited, for at least one night of privacy.

"I hear tell Sho-caw gonna leave guards outside all night," Zeena went on. "And 'stead of tribal dancing the next night, there gonna be none of that till next week, since the tribe in mourning for the dead *micco*."

Lanie heaved a huge sigh. Her limbs felt heavy, but her head was light. This was not what she had expected her wedding ceremony or wedding night to be—nor with whom. She and Justin were to have been wed in the great Saint Louis Cathedral in Jackson Square, and would have ridden back to Magnolia Hill in a rose-swagged carriage for a huge reception. The pillars and galleries of the mansion would have been garlanded with roses and camellias. The slaves would have all been given gifts and had their own celebration afterward with horns, drums and one-stringed fiddles. There would have been pink satin tables groaning under

Creole food and Paris champagne. There would have been
a huge reception line and dancing in the ballroom that
stretched the entire top floor of the house. Her *Beignet*
would have stood with her preparing her hair—and would
have been given her freedom the day her mistress surren-
dered her freedom to marry Justin Lyon. But suddenly,
Lanie knew none of that would ever be enough again. Jasmine should never have been a slave, nor the others! Justin
should never have been her fiancé!

Justin—her memories of his face seemed blurred. Instead, Josh's beloved, rugged face intruded—and then the
hard-eyed, devouring stare of the frightening Indian chief
Sho-caw! Quickly, she shook her head to clear it.

Lanie thanked Zeena for everything she had done for her
and grasped her hand. The woman seemed moved, though
she awkwardly tugged her hand back. Then Zeena tied the
calico tent flap up, to indicate they were ready. Sho-caw's
wife, Cho-fee, entered and then came a Seminole woman
with ashes smeared on her face and her hair wildly dishev-
eled. Her garments were torn and she was beadless but for
her single strand of life beads. Lanie's stomach turned over
at the sight of the haunted face.

"Who's that?" she mouthed to Zeena.

"The dead *micco*'s widow," Zeena said, making no attempt to whisper. "This here a place where the woman's
fambly more important than the man's. She the same clan
as Sho-caw and she here to show she agree he the new *micco*.
A widow always look like that for a whole year."

Lanie shuddered as the rhythmic beat of turtle-shell rattles began outside. When she was escorted to the door, she
was surprised to see that the village had assembled just outside. Copper bodies decked in rainbow hues parted like a sea
as Sho-caw approached with Josh behind him.

In height—almost in the brownness of their skin and
darkness of their hair—the two men could have been
brothers. And they had dressed Josh in close-fitting, gray-
brown deerskin leggings with side thongs and a rainbow
shirt. The outfit was much like Sho-caw's but for the sash
and turban. But Josh's face looked open, familiar, com-

forting. Show-caw's was closed and harsh and frightening. He marched Josh to the door of the *chickee* and took Josh's wrist to thrust his hand into hers while the tribe chanted Seminole words to the beat of the rattles.

"Now Ha-shay, means the sun, this your man," Sho-caw said to Lanie in quiet English only she and Josh could hear. His eyes searched Lanie's face, then dropped to the meager array of red glass beads draping her breast. Quick as lightning, he turned to Josh. "Ich-chaw, means the gun, guard her well from all harm and other men."

He turned and departed as he had come. Lanie stared after him while the villagers streamed toward the central square. Cho-fee and the frightening vision of the dead *micco* widow indicated they should go inside. Then they took their leave in Sho-caw's wake. Zeena untied the calico door curtain. She turned at the entrance with her hand on the flap to stare at Lanie and Josh, still holding hands, looking stunned by the swiftness and finality of it all.

"Lawsy, don't you two go do nothin' crazy now like 'temptin' to escape. Sho-caw out for blood since the massacre at Ope-hatchee. For some reason, you real lucky so far. I hope the Lord Jesus, he bless your marriage, Seminole or not," she added. The starkly colored flap trembled in the breeze as she stepped out and let it go.

After they ate the venison stew and bananas someone had left, they held to each other speechlessly for a long while. Then Josh cuddled Lanie in his lap while he sat on the floor with his back against a pole. This moment was so special, so precious. Yet, despite the comfort of his embrace, she had to know why he had almost suggested to Sho-caw he trade them to the pirates for guns.

"Josh, as frightening as this has been, I think we're better off here than to be traded to Gasparilla," she began, her voice wary. "Why ever did you suggest that to Sho-caw?"

"Gasparilla? I never said—" he started before he realized what she meant. "No, not to Gasparilla," he told her with a gentle shake. "I was going to suggest he trade us to a United States Navy ship, but he refused to listen. Besides, he hates and distrusts any sort of American troops."

"But what if the navy found out somehow you'd been living as a pirate? And why would the navy think we're important enough to trade for guns with the Seminoles? You told me these Indians are ready to go to war with the army and navy again."

"They are," he answered and pulled her into his close embrace so he wouldn't have to meet her earnest, trusting gaze. "It was just a desperate gamble. I'll have to think of something else." He still dared not tell her why the navy would gladly pay guns for him. The Indians might still question her in their overly persuasive way, and if they found out he was in the navy, they would kill them both. It was probably best he had not mentioned the navy to Sho-caw. He shuddered at the thought of Seminole torture again, especially for Lanie. Still, he intended to do everything he could to get them out of here in one piece.

"I won't hold you to this pagan marriage after we get back to New Orleans," she murmured against his chest. "It hardly means anything."

His arms tightened around her. "It means we can be together, and no Seminole's going to take you for his wife until we can get away from here and go to New Orleans."

She had another startling thought and sat upright. She stared into his deep brown, shadowy eyes. "They don't take more than one wife here, do they?"

"Do you have someone else in mind already? No, even with the way Sho-caw looks at you, I heard they don't. And I remember someone telling me they mutilate anyone who's unfaithful after marriage."

"Ugh!" She shuddered and put her head on his shoulder. This entire day had exhausted her, disturbed her deeply. Josh, her Ich-chaw, was right about Sho-caw looking at her. But the *micco*'s pointed stares were more akin to hatred than lust. And Lanie could not shake the vision of that wretched widow with her hair and face all smeared because her husband lay under the heavens in that strange burial she had stumbled on. Zeena's words haunted her: "I gotta find you some life beads tomorrow fo' sure, or the way these people think, you good as dead." These people hated the whites, wanted to torture and kill them as surely as the whites wanted to kill the Seminoles.

And yet, Lanie realized, the Seminoles sheltered and even married a runaway slave like Zeena. The whites she had known would have whipped and branded her. Perhaps that made the Seminoles less savage than the southern slave owners. Zeena's blessing on their marriage had touched her deeply, and the woman's tragedy of losing her man and her home had moved Lanie to her very soul. It had never occurred to Lanie to consider a black person's feelings before. Even Jasmine's—if she was honest with herself. She vowed that when she got home she would change that. It was yet another reason to get home safely!

"Josh," Lanie whispered in the growing dark, suddenly desperate for his strong touch, which made the complicated world so simple, "aren't you going to love your new bride?"

"I thought you'd never ask." His voice rasped so close it moved the tendrils of hair along her temple.

"When have I ever had to ask?"

"Things are different now. We're not on our own, and they say the Seminoles pass the power through the woman," he replied with a hint of a smile in his voice. She could not see it, but it still shimmered to her ears and heart through the darkness.

But Josh admitted to himself that he felt torn, even as he kissed Lanie. While he knew this Indian marriage would not be binding once they got back to the white man's civilization, a part of him wished it would. Yet his vows concerning Becky on the day of their marriage and on the day of her death still gripped him with a fierce hand. He almost hated himself for wanting Lanie just as fiercely.

They shared love still partly dressed, as if their Seminole garments could protect them from the hostile trap they were caught in. But the possessive hands, the desperate, almost feverish kisses knew no barriers between them. Instead of mounting her as he had always done, Josh pulled her upright into his lap again, but with her legs wrapped around his waist. He moved her, lifted her, until she saw what he intended. And then, in that mutual, wild, wonderful ride, everything else receded.

Nothing mattered but this man, her love for him. She hoped he felt the same. But then he spilled his seed again upon the ground rather than in her, and she felt not so much loved and protected as somehow strangely betrayed. She shuddered not just with the aftermath of passion, but with the fear that his lost wife, Rebecca, somehow still lay between them.

Chapter Nine

Their first week in the Seminole village passed quickly but disturbingly. Josh was taken out daily to hunt or scout with the men, as it was obvious he would not try to escape when Lanie was held under close surveillance by the village women every day. They kept her busy at various tasks— hoeing, sewing, watching children, carrying water, stirring cook pots. Only at night were she and Josh allowed to be together, and then it was with others always close around. And she wanted so badly to talk to him privately, to ask him the questions that had gone unasked in the marriage hut.

After the first night, they slept in the crowded, open-sided *chickee* of the wolf clan family. With Cho-fee, her old mother, *micco* Sho-caw, their ten-year-old son, Loko-see and two of Cho-fee's younger brothers who acted as Josh's guards nearby, there was no chance for a whispered conference about a possible escape. Even after the others slept they could not talk, for the women's mats were all toward the front and the men's toward the back.

Zeena's family lived in the next *chickee*, but unless some specific order for Lanie was to be translated, she saw too little of Zeena and never alone. If she and Josh tried to confer when they ate the evening meal, Zeena or even the shy Cho-fee would order tersely, "Seminole! No English!" It was obvious Sho-caw had ordered that their wedding night was the only time they would have alone.

Sho-caw, with his ruthless personality, dominated everyone in the tribe, especially his sweet-faced, stoic little wife.

One glance from Sho-caw and Cho-fee skittered to obey. Unless she was carrying out one of his orders, she was as jumpy and quiet as the rabbit she had been named for. Lanie began to wonder what good it did the Seminole women to have tribal power pass through their lineage if they had to obey a man's every whim.

Sho-caw kept strictly away from Lanie, but sometimes she felt his hawklike eyes study her. However much her daily work exhausted her, she found it nearly impossible to get a sound night's sleep in the *chickee* with Sho-caw, despite the fact that three others slept between her and the *micco*. Perhaps he hated her because she had dared to impersonate one of their sacred daughters of the sun.

But old Allapa-taw, Zeena's father-in-law, seemed kind enough to her. One day he showed her his herbal stores of bay, willow, cedar leaf, snakeroot and many other strange things he motioned her to touch for him as if he thought she could bestow a blessing. But he spoke no English, and she dare not do more than smile, nod over his treasures and hurry back to work.

Early on the eighth day, Zeena explained to Lanie that Sho-caw had decreed the day would be the hunt festival the tribe had delayed for the week of formal mourning for the dead *micco*. "Lawsy, you gonna see a real Seminole goings-on now," Zeena told her with a look over her shoulder, as if she were not allowed to be speaking long with her. "Hunting all morning—everybody helps. Lotta food and dancin' after the *muskogee* game. Wait till you see that wild mess!"

"Zeena," Lanie asked hurriedly, "have you heard anything about what is going to happen to Josh and me? Will we ever be allowed to leave?"

But Zeena's message was delivered. She pressed her lips together and looked over her shoulder again before she strode off to her *chickee*.

Despite Lanie's growing sense of unease, Lanie and Josh were caught up in the preparations for the hunt festival. From sunrise until noon all were busy, for everyone who wanted to be part of the *muskogee* game, dancing, or eating had to bring some item for the celebration. While the men hunted game, the women gathered berries, fruit and vegetables for the feast. The children squealed with delight as they scoured the area for mushrooms, firewood and wildflowers.

When the sun stood overhead, the men returned with deer and a black bear strung feet up on poles the men carried on their shoulders. Lanie picked Josh out instantly, and saw that his eyes, too, had skimmed the crowd for her. They nodded grimly across the cluster of people. She was starting to meet him when she saw Sho-caw's hard stare just a few yards away.

"Back with the women. Now!" he said in the first English she had heard from anyone but Josh's quick whispers and Zeena's commands since the first day in the village. Their stares held for a moment. She considered disobeying him, but then spun on her bare heels and went to stir the corn soup.

The pace of preparations accelerated as the women fixed the meal and the men got ready for the *muskogee* game. Cooking with Cho-fee, Lanie watched as the men trooped off for a ritual bath at the stream and the ceremonial drinking of something called *asi*. As always, Josh had to go with them, with Cho-fee's brothers at his side.

Soon the men were back. Each wore a breechclout with a wide, colored waistband to hold it in place and some sort of long, ceremonial animal tail in back. Leggings, shirts and turbans had disappeared. Powerful copper chests and muscular legs gleamed as some of the men began to daub each other from the waist up with white paint. Josh was the only one with any hair on his chest and legs. His body, like Sho-caw's, was left unpainted; the unpainted men would form one team. Lanie noticed Sho-caw still wore his *micco* sash over his naked chest, and that Josh was the only one without one of the tails the others sported. The men were proud as screeching, preening peacocks. The teams brought out their playing sticks, which had small thong nets on the end. Men pounded a supple sapling pole at each end of the open square to serve as goals while the ground was scuffed and cleared.

Shouting apparent insults, the two teams lined up in rows facing each other while all the women and children stopped preparations for the feast to watch. To Lanie's amazement, the men took turns scratching each other in a single decorative swoop from the back of the neck to the heels with an alligator jaw that drew ribbons of blood. When it came to Josh's turn, she bit her lip and turned away, but she knew better than to protest. Behind her, Zeena's voice whispered, "It just like going to a white man doctor. 'Stead o' leeches, that gator jaw get all the bad blood out." And then, in midafternoon, the melee began.

The women and children lined the square while old Allapa-taw ventured out between the two waiting rows of players and tossed a small leather ball high in the air and scrambled away. A violent, ten-minute struggle ensued before anyone was able to get the ball in play. Finally—with grunts, shouts, hits and kicks—the ball was on its way toward one set of poles or the other.

Lanie soon discovered the few rules of the rough-and-tumble game. Men couldn't touch the ball but had to catch it, carry it, fling it with their little nets on sticks.

She pressed in among the cheering crowd, urging Josh on. Considering he had never played the game before, he kept up well. Soon all the men glistened with sweat, except old Allapa-taw, who kept score along the sidelines by placing ten pegs, one per goal, in holes and then removing them until the game reached twenty. And then it began all over again—this time with any women who wanted to join the fray.

Lanie gasped in amazement as Zeena dived in to demand one of her husband's netted sticks, though most women played with the cup of a bare hand. The older boys joined in, too; Sho-caw's ten year old threw himself into a pile of writhing bodies. Even gentle Cho-fee darted in, but she soon left when the game became too rough. One woman's leg was broken, and she was carted off. It was obvious everyone on the square risked life and limb in the "wild mess" as Zeena had called it.

Then, for the first time in more than a week, Lanie realized no eyes were watching her. Maybe in this chaos she could get near Josh, find time to talk to him when everyone was so engrossed. She paced the sidelines looking for a path across the crowded, noisy square. Sho-caw was down the way, struggling for the ball in a pile of arms and legs, and Josh stood back, hands on knees, bent over, gasping for breath. How she wished they could flee to the coast together and leave all this behind!

She edged out along the fringe of the playing area and darted across the field, dodging several players waiting for passes of the ball. Down the way the ball exploded loose again. Shrieks and squeals rent the air as the crowd started her way, then sagged back. She cupped her hands and called "Ich-Chaw!" to get Josh's attention without screaming his name in English. He turned as if to search for her, then went under in the flowing copper wave chasing the ball.

She turned to skirt the chaos when a wall of bodies surged around her. They screamed; she screamed. She twisted around, went to her knees in the crush of people, then was instantly hauled up by hard hands.

"Josh—" she began at the familiar, strong touch. But she found herself picked up like a sack of cane in *micco* Sho-caw's sweaty, iron arms. "Oh!" she cried. "No, put me down!"

"*Halwuk!*" he cursed, and sprinted off the jumbled field with her clasped hard to him.

To her dismay, he charged past the sidelines and shouldered open the flap of the walled *chickee* where she and Josh had been taken that first day, the building she now knew was used for a council house or private meetings as well as a wedding night *chickee*. She shoved at his slick chest and pounded his shoulders.

He leaned down and dumped her on the matted floor. The back of her head thumped hard. He hunkered down beside her to glare into her terrified face. His big hand shot out to grasp her throat, but not enough to choke her. She felt dizzy. She froze on her back as if his eyes stabbed her to the floor.

"A woman who needs breaking but is hard to break," he said in his choppy English. "Like a whole handful of twigs together instead of just one! Bold spirit shines from your eyes. I could break you, Ha-shay, twig by twig. But I saw you in the sacred burial ground of the dead *micco*. You wanted his gun but did not take it. I spare you and your man for that. Not for the trade I will make for you. Not for the old man's hope you were a daughter of the sun. Not for the gold watch with the woman's face Ich-chaw gave me. Still, next time, perhaps I will not keep my hands only on your neck."

He rose to his full height to tower over her. He stared at her, sprawled trembling and speechless at his feet. "Stay out of the *muskogee* game where I have the right to touch you. Too bad you and your man soon be traded for the guns we need."

She gasped a sharp breath at that news. Had Josh given Sho-caw his precious watch to bribe him? "*Micco* Sho-caw, who will we be traded to?" she asked, but he whirled and went back to the game.

Lanie sat up slowly and rubbed her throat where his powerful hand had gripped her. And his words had gripped her, too: Sho-caw desired her and yet he detested her, too. They were to be traded for guns—but to whom and when? Perhaps Josh knew. He'd had this whole week hunting and scouting with Sho-caw to hear where they were being sent. She had to know!

She smoothed her garments and strolled nonchalantly along the edge of the square. A delay had been declared. Women limped off with their clothing smudged and their topknots of raven hair askew. They soon returned carrying bowls of soup or meat onto the playing field to their men, who'd collapsed where they were. Lanie saw Sho-caw, across the way, already being served by Cho-fee.

Quickly, she filled a bowl with venison and steaming squash and grabbed a hunk of corn bread for Josh. Head held high, she threaded her way through the tribe until she knelt beside the sweating, panting man they all called Ich-chaw. She ignored Josh's usual guards, who were seated just a few yards away. They, unlike Sho-caw, spoke not one word of English.

She sat and handed the food to him. "Josh," she whispered, "I just learned we're to be traded for guns. Did you know? Sho-caw told me."

His eyes widened in obvious surprise. "I had no idea. I had tried to talk to him, but— Sho-caw told you?" He read the fear on her face. "He didn't harm you, did he?"

"Not really, but I am more afraid of him than ever." She said no more about that, afraid Josh would take Sho-caw on if she told him that the *micco* had threatened her.

Josh ate slowly, but his mind raced. He prayed fervently that Sho-caw wasn't trading them to Gasparilla, or they were both as good as dead. He had to find out soon. He had not dared mention the navy, for he knew the Seminoles feared a trap. Besides, he could not risk Sho-caw's guessing he had anything to do with what the bitter *micco* called the "warriors of the white tribe," and whom he hated with such intensity. But Josh had told Sho-caw Lanie's father's name and city, hoping he, or even that damned Justin Lyon, had a ship out looking for her. Sho-caw had not responded, and Josh didn't dare get Lanie's hopes up.

Anyway, Josh thought with a heavy heart, he would have to let her go when they got out of here. There was no place for her in the real world with a man who lived as he had and was still wedded to regret and revenge. Lanie deserved better, so much better! But he couldn't bear to tell her all that, not here, not yet.

"Lanie, it's the best I can do to ask Sho-caw, but he trusts no whites." He stumbled through his explanation. "I'm going crazy, too, not being able to be alone with you. I feel so trapped here—I regret I can't do more quite yet . . ."

She got to her feet when one of his guards muttered something behind them. Damnation, she still could not read his moods! she thought. On Captiva, the man had shown he was an adept actor and liar, so who was real—Silver Swords or Josh Blair? Her captor or her lover? The man who loved her or the man who would always love another woman? She could tell he had distanced himself from her. Yet she could not bear to leave it. "Josh, I just need to know—" she began.

But her words were cut off with the usual grunted, "Seminole! No English!" Lanie and Josh moved guiltily apart. Cho-fee had obviously been sent over by Sho-caw, who glared at them from across the clearing. Silently, the Seminole woman tugged Lanie away by her wrist.

That night Lanie's head reverberated from her tormenting thoughts and the ceaseless pounding beat of the drums. She sat, cross-legged, next to old Allapa-taw, watching what Zeena had described as the animal hunt stomp dance. Zeena was now dancing with a reckless abandon that made her seem wild and free, and Lanie was hit with a pang of longing for Jasmine.

Josh sat across the way between his two guards. He seemed so acquiescent in their separation that Lanie had actually begun to wonder if he was not grateful they were always with him so he would not have to tell her he did not really love her. She could barely see his face in the darting firelight, but she imagined him sitting there, mysterious and austere, the way he had been when she first knew him.

She had been thinking. If she could retrieve her hidden cutlass, and if she told Josh she had it, would he be willing to chance running again? When they had been out on their own, she had believed in escape, in miracles. He had cared for her and loved her then. Besides, if Josh found out they were being sent to Gasparilla, they had no choice but to run, and she'd be ready with a weapon. Then, too, if she had her cutlass hidden within reach, the next time Sho-caw tried to threaten or seize her—

The steady thump, thump, thump of turtle-shell rattles on the women's ankles mingled with the squeal of wooden pipes and the hollow thud of skin-and-pot drums. All the dancers imitated individual animals with their steps and sounds: the croaking of the heron, the cry of the panther, the guttural bark of the alligator she recalled only too well. Sho-caw was impersonating the hawk for which he had been named. When the rhythm quickened, men and women, hands on each other's shoulders, circled around the fire in a stomping, writhing line. The song leader, a brave Lanie did not know, called out a bit of the song, and everyone repeated it in dissonant unison. It was miles and civilizations away from the balls of New Orleans or the melodic tunes she had so often sung at soirees in Magnolia Hill's lovely drawing room. But it was her chance to get the cutlass if she was careful.

She stood slowly and indicated to Allapa-taw she was going to lie down in the *chickee* for her pounding head. He merely nodded, glassy-eyed. She could sense that the old days of glory danced through his head better than this real dance. She only hoped he could not read her thoughts.

She lay on the sleeping mat on the floor of the *chickee*, wrapping her deerskin sleeping robe around her. She had to stay like this for a while in case someone checked. When she got the cutlass, she would also find her leather shoes under the dried leaves, too, for when she and Josh ran again. She prayed she could find them in the dark. At least the roaring central fire, built in a wheel design, threw wan, wavering light to the forest fringe, to help her find her things.

She feigned sleep when Cho-fee padded in and peered at her face. Lanie tried to breathe deeply and regularly until the Seminole woman left again. This was exactly what Lanie had hoped would happen—it would give her time before someone else looked in on her. Slowly, she rolled in her robe toward the open back of the *chickee*. She crept out into the shadowy hem of forest. The drums rolled on and the rattles made her fear a thousand rattlesnakes were ready to strike at her bare feet in the dark. That is what she would be in their strange hunting dance, she thought, a rattlesnake that would bare her fangs at the hawk Sho-caw in his leaping, soaring steps.

In the bushes near where she had put her gown and shoes, she fell on her knees to paw through dried leaves. Yes! A good sign. She left the gown and jammed the shoes on feet that were swollen too big for them from days of going barefoot with the Seminoles. She backed away from the noise and light.

She took a path she knew well now, toward Zeena's little patch of crops. Away from the blaze of fire, she saw the stars were out and a sickle of moon sliced the sky, curved like the cutlass blade its light would help her find. Surely, it was right here just off the path somewhere—just over here—under this bush.

"*Halwuk,*" a voice said. "You won't find your big knife there! I asked Zeena for it days ago. Zeena knows to obey her *micco*."

Lanie spun, her heart beating wilder than the drums. Sho-caw wore his costume of hawk feathers on a short shoulder cape over his bare chest and carried a club of large claws to imitate the hawk's talons. He wore fine deerskin leggings with feathered thongs. Hawk feathers protruded from his turban.

"Sho-caw! I just wanted to see if my big knife was still here. Besides, you said the Seminoles never steal," she dared, "so surely you would not take it."

"Will you lie to Sho-caw you did not mean to flee?" he challenged in return. He stalked her until she pressed against the rough trunk of a palmetto palm. In the shadows there was only darkness where his eyes should be.

"I did not mean to flee, but just see if the cutlass was still there," she insisted, amazed her voice sounded like her own. "Do you deny you are always watching me?" she accused, suddenly angry that he treated her like a slave to be ordered around and imprisoned, just as the pirates had. "But I will go back to the *chickee* now," she added.

"No. You have not learned to tell the truth yet. But tonight, you will."

She tried to scream, but his hands were quick and hard as he quieted and lifted her. She started to struggle, but he held his club of hawk talons so close to her face that she froze. The drums pounded as he strode swiftly with her the way she had come that first day from the burial spot.

No! He could not be taking her there! Josh said some Indians on Captiva sacrificed people. Did he intend that fate for her?

But Sho-caw did not carry her all the way to the burial clearing. He moved off the path into solid blackness. Leaves and fronds whipped at her; she closed her eyes. How foolish she had been to fear Josh's hard arms and quicksilver moods on Captiva. Her fear of Gasparilla's men was nothing next to her sudden surge of terror with this savage. He was going to torture her, to kill her as they'd intended to kill Josh!

"Please, Sho-caw. Please take me back," she managed in a quavering voice when he freed her mouth.

"Never beg," he insisted in taut tones. "Be strong, be proud. That is your heart spirit."

He put her on her feet and tossed his feathered cape under her before he pushed her down. He yanked her shoes from her feet and threw them into the bushes so she faced him entirely in Seminole garb. Silently, he sat beside her. She could hear the murmur of a stream somewhere nearby, and she could hear rattling fronds and the distant tattoo of drums. He was breathing hard. She sat on her haunches as if to jump to her feet, but she knew better than to try.

"I was fasting and guarding the *micco*'s grave. Then I saw you," he explained.

"Oh, you mean the day I first came." Her scattered thoughts settled. Perhaps there was a way to bargain with this dangerous man for her and Josh's safety and freedom. "Then you saw I honor the Seminole ways and did not harm the dead *micco*'s grave," she said. "Ich-chaw feels the same."

"One thing to honor a dead *micco* wanting peace with the whites. You—Ich-chaw, too—do not honor the live *micco*, Sho-caw. I want war. I should have killed you before I knew your power."

"My power? But I—"

He shoved her on her back and hovered over her, close but not touching her. His painted brow was inches from her wide, startled eyes.

"What power?" she demanded more quietly, when he continued to stare. "You do not allow—"

"The power to make me doubt the way things must be," he said. "The power to make me desire to have a woman with bold spirit in my *chickee* instead of gentle Cho-fee. A woman who wants war also!"

"But I cannot blame Cho-fee for desiring peace. I don't want war, either."

"You would if you were my woman! But I hate all whites. Do you think you could become Seminole if I pulled out all your sun-white hair?" he demanded.

She gasped as he lifted the hawk talons toward her face, then combed it through her hair. He tugged and pulled, but she did not flinch.

"Or could I make you Seminole by carving all that cloud-white skin away? By scratching out all your white woman's bad blood?" His voice went on as he ran the talons gently down her throat. She did not move but for the rapid pulse beat there. "No, nothing makes you Seminole," he went on. "Still, I desire a white woman for her strength and fury when I should be hating, be killing her."

He heaved the hawk's claw into the nearby foliage and sat up with his fists clasped around his bent knees. Her heart pounding, she sat up slowly and covered her legs with her skirt. He said nothing for a moment and stared off into the dark, moving night. The earth seemed alive with its own fears as a stiff breeze sprang up to brush the leaves faster and faster.

"May I go back now?" she asked quietly. "I will not try to run away."

He gave a snort and reached a quick, hard hand for her wrist. "Seminoles let young braves and girls enjoy each other's bodies. But never after they marry. Then it means mutilation. No one with wisdom shares a sleeping mat with another man's woman. So I made you marry quick. *Hal-wuk*," he said, his tone bitter, "and you a white woman! The squaws of the tribe kill a Seminole girl if she wants a white man. But will they kill their *micco* for wanting a white woman? And the Master of All Breath knows I shall lead my tribe to war against all whites. Then why, I ask the Master of All Breath, must I want you?"

He gave her a shake like a rag doll, but still she dared to say, "Perhaps your fierce desire for war against the whites is wrong."

At that, he yanked her closer and peered into her wide eyes with his slitted ones. "You would not say so. Not if you saw the massacres of *our* people for *our* land at Ope-hatchee. My brother and his family died when the whites came. But all the dead Seminoles are my brothers. I came to Ope-hatchee and found them. To the last child, lying dead in their blood! And on *our* land!" He roared and hit his chest with a hollow thud as he flung her away.

Tears stung her eyes. "I heard about the massacres. It's terrible, so wrong of the white man. But if you do the same to the whites I am very sorry for them, too."

"Sorry! *Halwuk*, woman!"

"You say that word all the time," she protested. "I was not at the massacre, and I do not want to steal your land!"

"*Halwuk* means 'it is bad, it is evil.' The massacre was *halwuk*, your lies are *halwuk*, the whites and you, too—" he raved.

"No! I am not!" she cried, so panicked she hardly knew what she was saying.

Quick as a cat, he kneeled and lifted her to her knees against him with his hands hard on her upper arms. Their noses almost touched. Their breath mingled and their eyes locked.

"Such defiance when I could kill you," he marveled, and she saw a quick flash of white teeth in the dark face. "A man should demand as many guns as stars in the sky for a woman such as you!"

"Then please do not trade us to the pirates! If you admire anything about me, do not give me to them to be ransomed and killed!"

A frown crushed his features. "Never beg, I said, and never tell a *micco* what he must do! But tell more—tell me why."

Grateful that he released her from his iron grip, she related the story of her capture from a ship owned by her fiancé, Justin Lyon, and of her imprisonment on Captiva. He shook his big head when he heard how Gasparilla promised her freedom but lied. She found herself downplaying Josh's role as her captor and stressing only how he had helped her escape.

She glanced at last into the darkness and then at the intent face of Sho-caw. Tears filled her eyes at all she and Josh had shared—and perhaps had lost now. "You are not trading us to Gasparilla, are you?" she asked.

"Will you agree not to tell anyone what I say? Not even your man?"

"Yes, I promise."

"Then we begin and end our trust with mingling blood," he declared and rose to find the talon club as if he had night eyes like a hawk. He returned with it, bared his wrist in the pale moonlight and drew the talons slowly down his skin to raise three parallel tracks of blood. She stared wonderingly at his stern face as he turned her arm up, scratched her and pressed his wet wrist to hers.

She started at the impact of that union as if it was somehow magical. He touched her nowhere else. She did not fear him physically at this moment, as she always had. Sho-caw had never tilted her insides and made her head spin as Josh did with his slightest look and touch, and yet something had grown between them, some unnameable bond, living and powerful. She tore her eyes away from his open gaze and stared at their wrists, bronze and ivory, pressed so strongly together.

"Now I will have your defiance and your fury with me," he pronounced solemnly. "Even when I share my sleeping mat with Cho-fee. And when I attack others with your pale skin." He cleared his throat as he moved his wrist and used some leaves to wipe the blood. "Your man, Ich-chaw, this Silver Swords you desire," he said slowly as he worked, "he told me your white name. Your father's name, too, and this Justin Lyon you were once promised to. Ich-chaw said trade you there."

"He asked you to trade us to Justin Lyon?" She gasped.

He nodded, his face grim. "I am trading both of you with that man we paid gold to before for guns—that man you say you were once promised to. That man Justin Lyon."

She pressed her hands to her breasts. "And then we'll be free!" she said, more to herself than him.

"Free of all but your other promise to marry that man before I made you marry Ich-chaw," he muttered.

But she hardly heeded his words. Salvation at last. Her heart sang. An easy trip to New Orleans in a Justin Lyon ship! No more threats of pirates or Seminoles or the tropic wilds! But then her mind realized what Sho-caw had said. Justin would expect a virgin fiancé in this trade, not one who had slept with a pirate and had married him in a pagan Seminole ceremony!

"So," Sho-caw said when she sat, dazed, and spoke no more, "this now makes a sadness for you. Pulled between two men as you have pulled me between two women. But we shall not speak ever of my desire for a woman of strength and fury at my side. I return to Cho-fee now, and you to your one man—or the other."

He helped her up, lifted his feathered hawk cape from the ground and swung it around his broad shoulders. "I chased you when you tried to escape," he told her. "A truth the tribe shall hear. Now I take you back among the Seminoles. We wait until the guns are at the coast. You will no longer sleep in the *chickee* of *micco* Sho-caw and his beloved wife Cho-fee." His voice hardened and rose as he spoke until it pierced her, knife-edged.

"But you know I will not try to escape now—"

"No one will know I told you these things. No one will know you took a blood vow not to tell. The *micco* must punish you for running. I will put you away until we leave for the coast. Then you shall think what to tell the man Justin Lyon you made another vow to once."

He reclaimed his hawk-talon club and pulled her swiftly along behind him in the darkness. The drums had begun again, or had they never stopped? The path grew brighter, moonlit first, then fire-lit. Her bare feet, toughened by work among the Seminoles, hardly felt the pine needles, sharp fronds or twigs. But she felt the chaos of reunion and loss. Joy shimmered in her at the hope of deliverance to Justin and home. Grief dragged her down with her threatened love for Josh. And a strange regret echoed through her stunned heart for the way Sho-caw had bared his soul to her and then walled it off in hatred once again.

Lanie spent the next four days alone in the council house, guarded. After Sho-caw had dragged her back during the hunt dance, he had announced to the tribe that he had hunted the best prey of all—a prisoner who existed only to be traded for guns for their war. Josh's face had shown shock; everyone else had danced and chanted harder. All night their noise had closed in on Lanie. Swamped by inner turmoil, she felt the council house walls—the entire world—press in on her, more suffocating than the carpet once wrapped around her as a child or the Little Hut where Silver Swords had locked her in on Captiva.

She spent long hours reasoning out what she must tell Josh, how she must try to win him back. She loved him, she ached for him, needed him, desired him. And yet he evidently was tied to another woman she could not even fight for him. And he had suggested Sho-caw trade them to Justin. That might mean more than just a desire for their safety. Josh might be more than willing to have her fiancé take her off his hands for good.

When it came to Justin Lyon, her thoughts careened and overturned just as wildly. After all, Justin had told as many lies as Sho-caw had truths. Josh had told her lies at first only from necessity to spy on Gasparilla. She forgave him for that, but she never could forgive Justin. And the Seminole had somehow traded for guns with him before! Each new truth she found out about her fiancé sickened her. Guns perhaps illicit slave trading with Lafitte—what had she gotten herself into when she'd said yes to Justin Lyon those eons ago before all this happened to her?

And what would Justin do with Josh if he learned that Josh was one of the pirates who had taken his ship and his fiancé—and bedded her into the bargain? Shoot him with those guns he evidently traded secretly? Or expose him to the authorities, who could imprison him or even hang him? It was common to put captured pirates on trial, and then she would be expected to testify against Josh. Whatever she said, it would all come out in court; her reputation would lie in shreds. Lanie shuddered at the thought of what that would do to her gentle mama. And it would be all for nothing, for nothing she could say would save Josh.

No, she would have to lie from the start. She, who hated lies, would be forced to lie to Justin to save Josh. Well, at least it would all be over fast, for she realized now that she could never marry Justin. After the precious hours spent in Silver Sword's arms, no man would ever measure up. She would have to tell Justin that she had changed her mind.

Lanie jerked from her mental turmoil when Zeena came in through the brightly hued door flap. Bundled in her arms, she carried the shoes Lanie thought she had lost for good and her faded blue gown.

"Guess it time you goin' to the coast, Ha-shay," the woman announced, but she did not look a bit happy over it. "A hundred rifles' worth, and barrels of that black silk powder, they say. Lawsy, I don't want no more war no way, not with my man, Wood-ko's daddy, fightin'."

Lanie got to her feet. Her heart thudded in her excitement and fear. "I don't want fighting, either, Zeena, believe me. Not against the Seminoles or the slaves. And I want to thank you for being kind to me. You've made me really miss a friend of mine I left behind, but I am going to send someone to save her. And—I will always remember you as a dear friend.

Zeena's eyes popped and she shook her head in bewilderment at this white woman claiming to be her friend. "After that first day, Zeena didn't do nothin' but what she was told," the tall woman insisted as she thrust Lanie's worn leather shoes and tattered gown at her. It was then Lanie decided it was best if Justin learned to see her in a new light, too. It might make whatever came later somehow easier. She donned the shoes Zeena held out, but said, "I would rather wear this Seminole clothing I have on—if the *micco* will allow it.''

After that, everything moved so fast that Lanie's head spun. In the village square, squaws and children gathered to see the two white people marched away for guns. Lanie glanced back, amazed that they had lived in the exotic village at all. Little Wood-Ko waved. Lanie called her thanks to Zeena, but the woman's face looked grieved. Cho-fee's gentle gaze followed Sho-caw's big form as he motioned the party of ten men and the captives to depart.

At last, fearing the look on Josh's face, Lanie peeked around bronze shoulders to where he stood, well-guarded, in the caravan. His dark eyes both questioned and comforted. She felt the impact of that look as if he held her warmly to him. She tore her teary eyes away from his face. She feared how much she loved him and how it would hurt to lose him if it ever came to that. Still, she intended to tell Justin Lyon she could never wed him. She vowed she would not look again at Josh or the village as they began their march to the coast. But when she glanced over her shoulder once more, his dark eyes were still on her. And the thick Florida vegetation had swallowed the Seminole Indian village whole.

Chapter Ten

On their march to the gulf coast, they stopped only once to rest. One of Cho-fee's younger brothers handed flat corn bread around, and everyone chewed in silence. Someone could have been mere yards away in the forest and not known the Indians were there. Braves went off into the bushes one at a time and returned. Lanie at last was allowed to have a private moment to herself.

During their respite, Lanie and Josh eyed each other. She could actually feel herself blush, just as if she was sitting on a tiny, gilded chair in the corner of her first ball waiting for him to approach her with a request for a dance. All this time Sho-caw ignored her, but she had the strangest feeling he wished to speak to her alone. The tension seemed as ready to snap as dry twigs underfoot. But Sho-caw only spoke a low command, and they started off again.

At last, thick mangroves loomed ahead, and Lanie was sure she could smell the sea. Her pulse, already pounding from the fast pace Sho-caw had set, accelerated in her excitement. Justin's ship would take her home! Magnolia Hill, Mama and Papa were just a few days away, after all this danger! And yet home could mean damnation as well as salvation—damnation of her love for Josh, a man she would always love.

They finally rested on a bone-hued sand beach littered with driftwood. Eagerly Lanie scanned the stretch of green, whitecapped Gulf of Mexico for a sign of a ship. She nearly jumped up and down when she spotted the bloom of big square sails tilting toward the shore. To her dismay, Sho-caw ordered Josh tied to a large driftwood tree trunk. Lanie stood nervously as Sho-caw approached her with another loop of rope while two of his braves built a signal fire.

"You know I will not run," she told him with head held high.

His sharp eyes did not meet the challenge of her stare as he scanned the sea. "I know nothing of what you have decided these last days," he said with a shrug of powerful shoulders. "I want the guns, and that is all."

"Is it? That and your revenge at some place called Ope-hatchee, I suppose," she dared quietly.

His voice matched her low pitch. "Even if you try to warn the Americans there, we will be first to attack." He indicated that she should put her wrists along a stout limb of driftwood trunk. She did as he said, but turned her wrist so he could see the scratches where they had mingled blood. He had tried so hard to avoid her eyes, but now his eyes jumped to meet her steady stare.

"I have come to hate being anyone's captive," she said. "And I tell you what you already know—that you must protect your tribe at all costs. If you attack Ope-hatchee, the whites will come looking for you, and too many of you will die."

"I tell this to you. You are captive to your feelings for Ich-chaw," he insisted, and nodded toward Josh. "Still, you must not let Justin Lyon know that until I have the guns. *Halwut*, woman, never give a *micco* advice. Your feelings for that man," he said, and nodded in Josh's direction again, "are written plain upon your face like smoke signals in the sky."

He lifted his big bronze hand, gesturing towards the coils of smoke that summoned Justin's ship closer to shore. Lanie saw that Sho-caw had Josh's precious gold watch secured to his sash with a leather thong. Sho-caw turned away, but he had not tied her hands. His words of her love for Josh were the last thing he ever said to her.

She knew better than to run to the longboat as it was rowed in from the anchored ship so some men could parley with Sho-caw and one other Seminole at the far end of the beach. But, as she squinted to pick out Justin, she saw he was not there. Perhaps he was not even aboard the vessel beyond the surf. That would mean a reprieve to settle everything with Josh. In one way that would be a relief, but why hadn't Justin come personally for her? Could it be he considered her sullied by her captivity among pirates and savages and did not intend to see her at all?

The Seminoles walked Lanie out to the open stretch of sand where Justin's men could see her. Lanie swept her windblown hair back from her eyes and managed a surreptitious, distant glance at Josh. His thick ebony hair with its startling silver slash was rumpled by the wind; how she longed to run her fingers through it. His mustache had grown much too long and shaggy, but he looked bold and unconquered even tied and guarded like that. He watched the action, too, his clear blue eyes slitted against the wind. Stark shadows highlighted the angles and planes of his strong cheek and jaw. If that had been Josh's ship, *he* would have come in to bargain directly for his woman, Lanie thought.

The business was soon enough completed. The men piled muskets on a square of canvas at Sho-caw's feet. Barrels of gunpowder swelled the stack of booty. The metal gun barrel Sho-caw examined closely glinted like pewter in the sun. He loaded one gun at random and shot it skyward, to down a soaring fish hawk in a spray of feathers. Then Josh, still tied with ropes, and Lanie, tied only with doubts, were escorted forward.

"Mademoiselle Melanie McVey?" the oily-haired, wiry man in charge of the landing party inquired in French with a brief bow. "Paul Chantal, Monsieur Lyon's captain of the *Barataria* at your service."

"Then where is Monsieur Lyon?" she asked, even as the captain helped her into the boat.

"He awaits on board," he informed her as he motioned Josh into the boat. Josh climbed in with his hands still tied in front of him. Before the captain could say otherwise, Josh sat beside her. Her eyes met Josh's steady stare.

"And why did Monsieur Lyon stay on board?" she pursued in French. Everyone else clambered quickly in, most of the sailors, a motley-looking crew, holding guns. Her gaze darted past Josh over Captain Chantal's rounded shoulder and linked with the stoic, silent Sho-caw's on the shore.

"But, *mademoiselle*," the captain was saying in loud French, "Monsieur Lyon stayed on board for safety's sake, of course. You can't believe these lying savages to make a deal. How do we know the red bastards will not try to pick us off like that osprey hawk on the way out, eh?"

"Didn't the Indian chief say he would not?" she demanded and pointed at Sho-caw, standing knee deep in the surf, watching as the sailors shoved off for the ship. "His word is good!"

Captain Chantal looked at her as if she had lost her mind. "Monsieur Lyon trusts him no more than a snake he should kill with his cane, of course," the man blustered.

Just as the waves smacking the prow sprayed her, so the smack of reality hit her, too. Had she been living in strange, foreign worlds of delusion? She had fallen in love with a pirate. She had felt the horrors of slavery firsthand. She had actually come to believe that a murdering savage's word was to be trusted. Of course, Justin would feel suspicious about Sho-caw and had taken all necessary precautions. Until recently, she would have thought it the wise thing, just as she never could have truly empathized with Zeena's fear of losing her home and loved ones again, or Jasmine's deepest feeling, until all this had happened.

The next wave bumped her hips into Josh's. She reached over to untie his hands despite Captain Chantal's protests, which she ignored.

"I cannot thank you enough for suggesting to Sho-caw that Lyon buy us," she whispered.

"I did it for both of us," Josh admitted, his eyes warm on her in the push of cool sea wind. "I've been planning too long to go back for Gasparilla on my own terms to ever go back to him as his captive. And I knew this was best for you."

She frowned at that, but it was not the time to discuss Justin, with Captain Chantal hovering so close. "I intend to go with you to rescue Jasmine, Serafina and the others!" she declared passionately.

His eyebrows shot up at that, and his nostrils flared as if he would like to hug her. Despite the sailors and Justin Lyon, she almost launched herself into his arms. Josh's next words, mouthed so quietly she alone could hear, thrilled her. "When you last untied me, we had just shared love for the first time, Lanie."

"Oh, yes, I know! Josh, we have to talk before—"

"Your esteemed fiancé Monsieur Lyon," Captain Chantal interrupted in French and leaned closer, "he will be so happy to see you safe, *mademoiselle*!" Lanie sat up straight and shifted slightly away from Josh on the narrow seat under the man's sharp perusal. She dropped the length of rope at their feet and held to the seat on either side of her as the chop of waves increased.

"Lanie, personal problems aside," Josh went on, ignoring the captain, "if Sho-caw's given you any hints about where he's going raiding, you've got to tell the authorities the minute you get a chance."

"I know. I—will. I do not want any more people ambushed and hurt," she admitted. She could not help thinking she was also speaking of herself and all that had happened to her since she had last been on one of Justin Lyon's ships.

Yet, as they bobbed along the wooden hull of the *Barataria*, she felt strangely sad that her great adventure with Josh was over. Was their love over, too? Perhaps when he saw she intended to break all ties to Justin, he would wed her in this other world also, and of his own accord. When she craned her neck to the ship's rail, she saw Justin leaning over, waving his gold-headed cane as if it were a magic wand.

Justin helped her up the last step of the rope ladder to the deck. "Ah, *ma chérie*, but look at you, brown as a berry!" he cried in the Creole French she had missed so much.

Ah, yes, she thought, she had missed that from him at least. Seeing him in the flesh again, she could see why he had once held an allure for her. Sleekly handsome, elegant, ever poised, so in charge of every situation. But she intended to see he was not in charge of her for very long.

He escorted her from the rail. He bestowed the briefest of light hugs, then held her hands out to the side and examined her minutely. She was surprised but relieved he did not kiss her lips. Josh was somewhere behind her, and she could not bear that he see that. Oh, damnation, how had she gotten herself into this predicament?

"How—well, quaint you look in that ridiculous savage *couture*," Justin murmured as he kissed her hand quickly. "*Ma chère* Melanie, rescued by her loyal fiancé at last!"

It jolted Lanie to be called Melanie again. Justin was the only one close to her who had always persisted in ignoring her pet name, as if she were a far different woman to him than to the others who loved her. And she did not need to be possessively called his fiancé again within earshot of Josh.

"Are Papa and Mama well?" The question spilled from her lips. "I have worried about them so, that they would think me dead or hurt! Is everything all right at Magnolia Hill?"

"Yes, things are fine, but for the distress about you. Your parents, they were devastated, of course, though they hardly mourned as much as I did, since I lost the loaded ship *and* my beloved."

She ignored the fact that he mentioned her after the loss of his ship. "But the pirates still have Jasmine and several other friends. We must rescue them!" she declared.

"Jasmine?" he repeated and looked taken aback. One eye flicked. "A valuable slave, but still just a slave, Melanie, and hardly worth this sort of expensive expedition—or such unladylike vehemence."

"She is worth it to me, Justin!" Her voice shook with anger for his attitude toward Jasmine after everything else she'd learned about him. "I declare, I have done a lot of thinking about things and—"

"But this," he interrupted and gawked behind her, "this is someone else who escaped from those pirates and Indian fiends?" he inquired as Captain Chantal escorted Josh onto the deck.

Her eyes met and held with Josh's bold stare. But she looked again at Justin and managed properly, "Monsieur Lyon, I am honored to introduce you to Monsieur Joshua Blair of New York City. His family was once in shipping, too. And yes—he was kept among Gasparilla's pirates and the Seminoles, also. I'm afraid he only speaks English."

She almost dared to introduce Josh as the man she had wed in a Seminole ceremony barely two weeks ago. But she was not sure what Josh thought of that now. She wished she had not vowed to him she would never hold him to that ceremony. How much she wanted to hold to him anyway she could!

Justin and Josh nodded stiffly and exchanged terse greetings. "Your servant, sir," in English.

Even barefoot, Josh stood slightly taller than the imperious, forty-one-year-old Justin Lyon. Justin's sleekly combed hair, trim side whiskers and carefully brushed mustache were auburn, gleaming red in the sun when he removed his top hat. His shoulders were broad, and he wore his immaculately tended garments with flair. His elegant checked cravat and the pleated cuffs he tugged down under his coat sleeves made Lanie and Josh feel as if they were dressed like ruffians. Justin was fastidious about cleanliness—something Lanie recalled with embarrassment as she and Josh stood under his sharp scrutiny rumpled, soiled and unkempt.

As the three of them surreptitiously examined each other under the patter of polite conversation, Justin handed his ubiquitous gold-headed cane to Captain Chantal as if the man were his valet, then clipped the end off a cheroot. The cigar was lit by a hovering crewman. The smoke bothered

Lanie's eyes even up here in the wind. And to think she had always loved the smell of Justin's expensive blends! She could not wait to get him alone to discuss how things had changed.

Justin politely introduced Josh and Lanie to his officers while he blew smoke rings, which were quickly snatched away by the breeze. Justin had only a skeleton crew on board, but then, after all, Lanie thought, this was not a real cargo ship. She noted that Josh seemed acutely interested in each man's title and function aboard ship. His eyes frequently roamed the deck as if to examine the rigging. Finally, Justin escorted them below to separate cabins to wash and change for dinner while he met with the captain. On deck, the big-bellied sails of the two-masted brigantine *Barataria* leaped to life as the boat moved northward along the Florida coast.

"*Sacré bleu*, you mean they were whispering intimately with each other as you rowed them out, Chantal?" Justin Lyon exploded in the privacy of his captain's cabin. "But of course, idiot that you are to speak only French, you caught none of their words!" he berated the man sarcastically as he paced in a circle around the sumptuous cabin the famous pirate Jean Lafitte had sometimes used.

Lyon prided himself in being secret partners with the man he considered to be the greatest privateer and local hero New Orleans had ever known. He displayed the monogram "J.L." they shared on his ships, his clothing and most of his precious possessions, as if it were some sort of sacred link between the two of them. Even now he tapped the head of his monogrammed cane along the table set for dinner with imported Sèvres china engraved on the gold band with the initials, and heavy tableware and delicate Bacarrat crystal etched with the same.

"I cannot help that, Monsieur Lyon! You should have asked Lafitte to spare another captain if you needed a fine translator, eh!" Captain Chantal dared with a nervous swipe at his slick hair.

"Ah, but where there's smoke there's fire, you fool," Lyon barked. "Be gone then, be gone. And not a word of my suspicions to anyone if you value your job and your life. My friend Jean Lafitte and I do not take kindly to parrots who talk on anyone's cue but ours!"

"Of course, of course, so you have told us all," Captain Chantal blurted. "I'll be in the wheelhouse if you require me again then, *monsieur*," he said and made a fast exit, relieved to be out of reach of Lyon's notorious heavy cane.

Lyon continued to pace, breathing hard. To the devil with the woman! If she had been despoiled, he would not marry her—despite her allure. Only her dowry of Magnolia Hill had made him offer marriage. Her defiant spirit and captivating beauty entranced him, but he was a man who had always gotten what he'd wanted without marriage. But he had wanted a legitimate heir for once, instead of that string of mixed-blood bastards his colored mistresses had given him. But if Melanie was smirched, then she must be discarded, like the mistresses he disposed of as if they were smoked cheroot stubs when he'd had enough of them. He and Lafitte were alike in that way, too—grand rogues, at home in any society, and suave paramours to the end!

He was angry at Melanie for the cost and trouble she'd put him through—not to mention the sullying of his good name with all the gossip that a rich, virgin fiancé captured by pirates had inspired at home. He locked the cabin door from inside and hurried to the side wall. He removed the small painting of Barataria Bay Lafitte had ordered done when the navy had made him move to Galveston Bay. Lyon carefully pulled the small plug of wood that allowed him to peer into the next small cabin, where he'd put Melanie.

Sacré bleu, what perfect timing! A grin split his lips and he licked them repeatedly as he stared. She was kneeling naked in a small wooden tub of water and washing herself all over with a square of cotton cloth.

Ah, that beautiful body was as stunning and seductive as he'd always imagined it! Never had he glimpsed such perfection, since his first love affair at age seventeen back in Lyon, France, before he had to flee. He had never deeply

cared for his first lover, Madame Sagan, of course, any
more than he had loved any of the beauties he'd later possessed as he might a lovely house or sleek ship. And madame had hardly been worth the cost; he'd had to shoot her
husband, who had found them together. Lyon shot him and
his second in the pistol duel just before the signal to fire. He
had been forced to leave France, but his life in French
America had been better than the life he could have had in
France under his real name. There, he would have been a
second son in his father's grand establishment at best. In
New Orleans, with his lucrative, covert partnership with
Lafitte, he *was* the grand establishment!

His eyes burned as he looked through the spyhole to ogle
Melanie's sweet flesh. His hand trembled on his monogrammed cane. He longed to plunder her as any pirate
might. The wanton, as innocent and cool as the river breeze
on the surface, did not fool him. He did not think for one
minute she had been gone for nearly three months in the
wilds and not been defiled. Now, she could never carry his
name and his legitimate children. But he would still have
her. He would take the defiant little coquette for his mistress until he tired of her.

Ah, but her skin was burnished golden in places that
made her pert, high breasts and twin globes of buttocks
erotically white in comparison. He'd always favored quadroon mistresses; there had even been one he'd kept for years,
until she fussed when he sold the third child she'd whelped.
The fruits of that union with the stunning quadroon had
come back to haunt him more than once, but at least that
problem seemed nicely taken care of by fate, since Lanie had
come back alone. Alone except for a damned bold-eyed
New Yorker named Joshua Blair.

With a string of whispered French curses, Lyon reluctantly plugged the peephole and rehung the painting. He
unlocked the cabin door and strode down the hall to the
small room where he'd put his unwelcome guest. He rapped
smartly on the door three times with his cane. "Blair, a word
with you before we sup."

The dark-haired Yankee opened the door. "Step in if it's that urgent," he said, strop and razor in hand. His gaze was hardly deferential. Lyon had grown to expect deferential gazes. He was bare-chested, and shaving soap covered his lean cheeks. Lyon shook his head to clear it of the stark memory of Melanie's body, sleek with soap and water in her private bath.

"A momentary word," Lyon informed the younger man and stepped past him into the small room. Joshua Blair closed the door and leaned against it. "I'll get right to the point, man to man," Lyon snapped as he tapped the head of his cane in the palm of one hand.

"Fine."

"I know the ways of the world, Blair. I demand to know what you are to my fiancé."

"Perhaps you'd best ask the lady. Man to man, I'm sure you'd admit women are harder to read than a ship's manifest, which declares a simple shipment of furniture when much more's involved."

"Meaning?" Lyon demanded, startled and off guard.

"Meaning what I said," Josh parried, carefully controlling his face and voice and his rampant desire to have it out with Lyon, by fists or swords. "You'd best ask the lady."

"You've had her, haven't you, you brazen bastard?" Lyon roared.

"Had her?" Josh countered as he flung himself away from the door, threw the razor and strop on the washstand and splashed the soap off his face. Suddenly he didn't trust himself with the razor in his hand. "Quite a touching way to refer to your fiancé, Lyon, as if she's a piece of goods you can ship and profit from."

"You'll not play games with me! I'll have you up on charges in New Orleans—or feed you to the sharks out here! I demand to know if you have abused and defiled my intended!"

Despite the fact that Lyon was holding the cane as a barrier, the younger man lunged at him to pin him to the door, with the cane pressed across his chest. "Abused? No! Defiled? No! It's only the leeches and hypocrites of the world like you that do that to women, Lyon! Now get away from me before I demand retribution on her behalf because of your vile insults! And if I hear you've taken any of this out on her, you'll have me to answer to!''

"How dare you slur me so, you bilge rat!" Lyon shrieked. He tried unsuccessfully to shove the cane back. "I have friends who would have you hanged from a yardarm faster than you could pee yourself in fear!"

"Then send your friends to see me, Lyon!" Josh challenged. "At least then I'll be able to deal with someone man to man!" He yanked the cane toward him, hauling Lyon away from the door. He swung it wide and gestured to the gasping man to leave. Lyon straightened, cursing the New Yorker under his breath in the French he thought the man didn't understand. He had meant from the moment he had met him to dispose of Blair; now he would make sure it was done painfully. Swinging on his heel, he stalked from the room.

Left alone, Josh Blair quickly donned the clean shirt and waistcoat laid out for him. He knew now that he had a lot to do in a very short time.

Ruffles, muslin flounces, real satin ribbons—Lanie reveled in them all as she struggled to hook the back of her gown without any help. It was kind of Justin to bring some clothes along for her in his haste, but perhaps her parents had insisted. This rose-hued muslin gown with off-the-shoulder pink puff sleeves felt so clean and elegant after these past three months. She could not wait for Monsieur Joshua Blair to see her dressed like this! She hadn't had stockings or underclothes since she had given up her last petticoat to make a sail when they fled Captiva.

She piled her hair on her head, though without Jasmine's clever touch, much of it cascaded down her neck before she was through. She examined her face in the first mirror she had seen in weeks. Unfortunately, Justin was right: she was brown as a berry. Mama, however happy she would be to see Lanie, would be horrified by the indelicacy of it all, Lanie thought with a tight little smile of joy at the thought of her family's reunion. But first, her reunion with Justin had to be completely settled. He would not take it well, of that she had no doubt. But she needed to tell him that, despite his rescue, she could no longer consider herself betrothed to him. She would pay him back somehow for the expense of this voyage and the guns he'd traded.

But nerves made her knees shake on the way to Justin's cabin. Her skirts seemed to swish loudly, and her flat silk pumps tapped to match the rattle of her thoughts. When she knocked on the door, Justin opened it instantly and she jumped.

"*Ma chérie*, how simply stunning you look, stunning! Come over here. I want to bask in your beauty and drink a toast to our future," he told her with a magnanimous smile as he escorted her to the elaborately set table. She glanced briefly out the porthole. She was surprised to see how close they were to shore still.

"To us and our glorious future, my Melanie," he toasted and clinked the crystal rim of his goblet to hers. But instead of taking a sip, she placed her glass on the table. Quickly, she stepped away as he reached for her.

"I cannot believe such luxury and beauty after the things I have seen," she began solemnly. She held the back of a carved chair to block him from embracing her. He studied her as her eyes dropped shyly, perhaps warily to the fine china, to fix on the monogram.

"I'm going to tell you something right out, so we can settle things between us," she told him. "In Gasparilla's camp, I heard you were partners with Jean Lafitte. I didn't want to believe it, but it almost cost me my life—and it did cost me my respect for you. And the gun trading with the Seminoles that is fueling these awful massacres—just more lucrative pirate's business to you, I suppose."

She fought to keep control of her voice, to get through her speech before he argued. "Justin, I cannot love or marry a man who does such things."

She glanced up to see his stunned face as his skin flushed with fury; she read no regret there at all. "And you would believe the word of such bilge-rat scum as Blair over my reputation at home! I am shocked, Melanie, shocked."

"You dare to deny it? I declare, I've become very adept in discovering when men are lying."

"I demand you explain that comment! A reference to Monsieur Blair, perhaps, but I can't abide the thought of your mingling with men like him!"

"Men like him! How dare you, when you—"

"You've been deluded, of course," Lyon insisted. He clipped and lit a cheroot, then quickly snuffed it out on a dinner plate. He began to pace, to give himself time to think how best to handle this. Too many people knew he had rescued Melanie and that Blair bastard—he couldn't get rid of them. Lafitte would throw fits if Lyon made waves with any of the society families of New Orleans whose goodwill he coveted. Lyon had ordered Blair's door locked and boarded up from the outside a half hour ago, but he had no intention of telling Lanie that. He did have every intention, however, of settling things thoroughly between them once and for all, and that was why he'd told his men to keep away until he summoned them.

"I've often wondered if women don't truly fancy a pirate or a savage in their beds," he said quietly as he strode up to her. She looked shocked and fearful at his change in tactics, and that aroused him even more. She'd always been so strong-willed, so spirited, like a fractious racing mare. Tonight, all night, he decided, he would loose that passion and use her wildness to suit his needs.

"Justin, I don't appreciate—"

"I promise you will appreciate all I'm going to do for you!" He seized her shoulders to stop her flight. He pressed her into the chair until it knocked onto the table and toppled goblets.

"Justin!"

"Don't you think I can read your simple little woman's mind? Whether by your own designs or not, you've bedded with that brazen bastard Blair and concocted all these lies about me, haven't you? Lies to clear your own conscience.

My, my, but I wonder what it was really like for you with Gasparilla's pirates. You and the hot-blooded Jasmine probably loved every minute of it!''

"Justin, stop it! You've no right to slander me, or Jasmine, either! You're the one I'm horrified about!" she insisted and began to struggle even harder.

"Would it arouse you to know I'm a pirate and in with Lafitte? That we're closest friends?" he asked as he stilled her thrashing. "That we like the same power, wealth and women?" he went on, pressing his florid face close to hers, his features suddenly swollen with lust.

"Stop it, stop it!" she screamed loud enough to summon the whole ship.

"*Ma chérie*, the men aboard are Lafitte's, and they obey my every order, as you shall. I only brought a few men along, so very few can hear your cries. Alas, your rather ragged-looking paramour is boarded in his room until I have him hanged for sullying your honor." He laughed, then dropped his voice again. "Now relax and enjoy this. Yes, Gasparilla's furious with Lafitte and me, if you are so enamored of the truth, but I'm the one who has you now. And if you fight me or cross me in any way, I'd hate to think of the accident that might befall you before we arrive home in port, before you get that little reunion with Mama and that father of yours, who fought me so on our betrothal.

"But if you'd just swear to cooperate," his slick voice, which she used to think was so entrancing, went on, "you could be my private mistress, though not my public wife. Perhaps I'll have to keep your friend Blair alive. If he's my captive I will be certain of your cooperation."

"No!" she screamed, despite his threats. "No more captives anymore, especially not yours!"

She freed a hand and raked her fingernails at his face. He shoved her on the chair, which had tipped over the ruined table. He reached for a small-bladed cheese knife and held its sharp point under her chin.

"Hold still until I tell you what to do," he muttered as he bit at her arched throat. His free hand slid heavily between her legs. He grasped the soft flesh of a bare, warm thigh above a stocking top and squeezed.

Despite the knife, she reached out and grabbed a heavy dinner plate. As he lifted his startled face, she shattered the delicate porcelain over his head.

He swore, reeled, staggered back. She rolled off the chair, but her mad scramble pulled the linen cloth to the floor with a clatter of dishes. He stalked her, spouting foul threats, which she hardly heard. She threw a goblet, then another plate.

He seized his gold-headed cane and came at her, swinging the cane. She ducked behind a chair; she screamed again. She ran for the door, but he grabbed her by one arm and threw her onto the bed, which was built in a little alcove. He shoved her arms over her head and jammed the cane across her wrists to hold them down. He knelt on her thrashing legs. And then the door smashed inward with a terrific crash; both looked up.

Josh dived low into the room, rolled over once on the floor, then leaped to his feet. He had a pistol and a sword, but he threw them down to haul Lyon off Lanie. He slammed Lyon hard into the wall once, again.

"Get some rope, a cravat, anything to tie him!" he yelled, as he hit Justin in the stomach and followed with a crisp right and left across the jaw. She jumped to obey. Still trembling, she ransacked the sea chests until she found Justin's immaculately laid out cravats.

"I heard you scream, but I was seeing to the crew and couldn't come right away. I was hoping a so-called gentleman wouldn't be so stupid as to harm you, but we'll have to do things another way," he gasped through ragged breaths as he forced Justin's arms behind his back and put out a hand for a cravat.

"What way?" she asked as she shoved her wild hair back. "And what about his crew?"

"There were only twelve, and two of those were guarding an empty, boarded-up cabin. They've all chosen, several at a time, to jump overboard. Come on! You and I are going to sail this untended ship to a place called Point of Rocks."

She watched smugly as Josh tied the illustrious Justin Lyon with his own cravats. "He admitted it was Lafitte's crew aboard this ship," she told him. "You were right about all that."

"Lafitte will get you both! He won't forgive this! But who the devil are you, then?" the battered Lyon muttered through a wobbly toothed jaw before Josh gagged him by stuffing a cravat in his mouth.

"Come on, Lanie, or this ship will pile up on a shoal," Josh ordered as he retrieved his weapons and ran from the cabin.

She stared at Lyon. She could not resist a poke of her slippered foot at the belly of the trussed, deceitful wretch she had actually promised to marry. At least all this treachery had cleared her conscience about Lyon.

"You know, Monsieur Lyon," she clipped out, "your morals are equal to a pirate's, but are much lower than a savage's, even one whose goal in life is massacre and revenge! And I cannot wait to share such news with the rest of New Orleans when we get this ship there!"

She ran up on deck with the thought that they were pirating this vessel from pirates. Had she really joined the band of brigands at last? All she wanted to pirate was Josh's heart away from his memories of the past and his thirst for revenge, which was as fierce as Sho-caw's.

On deck, the brigantine looked like a ghost ship, with only Josh running across the deck to reach the wheelhouse as they tilted into the stiff western breeze and the wheel spun madly. He meant for the two of them to control this entire ship, and she did not know the first thing about steering or sails!

"Too late!" Josh yelled back to her. "Grab something!"

She seized the rail as the ship shuddered, creaked. The towering web of spars and rigging shook; yardarms bounced and swayed. She thought the hull would split asunder beneath their feet. Lanie spilled to the deck and rolled wildly with the forward pitch as they ground to a shrieking, tilted halt on a shoal fifty yards from shore.

Chapter Eleven

When the *Barataria* ran aground on a submerged shoal, it listed coastward. Lanie grabbed the railing to stop rolling. Josh staggered toward her, pulling himself along the bulwarks.

"What are we going to do?" she cried. "Are we sinking?"

"Low tide, sandbars," he muttered as if he had not heard her. He helped her to her feet, and they leaned against the companionway entrance together. "We might float off at high tide tonight, but I don't want to stay here. Some of Lafitte's men I forced overboard may come this way along the shore and find us. Gasparilla might even be still searching this way."

"But are we sinking?" she repeated and grabbed his arm.

"No chance, Lanie, not you and I. Not after what we've been through!" he assured her in a sudden rush of exhilaration. They were not far from his rendezvous point with a naval ship, although the *Barataria* would not get them there. Still, at the idea of being alone with Lanie, heading toward his revenge and her safety, free of pirates and Seminoles at last, he almost cheered. They had nearly done it! He tugged her against his ribs with one arm around her waist to calm her panic.

"The ship won't sink here, Lanie. It's much too shallow. If you can manage, go below, see if you can find some food and bring it up," he ordered. "I'm going to try to free a

longboat for us. And stay away from your fiancé down
there!"

"My *former* fiancé," she corrected him with a smile suddenly as jaunty as the tilt of the deck. She almost laughed
with the delightful feel of freedom again—freedom with
Josh. The oppression that had settled on her when she met
Justin again had lifted. Now she only had to convince Josh
they should always be together no matter what was in their
pasts or their futures.

On impulse, she turned to kiss him. Startled at first by the
sudden move, he returned her caress heartily. As they kissed,
the ship shuddered and settled. "Oh!" she cried and
grabbed for the rail.

"It's nothing. The world always does that to me when we
kiss," he told her with a bright gleam in his blue eyes.
"Hurry back, then, and hold on," he ordered, as he patted
her bottom once and turned to try to winch down the closest dangling longboat.

She was certain things would be fine between them, she
comforted herself. He had never resisted her persuasions
yet, if it came to that. But she wanted him to want her in
many ways, for many reasons, as she did him. She wanted
him to love her and her alone. Confident and excited, despite the continued shuddering of the ship, she even
hummed the old Creole betrothal tune as she went down to
the galley to fetch the food.

Josh rowed north along the coast as the stranded *Barataria* seemed to drop behind the horizon. "Now we'll have
Jean Lafitte after us as well as Gasparilla," he told Lanie,
but he still seemed in a wonderful mood. She fed him the
cold chicken, cheese and plum *gateau* that had been meant
for Justin's sumptuous dinner. He stopped rowing to dig the
cork out of the wine bottle with the tip of his sword.

As the sun set across a red satin path into the sea, clumps
of clouds came in. Josh nosed the longboat ashore, and they
pulled the prow up high on the sand. He insisted they go
down the beach a little ways from the boat in case someone

stumbled on it. They settled on a quiet cove hidden from the gulf by a tumble of rocks as tall as a man.

Exhausted, he stretched out on sugar-soft sand. They were sheltered from the wind by the natural fortress. She sat primly at his side, smoothing her rose skirts over her knees as the last remnants of daylight faded. The surf sang its sweeping music through the rumble of distant thunder. Lanie had never felt happier or safer—and she was so in love with this man who had saved her from the world's dangers again and again.

"If your back muscles are sore from all that rowing, I could rub them," she ventured when he smiled at her but didn't speak.

"I'd love it. You owe me something for that well-timed rescue today."

"Well-timed?" she teased. "It seemed to me I'd been fighting him off and screaming for most of the day!" She watched him as he sat up to strip his black seaman's coat and high-collared shirt off. He looked as bronzed as an Indian; his curly chest hair dipped to a V-shape over his flat stomach as if to point toward his belt and the juncture of his hard thighs. He turned on his stomach in the sand, his hip against hers as she bent over to massage his shoulders and the corded ridges of his back.

"You can put more weight on me," he said. "I won't break."

"I believe I have noticed that," she said with a laughter-silvered voice as she got to her knees to push harder. Up and down, around. His smooth skin radiated warmth and strength to her kneading hands. The rocking motion she set up against him fluttered her stomach. She hesitated to break the spell of the jubilant mood they had shared at their escape from Seminoles and Justin, but she knew they needed to settle things. All that had happened that day seemed proof enough of his devotion. Only now, with the way she wanted to give herself to him again, she felt afraid. Physical love alone would never be enough for her—and she hoped it was not all that held him.

"Are you asleep?" she whispered.

"No." His voice seemed wary now, as if he had read her shifting mood from her touch. His back muscles tightened, then flexed before her hands dropped away. He rolled over and sat up to face her with his limp wrists over bent knees. She sat on her heels with her hands folded in her lap.

"We've been through so much together," she began, her voice quiet but unsteady. She could sense his ebullient mood had muted, too. He looked suddenly so solemn. "Yet sometimes I just do not know what you're thinking—about the future."

"I'm thinking that we need to do some serious talking about the past and present before we get to that. Lanie, in the Seminole village, I was fearful not only for our lives, but that Sho-caw desired you. I was willing to give him my father's watch to assure him of my friendship, but you were not part of the bargain. I just want to be certain he did not coerce you to—share anything else with him there."

"Only this," she said and pulled back her sleeve to show him the three scratches of their blood oath. "I made a vow I would tell no one some things he said. But I can tell you he's obsessed with a terrible desire for revenge because whites massacred some of his family."

"I can sympathize with that," Josh admitted, and his voice caught. He took her hand in the growing darkness. "The vows of secrecy you have to honor. But neither vows nor revenge are right unless bound by justice. Believe me, I've had a lot of time and trials to come to that realization. And that's what I need to talk to you about before tomorrow."

"What about tomorrow?" she asked. The questions she had held in too long spilled from her. "Why did we have to come to Point of Rocks? What happens now?"

She heard him take in a huge breath, then let it out slowly. "A ship will be stopping here for us, Lanie. By my reckoning, tomorrow is September 22. Tomorrow, as on that same date each month, a United States Navy ship will put in here, hoping to rendezvous with me. At least that was the plan more than a year ago when I first set out with a friend, Frank Reynolds, for Boca Grande."

He heard her gasp but he plunged on, "Frank and I had orders to play pirate for the United States Navy long enough to learn all there was to know about Gasparilla's methods and contacts before we came here and got help to lead an assault on his base. We got battered by a storm, and a rogue wave drowned Frank and cast me up on the beach with a broken leg where Serafina found me."

Lanie listened, stunned, swept along by his story, but questions flooded her mind. "But that story about your parents being killed?" she began.

"That is all true. That was one reason I volunteered for the dangerous assignment of gaining inside information about Gasparilla's camp. I had to know what had happened to them as well as help stop what he's been doing to other innocent Americans—like you and Jasmine."

She got to her knees, tugging her hand from him, and wrapped her arms around herself. She was suddenly chilled all over, and not from the approach of storm winds. "You're—you're an American sailor? Who are you really, Silver Swords?" she demanded, echoing Justin Lyon's question. She tried to pierce the darkness to catch every nuance of emotion on his face, but it was ghostly gray in the growing fog and mist.

"Mademoiselle Melanie McVey," he said in smooth French, "your devoted servant, Lieutenant Joshua Blair of the United States Navy. I am, and have been, at your service. And, despite what you may think, I had reasons for not telling you this earlier. Like you, but for a different reason, I have taken a solemn oath. I swore to keep my real identity secret until I could report to the navy—and I was afraid that if you knew everything, the pirates or the Seminoles might torture it out of you."

Relief, shock, dismay: the torture was that she did not know what she felt beyond being momentarily overwhelmed. "You—speak French. All that time and you didn't tell me. And—did you mean to meet this navy ship all the time, from the very beginning when we fled Captiva together?" she stammered. "And here I thought you had let me force you to leave because you wanted to help me—to be with me and protect and love me!"

He seemed to notice the chill in the stormy sky for the first time. He hastily donned his shirt and black seaman's coat as he explained, "The fact I was leaving for my own reasons doesn't mean I didn't want to help you. Protect you. Even love you, as best I could, Lanie. I told you the night we ran I wanted to help, but you wouldn't believe me."

"Believe you! Why should I have? How can I believe anything now, especially that you want to love me as best you can? And here I told Justin I could never trust him because he'd lied to me about himself!"

"I've hated myself for lying to you, Lanie, but I—maybe both of us—would be dead if I hadn't. After all, weren't you right to trust me? We're here, we're safe and—"

"Safe! Yes, but, Josh, lieutenant or whoever you are, I do not know you at all and I love you so—"

He pulled her into his embrace although he knew he should not touch her. His need and hers swirled wild as the storm winds. It should all end now that he had told her who he was, now that they were going back, he tried to convince himself. She would be safe. Jasmine and Serafina, too, he hoped. He would at last have his revenge. And then it would all be over. If only he could stop this desire to push her to the ground and make her his again when no woman could ever really be his at all!

He leaned forward and brushed his mustached lips against her ear, warmly stirring the tendrils of her wind-tossed hair. He moved his mouth along the slant of her cheekbones, across her lips, down her throat, which she arched for him in sudden surrender. Then, slowly, as she clung to him, he pulled her down on the soft sand in his embrace.

The sand still held the warmth of the sun. Her heart still held the heat of her love for this man. Whoever he was, whatever he had done or meant to do, she loved him with all her being. She needed him so desperately. She needed his promise that he would still want her when they went home, would court her, wed her. At the very least, she wanted his agreement she could follow him to the ends of the earth!

She clung to him. "Josh, nothing will change for us. We can put it all behind us! All the pain and our differences, the other people we thought we loved once—"

She felt him go rigid. He clamped her to him then held her off. She gripped his hand hard. The wedding ring she felt there was merely a thin band, but it seemed to loom as big as the rocks over her head. He sat up even as the first pelting drops of rain began.

"It's going to pour, Lanie," he said. "We've got to—"

"No! That isn't really it, is it? It's not rain, not your duty—not even me, is it? It's Becky—still here like a ghost, still in the way!"

"That's not true!" he insisted. "It's not just that anymore. Lanie," he cried, raising his voice as thunder rolled to drown him out, "it's so much more! I adore you, desire you, yes, love you, damn it! And that means if we wed and we shared a bed every night there would be every chance of our making a baby, and I can't allow that!"

"But I'm not afraid!"

"I am! Do you think I want to lose you and a child the way I did before? I can barely live with that once, but not again. Not with you, my sweetheart! I can take anything else this life has to offer and fight back, but not that, so—"

He said something else, but the clap of thunder drowned his words. Despite his denials and her arguments, he got to his feet and pulled her up. He hurried her under an overhang of rock as lightning repeatedly stabbed the sky.

Through her tears of frustration, fury and defeat, she gazed at his rugged profile, like the rocks, etched by lightning. Her Silver Swords, her Josh—a stranger's profile to her now. He had as good as said this was the end for them. He had even refused her embrace when she would have given herself to him so joyously. They stood there, unspeaking, awestruck at the storm.

Finally, when the noise and blinding flashes slackened, then swept inland, Lanie said, "We're both exhausted. Tomorrow when your friends come it will be a new day for us. Maybe after we save Jasmine and Serafina—"

He turned to her. He shook his head in wonder at her strength and resilience. Though she thought he was denying her desires again, she did not crumble.

"You're going to have to go with us to fight Gasparilla, Lanie, because I'm going to recommend to my superiors we sail to Boca Grande right away. But I won't let you put yourself in danger. You're not going with the United States Navy to storm Gasparilla's stronghold!"

"Lieutenant Blair," she dared, though her voice was not as strong as her heart would have it, "I have had quite enough of your telling me what I can and cannot do. I am no one's prisoner, no one's captive, nor ever shall be again. And neither will Jasmine, nor Serafina, nor Honorée, nor Celeste, nor anyone, if I can help it. And as for our previous discussion, we shall just see about that after these other matters are settled!"

She thought she saw the grim line of his mouth soften in the mist the rain had left behind. Her heart thrilled. He had shaken his head in such a final denial, but perhaps she could talk sense and reason to him after they rescued the others. He would have fewer burdens; he would change his mind then. And as to dying in childbirth, why, some women did that, of course, but not her! Her own mama had almost been lost twice trying to birth her first two babies, which had died right away, before her only living child was born, but she had survived. Lanie would have to convince him she was strong enough to live through anything, though sometimes, like now, she would much have preferred to just throw herself into his arms and sob and beg.

Her own happy family life and her love for Josh convinced her that motherhood would be worth the risk. She wanted to argue that they must not bypass certain joy for fear of possible sorrow. With the burden of losing Becky and their babe, poor Josh had been doing that for so long. But she could not bring that up again. Surely there would be a time for it later when reason and emotion together could prevail over his fear of failure and loss. She almost blurted it all out to him, but his commanding, detached tone, which she knew he struggled so hard for, kept her silent.

"I'll have to be up at first light tomorrow to spot the ship, Lanie. We'd best try to get some sleep."

They huddled on a thin stretch of dry sand under a rock, despite the forlorn dripping and the mist still swirling in the air. Stretched out, head to head, they were both as restless as the sea. He tossed and turned. She shifted positions and finally huddled with her knees pulled up, although she was not cold. At last, despite the tumble of her thoughts, she swam in sleep.

Her dreams tormented and delighted her. Somehow, she sensed she was in a dream, and yet she bid it on, closer, closer. She gave in to the sensations as she dreamed her Silver Swords flickered his tongue along her pouted lips, the way he had first taught her to kiss. He began to tease her senses alert with little forays of rubbing, massaging hands, first on her shoulders, her back, then her waist, her bottom, her thighs. He rotated his palms over her breasts until she almost cried out from the agony of her garments separating his skin from hers.

They slowly, carefully undressed each other in the tender dark and tossed their garments to the darting wind. No more storms, only the rush of hands and surf. Exposed skin, caressed by the brush of breeze, leaped to gooseflesh and then was warmed again. They came together after weeks apart, gently, deliberately, then with a hot, rampant desire that swamped them both.

She arched her back under the mastery of his hands and lips. He was everywhere along her skin, sweeping deep into her mind and heart. Only a pagan wedding ceremony that did not mean a thing—could it have made her so much more the wild, willing wanton? But she wanted him forever like this. And she wanted another wedding, a fine one at home and not on a windy beach where a ship would come and see them, take them away...

"I adore you, my sweetheart, adore you." Josh breathed hot against her soft flesh. "This moment is so perfect. I'll never love anyone as I do you! I want you. I want you to have my child—"

Each skim and clasp of flesh burned more alive and vibrant. They did not stop. She did not want to ever stop loving Josh. They pressed together, moving, melding in unison. He plunged over her, in her, and she drove him on to greater spiraling heights above the sea. They swooped and clung amidst the pounding waves, and he did not withdraw until they fulfilled each other's deepest desires forever to make one life—and a new one.

Minutes passed, and still they were reluctant to break the perfect union forged from all their trials and dangers. But the water flooded her face, and she fought to sit up in his arms. In his arms . . . where were his arms!

Lanie McVey jolted awake. She sat several feet from the sleeping man in the first blush of dawn. He did not touch her, had not touched her. The dream receded like the tide, and she knew the water on her face was only her own tears of longing. She was wet with perspiration, although a cooling breeze curled under their shelter. She still felt sated, floating, yet so desolate at the way he had refused her last night. But today was that new day she had promised him. Still trembling, she wrapped her skirt and petticoats around her like a shawl. She leaned against the rock and watched over him until he awoke.

When Josh sat up and stretched at sunrise, a three-masted square-rigged man-of-war stood at anchor in the gulf. Lanie was startled at the sight, but Josh ran up on the rocks to wave his jacket and shout greetings. At least, she thought, in this latest renaissance of Silver Swords, the man seemed to be telling the truth. She glanced around as if to say goodbye to a place they had shared alone on their travels to safety. But she still felt very determined as a longboat set immediately in for them, that she and Joshua Blair were not ever going to say goodbye.

She watched all the sharp salutes and his welcome among his crisply uniformed comrades. The seamen's striped shirts and the officers' blue waistcoats and white trousers sparkled in the morning sun. Each man greeted her politely, though most of them looked goggle-eyed that their long-lost

Lieutenant Blair had materialized at last, and with a tousle-haired, wrinkle-skirted young blonde.

On the scrubbed deck of the big *Norfolk*, Lanie took Josh's hand as he strode up to the deck. She watched as he snapped sharp salutes to the man-of-war's captain and to a lieutenant he seemed to know quite well. When formalities were ended, the stocky Captain Fisher welcomed her formally aboard, bowed and went below, evidently leaving her in Josh's care. Pigtailed seamen in striped shirts darted to their duties. Josh and Lieutenant Ingram grinned like boys and slapped each other on the back.

"Joshua, you old salt. Never thought we'd see you alive. And here you've traded Frank for a beautiful lady. Glad to make your acquaintance, ma'am," Clint Ingram said with an awkward bow that almost sent him spilling over his own feet when the tip of his sword hooked over the rail behind him.

"Clint, you know they gave me up to a year before you came looking for me," Josh said, then his words slowed. "Frank drowned, Clint, never even made it in to shore alive. There's a lot to tell after I have a briefing with the captain." Clint bowed his head in mourning for their lost friend, then jumped when Josh said, "So I'll ask you to escort Miss McVey below. Lanie, Clint and I went through midshipman's training and fought in the War of 1812 together."

"And haven't seen battle since, ma'am, except against these foul pirates, but I suppose there's a fight coming now, right, Joshua, old salt? Though word is," Clint said, and lowered his voice, "some Seminoles been kicking up their heels again at some place I can't recall."

"Not Ope-hatchee?" Lanie blurted.

"No, ma'am, though that's where there was a real bad battle last winter before the army cleaned out the nest of vipers there," Clint told her, solemn-faced.

"Ope-hatchee," Josh cut in. "Did Sho-caw say they were headed there with all those guns, Lanie?"

She wrapped her fingers around her right wrist where she could still feel the scars from Sho-caw's scratch. And yet he ad said even if she told the Americans, he and his braves 'ould attack at Ope-hatchee first. This war was wrong on oth sides. If Sho-caw attacked, Zeena might lose her man a battle and the whites would hunt down Sho-caw's tribe to ae last woman and child.

"Yes, Ope-hatchee, in revenge for what was done to his eople there," she said, her voice quiet. "But he said he 'ould get there first no matter if I told."

Josh turned away, and Lanie heard him ordering some-ne below to send men to warn the little settlement at Ope-atchee. She walked away and leaned on the ship's rail, ishing everything in life could be cut-and-dried, clearly ght or wrong. But there were all these frightening deci-ions to make somewhere in between, especially when one new the people involved and cared deeply for them, too.

Clint Ingram joined her at the rail. She turned to study im, this friend of Josh's. Clint was not tall, but he carried imself rigidly, with the same gun-barrel posture Josh had aken on since he had come aboard. Under his cocked hat, 'lint had blowaway brown hair and brown eyes and lashes, nd a pleasant, long face with a beak of Roman nose over a eek mustache and a narrow mouth.

"I'm sure you've been through a whole lot, ma'am, on ae run with Josh to get here. May I show you to your cabin ow? You'll want to freshen up, because Captain Fisher will equest your presence at the captain's table tonight—if you ill."

She nodded and took the arm he offered. His move-aents and words were sharp and quick, his eyes jumpy. 'lint Ingram seemed stiffly ill at ease with her, as if he had ot been around women much—or was it that he, too, re-aembered Josh's wife all too well? "So you are from New ork, too," she said.

"Yes, ma'am. Known Joshua since the terrible times his arents sailed away and never came back. My family's rved in the navy since the days of the War for Indepen-ence, ma'am. I volunteered to go with Joshua, you see, on iis rough pirate assignment, but Frank Reynolds got picked a my place," he went on as he escorted her below. In the narrow companionway, trying to give her a wide berth, h‹ scraped his sword along the wall and could not decid‹ whether to lead her down or let her precede him.

She liked Clint Ingram instinctively, and not only be cause he was a friend of Josh's, though the fashionabl‹ young ladies of New Orleans would call him a bumpkin o a bargeman behind his back. Perhaps some time she coul‹ talk to him further about Josh—and his first wife, whon Clint must have known. But there was no time. She patte‹ Clint Ingram's dark blue arm and bestowed a smile on him relieved to be on a friendly, safe ship at last.

That evening, Lanie enjoyed a lovely dinner with Josh Captain Fisher and his six lieutenants aboard the *Norfolk* Everyone marveled at her and Josh's stories of dangers anc escapes, which they told jumping in on each other, just a her parents did. It was as if they had lived together for years By mutual agreement, however, they omitted their real re lationship and their Seminole marriage. A necessity, o‹ course, Lanie told herself. And yet, despite the impropriet‹ of a young unwed woman journeying the tropic wilds witl their Lieutenant Blair, she hated the way it seemed that th‹ deepest ties they shared no longer existed. Didn't the tie remain as strong in Josh's mind as they did in her heart?

Their hosts clung to their every word. And then, at th conclusion of the meal as at the beginning, they toaste‹ Gasparilla's downfall and safe sea lanes for America.

Later, while Josh conferred with Captain Fisher again Lanie strolled the deck on Clint Ingram's arm discussing th‹ day's events. After Lanie and Josh were picked up, th Norfolk had sailed immediately to the stranded J.L. shi Barataria and found that someone had released Justin Lyo‹ and sailed off with him. There were other naval ships in th gulf that could have found the Barataria. But they woul‹ have left a skeleton crew behind, and not carted off th cabin furnishings, so it must have been a pirate vessel. Jos strongly suspected that it was another of Lafitte's ships. Th Norfolk left some men behind to try to get the ship off tl shoal and impound it for the navy.

By sunset the *Norfolk* had met and signaled two other navy ships, one small and innocent looking, the other sporting a checkerboard band of gunports along its hull. But Lanie still feared that Gasparilla's ships and guns could hold off the navy vessels, however sure these men seemed of victory. More than once she had heard the officers say they wanted as many pirates taken alive as possible—for public trials and hangings in New Orleans or New York.

"Quite a day, and yet more dangers to come," she said more to herself than to Clint as they stood at the ship's windswept rail. But she admitted only to herself how much she feared actually facing Boca Grande and Captiva again. It had to be done for the sake of justice and the women captives there, but it was awful to think of sailing in there again, navy or not. She did not hear the footsteps behind them; then she saw Josh tap Clint on his epauletted shoulder.

"May I cut in for this dance?" Josh ribbed his friend. The words were light, but the voice and face were solemn.

"Only if her mama agrees," Clint joked back, missing the tenor of his friend's tense mood. "Miss McVey was telling me she had a rather strict mama. But I realize you have a great deal to speak of, so I'll be about my duties. Miss McVey, good evening."

"Thank you for all your kindnesses, Lieutenant Ingram," Lanie called after him as he strolled off after a hasty bow, during which he inadvertently caught her skirts with the tip of his sword.

Josh looked absolutely devastating in a crisp blue and white uniform with gold piping and mirror-polished boots. "I feel you have a right to be informed of what's going to happen," Josh told her rather formally, and moved his big hand close to hers along the smooth oaken rail.

"Now, that's a change."

"Never mind. I know we've both been through some pretty rough things, but—"

"You are making that excuse so you can pretend there is no more to our relationship than we told everyone tonight. But there is, lieutenant."

"Yes, of course there is. I know that."

"Meanwhile, I will be able to help you tomorrow," sh
put in, triumphant at getting at least that admission. But sh
couldn't discuss marriage and babies and former lovers ou
here on the open deck. But when they got home and he cam
calling at Magnolia Hill—

He cleared his throat. She could tell she had riled him
even in the distant glow of the binnacle lamp. The shadow
along his lean cheeks deepened as he clenched his jaw; hi
lips tautened under his newly trimmed mustache. He looke
as if he would like to seize her where she stood, and she re
veled in the slightest hint that he still desired her.

She tore her eyes away to look out over the inky waters
"Say on, Joshua Blair, about tomorrow," she said, thoug
she would rather have thrown herself at him, all arms an
wild kisses.

"All right, then. As you wish. We are going to use th
small vessel as a decoy to lure Gasparilla out on the gul
where he'll be easier to handle. The armed vessel just ahea
of us, the *Columbia*, will be sailing further south to make
simultaneous raid on Jack Scarfield's men on Sanibel. I wa
able to give them the directions there, too."

"And if you sail in to shoot at Boca Grande as I hear
them say at dinner, what about Jasmine's safety? And ther
may be other innocent people there!"

"Do you think I haven't thought of that? Damn it, I'
even going to find it tough to fire on or arrest old Watch
man if he's still alive after Scarfield's raid, and Tortuga, too
Once you get to know people, it complicates simple hatre
and revenge!"

"Yes, I know," she said, reaching out to cover his han
with hers. They stood frozen at the rail like that for a mo
ment, only their hands and their eyes touching. The int
mate challenge in his gaze caught the light of the lamp, an
seared her heart. "Yes," she said again, but her voice caugh
so she only bobbed a stiff nod.

He cleared his throat again. "And so, if we lure Gaspar
illa or any ship out to take the bait, I'm leading a landin
party on foot to take Boca Grande," he went on. "I'll try t

see that the women are rescued if they're there, and if not we'll sail the smaller ship to Turtle Bay to see if there are any hostages who survived the raid and have been moved there."

He gave more details, but she heard little after he said he was going ashore. He would be recognized, a perfect target for those he had misled and betrayed!

"I'd like to request that you stay in your cabin during all this, but I know better," he was saying. "I remember well enough my first glimpse of you sneaking up on deck when Gasparilla's *Fortune* rammed the *Bonne Femme*. I'm only asking you to be careful tomorrow—and for this."

Before she could resist, he reached for her and pulled her to him for a hard kiss. His hands, between her shoulder blades and on the small of her back, pressed her to him full length; his lips claimed hers with power and determination. Her head swam. Her body soared. But instantly he released her.

"Wish me luck, Lanie," he said simply when she just stared at him. "I know I've lied about a lot, but never about loving you. About all the other—the future—I'm sorry."

"Josh, I cannot see why—"

"I know." He cut her off. "Good night."

He spun on his heel and was gone with a gleam of silver sword.

Chapter Twelve

September 23, 1821, dawned hot and clear. The sea looked lovely, calm and innocent; the blur of beige and green Florida shoreline hovered in morning mist. The American flag at the stern of the man-of-war *Norfolk* lay lank and still. The sun seemed suspended on a tip of bare yardarm just over Lanie's head.

Wearing an officer's cocked hat, which Clint Ingram had brought her for shade, she stood holding a brass and wood spyglass, waiting for the action to start. During the night the big gunship *Columbia* had set out for Jack Scarfield's camp on Sanibel. And just at dawn, the smaller *Reliant* had sailed past the *Norfolk* flying the British Union Jack as if it were a merchant ship, to lure Gasparilla from his lair just miles ahead. If Gasparilla took the bait, the *Norfolk* would swoop in to help the *Reliant*.

Everyone waited tensely aboard the *Norfolk* for a signal from the *Reliant* that she was being attacked. Sailors balanced on their bellies across the lofty yards, waiting to unfurl sail. Officers peered expectantly southward, though they could no longer see the *Reliant* around the curve of shore. And then there was a single boom of distant cannon. Gasparilla must have gone for the lure!

"Crack on sail! All of it! Step hearty now!" Lanie heard Captain Fisher order, then the bos'n repeated his words through his brass speaking trumpet. Sailors untied and dropped canvas. Even in the fitful, feeble breeze, the big sails stirred to drag the vessel forward. As soon as they were out from the hook of land, Lanie saw the action ahead. Gasparilla's favorite schooner *Fortune*, which she recognized only too well, sailed on the ebb tide for the apparently becalmed decoy *Reliant*.

A breeze sprang up to take the *Norfolk* faster, faster. The flag at Lanie's back flapped and crackled. She peered alternately through the spyglass Captain Fisher had loaned her at Josh, standing on the prow, or at the unfolding drama. Soon the innocent-looking *Reliant* would drop her false side to show her four swivel guns and hoist her true colors, the bright stars and stripes. The pirates, evidently still intent on their prey, had not noticed the larger, fully armed man-of-war making straight for them. They would be in close when the battle was enjoined, Lanie thought. It would be as bad as that day the *Fortune* had come right up to take the *Bonne Femme*, and she had looked into the eyes of the blood-lusting pirates!

"Miss McVey, ma'am." Clint Ingram startled her. He had come up beside her when she'd been intently looking through her spyglass. "Joshua says you're to go below if the big guns start."

"I will be careful," she informed Clint, touched that Josh had given her a thought amidst all his worries. "But you may also inform Lieutenant Blair that I am quite done with taking orders, from reformed pirates or navy lieutenants or my parents. Perhaps someday from a husband, and even that is yet to be seen."

Clint looked taken aback. He touched his hand to his hat so hard it went cockeyed. "Well, yes, ma'am, I can tell him that," he clipped out and hurried off with sword clanking.

She went back to worrying that Josh would be a clear target for any pirate sniper who recognized him. He and all his friends were too obvious in those uniforms for anyone wanting to pick off an officer. She wished there was the time and privacy to pull him aside and settle everything—just in case something dire happened. He had kissed her last night, and she had responded. Yet that was not the same as her giving him a good-luck kiss of her own.

She felt beating bird wings in her stomach for him as the two naval ships closed on Gasparilla. She saw clearly in the small glass, which brought everything close, that the pirates had discovered the trap. Shrill shrieks and battle cries went up, like the cries she had heard before the attack on the *Bonne Femme*. But this time their swivel guns and glinting cutlasses stood against the cannon of the navy. Surely Josh's plan to take them alive for trial would succeed now that they realized they were outmanned and outgunned. Lanie shivered with alarm at the thought of facing Gasparilla again under any circumstances. But then chaos crashed all around.

As if he wanted to be blown from the water, Gasparilla's swivel gun raked the *Reliant*, which belched two cannon balls into the *Fortune* below her waterline. The *Norfolk* came about on the quickening breeze, and the deck under Lanie's feet shuddered as they launched a broadside to halt the *Fortune*'s deadly fire.

Sulfur smoke seared Lanie's nostrils as she clung to the stern rail and tried to pick out pirates she might recognize through the drifting smoke. Some were wounded, and a dead man was draped over the rail like a piece of cloth. Others jumped as the once sleek, swift *Fortune* began to list. Pirate vessels were meant to chase and capture, not stand and fight. And then, in Lanie's circle of glass, Gasparilla's face leaped into her view along the rail of his ship.

She gasped aloud. She almost could not bear to look at that demonic, tormenting face, which she had hoped never to see again. The nightmare of her capture and degradation on Boca Grande hit her like a fist in her knotted belly. She wanted to flee, but she kept her glass steady.

It was like watching a scene in a grotesque play. Lanie could tell the pirate chief knew he was trapped, just as he had trapped so many others. He glared and shook his raised fist at the *Norfolk*. Lanie lowered the spyglass to be certain he could not be as close as he looked. When she lifted it again, she cried out. Gasparilla was wrapping a length of heavy chain around his waist, around and around. Realizing what he intended, she lifted her skirts and tore toward the prow of the ship, shouting Josh's name.

Josh stood with Captain Fisher at the rail, watching, pointing, gesturing. "Josh!" she cried. "He's going to kill himself! He's going to jump!" Halfway along the length of the ship, she stopped and stared with all the others as the pirate Gasparilla leaped over the side of his ship and sank immediately from sight.

She stared at the bubbles in the water where he had disappeared even as the *Reliant* edged closer to the sinking *Fortune* to take some swimming pirates prisoner. But the *Norfolk* wheeled away toward Boca Grande, by way of Gasparilla Pass.

"So you watched it all on deck despite my warning," Josh said close behind her. She turned and faced him. "I heard you call me, but there was no way to stop him, Lanie. He chose to die as violently as he lived, and on his terms."

"I just wanted to tell you—what I saw he was going to do," she said, still stunned.

"I should have known better than to think you'd take my advice to go below," he muttered. "But you will go down now, until we're sure that swivel gun Gasparilla has mounted on the crest above the pass isn't going to rake our decks."

He didn't wait for her to move, but grabbed her elbow and marched her to the companionway and down the steps. "It's better than his getting away," he said, almost as if to himself, "but I read him wrong. I didn't think he'd do that. It's going to be harder to shoot men ashore, since the two are gone who directly harmed my parents."

Her heart went out to this man she loved as she thought of all he had faced and conquered. But she was afraid for him now. She could not bear to have him walk ashore in that hornets' nest, even with Gasparilla dead. She turned at the open door to her cabin and met his worried gaze. She knew she had to comfort him and send him off bold and brave, despite what troubles still stood between them.

"I want you to know how proud I am of all you've done, Josh. You've risked your life to live here with them, and all for this day of justice. You have worked for everyone by

Silver Swords

stopping the robbery, capture and murder, which have lasted too long."

He looked surprised. His eyes held hers in a sudden soft caress. "Thank you, Lanie. Whatever happens, thank you for that. And, if you're willing, when the worst of this is done, I told the ship's surgeon to ask you to help him with the wounded. He'll be down for you later, but you'll have to forgive the despicable Silver Swords once more for locking you in. The cabin's not too small. Don't be afraid. Just look out the porthole at the sky."

She moved so quickly it took him off guard. She threw her arms around his neck and kissed him full on the mouth. For one moment he responded hotly as if they had all the time in the world. Then he pushed her gently away; his intense gaze raked her. He looked as if he would speak, but he closed the door and turned the key in the lock.

"Joshua Blair," she cried and hit her fists on the door as she heard him walk away, "you had better take good care of Jasmine and Serafina! And don't trust Watchman not to shoot you in the back! And Honorée and Augusta—"

Her frenzied words were stopped by gunfire rattling across the deck boards overhead. She leaned her forehead on the door, a chill running through her as she thought of the danger Josh and his men still faced. But as she heard and felt the might of the *Norfolk*'s guns answering the challenge, she steadied herself to wait in the little cabin. She sank on the narrow cot to pray and wait.

The big booms of the cannons muted to the crackle of smaller arms. Lanie heard the creak of the winches lowering longboats. Luckily, her small porthole looked out on the beach at Boca Grande, so she could see what was happening. She watched Josh lead three longboats of marines ashore. Like a returning nightmare, the stockade, jetty, warehouses and scattered huts of Boca Grande drifted at her through the puffs of gray gunfire. She picked out the hut where Silver Swords had taken her and Jasmine that first day. She prayed with her eyes wide open now, so as not to miss a bit of action through her spyglass.

Confusion reigned ashore. Groups and individuals ran here and there. Occasionally, bodies crumpled like dark stones to litter the ground. Flames curled up from the warehouses and from Gasparilla's sprawling home, and she wondered if the fleeing pirates had fired them. But then she picked out separate forms holding flaming torches. Women! Six, no eight women running down to the beach with pine torches in their hands. She squinted to pick out familiar forms, but could not recognize one of them. Marines ran from hut to hut, herding the women and children into the square. Many must have fled into the tropical wilderness. Dogs ran in circles, barking at the attacker's heels.

Lanie nearly jumped through the tiny porthole when a rap rattled her door. "Yes, I'm here." She hurried to it. Mr. Forbes, the young, freckle-faced surgeon, stood there sheepishly with her cabin key in his hand.

"Pardon, Miss McVey, but it's safe ashore now and Lieutenant Blair said I was to ask if you would lend a hand there. I'm going now."

Trembling, she went with him. She craned her neck to watch the action all the way in. The marines had quite a group of prisoners. The woman with the torches had been forced to throw them in the surf. Lanie's heart beat faster as she saw Josh emerge from a hut to stride for their boat and help them drag it ashore.

"One injured among those women, Gasparilla's harem there," he informed Forbes. "It's Pamela Ramsay, Lanie," he added as he helped her out of the boat.

"Pamela—in his harem?" she gasped. "But what about the others from Captiva—Jasmine and—"

"Help Forbes," he ordered. "I haven't seen a one, but I'm looking."

The women with the torches had been Gasparilla's harem, Lanie marveled as she followed Forbes to the hut Josh had pointed out. And there, in a tattered yellow gown with the left side of its waistline soaked with blood, lay a wide-eyed Pamela Ramsay. Forbes bent over her and opened his canvas wrap of supplies while Lanie knelt at her side.

"I can't believe all this!" Pamela gasped out, obviously in pain. "Silver Swords and you came back to this hellhole. My ransom never came. It never came, so Gasparilla took me for his harem. And it was awful—"

"We are going to help you, Pamela. You are going to be all right," Lanie promised and took her hand.

"Never be all right again, McVey, never!" She panted and gripped Lanie's fingers so tightly they went white and numb. "You don't know what—that man was really like—and I thought I could use him to get—" She jumped as Forbes cut away a piece of gown to examine her wound.

"It's all right, Pamela. You can forget Gasparilla now."

"Not too bad. Went right through," Forbes muttered to himself as he bent close over the wound.

"Tell me what to do. I can help," Lanie told him.

"Just talk to her. You're doing fine."

"What happened to the others from Captiva?" Lanie asked Pamela. Then Forbes swabbed her wound, and her eyes rolled up in her head and she went limp.

"She's not dead?" Lanie cried.

"Fainted. Better this way," he told her. "Here, take this roll of bandages and these scissors. Go out and wrap anyone who's bleeding until I get to them."

She did as he said, going from one marine to the other. She gasped when she stepped over fat Gunner Joe's corpse, sprawled on the ground with a pistol in his hand as if he still planned to rise and shoot. The marines were burning the empty thatch huts to the ground. Josh appeared again, smoke-smudged and limping.

"Are you shot?" she cried. Sword still raised, pistol in the other hand, he turned and saw her.

"It's nothing," he said, "though if we had more time I'd love some compassionate tending. Old Emma's dead by the warehouse fire," he went on in the same breath. "I think she poisoned herself with some of her own concoctions. I hear Tortuga took Jasmine in after I disappeared and has her in a hut up the beach. They've probably run off, but I'm going to check."

"Jasmine! I'll go, too!"

He turned, and she thought he was going to order her to stay, but instead he said, "Let me lean on you until this damn wound stops bleeding."

They walked unsteadily on the crunchy sand away from the subdued village of Boca Grande. A few pirates had always kept huts down the curve of cove. Josh searched them methodically, making Lanie stand back as he poked his gun inside. The first two were deserted, and he fired them both with his flint box. In the third they found Jasmine kneeling on the floor over Tortuga's sprawled, bloody body.

"Jasmine!" Lanie cried and vaulted forward to hug her, but Josh's hard hand pulled her back. Slowly, Jasmine lifted her dazed, tear-slick face.

"I shot him," she whispered, her wild eyes darting from one to the other. "He was going to kill me so you couldn't rescue me. He said he loved me, adored me, but he wanted to kill me. I—I thought you only kill people you hate. I shot him before he shot me."

"It's all right, Jasmine," Josh told her. "This whole nightmare's all over now."

"Bah, it will never be over! He looked so awful at me while he died! There's just one man I want to kill, and not this one, but he was going to—"

Lanie shook Josh's restraining hand free and knelt beside her friend. "Gasparilla's dead," she comforted as she reached for Jasmine's shoulders to pull her away from Tortuga's body. "We have come to take you home. You have things to do there, a new life waiting in New Orleans. You're going to be free, Jasmine, I promise, and not because I'm marrying Justin Lyon, because I'm not!"

Jasmine tore her gaze away from Tortuga's staring face as Josh bent over and closed his eyes. "You're not?" she asked. "You and Sil—"

"No, it isn't that," Lanie told her quickly, fighting to keep bitter regret from her voice.

"Jasmine," Josh cut in, "where are the other women from the Captiva compound? We've only seen Pamela Ramsay."

Jasmine wiped at her tears with a hem of jade satin petticoat Lanie recognized as one part of her lost trousseau. "I heard a couple got killed in the raid where you all disappeared. I'm not sure who. A few got moved to Turtle Bay. There's a new woman off a ship they just took, too. But Serafina's been back here, though she sure enough regrets it."

"Why?" Josh demanded. "What's happened?"

"She moved into her old hut to wait for you to come back," Jasmine said as she got slowly to her feet with Lanie's help. Her voice seemed lifeless. "I told her come live here where Tortuga could protect her, too, but she wouldn't. Bah." She shook her head and shuddered. "Some of the worst sort been going out there at night, and if she'd run they'd drag her back—"

But Josh, limping and dripping a trail of blood, was already halfway out the door at a run.

He had a good start down the beach, but Lanie was not far behind. She watched him drag his wounded leg more and more. Jasmine hurried after him, too, but then just slumped in a stand of sea oats and stared after them, her thoughts her own.

"Serafina!" he called. "Serafina, it's Sil! Are you here? I've come back to take you away!"

That passionate cry seared Lanie's soul, and she stopped on a gentle dune overlooking the pitiful hut. His concern for Serafina echoed her own, and she winced at the thought of what that loving, pathetic woman might have gone through bereft of the protection of Silver Swords. Where was she now?

"She's not here, Lanie," Josh told her when she caught up to him. "Those foul bastards went back to abusing her, and something's happened. I'm going to look around."

"Let me bind your leg first. You're losing too much blood. Then we'll look for her together," she insisted.

He let her wrap his leg. For an hour they combed the thickets off the shore, calling her name. "Maybe Jasmine was wrong," Lanie suggested. "Maybe Serafina went to Turtle Bay to cook for the captives."

"No," he told her as he gazed helplessly around at the forbidding, thick foliage. "The ashes outside her hut were still warm from breakfast, and inside was the flat corn bread she always made. Hell, I can't spend more time here. I'm going to make a crutch to take the weight off this leg and we'll go back."

They discovered that male prisoners had already been taken aboard the *Norfolk* and put in the brig as Josh had ordered. The women and children were told that a naval ship would arrive sometime next week to take them to Cuba, where most of them were from. The wounded marines rowed out last. Jasmine and the injured Pamela Ramsay were rowed aboard to share Lanie's cabin. The surgeon Forbes, Josh with his boot off and leg wrapped and Lanie were in the last boat to shove off. Behind them, Gasparilla's once lawless town of Boca Grande lay in smoldering ruins but for three huts and the crops they'd spared for the women and children who still stood on the shore cursing at them in whatever dialect or language came to mind.

In the longboat, Lanie moved over so Josh could prop his leg on the seat beside her. The day had made her feel as close to him as she had when they fled the pirates together. And yet she feared that on the ship and then in New Orleans, he would build those barriers between them again. She sighed and gazed shoreward. Then she sat up straight, squinting into the noon sun and shading her eyes with her hand.

"Josh, there on the shore, beyond those screeching women! That girl running and waving her palmetto hat—"

He looked. He yelled, "Halt this boat and put back in! You're right, Lanie. That's got to be Serafina!"

"It is! It is!" she cried as tears drenched her lashes.

Several of the pirates' women screamed at the running girl and shook their fists as she tore past them. Despite his leg, Josh was out of the boat the minute it crunched on the sand. Lanie scrambled after him while Forbes gawked. Lanie stood back as Serafina flew toward them on the slick, wave-washed shore. Her face was bruised, an eye blackened. Her eyes were streaming, but the sad mouth was smiling. Josh held his arms out and she smacked against him to hide her face against the lapels of his dirtied uniform.

"I ran away when it all started. I didn't know it was you!" Serafina cried, her stilted voice muffled against him.

Her heart full, Lanie stood in the surf until Serafina finally glanced her way. The girl opened her mouth to speak. Nothing but a strangled little sound came out.

"He's hurt his leg again, Serafina," was all Lanie could think of to say at first. "Every time he comes ashore, he hurts his leg. I declare you're going to have to keep an eye on him again. And if you'll come to New Orleans with me, I'll find a home for you." Serafina looked startled and uncertain, and impulsively Lanie pulled her into a hug.

When Serafina finally pulled shyly back, she was smiling a little. "Thank you for letting him come back," she said. "I did not think he would come back if he had you."

"I do not have him, Serafina," Lanie said quietly as Forbes helped Josh into the boat. She felt desperate to change the subject. "But I am grateful to you, too, for all you taught me about living off the land. It saved us when we ran from here. And Jasmine's all right, too. Come aboard the ship now, and we'll all be together," she promised, but her voice finally broke.

Lanie let Serafina sit in her seat with Josh's propped, sopping wet foot cradled next to her. She knew they were going to Turtle Bay to rescue the captives. But suddenly, everything that had happened descended to drain her strength. Her eyes on her hands folded in her lap, she felt as afraid as she had that first day when she had been taken to the captives' compound. Only this time, her fear was not that Silver Swords would keep her captive, but that he would free her, leaving her lost and alone.

At Turtle Bay their task was easier. One boatload of marines went ashore armed, but came back with four women and the word that the guards must have deserted and run into the heart of the island. Joyously, Lanie greeted Honorée Clemenceau, Celeste Beaupré and Augusta, Lady Wyndham. A new red-haired Spaniard was with them, who

had only been there for a week. Augusta told them Doña
Inez and Doña Maria had died in Jack Scarfield's raid.
When everyone was settled below with Serafina and Jasmine's help, Lanie headed for the galley to help Forbes, who
was still tending the wounded men.

In the doorway, she overheard an eager young marine
who had led the landing party at Turtle Bay report to Josh.
"I just know I could catch those pirates who escaped, lieutenant. Would you believe one of them dropped some loot
as he ran? Four pocket watches one after the other Clancey
brought back. I bet we could follow that one's trail and nail
him for what he's done!"

"I appreciate your zeal, Keller, but we're going to cast off.
We have what we came for," he told the men. "A string of
pocket watches, you say." As Josh dismissed the man with
praise for a job well done, his eyes lifted to see Lanie.

"A string of watches, imagine that," she said, not moving from where she leaned her shoulder on the door frame.

"You caught me," he said, his blue eyes holding her green
ones.

"Old Watchman could easily have shot that overeager
boy if he went after him in that tropic wilderness," she said.
"I'm grateful it is all over at last. But, Josh, there are just
some things that cannot—cannot really be over!"

He took several slow steps toward her, favoring his
wounded leg, and gently grasped her wrist in one big, warm
hand. "I know. But I can't help it right now with everything else happening."

She tilted her chin up to gaze directly into his narrowed
eyes. They seemed to shutter his inner self from her, and
that panicked her. "There will always be 'everything else'
happening, Josh," she told him, her voice deliberately low.
"We need to talk now."

"Have you thought about the fact I will be sent to sea
again when we get back?" he argued quietly. "Our whole
life might be separations. And what if I die in the line of
duty sometime?"

"Then I would grieve until the day I died, but I would never, never regret the joys of life we had shared and not squandered in the meantime!"

His eyes misted. His nostrils flared as he fought to keep back tears of mingled fear and longing. "You're so bold, sweetheart. Everything looks so easy to you."

"I have learned that nothing worthwhile is easy, Josh, my love. That is not what I said. Just think about it—think about us," she pleaded.

"I do, Lanie. All the time." His gaze caressed her, and she almost threw herself against him despite the curious men across the room. His voice was the merest fervent whisper now. "But I'm so damned afraid my passion for you—our love—might destroy things—destroy you as completely as we wiped out that whole tropical pirate world that thought it was so safe."

"But don't you see, Josh?" she said, her voice shaky despite how strong she meant it to sound. "You're destroying me now—us, our love, all we've had. You're still running and you've never stopped long enough to realize that the risks of living beat the fear of dying anytime. I've learned that the hard way out in the wilds running from dangers, but what have you really learned?"

He stood silently, not answering her, and she knew she would break into sobs before them all. She tugged her arm away and hurried from the room where other conversations lulled and too many eyes peered their way.

So she did not hear the final words Josh mouthed. "I have learned I will love you forever and so must let you go."

During the three-day sail to New Orleans, Clint Ingram was in heaven. He fetched things for Augusta, Celeste and Honorée and escorted them around the deck. Even the saber-tongued, convalescing Pamela had him going in circles with demands that Josh visit her in Lanie's cabin. But Clint politely turned her down each time at Josh's bequest, saying Josh could not walk on his leg, which Forbes had finally dug a bullet from. Soon Clint as well as Josh avoided Pamela, and Serafina did all the fetching for her.

Jasmine, broodingly, kept to herself. She spent so much time staring over the rail into the rolling waves that Lanie had several sailors watch her closely. She tried to talk with Jasmine but came up against the wall of her resistance until Lanie thought she would scream. She could not bear to lose Jasmine—not when she seemed to be losing Josh! Lanie wanted so badly to explain to her friend how this entire experience had changed her, made her grow up, see things through other people's eyes. She wanted desperately to assure Jasmine they would always be friends, but Jasmine seemed so withdrawn. Both Forbes and Josh had suggested Lanie give Jasmine time to rest and heal. Back home in New Orleans, Lanie thought, when Jasmine saw that she was really free at last and escaped her bad memories, things would be different then.

Serafina stuck close to Lanie, and the only row at all in these crowded conditions was when Lanie walked into the cabin and overheard Pamela taunting Serafina. Quietly, Lanie asked Serafina to step outside. Hands on hips, she glared down at the woman who lounged half dressed on her narrow cot.

"You leave Serafina alone!" Lanie warned Pamela. "She has never done one blessed thing to deserve such treatment from you! And she's certainly not to blame for the wound in your body or the ones in your heart!"

"I have no wounds in my heart, McVey! Best worry about yourself for that. You think I don't know how you and Sil carried on in the wilds? And I don't hear he's asked you to be his faithful wife, even if he did turn out to be a damned upstanding soldier boy!"

Pamela's taunts sliced deep. "You're a pitiful, bitter woman, Pamela. And you're the one with an ugly mouth, not Serafina," was the best Lanie could manage. Tears obscured her gaze to make two furious Pamelas. Lanie spun away and closed the door on the ranting woman. But in the hall she smacked right into the eavesdropping Serafina. The two women grabbed each other's arms to steady themselves, then let go and stepped back.

"Sil, he—I mean Joshua," Serafina said, "he does love you, Señorita Lanie, I know he does. I have always seen this," she insisted, even though the droop of her face gave away her own disappointment at her words. Serafina's kindness helped to heal the hurt Pamela had inflicted. Touched, Lanie grasped the girl's hands.

"I just don't know, Serafina. I thought so once," she admitted, and her voice trailed off. "But I do know he's always admired and been grateful to you. There is no doubt about that, at least, and—"

"But that," Serafina interrupted and tugged her hands back, "to be admired—he is grateful. *That* is not what a woman really wants from a man!"

Horrified at what she had blurted, Serafina clapped her hands over her mouth. Her eyes, wide as saucers, stared into Lanie's.

"No, Serafina. No, it is not. And, although you probably do not believe this, I tell you I understand your sadness. I know it is terribly hard to want something—someone—badly and have no real hope..."

Her words trailed off. Lanie leaned wearily on the wall. Did she have one shred more hope to have Josh than this poor, sweet, adoring girl did? But there was no one she could say that to—not even Jasmine, who seemed to have turned from her. And certainly not dear Serafina, who loved him hopelessly, too.

"Now, listen, Serafina, don't go into the cabin alone, or Pamela will bite your head off," Lanie said, changing the subject abruptly and hurrying away.

Behind her, Serafina sat for a long time at the bottom of the steps, her head in her hands. She would give anything, she thought, to be Señorita Lanie for one minute and be free to go to Sil. And then he would look into her beautiful face and love her with all his heart and his body, too. She wished fiercely she did not care for Señorita Lanie, too. But there seemed to be something keeping Señorita Lanie and Sil apart, despite the fire in their eyes when they looked at one another. Since Serafina would never have the man she loved

more than life itself, maybe she could go on living if Señorita Lanie didn't have him, either.

To everyone's surprise, the *Norfolk*, with the little *Reliant* right behind, sailed into the port of New Orleans to a
festive heroes' welcome. The *Columbia*, her hold full of
Jack Scarfield's men, had returned the day before to announce that other pirate-hunting ships followed. All along
the banks of the tawny Mississippi's wharfs and docks,
people stood and cheered. Steamboats shrieked their whistles; crude Kentuckians hallooed from their flatboats. Slaves
loading barges wiped their brows and waved bright ker-
chiefs while draymen along the bank yelled. The bustling
city of gulf and ocean trade rejoiced that their livelihoods
were being made safe with the capture of pirates who had
sapped their profits for years.

"I'll bet there's only one merchant not glad to see us today—if Justin Lyon's made it back here somehow," Josh
told Lanie as she stood between him and Jasmine at the rail
staring at the raucous welcome. "And if he turns up, you
send word to me, Lanie. I want him for questioning, at the
very least."

"Meaning I will not be seeing you in person to tell you?"

"Captain Fisher thinks I'll be sent out very soon."

"Very soon. I see."

"I don't think you do, Lanie. You need time. I do, too."

"Time for what, lieutenant?" she dared, but then looked
pointedly away. What was the use of trying to discuss all she
felt with the entire city gawking? Besides, he was not willing to meet her partway.

She bit her lip to fight back tears. The man at the rail beside her managed to look grim during this welcome, even
when he heard some of the people cheering his name. To her
relief, strength and logic flooded in when Jasmine reached
over to pat her hand.

"Justin Lyon won't dare show his face here ever again,"
Lanie declared to both Josh and Jasmine. Jasmine's touch
tightened on her hand, but Lanie was intent on Josh again.
She would show him that she was not a woman to beg, even

if these were the last minutes they could speak for—well, she
didn't know how long. "Besides, lieutenant, I'd have him
arrested," she added.

"Leave everything to me," was the last thing he said to
her.

The minute they were docked, a well-decorated contin-
gency of naval brass boarded, and salutes went all around.
Josh was instantly surrounded and congratulated. Lanie
heard his name called out by folk along the wharf, stevedores and Creole gentlemen alike. Clint Ingram fought his
way through the crowd on the *Norfolk*'s deck and actually
pecked a kiss on Honorée's cheek while she blushed and
giggled. Lanie was taken aback. Shy Honorée's eyes sparkled, and Clint hardly seemed the bumbler now. Lanie
craned her neck to try to spot Josh in the press of people,
but he was hidden by a wall of cocked naval hats, braid and
plumes.

She kept scanning the crowd on the dock for her parents.
But it was a veritable potpourri of people along the naval
wharf where they had tied up. Barkers sold flowers from
barrows and hawked delicacies from oyster booths piled
with pyramids of shiny shells. Children jigged for pennies
while women sold ginger beer, kept cool in tubs of water,
and piquant redfish stew, which Lanie could smell from the
ship. On the sidewalks under the wrought-iron lacework
balconies, black women with striped tignons on their heads
peddled strong chicory coffee from pots in wicker baskets.
Everyone milled around together—bankers and quad-
roons, soldiers and priests, harlots and frontiersmen.

Suddenly, despite the throngs of people and even Jasmine at her side, Lanie felt very much alone. This wasn't the
way she had imagined things ending with Josh. She might
never see him again. But then she heard a familiar voice,
deep and resonant. A voice always tinged with a bit of Irish
brogue whether speaking English or French. She jerked her
head around. Jasmine had heard him, too; she was squinting into the crowd.

Lanie turned with arms outspread. "Papa!"

"My darling Lanie!"

She burst into tears at last, then fought to stifle them. Her father held her tight to his barrel chest while Jasmine sniffled at her shoulder. "Mama's waiting at Magnolia Hill," he managed, his voice thick. "You know what she thinks of common crowds."

Lanie nodded wildly through her tears. She was finally home at last. And yet, despite her joy, she would have given anything to be leaving on Josh's arm instead.

Chapter Thirteen

Lanie McVey paced across the flowered Aubusson carpet in her big bedroom at Magnolia Hill. Workers were burning the cane fields in preparation for the harvest next week, and sweet smoke tinged the air even here with the punkah fan revolving on the sixteen-foot-high ceiling. Lanie was restless. She would much rather be out with Papa overseeing the purging of the cane fields, which left the weed- and rodent-choked crop standing straight and tall as a man for unhindered cutting. Actually, if the truth were known—and she had not told her parents everything she had shared with her Silver Swords—she would rather be with Josh scouring the gulf for remnants of Florida pirates.

She reached mechanically for the row of bell pulls, which summoned the servants, but she stopped herself before she yanked the silk cord for Jasmine. Old habits died hard, but not fast enough! Jasmine Bouchet was a free woman now, along with her field hand brother Sam, whom Papa had purchased from the Bouchet plantation. Despite the fact that there would be no wedding for Melanie McVey at Magnolia Hill, her dear *Beignet* was free to go. Lanie's parents had been so relieved to have their daughter returned to them two weeks ago that they had promised her any gift she wanted. Jasmine's and Sam's freedom had been her request. That had not surprised them, but the deeper changes in her had.

She was more serious, more actively concerned with other people. Yet she also seemed withdrawn, and they read the

signs well for that. Yes, she had told them when they finally asked, she did love the man who had rescued her,
whom they had never yet met. No, there were no plans for
marriage, although—and here Mama had swayed on her
feet with an attack of the vapors—she would gladly follow
that man anywhere if he but asked her.

But what surprised them most in the new Lanie was her
passion for what Papa called "Yankee, liberal, masculine,
dangerous political causes," which she espoused to anyone
who would listen—complete repudiation of Jean Lafitte and
any businessman dealing with him, peace and land ap-
peasement with the savage Seminoles, no more chasing of
runaway slaves, no more selling or trading of slaves, grad-
ual emancipation of slaves already bought and paid for.

Finally Papa, who had freed a great many faithful servants over the years, suddenly thought it best to strike a deal
with his zealous daughter. The McVeys would work toward
these goals with their own slaves at Magnolia Hill and hope
others saw their humanity and increased productivity as a
guiding light.

It had not been enough, but Lanie could see her papa's
side, too. When everyone saw how well people like Jasmine
and her brother Sam would do with the sachet and potpourri shop Lanie was supporting financially with some of
her inheritance, which Papa had given her, they, too, would
free slaves—and pay them salaries until they got on their
feet. Jasmine was packing to move to New Orleans to open
the shop. Lanie knew she would miss her desperately, but
she had to give her that freedom.

Her bell-shaped canary-colored percale skirts and petticoats rustling, Lanie darted another look out the window
toward the distant burning cane fields. Beyond the row of
Doric columns and sweep of ironwork outside her second-
story window, past the camphor and magnolia trees grac-
ing the gardens and lawns, workers torched the forty-acre
squares of tall, tasseled cane one at a time. Irrigation ditches
eventually contained the cackling, crackling race of flames
billowing black smoke. When each conflagration died

down, in a quarter hour or so, the men moved to the next block, and fires crept once again across the heavens.

Lanie sat on the windowsill. She swung one foot fretfully and brooded. She still worried about Zeena and the Seminoles, who were at war again. She missed Josh terribly and feared it was more his devotion to a dead woman than devotion to his duty that was keeping him away.

Her eyes roamed her familiar bedroom as if she would find comfort there. Her sunny, breezy room was spacious, with its lofty proportions of the grand Deep South Empire furniture such as Justin Lyon used to import and sell. The posts on her white ruffled bed were nearly the size of her waist, and reached almost to the ceiling; the massive rosewood armoire and marble-topped table balanced the scale and elegance of the sixteen-room mansion. This room had always been her refuge. But now she felt as closed in as she had in the Little Hut that day at the Captiva compound. She needed desperately to share all this with her best friend, and after today she wouldn't be able to so easily.

She hurried from the room and down the hall to the servants' back stairs and climbed to the top floor under the dormer windows. Here, in slant-sided cubicles, eight house servants shared rooms so they were always within closer call than they would be if they lived in the slave street out back. The door to Jasmine's dim, narrow room stood ajar. She had a pile of things on the small, low bed and knelt on a rag rug sorting through a wooden chest in the corner. Lanie rapped on the door, and Jasmine turned around with the look of a startled fawn.

"You could've rung for me, Miz Lanie."

"It's to be just Lanie now, Jasmine. You agreed," Lanie insisted and stepped in. "Besides, friends don't ring for each other. They just—visit."

"Old ways die hard," Jasmine said as she bent again to lift out a woolen paisley shawl.

"They're burning the cane, can you smell it? I wish we could go out to watch closer!"

Jasmine stood at last to face her and tossed the shawl on the sunken mattress. "Reckon you could if you want. You always been free."

Lanie sighed. "Not really. Tell that to the people of New Orleans who all wonder if I am a fallen woman now and give me sideways looks when I go shopping at Madame Olympe's. Tell it to Papa or Mama, or—damnation, to my own heart."

Jasmine, in her best gown of beige and brown calico with dark braid and ribbon trim, rested her hands on the taller woman's shoulder. "Still that bad, missing him, now you been back home a while?" she asked, as if she had read Lanie's mind. "Funny how one man goes changin' one woman's life, sometimes for good, and sometimes—just the other way, whether it be a lover—or even a father—"

Their eyes held, brown to green, but there was no jesting as there had been in the old days to lighten the mood. They had both been through too much these past few months to ever go back.

"I'm gonna miss you something awful," Jasmine blurted, "and I'll never thank you enough from both Sam and me. And, *voilà*, I guess I better get back to my fine Creole French if I'm going to sell sweet scents to the *belles mademoiselles* in town," she added with a forced laugh.

She spun away to thrust her goods into a big wicker basket while Lanie watched. "But don't miss me too much," Lanie told her, "as I intend to be in to visit your shop. And you and Sam will have to come out here to get the flowers from the gardens to dry and all. And I declare, I will still always think of you—Jasmine, what is that! Where did you get a gun?"

Jasmine grabbed the pistol that had fallen out of her meager pile of garments and jammed it in the basket. "To tell true," she admitted sheepishly without meeting Lanie's eyes, "I had it for a while. It's not loaded," she lied. She regretted misleading Miz Lanie, but there was one reason they could not share everything as true friends yet. "Honest, I found it, and I'm just gonna use it in case anyone ever tries to take away all you give Sam and me, Miz—Lanie, I mean. Free people got rights to protect themselves!''

"Well, yes, that's true. But I want everything to go so smoothly for you and Sam so you can be models for others I intend to sponsor. Jasmine, we are friends now for good, aren't we? And you'd tell me your deepest feelings and fears, just the way I've told you mine about Josh?''

Jasmine turned to put her hands on Lanie's shoulders again. "I want us to be friends always," she promised, but ignored the last question. Her eyes misted. How she longed to blurt it all out to Lanie, about the man she would gladly die for and could not have because of the man she must kill. But, considering who the man was the gun was meant for, she just couldn't—not quite yet. And besides, Miz Lanie couldn't really understand; she had never been a slave. Deep in her heart, Jasmine knew she still held that against her. The tearful women hugged silently, then both jumped at a knock on Jasmine's door.

They turned to find Serafina there. Although the girl's cleverness was better suited to the kitchens than a lady's *toilette* or *boudoir*, Lanie had refused to banish Serafina to a life of cooking, and the girl moved around the house in the nebulous position of companion and maid, as Jasmine once had. Besides, Serafina moped as much as her mistress did about Josh's being sent away without more than a four-line note to Lanie about his promotion to captain of his own ship and his being immediately ordered to sea.

"Oh, here you be, Miss Lanie," Serafina said with no attempt to cover her mouth as she used to. "Miss Adrienne and your papa, they say to 'request Miss Lanie's presence in the drawing room,'" Serafina told her with the funny little curtsy she had learned from lady Augusta, who had sailed home to London. Honorée Clemenceau was the only former Captiva guest left at Magnolia Hill. She spent a good deal of her time pining for Clint Ingram, who had been sent to northern Florida to help suppress another Seminole uprising. Honorée's longing for Clint depressed Lanie at times just as much as her and Serafina's yearning for Josh!

"Papa's in from the fields while they're burning?" Lanie asked the girl, who only shrugged. She left Serafina to help Jasmine finish her packing and hurried downstairs.

At the bottom of the curve of the first-floor staircase, Lanie paused. Her parents' voices were raised, so she could hear them even through the thick double mahogany doors. She stared at her own frowning image in the gilt-framed French mirror, which also reflected a matched pair of tall Dresden vases. She could not recall hearing her mother's voice raised before, though Papa's sounded much as usual.

"But I declare we don't really know everything that has happened between them, Michael." Adrienne McVey's musical French words were edged with a rare strident tone. "Perhaps we should request that naval officer's presence here—say at the coming harvest ball—so we can decide for ourselves what really is the state of affairs between them! After all, he is rather a New Orleans hero."

"My own dear colleen," Michael McVey addressed his wife with his familiar endearment for her, "she's brooding over the man, I tell you, and we don't need to spy on them at the ball to discover that. It's certainly not Justin Lyon's loss—and good riddance to him!"

"I only know I will not allow our daughter, our only child and heir, Michael, to be courted by someone even remotely unsuitable, not after this debacle with Monsieur Lyon."

"Now, my dearest colleen—" Papa protested only to be buried in the continuing deluge of polished, passionate French.

"Hear me out, Michael! I do not credit some pagan Indian ceremony we finally pried out of Lanie as either lawful or moral. It is obvious neither Lanie nor that naval hero put stock in that sham of a marriage. At first I was relieved he has not been here to make some claim on her, but I really believe we must invite him for Lanie's sake. And now that Justin Lyon is back in town—"

Lanie gasped. Justin was back? But the navy had a warrant out for his detainment for questioning. At least he would not dare come here, or Papa would challenge him to a duel. She had not been able to stomach telling her parents

that Justin had tried to press his advances on her in the cabin
of his ship. But she had told them he had admitted to all
sorts of attachments to Lafitte as well as selling guns to the
Seminoles. And that slur on their daughter's reputation
through her betrothal was much more than sent some men
to the dueling gardens of St. Anthony, near Saint Louis
Cathedral, in this hot-tempered, honor-bound town.

Lanie hurried down the steps and rapped with the painted
porcelain knocker. When she entered, the scene was ach-
ingly familiar. She marveled anew that her parents could
share such passion in private and yet be so proper and polite when anyone—including their own child—entered.

"My dearest," Adrienne McVey greeted her. Miss Adrienne was known to people on the great neighboring sugar
plantations as "iron magnolia" for more than one reason.
Despite her mild-mannered ways, she always knew what she
wanted, and she always got it, including an "unsuitable"
non-Creole husband. But during the years Michael McVey
had won her family over with his charm. Still a stunning
woman at forty-four, Adrienne had auburn hair and pale-
green eyes. She stood a petite five foot three inches, a
smaller, demurer version of her vibrant daughter. Even now
her graceful hands were busy with a lap full of embroidery
and her ramrod-stiff back never touched the brocade chair
as she tilted her cheek up to be kissed.

"I declare," she observed to Lanie with a hint of a nod,
"that little Serafina of yours took a good while to find
you."

"Just seeing if Jasmine needed help, Mama," Lanie said
as she pecked a kiss on the powdered, silken cheek and
smiled at her father. She longed to demand to know all
about Justin's return and to remonstrate their discussing her
and Josh that way, but she had no intention of letting them
know she had added eavesdropping to her heathenish ways.

Michael McVey stood in his field clothes with his kelly-
green hat in his hands—always a touch of Irish green, no
matter how properly and elegantly he dressed. He was
handsome yet, though he had gone rather stout and jowly
at age fifty-four. His square jaw was etched with silvered

chin whiskers, which used to be as blond as Lanie's tresses. He always walked and talked with a heady mixture of authority and élan. And Michael McVey always looked a person—man, woman or daughter—straight in the eye.

"Your mother and I were just discussing if you wouldn't like us to invite Captain Blair to the harvest ball—if he's back in town by then, of course. But it's for another reason I've come in out of the fields today when I need to be there, Lanie. It seems we've a bit of a problem here, and I told your mama you ought to be informed immediately. Justin Lyon has dared to send a slave out from town with the news he's coming to call at any moment."

"Calling? Here? On me?"

"Perhaps on me. At any rate I'm going out to wait for him on the front steps to tell him he's not welcome and can name his weapons and meet me in the dueling gardens if he dares."

"Now, Michael—"

"Now, Papa, you can't—" Both women spoke at once.

"For the love of St. Patrick, both of you listen to me!" he said. "There's something I should have told both of you earlier about the man—the real reason I never wanted him to wed my flesh and blood—and I should have stopped him for it, too, but it's not for the ears of ladies."

"Then, Mr. McVey, I declare, we don't need to hear it now," Mama protested, and her nimble fingers did not stop embroidering.

But Lanie was bursting to know. How could Mama just sit there, eyes properly down, voice controlled as if she had never yelled a bit at Papa earlier? How could she call him Mr. McVey in front of their very own daughter as if they had barely met, as if they had never shared love together?

"Damnation, Papa, just tell us!" Lanie blurted.

Mama gasped as though she had pierced her finger, and Papa colored at hearing his favorite oath tossed back in his face.

"Lanie, that is most indelicate," Mama protested, "and I insist that—"

"No, Mrs. McVey, it's most indelicate I haven't told all of what I knew before," Papa cut her off. "And if it's not for your ears, I'll tell Lanie, as she has to know so we can clear the air before that Captain Blair returns from wherever they've sent him so I can't even settle things with him, either."

"I am the one who needs to settle things with Captain Blair, not you, Papa," Lanie stated. "But tell us about Justin Lyon."

"I shall stay, too," Mama said, her voice as stiff as her back. "Say on, Mr. McVey."

"Lanie, I'm sorry your misfortunes with the pirates made this explanation almost too late," Michael McVey said and crossed the room to put a hand on her shoulder. Lanie could smell the sweet smoke of the sugarcane field on his clothes and hair. "Justin Lyon's a devil of a man, but, I swear by St. Patrick, I didn't know he was in with Lafitte's pirates or selling guns when I allowed you to accept his hand. But I do know, and should have told you long ago, that the man's had a string of mulatto and quadroon mistresses over the years, and planted his seed in most of the slave girls on his plantation and the Bouchets'. But I never let him touch a one of ours here."

That revelation made Mama look up from her work, and fan her face with it, too. "Disgraceful!" was all she managed.

"And a practice he'd not be likely to stop even if he took to wife the most beautiful woman in all of Louisiana," Papa went on, his voice a sad whisper.

But Lanie's mind ran beyond her own predicament. "And that is no doubt why Jasmine hated him," she said. "She knew he used slave women that way. Perhaps that time he was chasing her and I stopped him, he meant to hurt her. She's been too ashamed to tell me, especially when I insisted on getting betrothed to him. And to save my feelings, she never told me. Thank you for the truth, Papa. Thank you both for trusting me. I've got to run up to Jasmine now."

She rushed from the room, her thoughts racing as fast as her feet. Dear Jasmine had been trying to protect her without slandering Justin, but she should have told her everything! After all the terrible things she had been through during their captivity, she could understand how Jasmine felt.

Under a sky boiling with black cane smoke, Jasmine handed her wicker basket to her bulky-shouldered, field-dark brother Sam. The McVeys had loaned them a wagon and horse to take their many baskets, boxes and personal items to town. The boxes contained things they would need to start their business. Jasmine glanced at the big house with a mixture of regret and resentment. But she was thoroughly touched by the things the McVeys had bestowed on her to set up the little shop. As bad as their captivity in Florida had been, some good had surely come out of it for her and Lanie. And how wonderful to have dear, protective Sam with her after all these years of separation. She owed Lanie and her family for that!

Jasmine was so deep in thought that, at first, she did not hear the horses' hooves on the lane. She glanced up, gasped, then reached into the wicker basket Sam had just stowed on the wagon.

"Hey, girl, what you doin' messin' up all my hard work," he scolded, then halted at the look of hatred on Jasmine's face. He craned his head to see who she stared at. He cussed under his breath when he saw it was Justin Lyon. Not only was the man wanted by the authorities, but brother and sister had hated him for years. Sam stood with mouth agape as Jasmine took on Justin Lyon.

"So—you here!" Jasmine's voice startled Lyon as he dismounted with his two companions. "At last, a happy little family reunion!"

Justin glanced nervously at Sam, whom he hadn't seen for years, then at the girl. He hadn't noticed her behind the wagon. She'd always been trouble, damn her. She clasped a paisley shawl around her, as if she hid something in it.

"Out of my way, darkie girl!" he ordered, but his voice shook at the look on her face. "My business here is certainly not with the likes of you!"

"'Course not. Never was!" she shouted. She didn't care if everyone heard now. Today was the end of all her trials. "Not with a man who sold our mama off like some old horse. And after she was fool enough to adore you and give you three fine children."

"Three darkie slaves," he goaded.

"Three fine human beings, and two of them now freed," she answered. This felt so good, even through the jagged, grinding pain, which she had bottled up for years. She was truly liberated at last! "Freed to tell the world all about the real you, Monsieur Lyon *le bâtard*, the same way my friend Miz Lanie told the whole world what you did with that pirate Lafitte. The same way the navy's gonna find you and arrest you—or so they think."

"Get out of my way, you uppity black bitch!" Lyon said, and reached for his gold-headed cane. "You always did need a good beating—your fancy mistress, too!"

"You as good as killed our mama, *bâtard*!" Jasmine's words rent the air. He gasped when he saw the gun she had under her shawl, now pointed right at him.

Sam saw it, too, and said, "Jasmine, girl, easy now. Put that thing down. He a white boss, he a masser, and our daddy!" The big man clambered from the wagon as fast as he could.

"No! He's none of those things! He's no one's master now!" she screamed.

It all happened so fast. Jasmine heard Lanie shout her name and Lyon's from the veranda behind her. Lyon lifted his cane to hit her the way he had so many times—Mama, too. Sam lunged at her, and the gun roared and slammed her hand into her ribs. Lyon swung the cane at her once, twice, and she went down under its fierce blows. Hadn't she shot him? Suddenly, Lanie stood over her, her fists flailing at Lyon, grabbing for the cane, clinging to it. Then Michael McVey pulled Lyon off Lanie. But when Jasmine lifted her head, she saw that Sam was down. He writhed on the gravel walk. There was a bright red stain on his upper chest.

"Sam! Sam," Jasmine shrieked. "Not Sam! Not Sam!" She scrambled to her knees to throw herself over him.

Lanie heard Mama come out on the veranda and call for help. For one moment Lanie stared in shock at the human wreckage of Jasmine's secret. Then she knelt to pull Jasmine into her arms, to hold her off the wounded man. Lanie had heard Sam and Jasmine say Lyon was their daddy! So this was Jasmine's dark secret! Oh, why had she never guessed?

At that moment hoofbeats sounded up the oak-lined lane. Riders—riders all in white and blue. Navy men with Josh at their head.

Lanie grappled the shrieking Jasmine to her to keep her from clawing out Lyon's eyes.

"I hate you, Lyon, hate you!" she was screaming. "You killed her, killed my mother. Sam! Sam, I didn't mean to shoot you—not you—I told Mama I'd never tell, but I had to—had to—"

Lanie gaped at Josh as he dismounted. His eyes took in the jumble of people. "Arrest Lyon," he ordered the man behind him. "Jasmine, quiet now," he insisted, and the young woman obeyed. "What happened here, Lanie?" he asked as he knelt over the wounded man just as Adrienne McVey and two servants bustled down the veranda steps with cloths and water.

"That's Sam, Jasmine's brother," Lanie told him. "She accidentally shot him."

Jasmine fought and bucked in Lanie's arms. Josh held the moaning Sam as Lanie's mama knelt in the grass to staunch the blood with a fistful of cotton.

Serafina appeared, and together she and Lanie helped the sobbing Jasmine onto the shaded veranda. "Sam will be all right!" Lanie comforted her, pulling her head against her shoulder. "So that's why you always hated Lyon so much. He hurt your mama."

Jasmine's hysteria suddenly quieted, and she sat up straight on the padded wooden bench between Lanie and

Serafina. Her contorted face glazed with tears, Jasmine managed to say, "I thought I'd never tell. That horrible, horrible man was—is—my father."

Lanie sat and gripped Jasmine's hands in her lap. "You should have told me. I know I can't really grasp the horrible life you slave women have been through, Jasmine. It's beyond my comprehension, but not my love."

Jasmine's eyes lifted to link with Lanie's. Jasmine's inner terrors shifted and settled. And, for the first time in the long years since she'd been sent away from Mama, she felt comforted.

Over Jasmine's shoulder, Lanie glanced at Josh bent over the wounded man, shoulder to shoulder with her mother, while Papa leaned over them both. She was relieved to see that Josh's men had taken the furious Lyon and his two cronies into custody. She started when Jasmine spoke again, her voice calm.

"I couldn't tell you all before what I swore when my mama died. Bah, it wasn't what you think, but I know I can trust you now. My mama, the beautiful Nola Bouchet, she loved him—actually loved Justin Lyon!" she said in awe, her voice trembling. "He kept her in luxury for years in town, like the best pampered mistress, let her keep me there as a child. But when she bore Sam, he made her send us to the Bouchet plantation where he got her. And when she bore him a second son, he just went and broke her heart."

Jasmine glanced up, then looked at her knees. She shook her head unbelievingly as the memories cascaded over her. "He sold the baby off clear to Alabama. He sent Mama to be a slave after how he'd kept her, but not to the Bouchets, not where she could be near us. I found out where she was and ran away to see her. I found her dying—dying and still in love with that bastard. I swore I'd never tell no one the truth. But," she gasped out through a new deluge of sobs, "I never swore to her—I wouldn't kill him—for all he done." She grasped Lanie's hand in an iron grip. "But I couldn't bear to sacrifice you to him—and now poor Sam."

"If only you had told me sooner, Jasmine. I never would have thought to wed him then! But," she admitted, "I guess

I couldn't really grasp everything you felt until I'd suffered, too. To love a man who hurts you—I want to help you, Jasmine, but I need your help so badly, too—''

Jasmine nodded wildly through her tears. "Now you had your freedom taken, too—now we really know what we mean to each other!" Jasmine choked out, but could not go on as the two women embraced and held hard to each other at last.

Serafina and Lanie still sat beside Jasmine when Captain Joshua Blair rose to his feet on the lawn. He glanced at the veranda, then excused himself to Lanie's parents and climbed the steps. His eyes darted from Lanie to Serafina, then to the distraught Jasmine.

"Lanie, Jasmine, Serafina," he said and nodded to each woman in turn with his cocked and braided hat in his hand. "The moment I got back I heard Lyon was coming here. I came out right away—just barely too late."

He looked so fine, Lanie thought, with the captain's shoulder braid and new epaulets. Each breath she took with him so close made her ache with longing.

"Jasmine, the bullet went clean through him, and seems to have missed the lung," Josh said. "I've seen worse. If you calm down, you can go help Mrs. McVey nurse him."

"He's going to be all right? And that bastard—my father!"

"Lyon? Is that it then? He's going in for questioning and probably worse. Nice of him to return to town the same day I did so I had the honor," he said, as his eyes met Lanie's in some unspoken message. "I regret, Lanie, this is not a social call." She nodded, her hands still tightly grasping Jasmine's. Jasmine needed her now, she thought, and she had to put aside for a while her need for this man.

Josh turned to Jasmine. "I understand you and the wounded man have your freedom, Jasmine. I intend to tell the civil authorities this was an accidental shooting, and I'll take your pistol with me. When he's better you can both be on your way to the city, but you—all of you—will leave justice against Lyon to me. Serafina, you look like you've been treated very well. Until another day, then, ladies."

Serafina cried aloud with disappointment and darted down the stairs to have another word with Josh while Lanie sat with her arm around Jasmine's trembling shoulders. Together she and Jasmine watched Josh touch his hat and nod to her parents, then order his men to move out. Lanie felt devastated. Still no word to her. It was almost starting to seem that he meant to leave forever. And yet he'd helped save the day for her and Jasmine again. And for Papa, too, who would have challenged Justin to a duel and perhaps lost.

The officers and their prisoners rode down the tree-lined lane toward the road by the river. As Jasmine started down the steps to follow the makeshift stretcher they had laid Sam on, she turned to Lanie.

"I wouldn't hate him so much if she hadn't still loved him when she died—after all he did to her," she tried to explain. She lifted her hands hopelessly then slapped them down to her sides. "And there's still so much between you and that man Silver Swords," she added, then frowned as if she didn't know what else to say. "You be careful!" she added and shook her head. "And if you need a friend— Bah, more has burned hot and quick than cane here today—that's all."

Lanie stood, gripping the wrought-iron rail, as Jasmine hurried shakily down the veranda steps to follow her wounded brother. Serafina ran partway down the lane in Josh's dust before she came slowly back.

"Ouch, Serafina!" Lanie cried as the girl yanked another snarl in her hair the day a much improved Sam and Jasmine had finally left Magnolia Hill for New Orleans. "Here, let me have the brush. I can do it."

"Sorry. I did think the flowers pretty in your hair. But I had to tie them in," Serafina admitted with a shrug and a roll of her big brown eyes.

"Pinning would have been quite enough," Lanie told the girl and eyed her in the mirror. The look on Serafina's face suggested she indeed might have liked to pin the flowers right to her mistress's skull. Lanie sighed. This was not working out. Too much—one man too much—stood between their living this close every day.

"Serafina, I know you have not been happy here," she began and turned to face the girl as she continued to brush her hair. "Your skill is really with herbs and flowers and food."

"It isn't that," Serafina said and shifted from one foot to the other with her fists grabbing wads of skirt. "He still loves you, doesn't he?"

"I hardly think one brief visit here with my parents in the room before he sailed again testifies to that. But, in honesty, Serafina, I hope so," Lanie admitted and put the brush in her lap.

Serafina sighed, and tears instantly hovered on her lashes when she blinked. "I knew it from the first. It was like lightning on the dark gulf at night when you looked at each other. I was never right for him anyway. I knew that, Señorita Lanie. But when he had no one and I was in his house, taking care of his meals—those weeks his leg did heal—he was mine then in my heart."

"Of course. I do understand," Lanie managed.

"I did think at first to be near him—even if he looked at you that way no man looks at Serafina—it was enough. But no, inside, I did want more from him. My woman's heart never knows my face looks this way. So, perhaps I could go to town and help Jasmine in her shop—at least until her brother is really strong again, yes?"

"If that is what you would like."

A deep sigh shook the girl's shoulders. "Since I will never be you, it is what I would like second best," she said, and fled before Lanie could put her arms around her.

Chapter Fourteen

After a fitting at Madame Olympe's for her harvest ball gown, Lanie asked the driver of the Magnolia Hill barouche to go around to Jasmine's sachet shop on the way home. She had not visited there since Serafina had gone to work with Jasmine last week. She hated for Serafina to be so unhappy over a man she could never really have, but then Lanie did not have him, either. The Gulf of Mexico had him right now, and she prayed his days away from her would make him yearn for her half as much as she did for him.

Lanie alighted from the barouche in front of the Belle Millinery Shoppe because there was, of all things, a bulky livery wagon parked in front of Jasmine's Sachets and Potpourris. Lively guitar music emanated from the milliner's shop. The wagon in front of Jasmine's announced in bold red letters, "Desso Ross. Horses. Wagons. Stables. By the Docks."

Lanie breathed deeply of the balmy autumn air tinged with Jasmine's flowered scents as she gazed in the window. Everything was balanced and beautiful in the display spread over draped folds of white satin, just as anything Jasmine touched had always been. Lanie gathered her skirts close and stepped in the door. To her surprise, the small outer sales room was deserted. But she heard Jasmine's voice—and a man's—from within.

Embarrassed and surprised by the passionate tenor of the voices, Lanie strolled in and nervously bent to sniff the fragrant potpourri in each wicker basket on the polished

wooden counter. That was not Sam's voice, she thought.
And where was Serafina?

"I told you all, Mr. Ross, nothing's changed! I got duties here, and there's things about me you don't even know
and don't want to!" Jasmine was insisting. "Just because
I'm free from slavery doesn't mean I'm free from private,
personal obligations."

"We all got those, Jasmine, gal, but I'm willing to help.
And you gotta admit you could use someone to deliver your
big orders in a wagon," his rich voice soothed.

"It doesn't take wagons to deliver the dry petals I sell
here. And that's what I've got a big, strapping brother for,
anyway." Jasmine retorted, but Lanie heard that charac-
teristic waver in her voice that always signaled she wanted
something out of reach very badly. Lanie edged toward the
brown silk curtain hiding the back room, wondering if she
should knock to announce her presence.

"But a brother, big and strapping though he might be,
ain't what I'm wanting to be to you at all. There never been
anyone else serious for me all those years, Jasmine Bouchet,
and if you'd just give us a chance," the man's earnest voice
plunged on.

Lanie was listening unashamedly. Who was this Mr.
Ross? Whenever could Jasmine have had time to meet him
all those years ago? Could it be he was the phantom lover
that kept Jasmine from being a virgin the day the pirates had
auctioned her off at Boca Grande? She had never asked
Jasmine about that.

"Desso, please," Jasmine said, her voice quavering.
"You just making this real hard for me. I still got unfin-
ished business I can't discuss. Desso, don't!" she cried and
exploded through the curtain almost directly into Lanie.

"Oh!" Jasmine cried in surprise at seeing her friend and
in dismay at having to shake Desso's warm, sure hands off
her arms.

"Sorry!" Desso growled at both women with a frown.

Lanie mouthed the word. "Damnation!" even as Jasmine hurled herself into her arms. Desso Ross tipped his hat
to both of them and beat a hasty, huffy retreat.

"Who was that?" Lanie asked as Jasmine pulled back from her embrace and smoothed her brown calico sleeves.

"An old acquaintance."

"I declare, he doesn't look much over thirty-five to me."

"Don't joke, Lanie. It's dead serious. I suppose you overheard."

"Some, yes."

"I knew him once before I knew you, and I never quite got over him. And if he isn't the smoothest, most persuasive man I've ever known I don't know who is."

"The elusive Captain Blair," Lanie put in.

"Bah, then we both got it bad," Jasmine admitted and strolled over to rearrange rows of heart-shaped satin sachets in a flat basket on the counter. "We both want our men bad, and there's something in the blasted way."

"Jasmine," Lanie said and touched her arm, "you're still not thinking of getting even with Lyon, are you? The navy's got him locked up, maybe for a long while, and I would advise you to go on living. And if that means a chance to share your life with this Desso Ross, and if you really love him, don't let it pass you by. Well," she said and turned away, "that's the voice of reason if not experience speaking. How is Sam? And where is Serafina? I have a present for her."

"Sam's out delivering, and Serafina's next door at the milliner's—with a man," Jasmine said and tried a smile.

"Serafina with a man?" Lanie could not repress a grin of excitement and relief, which they both shared.

"She's been helping me in more ways than one. She's been getting free ribbons and lace clippings for me from the milliner's scraps because of the shop boy, the milliner's nephew. He comes over here to sweep the shop for free 'cause of Serafina. And she dances next door for him, you see, and—"

"Now, slow down a minute!" Lanie demanded with her palms raised. "Do you think she would mind if I went over with this present for her? I've got to admit I am really curious."

"Hear that guitar music?" Jasmine said and pointed at the wall the two shops shared. Lanie nodded. It was the same wild beat that had spilled out into the street when she arrived.

"The fandango," they said together.

"Every day when Madame Loiselle, the milliner, goes out," Jasmine said. "Just Serafina, the fandango and the one who's helping her forget her Silver Swords. I swear, Lanie, she's finally got herself someone who can return all that pent-up love. I gotta sit with the shop, but she won't mind if you go on over."

Clutching her net purse with the gift for Serafina, Lanie stepped into the street and hurried next door. A bell announcing her arrival tinkled overhead but went unheard, covered by the swell and crash of guitar music. She strode behind the counter and peered into the back room.

Serafina, a peacock feather in her teeth, wild, coal-black hair flying, skirt whirling to reveal a flash of bare leg to above the knee, cavorted wildly on the milliner's cutting table. Ribbons, bits of lace and velvet flew to the floor each time she spun. She clapped her hands and stomped while a red-haired, lanky, freckled boy of about twenty with big hands propped one foot on the sewing chair and strummed an old guitar for all it was worth. He threw back his head and shouted a laugh of pure joy as he watched Serafina twirl. They both looked enraptured, transported. Lanie was startled at the scene, but smiled despite her surprise. At least Jasmine and Serafina had adoring men pursuing them these days, while she felt so desolate and alone.

"Hello, Serafina!" she called in a slight pause as she waved and stepped in.

The music stopped; the passionate chords reverberated in the air. Serafina's skirts settled as she stopped. But rather than being contrite or embarrassed, as the old Serafina would have been, the girl stared, surprised at first, hands propped on shapely hips.

"Oh, Señorita Lanie," she greeted her, her words slightly slurred from the feather in her mouth, which she plucked out hurriedly. "Better days are here than the ones I danced in Gasparilla's kingdom, no? This is my new friend's kingdom," the girl declared proudly with a wink at the gawking, lanky lad. "My old friend, Señorita Lanie, this is my new friend, Vergil Crothers," Serafina declared grandly with a sweep of skirt and feather.

"I'm pleased to meet you, Vergil, and sorry to spoil your fun," Lanie told him. "I declare, I just don't want Serafina falling off and breaking one of those beautiful dancing legs."

The boy nodded with a flash of smile as he helped Serafina step to the chair then down to the littered floor, proud as a deposed queen. Lanie marveled that Serafina returned his smile without covering her mouth, even with the feather.

"Glad to meet you, too, Miss Lanie," Vergil replied solemnly. "I heard a lot about your adventures, I did—all of you in that pirate's village." Lanie wondered what Serafina had told him of her hero, Silver Swords. But, despite Lanie's aching need for Josh, warmth and joy tinged the air here.

"I always thought Serafina was one of the cleverest people I ever knew with her hands and her feet, too," Lanie said. "And I think Serafina's a wonderful cook."

"Me, too," Vergil blurted with an even wider grin. "Serafina's just plain wonderful!"

But it was Serafina Lanie studied now. At each glance and word from Vergil, Serafina obviously fought a battle with herself whether to trust his adoration or run from it. Lanie prayed that, unlike Josh, she would not run.

Tears crowded Lanie's eyes as Serafina returned the boy's stare. Suddenly, Lanie felt out of place in their little world of blatant happiness. She moved a few steps toward the door. Then she saw that Vergil limped as he moved closer to Serafina. It struck Lanie there was something fated about Vergil's limp while Serafina danced so assuredly; something exactly right about his sweet, perfect smile when Serafina's mouth was the way it was.

"Oh, I almost forgot," Lanie said apologetically as they looked her way. She hastily pulled a small package from her netted bag. "Two tortoiseshell combs to keep your hair back when you dance for Vergil."

With sparkling eyes, Serafina hurried over to accept the gift. She thrust both combs into her bounteous hair, then pirouetted once before she hugged Lanie shyly.

"You deserve him, Serafina," Lanie whispered to her. "And I'm telling you, Vergil adores you. Serafina, he looks at you with gulf lightning in his eyes!"

Serafina's gaze widened. Surprised, then delighted at that thought when she had always declared that was the way her Sil looked at Lanie, she nodded. Her hands lifted to the new tortoiseshell combs. "Yes," she managed. "And I can never thank you enough for—for this gift," the girl said, her eyes liquid with unshed tears as Lanie made her farewells to them and left them to their love.

The folding top over her seat kept the hot sun from all but Lanie's knees as the barouche pulled away from Jasmine's shop to head home an hour later. Lanie leaned against the padded leather, her eyes closed, her thoughts flying. Both Jasmine and Serafina had men hotly pursuing them. After all those exciting days with Josh, those nights of sharing love, she had nothing but vibrant, taunting memories. She had thrown herself into the things she believed in, but even friends and dearly held beliefs were not enough to fill her life, not after Josh. This horrible waiting for the navy to send him back again so they could settle things somehow was sapping her strength and her confidence that all would work out well.

Her eyes flew open when the carriage slowed on the busy street. Crowd noise rumbled in the air like thunder. She heard one man's shrill cry above the rest. She saw that they had been caught in a press of people near the posh Saint Louis Hotel where slaves, who could no longer be imported legally, were still bought and sold. The crowd, mostly men, was gathered around a four-foot-high platform. A fat man was calling out the price and description of those to be auctioned. The memory of the scene at Gasparilla's Boca Grande where Jasmine had been sold leaped into Lanie's head. But it was the sight of a tall woman and her girl child awaiting their turn on the raised block that made Lanie gasp.

"Bids will start at one hundred for the pair." The barker's voice carried to her. "But we can sell 'em separate if you like."

"Stop!" Lanie called to her driver over the creak of wheels. "Stop this carriage!"

She was already gathering her skirts and clambering down the single step to the rutted, dirty street before the carriage jerked to a halt. Gingerly at first, then with increasing vigor, she plunged into the milling crowd. She bumped someone and apologized, but kept her eyes on the platform. That woman and child—they looked like Zeena and her Wood-ko!

She made her way closer, saying "Excuse me" and "Let me pass, please." She heard the crowd buzz her name. She thrust aside thoughts that her already scandal-tinged reputation would be further blackened.

"This prime pair real hardened workers, both of 'em," the barker was bellowing over the noise. "Anyone want a closer look, come on up." He saw Lanie for the first time when she climbed the steps. He shook his head and held up one hand.

But Lanie ignored his warning. They had kept her from Jasmine the day she was auctioned off at Boca Grande. They were not going to keep her from helping this woman who looked like Zeena. Zeena! It really *was* Zeena, though the beautiful ribboned Seminole garb had been exchanged for a ragged calico gown and her tribal beads for a strap and chain link around her neck. Zeena stood with her face impassive, her chin held high. If it were not for her grip on the child's hand, Lanie would have thought she was a carved ebony statue.

"Zeena! Zeena, it's me! It's Ha-shay!" Lanie cried.

The auctioneer gaped and muttered an oath. Zeena's head pivoted toward Lanie. Her eyes widened and her lower lip dropped. The trembling Wood-ko stopped crying. Heedless of the chaos her appearance on the slave platform was causing, Lanie hugged the rigid woman to her.

"I was afraid something awful had happened to you—afraid you were dead," she told the astounded woman and tried to ignore the barker's furious sputterings. When he finally took her arm to escort her away, she shook his hand off and turned to Zeena.

"The worst happened to the village," Zeena whispered so the auctioneer would not hear. "Don't know 'bout my man, Sho-caw and the rest. Their war party went off to Ope-hatchee with the guns they got for you. But while they all gone, bounty hunters come lookin' for our village. They kilt and scattered us—old Allapa-taw dead, Cho-fee run off. 'Course they brung Wood-ko and me back as 'scaped slaves. Oh, Ha-shay, I hope it ain't my running away brung those killers to the village!"

"Of course it wasn't. You did all you could to be a good Seminole!" Lanie whispered. "I am going to help you—buy you if I must. Don't you worry!"

"Now you all just hold it here," the auctioneer bellowed over the mounting murmurs of the crowd. "See here, young woman. This here is man's work, and when I said people could have a closer look I didn't mean no ladies, so— Oh, I recognize you now, Miss McVey. Your papa hereabouts, too?" he asked and craned his neck as if hoping Mr. McVey would swoop in to drag Lanie off.

"No, my father is not here today. But he approves of my bringing this woman and her child to Magnolia Hill. You see, she was of great help to me in my captivity, so she deserves her freedom. I must take them with me right now. Their price will be forthcoming, sir."

"Now see here, Miss McVey, they're up for auction for a reason, so's they can be punished for running and fetch the best price. No absentee bidding. And I don't think your papa would stand for a lady causing such a scene."

"Such a scene, as you put it, sir, is disgraceful, and I am the one who does not like it and will not stand for it!" Lanie exploded before she grabbed control of herself again. She had meant to use honey rather than vinegar if possible, but she had absolutely no intention of deserting Zeena.

"Sorry, ma'am," the man insisted. "You gonna have to just clear the platform. This here Negress escaped sure as shooting off some plantation, but won't tell where from. She's on the block to the highest bidder, so you just take yourself off if you're not bidding. She deserves to be sold and she's gonna be, I tell you."

"No!" Lanie said. "She deserves to be free! They all do!" she said, her face thrust inches from the lout's startled countenance. If only Josh were not out of town, she moaned silently. But an inspiration came to her as if he actually stood by her side. For the first time in days she felt less deserted and lonely.

"Besides," she told the beet-faced auctioneer, "this woman is wanted for questioning by the United States Navy about the Seminole wars. Captain Joshua Blair needs her as a witness against—gun sellers and such. And I certainly hope during her testimony she won't have to say you got her illegally or abused her either, not a United States Navy witness! You see, I've been a prisoner in Florida, rescued by the navy just as this woman should have been. You do know about that and who I am, I assume, sir."

Lanie was trembling inside, both with fury and with fear she would not be able to save Zeena. Now she had publicly flaunted her scandalous past, which the whole town whispered of. Dear God, she prayed, at least let her questionable reputation be good for something! And she'd thrown Josh's reputation on the line, although she had no idea when he would return or what he would say about her actions.

"Well, look, ma'am, Miss McVey, I mean, I can mebbe postpone her sale a bit, till she's questioned by the navy and returned to me. But she's worth good money, and she's mine to sell real legal."

"Just tell everyone there's been a mistake, and she'll be at Magnolia Plantation. I'll send you the money for her, and she'll put in a real kind word for you with the authorities, though they're so all fired angry at anyone dealing with illicit goods lately, just like this crowd is."

The auctioneer gasped air like a fish. Protests from the crowd to resume the auction were swelling. The man sputtered and put his hands on his pear-shaped hips. He knew there was just one thing New Orleans crowds had been touchy about lately, and that was the debt they owed the United States Navy for keeping pirates away from their shipping lanes.

"But she's goods and chattel!" the auctioneer protested, this time more quietly. At the tone of his voice, Lanie sensed his wavering. "This ain't legal or ethical at all!" he whispered. He held his hands up to silence the crowd, then hissed at her, "At least the little pickaninny stays, and I'll sell her alone, then!"

"You evidently do not know how the navy questions people," Lanie dared. "The child may be able to tell them something about the Seminoles—and the treatment they've received in New Orleans, too." She risked it all—this man's greed, the crowd's mutterings, whatever tattered remnants of her reputation remained—by stooping to lift the child into her arms. "You'll get your money from Magnolia Hill and your thanks from the navy, too," she dared to throw over her shoulder as her parting shot as she led the shocked Zeena from the platform.

Lanie sensed the man wanted to chase them and drag them back. But as she shoved through the tightly packed crowd toward the barouche, she heard the auctioneer shout, "A little confusion about what's next in the order of things, that's all. Seems the McVey plantation had a claim on those two and the navy's been looking for them, too. Anything for the navy that's gonna rid our seas of pirates so our city trading ships get through!" were the last words Lanie heard before the crowd cheered to drown out his words.

But she still felt hundreds of eyes boring in her back. She was Melanie McVey, the woman who had lived in the wilds with pirates and Indians and a man she had not been wed to and had not married since. Melanie McVey, who had publicly repudiated Justin Lyon and who pranced into slave auctions to hug escaped slaves and insist that the very economic backbone of plantation society, which had bred her, was rotten. It was obvious to most people that she was either a fallen woman or that the Florida sun had done something strange to her brain as well as her skin! A few at the fringe of the crowd even jumped back from her as if she were contaminated or demented. But when she glimpsed the relief on Zeena's face and felt Wood-ko's trusting arms around her neck, her action was worth any price.

"Get in the carriage and take Wood-ko," Lanie told Zeena, and her voice shook for the first time. Her driver, his eyes wide as saucers, looked surprised and shaken. But he helped the women up, then climbed to his seat and grabbed the reins. He clucked to the horses. It was then, as Lanie leaned back limply in the seat, her eyes met those of the man she had seen at Jasmine's earlier that day. He had evidently been passing in his livery stable wagon and pulled up to see what was happening. Amidst all the hostile eyes, Desso Ross shot her a wide grin across the crowd. Then he clasped his hands above his head and wagged them up and down in jubilation at her victory.

Jasmine had been supposed to return to Magnolia Hill for the sugarcane ball a few days later, but instead, after she had already dressed herself in her finest canary-yellow gown to attend, sent Sam at the last moment with a note to Lanie.

"I don't want to let you down, Lanie," the note read, "but you're going to be with Josh tonight and, thanks to some things you said the other day, there's someone I need to be with, too. I know you understand. Desso Ross, he's got his pride, but he's going to have me, too—if he still wants me. Love to my dearest friend, Jasmine."

Just at dusk, Jasmine closed her shop and left Serafina talking with Vergil in the tiny back parlor. Her heart thudding in her breast, she headed toward the docks.

She'd forgotten how bad this neighborhood could be at dark, with white stevedores strolling here and there, but she kept her eyes down and hurried on. Funny, how a little thing like walking with her chin up and eyes lifted was something she'd done since Lanie got her freed. And when Sam had told her what folks were saying in the streets about Miss Melanie McVey marching right up on that slave platform to save a black woman and her child on the auction block, that had made her proud all over again! Despite the curious looks she got from some passersby, she lifted her head and looked straight ahead again.

Her heart pounded as she got closer to the swinging sign with Desso's name painted on it, big as you please. Desso deserved a woman who was already freed so he wouldn't have to spend his sweat-earned money buying her, like he said he'd do when she first met him. Eight years since he'd brought her back after Mama died of heartbreak over that bastard Justin Lyon, but there was no place for hatred on this night. Only, she hoped, for love.

The big doors where the horses and wagons went in and out were barred and dark. But there was a single window in the narrow door, and a lantern just on the other side. It dazzled her eyes just as the looming possibilities dazzled her heart. But what if Desso had asked another woman to-night? What if her heartless treatment of him all this time and her tart tongue the other day had made him forsake those few happy hours they'd had?

The door was ajar, and it creaked open at her touch. Despite the scent of horses, the place smelled wonderful to her, since it evoked such precious memories of comfort and refuge—and passion.

"Desso? Desso Ross, you here?" her voice came out the merest croak.

She heard feet on the steps. "We closed, 'less it's an emergency!" a voice called. At the bottom step he just stopped and stared. The lantern wafted pale yellow light across her expectant face and caressed her buttercup gown, meant for Magnolia Hill's fine sugarcane ball. She had no idea how beautiful she looked to him; he could tell by her enraptured face how he looked to her. She found her voice at last.

"Can't say I came for a horse or carriage. 'Course I figure I do have a mighty big debt to pay to one Desso Ross, and it's been a while, so if there's any interest due—"

"My interest always been due you, Jasmine Bouchet. Well, can't believe it's really you come calling," he managed. His voice trembled, too. He reached out slowly to take her hands. "Getting dark outside. Fine-looking gal like you shouldn't be out in the street without no special escort. Come on up, then. Just having my dinner."

He latched the door with a shaky hand, and she boldly climbed the stairs with him. The years rolled away, but her long-denied feelings for this man rolled back to make her knees like water. Her eyes darted quickly once around his small slant-roofed parlor. His lumpy old settee was still there, but she had a nicer one at the shop that would fit right in here. She only prayed she'd fit right in, too.

"Desso, about everything, I'm sorry," she began as they faced each other awkwardly in the middle of the crowded room. The place suddenly seemed like a palace to her. She opened her mouth to say more, but evidently that was all she needed.

"I'm telling you something, my beautiful gal," Desso said, and wagged a finger at her. "This time you staying for more than one or two nights, you hear?"

"I hear," she said and grinned despite the tears that threatened.

"Well, now," he breathed. "But I mean marriage, too, so you don't go running off anywhere without me, 'cept to that nice sachet shop you got."

"With both our businesses—and us both free—we'll own this city in a year or two," she told him jauntily, her exhilaration at his words coursing through her.

"We both free all right," he said, "but I'm never gonna be free from you. Don't want to be, neither, you hear?"

"I hear, Desso, and it sounds like finally coming home to me."

That was all it took after all those years. And all the pain and separation were banished when they came together in a wild embrace of hands and lips and endearments. Soon, not even her golden gown came between them in the long-delayed celebration of their love.

Chapter Fifteen

The night of the sugarcane ball, the spacious rooms of Magnolia Hill sparkled in the darkness with crystal chandeliers, hanging lanterns and candelabra. In the third-floor ballroom, which ran the length of the house, Jasmine's sweet sachets were strung amidst garlands of gardenias wafting waves of fragrance in the mild October air.

Everyone danced and ate and gawked at the two young people who had defied pirates, Indians and the wilds of Florida. Or so Lanie's friend Honorée found herself telling a pressing crowd who could not wait to hear all about Gasparilla's captives on Captiva from one who had been there, too.

"And Captain Blair was actually the women's jailer there—yours and Lanie's?" one plump women asked Honorée, and fanned her face so hard her pink-plumed headdress flapped. She could hardly fathom being the handsome Captain Blair's prisoner on some tropic isle no matter how Lanie's mama stressed Captain Blair's parents had once been in shipping in civilized New York.

"Did the captain have to duel with that pirate Gas-what's-his-name *and* that deceitful Justin Lyon?" another avid matron demanded with a tap of gloved fingers on the younger woman's arm.

The questions washed over Honorée in a torrent. "I simply must know, my dear—is there a betrothal announcement forthcoming. I mean, after all that time spent wandering around out there alone?"

"And is it true that the greatest pirate of all, Jean Lafitte, is willing to help the army and navy fight the Seminoles just as he fought the British once, and that's why the navy is going to see him in Galveston?"

With a smiling face and smooth excuses, Lanie extricated the flustered Honorée from the onslaught of inquisitors and walked her to the food tables. Lanie knew Honorée was especially worried about the absence of her beau, Clint Ingram, so she tried to keep a good eye on her all evening. Clint had been sent to northern Florida to see that the Seminoles were not harassing the coast now that the pirates had been cleaned out. At least, Lanie chided herself, she did not have to actually worry for Josh's safety, but Clint's return was several days overdue to fret poor Honorée.

"Bless you for my rescue—again, my friend," Honorée said, her china complexion burnished from the heat of battle. "Some of those people just do not let up, and they have a few things that really happened rather confused. And I'm afraid they are treating your Josh the same way over there," she told Lanie as they watched a circle of animated matrons and their starry-eyed daughters surround Josh with their flutterings and questions.

Lanie's first impulse was to charge over to help him, but he was obviously adept at his own rescues. Besides, her emotions were rubbed raw by everything that seemed to be keeping them apart. Every time she even glanced his way, her heart hammered and her mouth went dry as cotton with longing to call out to him. Other people received his glances now. Even his talking to others hurt her when they had so much to settle. Somewhere, somehow, she needed time with him alone this evening, and she had not found it yet. It all welled up so agonizingly inside her that she wanted to scream at everyone to get out of her house so she and Josh could be alone. And yet she talked, she nodded, she smiled somehow through the creeping cold numbness of fear that nothing would be settled between them, and he would simply leave her again.

It tormented her, too, that everything except what mattered most to her in life had gone smoothly tonight. Josh had gotten on well with her parents. In fact, he seemed more their guest than hers as they plied him with compliments and introduced him to their friends. Josh had been more than attentive to her tonight before they had been separated by swarms of guests; his blue eyes had caressed her to make every nerve vibrate. And he had told her they had much to discuss before she brought it up.

But all that promise just out of her reach seemed to only torment her with its closeness—a precious gem dangled but not to be touched or possessed. Lanie had been happy after reading Jasmine's note, which hinted she would be reconciled to her Desso Ross this evening, yet it just made her and Josh seem more estranged by comparison. And all that pain knifed deep inside her with each breath she took.

Still she managed to link her arm in Honorée's as they made their way determinedly toward Josh's little coterie across the room. People strolled along the buffet tables, which were carpeted with food. Covered dishes of spicy shrimp *étouffée*, mirliton pears stuffed with ham and other Creole dishes stretched for yards. In the corner three-tiered Sèvres platters displayed various cakes and pralines. Next to that, huge crystal bowls swirled with iced punches. Lanie had arranged for the same food to be sent out to the slaves, and she had put Zeena, whom she was paying to oversee Jasmine's flower gardens, in charge of it all. Between each waltz, she could hear the noise from the slaves' celebration in back. They, at least, seemed happy and content.

But Lanie could have flown the rest of the way across the polished parquet floor when Josh excused himself from his group and walked straight to her to request the next waltz. Bareheaded, he looked so dashing in his crisp formal white, blue and gold uniform. After chatting with Honorée, he bent to kiss Lanie's flushed, trembling cheek before he escorted her to the dance floor.

Josh was having trouble remaining calm and cool. Lanie looked so dazzling tonight as his gaze swept her. The sea-green satin gown matched her eyes and highlighted the emeralds, which flashed at her earlobes and slender throat. The bell-shaped skirts, puff sleeves and off-the-shoulder neckline dripped lace and ribbons. Entwined gardenias swept back her sun-gilded hair in the soft lantern glow. Yet a deep sadness emanated from her beautiful face, and he silently cursed himself once again for causing that pain.

He had never desired her quite so much, this loving and lovely woman, he told himself as his eyes devoured her. He had tried to talk himself into the courage and the words to give her up, but he would never escape the love he bore her. He had discovered that even out on the freedom of the ocean, pursuing his sworn duty, he was still captive to that love. He felt drawn to her like helpless iron filings to a powerful magnet. Her inner spirit awed him, as did her outer beauty. Her innate generosity and her impulses to help those less fortunate had bloomed to a powerful desire for justice, and he admired that more than he could ever tell her.

But he must tell her all this tonight, he chided himself, before he was sent to sea again tomorrow. Perhaps he could take the risk of making their love legal. Lanie had conquered great odds, both physical and mental, when they had fled through Florida. Surely, her health would keep her safe, even with the risk of childbirth, through their marriage. After all, what had happened to his dear, dead Becky had perhaps been from a flaw in her delicate health, or in her family. It would never happen to his "indelicate" Lanie.

He led her around the dance floor, and they spun so smoothly she imagined they were on their little raft again. They glided and dipped, around and around. She felt dizzy with love. She longed for him to twirl her right downstairs and out onto the veranda and over the dark horizons to his ship and wherever it would take them.

"We have come so far together," she began shakily, her eyes locked with his. It was suddenly as if no one else was in the room—in the entire world—at all.

He nearly missed a step. It seemed she had read his mind. "And, even after the shameful way I've treated you, you've no doubts we should go farther?" he asked tremulously.

"No doubts. But you?"

In answer, he whispered the words she knew he had recited just for her that one dark night on Captiva:

"Doubt thou the stars are fire;
Doubt that the sun doth move;
Doubt truth to be a liar;
But never doubt I love."

"I think I'm ready for us to go on." His voice faltered. "Together. Forever. No matter—what happens."

The waltz ended, and they stood arm in arm, smiling at each other, then, dazedly, at the crowd. As the floor emptied to make room for a group dance, people stared and applauded; many secretly envied the handsome couple, not in spite of their wild adventures, but for them. Lanie blushed, and Josh shook his head in surprise at how everyone made them feel the matched pair, the chosen ones. And weren't they now? he thought. As soon as he found the words to propose to her, the whole universe would smile, too. Then, as if they were alone, he led her from the crowded room onto the balcony, where the music was fainter and the breeze was sweet from the window. It was dim here, for the light of the blazing candles did not reach this private place.

Lanie's knees wobbled with emotion. She leaned her shoulder slightly against his chest and drank him in with all her senses. He rested one hand on the small of her back; his gentle touch there spread warmth to all her limbs. His other hand held her gloved fingers. He smelled wonderful, she thought, like leather and the sea and—just like her alluring Josh.

"This time apart," he began. He looked down almost guiltily at her hand, which he held so hard he almost crushed her fingers. "It's been awful for me, too, but—God forgive me, Lanie—maybe I needed it to wake me up."

"It has been awful, Josh, not knowing if you cared anymore."

He looked up, dumbstruck. "Not cared! Just the opposite! You've never really seen it that way, though I've tried to explain."

"I am weary of explanations, weary of waiting and longing for you. Josh, I do not want explanations or apologies or excuses. I just want you!"

He swept her hard against him, and they kissed as they had those wild pagan times riding the cresting surf or pressed together in the tropical night. His mouth crushed hers, but she met his possessive caress with demands of her own. Now, at last, she told herself, they would never part again—not really part, even when he went to sea. She clung to his epauletted shoulders, dizzy at the thought of really belonging to Josh at last, her silently suffering Silver Swords. They had so much to do—more of this, more talking, more vows of eternal love, which they had never quite had a chance to make yet.

Even as she reached up to pull his lips closer, she decided they would leave the party no matter what her parents and everyone else thought. She could say they were going out back to visit the slave party. They could talk and love and kiss like this forever!

"Josh." The voice startled them. "Sorry, old man, but I—" Clint Ingram said.

Lanie and Josh moved dazedly apart. Clint had evidently passed them on the stairs and peeked in the ballroom before he had seen them in the shadows. His long, serious face was framed by the sea of heads through the entrance behind him. Honorée had spotted Clint from inside and came hurrying out to hug him.

Josh found his voice. "Clint, I'm so glad you're safe!" They exchanged smart salutes, then clapped each other on the back before Clint bent hastily over Lanie's hand and kissed Honorée once more.

"Good evening, ma'am," Clint addressed Lanie. "Sorry to interrupt like this, but it's urgent," he said to Josh and shot him a look Lanie could not read. It was not embarrassment, which she expected on Clint's face, and the word *urgent* terrified her when she and Josh were newly reconciled.

"Orders to report news to you forthwith." Clint's sharp tone cut off a deluge of questions from the crowd that had assembled, "and not much of it good."

Josh made an apology to Lanie and Honorée and started to usher Clint down the stairs to get his report. But Lanie heard Clint's words. "It all concerns Lanie, too, captain," and she went down the curve of staircase after them so fast her skirts swept the steps behind her. Honorée followed halfway to the second-floor landing, and peered over the balcony at them.

"First," Clint told them and fished in his waistcoat for something, "I'd better give you this, Josh." In his big hand, he held out a pocket watch just like Josh's.

"It has J.B. on it!" Lanie gasped. "Josh, your watch! But—Sho-caw had it last!"

Clint snapped the case open and all three of them stared at the familiar painted portrait of Josh's mother. "I recognized this from remembering how lovely she looked when I knew her, Josh, not from the initials on it," Clint told them. He cleared his throat and his sword clanked into Josh's as he shifted feet. "I found it at the scene of the Indian attack we investigated at Ope-hatchee—on a dead Seminole war chief."

Lanie's eyes met Josh's. "Sho-caw dead," she managed, and her insides twisted. Now Zeena had her answer about the fate of the Seminole village men.

"Any Indians taken alive there?" Josh asked Lanie's question for her, and reached out for the watch.

"Not a one." Clint's quiet words pierced Lanie as her legs gave way and she sank on the stairs in a puff of green satin skirts. Quietly, Honorée joined the group and bent to touch Lanie's shoulder. "The Seminole braves killed a lot of whites," Clint told Josh, "but they were overwhelmed despite the audacity and cleverness of the raid."

As Clint told Josh other details, Lanie peeled back the white kid glove from her right wrist. She stared at the threadlike white scars she would always bear from the night Sho-caw and she mingled blood and thoughts. Perhaps that was the closest he had ever come to trusting a white person, the night he had declared all Seminoles were his brothers. She had felt that way, too, she realized, about the Seminoles, about the slaves. But perhaps there was little hope she could ever do much to save either. For Sho-caw's hatred and his bloody revenge, he was gone. But she was trying so desperately to help Jasmine, Sam, now Zeena. Gratefully, she grasped Josh's arm when he leaned down to help her to her feet.

"The other thing's the real reason I rode right out, Josh," he said. "Sorry to tell you this at such a fine event, but someone's sprung your prisoner Lyon right out of the brig on the ship."

"Lyon!" Josh shouted. "But how in blazes—" he clipped out before he realized that Lanie's parents leaned over the balcony to see where their guests of honor had gone. "He'll probably flee the city, but I've got to head back to search anyway," he told Lanie.

He escorted her up the steps to her parents to bid them a hasty farewell. They understood when they heard Lyon was loose again. He thanked them for a lovely night and told them he was putting guards at the bottom of the lane by the levee landing in case anyone unwelcome came calling.

"I declare, we'll be careful," Mama assured him when he bent over her hand. "Our Lanie and her happiness are the most important thing in the world to Mr. McVey and me. You see, Captain Blair, when you lose two other babes in childbirth, you know the worth of the one child God allows you to keep."

Lanie gasped and the elder McVeys frowned at how Josh's bronze face blanched pale as his shirt at Mama's revelation. But he managed to curtly summon several navy men to him and assign them to guard the entrance to the lane all night.

"Josh, please," Lanie insisted as he bowed again to her parents and started away, "I'll walk you out."

They hurried downstairs and outside, with Clint and Honorée arm in arm just ahead of them. On the lighted veranda, when Josh's shaky hands pulled Lanie into the shadow of a pillar, her heart soared despite the terrible news they'd had tonight. How she wanted to assure him that they could overcome anything together. Justin would be found. She would hurry to comfort Zeena and little Wood-ko. Mama's words about her lost babes should not remind him of his own grief. But his words shattered all her strength and hope before she could speak.

"Forget me, Lanie. I'm not the man for you, with my duty always taking me away. I greatly admire and will always love you, but our marriage would not be fair to you. I cannot risk it—especially not now, when—after what your mother said."

"I told you before, I'm not afraid!" she insisted. "Not of marriage, of childbirth, of anything! There is a great lot of grief in this life, my love, but we have to seize what happiness we can. You're no coward, and yet—"

"Only a coward in that I could never bear to lose you by causing your death. Losing you this way is surely better," he choked out, his voice almost a sob. He shook his head, swooped a kiss on her cheek, disengaged her hands from his cuffs and hurried down the steps with a rattle of his silver sword. She stood there, too stunned and bereft to move, until Honorée came to put her arms around her while the men's horses thudded down the lane into the darkness.

Jasmine and Desso had loved and talked for hours, until she insisted he take her home to tell Serafina and Sam their plans and prepare for the wedding. Desso had told her his firsthand view of Miss Lanie rescuing the slave and her child from the public auction block; Jasmine had told him all about their captivity and rescue, and how Miz Lanie had become just Lanie. She had even shared with Desso all about Justin Lyon and her vow of revenge. But her love for Desso had settled that at last in her heart. Her own love fulfilled would make up for Mama's poor, warped love for Justin Lyon. After all, she would never lay eyes on him again.

It was late that night when Desso rode her home on the back of a mare from the stables. They had made their plans for a simple wedding the next afternoon. Only a few friends of Desso's, along with Sam, Serafina and Vergil and, of course, Lanie would be asked. They weren't certain whether they would live above the stables or the shop. As long as they were together, nothing else mattered. As he helped her down in the tiny lane behind the shop, Jasmine was so stunned by the sweep of perfect happiness she was afraid to blink in case it would all explode to the nothingness of a dream.

"You have a good sleep 'cause tomorrow night's your wedding night," Desso told her, his voice still husky from whispered love words and that delicious way he had of talking to her while he touched her everywhere. He pulled her close for a final kiss, and she melted against him. Her arms entwined around his lean waist again to bind him to her. His sweet tongue plundered as if they had all the time in the world—and didn't they?

"Mmm, Desso, you're gonna make me forget myself and ask you in, and what if Serafina or Sam wakes up then?"

"Guess we'd teach them a thing or two!" Desso patted her bottom through her wrinkled yellow skirts. He chuckled at his thoughts of the morrow, then dropped a light kiss and a quick flicker of tongue between her fluted collarbones before he swung regretfully up on the horse's back. He shot her a white smile that lit the dark with its allure and promise, then clucked to the horse and rode away down the alley.

Jasmine blinked back tears of joy and breathed a huge sigh. She only hoped things had worked out as well at Lanie's reunion with Josh tonight. Lanie deserved to be this happy, too.

Jasmine shoved the narrow back door open and went in. She was surprised Sam and Serafina had not left a lantern burning for her. Perhaps Sam had stayed the night at Magnolia Hill where the slaves would be celebrating, too. But surely Vergil had gone next door, and Serafina was in bed by now. She slept just around the corner in a tiny room with one high window.

She heard a sound, then sensed movement in the darkness. "Serafina?" she whispered. But then her foot bumped a big form on the floor. She gasped out Sam's name as she bent over him. He lay bloodied and beaten, his eyes white in his face, and he was bound and gagged. The terror of the day she accidentally shot him leaped at her from the darkness as someone grabbed her and slammed her to the wall.

Hard hands held her, muffled her cry. Where was Serafina? Her eyes rolled in fear as a strange man's ghostly face bent close and his hand pressed her lips against her bared teeth to quiet her.

"Finally come home from cattin', eh, blackie?" her captor whispered in bayou French. "Monsieur Lyon would have been in a real temper if we only showed up with the white McVey bitch instead of both he wanted, eh. Tie her good and stuff her in that sack, Pierre. We've got a good ride ahead of us in the wagon to Magnolia Hill."

Lanie pulled her pale blue satin wrapper close around her batiste nightgown and stopped her pacing to gaze out her bedroom window across the moonlit front lawns of Magnolia Hill. She couldn't sleep despite the silence of the house after the bustle of the ball. Everything unwound through her mind from the beginning. Fear and anger the day Gasparilla took the ship, when she first saw Josh, hanging in the rigging like a demon possessed. And he had possessed her, body and soul.

She recalled the others she had known who had been prisoners one way or the other: Jasmine, Honorée, Pamela, Zeena, even Serafina. Why couldn't people be happy and free? Jasmine was, now, but Jasmine's father was Justin Lyon, a defiling madman who worshiped the notorious pirate Jean Lafitte. And her beloved, brave Josh was a prisoner of his own guilt and fear.

She almost started at a faint movement of her bedroom door. As it opened soundlessly, she stepped against the wall so as not to be seen in front of the window. A petite woman's form. No doubt only Mama looking in to see if she were asleep after everything tonight. No, not Mama. The woman with a dark shawl over her head approached the bed before she saw that no one was in it. Lanie's eyes were so attuned to the darkness that she recognized who it was as the shawl fell from her head.

"Serafina?" she whispered.

The girl sprang back. "Oh," she said, "I did think you were not here."

"Whatever are you doing out here from town at this hour? How did you get past the guards and into the house?" Lanie demanded as she took a step toward her.

"Miss Jasmine, she need your help and—"

"Jasmine? Did Lyon come to see her? Is she all right?"

"She say tell you about Lyon, he has no money now because of the navy taking his plantation, his business. His men tell Jasmine to get money from you. His men say he will leave New Orleans for good if he has money. So Jasmine say come to you."

Lanie grabbed Serafina's wrist. "His men say? But where are Lyon and these men of his?"

"His men waiting in town with Miss Jasmine, but one brought me here. He opened the back door somehow. Lyon, he gone somewhere out of town," she cried as she tried to extricate her wrist from Lanie's strong grip.

Lanie released her to scramble into the first gown she yanked from her armoire. "I've got to get to Josh's men, the ones he left down the lane by the levee," she told the quaking girl. "They've got to tell Josh to help Jasmine. We will have them arrest that blackguard who brought you, too. You say he's in back?"

"Yes, but they want money for Miss Jasmine's life, and you bring it," Serafina insisted. "They got Sam all tied up and Jasmine, too, but one brought me here to tell you," she repeated as if she had memorized a speech.

"All right, all right. Now listen to me. Go and wake my father and tell him what happened. I am going to sneak out the front and go down the lane to tell Josh's men. They can catch that man at the back and go into town to rescue Jasmine and Sam." She held Serafina by her shoulders and peered close at her face. Tears glazed the cheeks and crooked mouth. It was not like Serafina not to meet her eyes. "Please, Serafina, do as I say. Go on!"

Lanie threw a short cloak around her still unhooked gown and from her dressing table seized the flat velvet box that contained the emeralds she had worn that night. She had no eady money, but if the man outside saw her and she had to tall or bribe him, these would have to do. She jammed lippers on her feet and hurried Serafina out into the hall .head of her. For one moment, when she saw the girl waver .gain, Lanie wondered if Serafina meant to defy her. "Sec-•nd door on the right down the hall," she whispered. "Don't be afraid, please, Serafina. Go on!"

Lanie hurried down the front stairs and quietly slid the •olt on the front door. Clutching the jewel box close to her •reasts, she stepped into the blowing night and closed the •oor. Papa would be close behind. She only hoped he did .ot light lamps or make noise until the man at the back was .aptured. She hurried across the veranda and down the teps. And right into a circle of four men who jumped up at .er from the magnolia bushes.

"No sounds, no scream," a voice hissed, and a pistol •arrel glinted dull pewter in the moonlight.

"Just like flushing a pretty partridge from the brush," nother said. "Told you that scar-mouth *femme* would do : if we made it clear we'd kill the quadroon if she didn't."

Lanie's head spun. "Who are you?" she demanded. "Serafina said—"

"Said what she was 'sposed to say. Lyon told us don't •other bringing the feisty little quadroon slut to Galveston .live if it's a bother, so she's our gambling chip," the bulky .an said, more to his friends than Lanie. "But we get more f we show up with both of you."

Lanie saw two more men, one pulling a trussed, gagged, vide-eyed Jasmine forward, and one with a hand clamped •ver Serafina's mouth. Lanie tried to run and scream. A .an's hand came at her with a pistol butt. He banged her on he side of the head, and she crumpled to the grass.

On hands and knees, she fought the blackness, the red •ain. Through a rolling fog, she heard him threaten to hit .er again, to kill Jasmine and Serafina if she did not obey. Iard hands lifted her and put her over someone's shoul-er. They jammed a piece of cloth in her mouth and tied her ands tightly. By the time she realized Serafina, under

threats to Jasmine's life, had never summoned Papa at a[
she knew her own life was probably forfeit now, too.

"Well, lookee here," a voice whispered in the poor bayo
French these men spoke, "she brung us some emeralds fc
our troubles. Come on, boys, out through the back bayou
like we come. We're off for Lyon and Lafitte at Galvesto
with our three little pigeons."

Lanie fought to stay conscious as the lawns, gravel patl
and canefield stubble of Magnolia Hill crunched by und
her captors' feet. A prisoner, her stunned mind taunted he
Captive again, freedom gone for Jasmine and Serafina, toc
They traversed a ditch and the marshy bank of bayo
through the woods of giant live oaks where she had playe
as a child.

The man plopped her in one of the flat wooden pirogue
the shallow, long boats bayou people swore would float o
a dew in the swamps and twisting rivers of the bayou. Di:
zily, her head screaming pain from the blow of the pisto
she watched as Jasmine and Serafina were deposited lik
sacks of cane in the other pirogue. The six men scramble
in, three to a pirogue. By moonlight, they pushed silentl
out into the ebony labyrinth of the bayous.

They traveled for what seemed an eternity. The men I
pine-knot torches, and sharp shadows loomed from th
depths as they poled away from Magnolia Hill. Lanie trie
to clear her head, to reason out possibilities of escape, bu
quite simply, there were none. Lyon's men—or Lafitte's, sh
was not sure since they spoke of "Jean" as much as "Ju
tin"—were brutal, uncaring, and just doing a job. How kin
and protective her Silver Swords had been all along com
pared to this.

When she could, she tried to catch Serafina's or Ja
mine's eyes to send them courage. But the pine torch ligl
only reflected the paired red eyes of huge bullfrogs and a
ligators lurking in the inky waters. The skilled bayou me
wove their way past clumps and clusters of land, then a hal
submerged forest of twisted cypress knees. Ferns, creepe
and silvery Spanish moss grabbed at Lanie as the boa

turned down another channel. The men hacked at brush sometimes and poled through mazes of water hyacinths.

Lanie's stomach twisted with nerves, her heart with fear. In a lagoon hemmed by canebrake, they disturbed a rookery of white egrets, which shot skyward from the trees. When dawn came it seemed as sluggish and amber as the water—thick as gumbo with ooze, roots and decaying life—which lay all around them. Lanie cried silently for herself, for Jasmine, for Serafina, for all those separated from the ones they loved, once they had glimpsed perfect happiness.

Finally, the bayou flowed faster toward the sea, and she smelled the ocean above the rank vegetation and heady smell of muscadine trees. And when the primordial bayou finally emptied itself into the sea, a ship was waiting just off shore—a ship boldly painted on the side with Justin Lyon's and Jean Lafitte's famed monogram, "J.L."

Two days later, the three women were unloaded from the ship five miles from Lafitte's pirate town at Galveston Bay. They were taken on horseback a roundabout way to an unpainted clapboard house, hidden in mangrove thickets a mile from the beach. Lanie soon understood that this was the private retreat of Jean Lafitte, away from his warehouses and his crews' village on the shore. And, she learned, it was serving its secretive purpose well, because American naval ships were in the harbor while their officers oversaw the loading of Lafitte's personal goods for his forced exodus from the gulf coast region.

Lanie's heart pounded in her chest as she strained to hear everything she could while she, Jasmine and Serafina were tied to chairs and ignored in the bustle of final packing. Navy ships in the harbor! Rescue was so close, if only they could escape!

"I told Lyon his pigeons were here but not about the emeralds. We'll split those later," she heard one of their captors tell another. "I've half a mind to tell Lyon we couldn't get the quadroon out of New Orleans alive. I could smuggle her aboard the ship in a trunk before we leave today. Get good coin for passing her around to the boys all the way to South America.''

''The blond one, too, but Lyon's got some kind of idea of his own for her, I guess,'' another man said before he moved away to help pack the last of Lafitte's goods in big chests, which men carted off at regular intervals.

Her eyes scanned the room for possible sharp edges she could use to saw through her ropes. The only cutlasses or knives she saw were securely thrust in the belts or scabbards of the men who packed and carried. If there were only some way to send word to the navy men on the shore that she was a prisoner! Or was there any chance Josh might think she had been brought here? Would he come looking himself?

''Lyon's here!'' she heard someone call outside just before she heard Justin Lyon's voice. All three women stared at the doorway as he filled it. The sharp smell of his cheroot wafted in ahead of him.

''*Sacré bleu,*'' he chortled and tapped his gold-headed cane on his leg. ''My own little former fiancé, Miss Melanie, and my brazen, murdering hussy of a slave daughter just where Lafitte and I want them.''

Chapter Sixteen

Despite her gag, Jasmine screamed at Justin Lyon. He strode in as if he owned the world, immaculately dressed as usual, especially compared to the other sweating, hard-working men who traipsed in and out. Lyon bent over Jasmine and blew a smoke ring directly in her face. When she glared at him defiantly, he thrust her head back with his cane across her throat while she sucked in desperate breaths through her gag.

"Lafitte used to sell slaves like you for a dollar a pound, black ivory smuggling, he called it. But you're my gift to him, an exotic whore to take along when he sets sail. You know, that was why I bought you back years ago. For him. You're good for nothing but pleasuring a man in bed as your mother did. I should never have let poor Nola name you Jasmine, because it was my favorite scent she always wore to bed. And I certainly never should have let Miss Melanie here have you as a gift, even before she got her stupid ideas about your freedom, you filthy little slut." He snorted in derision, and his voice dripped contempt. "Freedom for you and that field darkie Sam is the most asinine thing I've ever heard!"

He kept the cane against Jasmine's throat until her eyes popped and she went limp. Finally, he released her and swung to face Lanie, who tried to protest through her gag.

"*Ma chérie*, so good to see you, so good," he mocked. "You owed me loyalty and obedience before, but now you owe me so much more. That bastard Joshua Blair has impounded all my wealth and goods, but he'll pay, just as you will, starting with this.''

He yanked her gag down, grabbed a handful of her wild tresses and slammed her head against the chair. He ground his mouth to hers until she thought her neck would break. When she was certain she would faint or be ill, he released her suddenly and stepped back, panting. While she sucked in great, ragged breaths, he threw his cheroot stub down and ground it out under his heel.

"You foul, defiling—" Lanie began when she got her breath.

"Curse me all you want, woman, but don't think I have personal designs on such a wanton as you. No, no, you're no longer worthy. I've planned something appropriate to your talents—and I will be returning you to your dear Captain Blair."

"You will? When?"

He laughed in her face and smacked his cane rhythmically against her bound thighs as he answered. "When? After every last man on one of Lafitte's ships departing today has had you en route to South America. Personally, I'd sooner couple with this scar-lip girl here. I don't know why they brought her, but she'll be easy to get rid of."

Lanie beat down her fear of his threats. Somehow she was going to escape this just as she had Gasparilla! And this time she would take Jasmine and Serafina with her!

"Serafina has done nothing," Lanie began, choosing her words carefully, calmly. "She has no part in your quarrels with Jasmine or me. If you intend such dreadful fates for us, at least send Serafina to Captain Blair to tell him. She has done nothing to harm or defy you."

"At least you admit you have, woman."

"I admit I loathe your foul touch and demented character more than I ever thought possible," she dared in the only gamble she could think to take.

He fell for the ploy. Cursing her in a torrent of French, he yanked out a small knife and cut her free of the chair. He hauled her to her feet and anchored her against him with a handful of her hair. "You know, I believe I'll beat both you and my black-skinned, black-souled daughter within an inch of your lives before I give her to Lafitte and you to his crew. Jean Lafitte and I cannot abide defiance and disobedience, you little bitch!''

Her feet still hobbled, her hands still tied, he shoved her flat on her face on the floor and lifted his cane to strike her. Lanie tensed against the blow, but it never fell. After he hit her she would pretend to go limp. Untied from the chair, she might be able to grab a weapon.

"Hold!" a shrill man's voice came in French. "You're a damn fool, Lyon! No one who does business with me beats a woman. And I've heard the last of your bragging about being my bosom friend. It is you who have caused the navy to throw me out of my last American refuge here in Galveston!"

Lanie's cheek scraped the rough rug as she turned her neck to see the speaker, whom she assumed must be Jean Lafitte. From her vantage point on the floor, her wide eyes took in two dusty boots, black trousers and a battered blue frock coat. A stark white shirt and cravat set off the man's swarthy complexion and snapping black eyes. Sleek eyebrows, thin mustache and slick ebony hair brushed slightly forward at brow and temples reminded her of etchings of Napoleon. A single small gold hoop glittered in his right earlobe. He looked to be about forty, near Lyon's age. Everyone quieted, and stared. Jean Lafitte, short and slight as he was, commanded attention and instantly dominated the room.

"Loose her, I said, you lily-livered devil. The others, too!" Lafitte clipped out with a slash of his hand.

Lyon hauled the shaky Lanie to her feet. "But I brought the quadroon for you, Jean, a gift. I know your tastes in women as well as my own," he boasted.

Lafitte sat in a fourth chair and propped his booted feet on a trunk awaiting its turn to be carried out. He looked exhausted and drawn.

"You know nothing of the sort. You do not even know you have become a liability to me in my business, Lyon. To me business is always business. You abuse your own daughter and the woman once your fiancé. You sicken me. And, as I said, untie the ladies," he added with a flick of a hand in their direction.

Lanie breathed a sigh of relief. This man had changed all the rules in this dangerous world with a mere look and word. He seemed so sane compared to the volatile, unpredictable Gasparilla or the demented Lyon. Here, perhaps, was a man she could do business with.

Lyon scrambled to obey Lafitte, first cutting Serafina's bonds. She darted to untie Lanie. Lyon then stood his ground, nervously cradling his cane before the glaring, slouched Lafitte. Lafitte's black eyes pierced them all, one at a time, Lanie noted, as if he were weighing them all in some balance.

"But, but . . . you and I have been wonderful partners, Jean, wonderful," Lyon protested, his voice suddenly pleading. "J.L. and J.L., together all the way! And we will be again in South America where we're going, as soon as you set us both up there."

"Ah, but even before this catastrophe, I wearied of setting you up. Of your hanging on. Of your imitating me with your brags and your tiresome monogram. Of your telling the navy men in New Orleans all about me before I could have you freed. I needed a private partner, not a public, piratical one!"

"Monsieur Lafitte," Lanie said as Serafina bent to untie Jasmine. "I am Melanie McVey of Magnolia Hill Plantation east of New Orleans, and this man abducted me and my two friends. He's made dire threats to us. But if you would only turn us over to the navy, we would tell them you saved us. Captain Joshua Blair, stationed in New Orleans, is a good friend of mine, you see."

"I do see," Jean Lafitte told Lanie cryptically. He stared at her with hooded eyes. "And forgive me for not arising properly and kissing your lovely hand, Mademoiselle McVey. Your precious navy is ordering us out today before they burn us out. It has caused my rather short temper. And, quite frankly," he went on as his booted feet hit the floor and he rose at last in a catlike stretch, "it is not only Monsieur Lyon here at fault. His carelessness has brought the navy here, but you have, too.''

''I—but you mean they have come looking for us?''

Lafitte shrugged and his mustache lifted in the hint of an admiring smile, although his thin lips seemed rigid. ''I'm afraid so. As a gentleman, I'd like to release you to them. But I have other necessary plans for you all. Business plans.'' He drew each word out. He tugged at his earring then shrugged again as his eyes went thoroughly over her. ''*C'est la vie* my beautiful Mademoiselle McVey. Such is life. I myself have learned this the hard way.'' He turned from her and called out, ''Men! To me!'' Three barrel-chested louts who had been carting trunks all afternoon burst in the open door as if they had been hovering just outside. ''Take Monsieur Lyon to the bayou alligator pit. Be certain no trace is found of him or his monogrammed clothing or cane. I,'' he went smoothly on over Lyon's shocked gasp, ''shall deal with the ladies.'' Lafitte drew a tiny pistol from his blue waistcoat and leaned beside the door with his arms crossed on his chest as the three men dragged the pleading, struggling Justin Lyon out.

''Mademoiselle McVey, step over here with me first, please,'' he said politely with a slight bow and a flick of his free hand. He indicated the door to another room, which looked bare as boards. Slowly, her mind racing for a way out her body could not take, she obeyed.

Lanie glanced out the door as two of Lafitte's men gagged Justin Lyon and pulled his hands behind his back to march him into the thicket. Behind her in the main room of the house, the third man guarded Serafina and Jasmine with a gun. Lanie stopped at the doorway of the side room.

''You cannot just murder Lyon like that!'' she protested.

''Execute,'' he corrected. ''Once again, a business necessity.''

''Business it is then,'' she dared, her eyes defiantly meeting Lafitte's bayou black ones. ''I will pay you for our lives.''

''Inside,'' he ordered curtly. To her relief, he put the pistol in his belt, so she obeyed. He closed the door quietly behind them. "A tempting offer, pay from such a beauty," he told her with a twist of lips that might be a smile. "I accept, but only on my terms."

"I cannot allow that."

"I regret I have no time to bargain with you. Such a lovely opponent. Brains and brazenness as well as beauty. That may scare someone of Lyon's ilk, but not Lafitte. He was never as like Lafitte as he deluded himself. Now, I give you your lives," he went on quickly, his black eyes boring into hers. "But you and your friends are leaving for South America with me and my men this afternoon, *mademoiselle.*"

"No, I cannot—we cannot. Please, I will explain everything to the navy. If you just leave us behind, they can take us back safely!"

He shrugged, though he studied her intently. "I'm afraid not. You see, your Captain Blair is on the shore, and he cannot know a thing of this until my ships are too far out at sea to chase."

"He's here? But then—"

"But then that changes nothing. Those United States Navy men must not think I traffic in white women as I used to in smuggled slaves. With Lyon's unfortunate departure, they may not believe I meant you no harm, and who knows what you'd tell them when you're free. That bastard's told them enough already. I prefer to send you back to them after I am entirely out of their reach."

His gaze, usually so guarded, raked her, and she took a step back only to find herself pinned between him and the wall. "*C'est la vie*, my beauty," he told her. "You must learn to accept the fate life deals you and not struggle so hard against it. Ah, but I envy ones like you who think it is worth it to fight. It makes life so much more exciting. But you are going along with me. I must lock the three of you in here now. My men shall soon dispose of Lyon. Then they will take you down the shore several miles until my ship can pick you up later. Too dangerous to smuggle you to the dock in one of these trunks. Your precious Captain Blair might stop us."

"Please, just release us! I will not go with you!" she insisted before she seized hold of her self-control again.

"But I flatter you by even telling you these things," he assured her with a sweep of both hands. "And do not gaze on me that way. I have never forced a women to submit to my advances. Never had to," he said with a sly smile.

"Send us back to New Orleans then, and we will say we were held by Lyon in the bayous but escaped when he fell in the pit." Tears stung her eyelids; her heart galloped. She could not be so close to Josh and be sent away! "I love Josh Blair more than life!" she cried.

"Never tell a man that about his enemy, my beauty. In South America, you will live like a queen until I send you back someday. I have riches hidden beyond belief. Perhaps we shall even come to an understanding between us. But not now. I tell you these things so you can calm the other women. Convince them that obeying me is the only way," he said and tugged at his gold ear hoop.

"And they used to believe in New Orleans you were such a hero and a gentleman!" she spat at him.

He gave a sad little smile and leaned his shoulder on the door, looking defeated and tired again. "I saw you once in the city several years ago," he said as if he had all the time in the world. "You intrigued me even then, you know. You were shopping on the rue Royale. So lovely, so proper a lady, I thought at first. But your eyes kept straying from things your mama showed you. You wanted something else, some adventure in your life. You were rare, special. Never, I thought even then, could that woman just be business to a man. And now I imagine such a woman at my side at sea. I imagine some day she will say, 'Do not send me away, Jean. Let me stay with you!' "

His words and dreams tormented her with their echo of her passions for Josh. "Never! You're as insane as Lyon!" she cried. "Just like Gasparilla!"

He leaped like a panther to press her shoulders against the wall. "Never, never say my name in the same breath with either man. Not Lafitte!" he ordered, his voice harsh with pride. But he released her and stood back. "I put you in charge of those two women," he said, with a toss of his head at the door. "If I were only in charge of you this day, this life would not stretch out so wretched before me!"

He yanked open the door and ordered the guard to put Jasmine and Serafina in with Lanie. Even as the women hugged each other, Lanie heard Lafitte's fading voice giving curt orders outside. Then the door slammed and the bolt grated shut on their little prison.

"There's no time for all this!" Lanie whispered as Jasmine hugged her and Serafina clung to them both.

"I never can thank you enough, Miss Lanie!" the girl told her, her eyes shining like brook pebbles.

"Don't thank me yet," Lanie insisted. "We are hardly out of here."

"But I mean," she said, "thank you for speaking to save my life to Monsieur Lyon out there before! You said send me back to Josh when it is you who loves him so much. For a chance to go back to my Vergil, I am your friend forever!"

"Vergil! Then we have to get *you* out of here at least! And Jasmine—what about you and Desso?"

Jasmine told her briefly, then added, "Bah, now that we got our chance for marriage and happiness, he's gonna think I let him down again! And how about what you and Josh—"

"No time for that now, my friends. Maybe never if we don't get out of here somehow. Lafitte's taking us to South America with him," she told them grimly.

Tears streamed down Jasmine's cheeks, but Lanie soon realized it was not from fear she'd never see Desso again. Jasmine kept glancing out the window. "You cannot see it from here, can you?" she finally asked. "The alligator pit?"

"No. They took him into the thicket. I am so sorry, my *Beignet*," she said and went over to squeeze her arm.

"I wouldn't cry if Mama hadn't loved him to the end. I'm not crying for him," she insisted vehemently, though they both knew, at last, that the daughter's tears were for the loss of her father—long years ago—too.

"Then that's enough for now," Lanie told her firmly. "Somehow, we are getting out of here and down to the navy men watching the loading on the shore! Lafitte said Josh is there!"

Time dragged. A man they had not seen before boarded up their single window with four pieces of wood, though they could still peek out. Voices came and went; they could see men toting chests and boxes from the house. Lanie worked feverishly to pick the lock with a whalebone hairpin. She had gotten out of her room more than once in her childhood after she had been incarcerated for doing something indelicate. Amazingly, the handle soon turned all the way, but they dared not run yet, with people still going in and out. At last, Serafina reported Lyon's two captors had returned without him.

"Then we're doomed," Lanie groaned, raking her hands helplessly through her mussed hair. "They are supposed to take us to some distant shore to wait for Lafitte's ship."

"But all the men, and the three of them, they are walking away!" Serafina cried.

They peered out the cracks between the boards on the window, then scrambled to the door and listened. No voices, no sounds in the house. A plan Lafitte had inadvertently suggested came to Lanie, though the challenge of it staggered the remnants of her courage. She knocked on the door. No answer. She turned to face the excited Jasmine and Serafina. Lafitte had told her to control her friends, and she meant to do just that. But she also had to control her own fears.

"We have to act quickly," she whispered. "We are going to take some things out of three trunks and climb in ourselves. When they carry us down near the shore or up the ship's gangplank, scream for help to the navy men."

Serafina nodded wildly, but Jasmine grabbed Lanie's trembling arm. She did not speak, but her love and admiration washed over Lanie. Jasmine knew Lanie's terror of closed places. Yet this was the only way. No running into the deadly swamps, no dangerous mad dash down to the shore just because closed places devastated her. Jasmine knew her dear friend Lanie would do the impossible to save them all.

Lanie quietly opened the door to the main room, then locked it behind them so the men would think they were still closed in there. Their hearts pounding, they yanked open three of the chests still in the room. They grabbed garments and jammed them up the fireplace chimney. Jasmine lowered the lid on Serafina's frightened face.

"I'll close you in," Jasmine told Lanie. "Don't be afraid. No matter what, I just want to tell you—" Her voice broke. There was no time. She hugged Lanie hard. They heard men's voices. Lanie climbed in and Jasmine closed the lid on her just before Lanie heard her climb into another trunk.

To Lanie's relief, there was no outcry from the men, no trying of the locked door, no sudden search for escaped prisoners. Either they thought the women were still locked in the room or their captors had not come back for them yet.

But there seemed to be no air in the trunk, Lanie thought. Her first impulse was to claw her way out, even as men lifted the trunk. She bumped her head. She held her breath, then breathed slowly, shallowly. It made no difference whether her eyes were open or closed: the solid, smothering blackness was the same.

She felt her pulse racing, heard her heart beating very loudly. She fought to picture light, airy places—the spacious, rolling fields of cane, the open, sunlit sea with Josh. But panic pounded her. She was rolled in that carpet again as a child. She knew she would die. She was trapped in the Little Hut on Captiva. Gasparilla had her and he would keep her here forever. Sho-caw had carried her out into the night, and the blackness of his hatred closed all around. Josh! He was dying of yellow fever! She was losing Josh! Josh was afraid to marry her. But she had to tell him she would not die—not unless he turned away from her forever! She fought back the dark images, tried to steady herself by gripping her arms around her bent knees. It was an eternity to the shore.

"More of Lafitte's private goods?" a voice asked. "Blimey, doesn't matter which ship. Oh, here comes Lafitte. We'll ask him."

Lanie's blood raged in her ears. Lafitte's man might look inside! Was she near any navy men? There were no voices in English yet. How far away was Josh? Should she scream or try to get out and run? Would Lafitte shoot her? And then she was delivered once again by the man she would always love.

"You've got enough clothing trunks for an army, Lafitte." Josh's voice came muffled to her ears. "And I still insist on searching your holds again after they're loaded for the abducted women as well as for Lyon."

Lanie exploded out of the trunk so fast the two carriers yelped and dropped it. She spilled out on the rough dock boards along the sand, gasping for air, blinking in the slant of sun.

"What the hell! Lanie! Damn you, Lafitte!" Josh shouted and held her tight in his arms.

"Ah, but she ruined my surprise for you!" Lafitte insisted, all smiles as he slapped Josh on the back. "I'd hoped not to surprise you until she was on the deck of the ship."

"Serafina and Jasmine are in other trunks." Lanie gasped and squinted in the glare of light to find them.

"You see," Lafitte told the furious yet joyous Captain Joshua Blair, "I saved the three of them from Justin Lyon. He had terrible plans for them. True, yes, Mademoiselle McVey?"

Lanie's wide green eyes met Lafitte's narrowed black ones. "True," she managed. Her mind raced. She could not mislead Josh. Lafitte had not meant for her to escape—had he? Of course, the guards had suddenly disappeared, and she had picked the lock so simply. The three trunks were just sitting there, filled only with clothes so easy to pull out, and Lafitte himself had given her the idea.

"You see," Lafitte explained to Josh in a rush as officers led a shaken Jasmine and Serafina toward them from down the dock where Lafitte's three other ships awaited. "I thought it best the women sail back to New Orleans with you. Since I'm heading south, I mean," he said and shook his head. "I'm pleased they took advantage of the trunks I left for them to stay hidden away until the dock."

"Now see here, Lafitte!" Josh argued. The man was lying, of course, Lanie thought. He had boarded up their window. He had told his men to watch them. Or had he known she really would die before she would belong to another pirate than her own beloved Silver Swords?

"She spoke of how much she loved you when we talked," Lafitte told Josh as if to waylay his questions. "You are a very fortunate man, Captain Blair." He gave a shrug and tugged at his ear hoop. "Remember my advice, Mademoiselle McVey," he told her smoothly, as his dark eyes glittered with reflected sunlight. "Life is much more exciting when you think you can fight fate. *Adieu*."

Before either she or Josh could say another word, he turned to his men and shouted, "All loaded! Torch the buildings! Get the last things aboard! We sail before the sun goes down!" And he strode away from the dock, his black boots crunching sand.

"Lanie, are you really all right!" Josh demanded as he looked her over. "Lafitte and his men didn't hurt you?"

"No, though Lyon's men, who took us from Magnolia Hill, were brutal. We can identify them if they are here somewhere."

"And is that wily devil telling the truth about letting you escape? It seems New Orleans can't decide yet whether he's hero or villain."

"Did he let us? Yes and no. But maybe none of that matters now. Lyon's dead, Josh. Lafitte had his men throw him into an alligator pit when Lafitte heard what Lyon had planned for us." She explained hurriedly to him from the beginning. She wondered if the gentleman pirate Lafitte, once hero of New Orleans when he helped save the city from British attack, had meant to let her go. But she did know one thing for sure, and that was that she was not going to let Josh let her go—ever again!

"I've got orders to let him sail, but I'm going to find out, that's damn sure!" Josh cracked out and started away, but Lanie grabbed his arm.

"Josh, wait. I think we have both learned there must be an end to hatred and revenge somewhere, or there would be no love in the world at all. Jasmine agrees now," she added, and looked at her friends. Jasmine only nodded, but put her arm around Serafina to take her up the naval ship's gangplank.

Josh faced away from Lanie in the sand, watching Lafitte's men scurry like rats up their gangplanks to cast off. Behind them on the shore, buildings went up in a whoosh of flames, just as they had the day the stockade at Captiva burned and the day the navy raided Boca Grande.

Josh thought of how he had lived his early years for revenge against Gasparilla and then against all pirates. How he'd hated Lyon and Lafitte, whom he'd wanted to destroy, too, for what they stood for. But Lafitte had saved Lanie and rid the world of Lyon. He thought of the hatred many whites felt for the Seminoles and the Seminoles for the whites. Another full-scale war was looming, and he knew it was all wrong. Death caused by someone else was to be avoided at all costs. And that was why he hesitated even now when he knew Lanie was looking at him so hopefully. After what he had heard her mother say about her own two babes dying like his and Becky's daughter, he could not propose to Lanie. In these past few days when he thought she might be dead, pain and past ghosts had staggered him.

"I'm going to get you safely home, Lanie. You'll be safe there in the future," he said, and the painful edge to his voice filled her with foreboding. She stepped toward him and turned him to face her on the shore with ashes swirling around them in the wind.

"I feel we've been here before, Josh—not this place, but this situation," she began. "And I cannot bear your running away from me, not again. Go to the ends of the earth if you want, but I'll be right behind you, Josh. If not really there, then in your thoughts and heart. And I will not ever let you go!"

His face looked carved from stone; his voice cut sword sharp. "I want you safe the rest of your life, I said, and I don't just mean from pirates. We're all out of those at last, I think."

"Don't bother to try to change the topic, Josh. You want me safe from ever dying in birthing your child, that's what you mean, isn't it?" she demanded.

"Exactly," he clipped out, his face paling at the agony coming for both of them when he held his ground.

"So you'd rather I go back to Magnolia Hill and wed someone else and die bearing *his* child, is that it? You think you have the future all figured out like some fortune-teller? Just go wed a man I wouldn't love, of course, because I love you and always will." She knew her voice was rising shrilly, but she plunged on. "So we can both be eternally unhappy apart while I marry someone I could never care for, or even bear to have touch me the way you do, and—"

He looked absolutely stricken. The idea of someone else even thinking of or looking at Lanie the way he did sickened him. And if any other man so much as touched her— He felt himself vibrate with smothered violence.

"I didn't mean—" he began, but she did not intend to let him retreat into his convoluted tragic evasions or escapes.

"Don't you understand that women cannot just turn off their love for a man, Joshua Blair? Do you think that your mother would not have wed your father if she had been able to look ahead and see that he would die before her eyes someday? No, she would have loved and wed him and treasured every moment they had together anyway! Would your Becky have refused your proposal? I didn't know her, but she must have been wonderfully giving and strong for you to love her so all these years! Would my mother have turned my father down, a rogue of an Irishman she married against her beloved Creole family's wishes, if she could have seen two lost babies she'd bear him someday? No, because she loved him, and besides, she has a healthy child now!"

"Lanie, please, just—"

"That's the way women are, Josh!" she interrupted. "Like Lafitte said, life's much more exciting—and dear too—if you think you can fight fate. And I do, Josh! And I refuse to run away from love for fear of the pain of possibly parting someday. I'll take what I can get, every second, and not squander one more moment!''

Out of breath, she stared defiantly into his stunned face. "I—I've hated and blamed myself so long—" he stammered. "You're so much stronger and bolder, Lanie."

"But you see, my darling, none of that, not losing your parents or your wife and baby was ever your fault," she said quietly, and took a step closer. She ached to touch him, to hug him to her and soothe away his deep-rooted pain and fears. "And if something dire happens in the future to us, saying yes to love clears you of any blame, not the opposite."

She saw his big body tremble and tears glisten on his sooty face in those little white crinkle marks he had from squinting into the sun. She felt the two of them balanced, suspended on the fulcrum of a compass that fought to find true north and stop its hapless spinning.

But then Josh lifted one hand to her. He took one unsteady step in the sand, and then a larger one. The corners of his lips, which had been pressed so tautly together in denial, hinted ever so slightly at a smile to come.

She clung to him, and he swung her around, once, twice, before they collapsed into the swirl of sand their feet had made. "Lanie, Lanie, I've always loved you. Thank God you were strong enough to save me, save us both!"

"Just you try to get away!" she choked out through a flood of tears she could not stem. Strong! She had never felt so shaken and weak in her life as she sobbed against his chest while he crushed her to him.

"Wait, Lanie, wait!" he insisted, and lifted her glazed face to his. "I swear I'll ask you again later, more properly, but tell me you will be my wife!"

"Yes, yes, yes!" she cried, nuzzling her wet, sooty face against his warm neck, stiff high-collared uniform be damned.

"It's settled then, for good," he said, and in his voice suddenly was that old commanding tone. "For good." He pulled her to her feet. He took her hands and stood her away from him. Their eyes held in the dancing fire glow. Then he slowly removed from his finger the small gold ring that had so long bound him to a hollow, empty life. He dropped the gold band on the sand and pushed it firmly down with his boot.

"Everything new starts here and now for us," he told her solemnly. "I love you, Lanie. I have from the first, and I always will. We're going to live and love with joy till death us do part."

For once, words failed her. But she nodded and kissed him again and again as he lifted her and carried her down the shore and up the gangplank to his ship. From there, they watched Lafitte's fleet sail away with an escort of two United States Navy men-of-war following them. Lafitte's pirate lair burned to raw reds and oranges until it was only ashes in the wind, like everything bad in their pasts.

On their wedding day, December 16, 1821, the New Orleans sky was silver with unspent rain, but it did not matter. Everyone's heart was full that day, and the city had turned out to welcome their own Melanie McVey and the naval hero, Captain Joshua Blair, who had made the southern sea safe for America. The fact that it had taken them a long time to announce their wedding—well, what of that? The bride's tiny waist made it obvious to the citizens of New Orleans that there was no necessity for this match but *vive l' amour!*

En route from Magnolia Hill to the cathedral, Lanie, Papa and Mama rode in the first carriage, which was festooned with swags of gardenias and Zeena's flowers. The barouche had its folding gray top up in case raindrops began. Lanie's lace train filled most of the seat by Mama across from her and Papa. Her bridal gown was cream satin with triple tiers of lace edging the neckline, hem and wrist-length cuffs. A single strand of pearls and pearl eardrop echoed the luminous, perfect skin of her face, bare throat and shoulders. She wore her pale gold hair loose down he back under a wreath of flowers, which held the train. Just for today, Jasmine had done her hair.

As elegant as everything was, Lanie could not help but think that she would have been content to wed Josh—her beloved Silver Swords—barefooted on some southern beach or on the deck of a ship bound anywhere. After the ceremony, they were setting sail for their new life in New York City, where Josh would be a ranking officer in the fleet. Serafina and Vergil, wed last week, were going, too, but Jasmine and her husband, Desso, were staying here, and that was the only great regret in this lovely day.

The city swept by, all brick, pastel plaster and iron-embroidered balconies dripping flowers. Amazed to see crowds on the banquettes along the narrow streets as they neared Jackson Square with its white Spanish-style cathedral, Lanie waved joyously to people whether she knew them or not.

Josh, with their supporters, Clint Ingram and Honorée, rode in the next carriage. Josh and Clint looked dazzling in full-dress navy-blue and white uniforms with glistening swords and feathered cocked hats. Despite the overcast sky, their gold braid, buttons and epaulets seemed to glitter. The third bridal carriage bore Jasmine and Desso and Serafina and Vergil, who blushed more than anyone else. The four smiled and waved as if they were going to their own wedding or at least their coronation. Others of the household staff, including Zeena with a bright red silk turban on her head, came in Desso's bedecked livery wagon bringing up the rear. The McVeys had feted everyone at a huge reception at Magnolia Hill last night, since Josh and Lanie were sailing directly after the ceremony to make Josh's required arrival at New York.

Mr. and Mrs. Joshua McVey emerged after their formal, hour-long wedding ceremony from the grand Saint Louis Cathedral under a tunnel of arched silver swords held by naval officers. Those waiting on the muddy parade ground of Jackson Square exploded in cheers and applause. Holding hands tightly, the bridal couple dashed for the barouche through a shower of rice to challenge the raindrops.

Near the waiting carriages, Lanie saw that Jasmine held
Desso's arm tightly with one hand as she tossed fragrant
potpourri petals with the other. Honorée clasped Clint's
arm; Serafina stood next to Vergil, who gazed only at her.
Zeena, with wide-eyed, waving Wood-ko in her arms, smiled
and cheered.

Lanie and Josh hugged or shook hands with everyone in
reach. Then Jasmine and Lanie embraced again. Jasmine's
eyes were streaming tears despite her smile.

"I never thought I'd be so happy," she murmured in
Lanie's ear. "For both me and my best friend. Freedom and
now love, too—it's heaven on earth. But I'm gonna miss
you something awful! Now, you promised me," she went on
as Lanie's parents joined them, "you all gonna send for me
first time you having a child! Zeena and Serafina can come,
too, and we'll drink bumboo and make some kind of party
out of it!" she declared, but her hand clung desperately to
Lanie's gloved wrist.

At Jasmine's impassioned words, Lanie's worried gaze
met Josh's, but he did not flinch at the mention of a child.

"All that worries me," he said, straight-faced, "is that
any child of ours will have its mother's temper and my
looks."

"My temper!" Lanie cried, but she smiled at Josh with
her eyes and heart, too, for that bravado. They would face
the future like this—a few tears, perhaps, but smiles and
optimism for a life waiting out there for them together!

Papa kissed her cheek and Mama fussed over Lanie's veil.
At the parting from her daughter for a while, the Iron
Magnolia was in tears, too. But she managed a smile at them
as Papa closed the carriage door.

"Don't forget your yearly visits you promised, children.
You'll be glad to see more paid workers every year, Lanie!"
Papa added. "Be happy always, just like your mama and
me," he added and put his arm around his wife. "Driver, to
the docks! We'll be right behind."

Josh and Lanie bounced in the seat as the carriage rolled
away through the crowd. Lanie glanced down, half surprised by the large marquise-cut diamond on her left hand.

Josh's sword pressed against her leg as they rounded a corner.

"Better watch that weapon, pirate of my heart," she told him. "I declare I can wield a pretty good cutlass if I have to, you know."

He grinned and his brown eyes lit with love. "So I recall. And I recall what happened after I took it from you," he said, smugly and cupped a big hand gently over her satin knee.

"Just a little tussle in the surf," she teased, but the familiar delicate butterflies of desire for this man fluttered their velvet wings inside her.

He leaned closer. "And then so much more happened. And much more to come," he whispered and took her lips.

Lanie gave them gladly as she would her whole life. And just then, sunlight leaped in the barouche window to light her diamond and his sword to shining silver.

Epilogue

Magnolia Hill Plantation
Ten years later

I'm so grateful you and the family visit us every year," Papa told Lanie, and patted her hand on his shoulder. Her parents sat on the veranda just after dark, and she was bidding them good-night. Josh had gone upstairs ahead of her to stop their eldest, Charlie, from screeching and running in the halls with a stalk of cane brandished like a sword to scare their other two children.

"Part of being wed to a man of the sea, Papa. Josh always knew the McVey cane ditches led to the river and the river to the sea, and back again." She smiled to see that Mama had slumped against the back of her pillowed wicker chair. Chasing and holding her three lively grandchildren all day had wilted even her steely spirit.

"Finally got Charlie to settle down," Josh reported when he rejoined them. "He dropped off to sleep like a stone. Maybe it was crazy of us to tell him the Gasparilla story when he sailed around Florida this year, sweetheart. He's been playing pirate ever since.

"I don't mind so long as he knows Gasparilla was not the hero and you were," Lanie said as she went to stand by Josh in the doorway. "And I will not have him holding Andrew and Sarah prisoner!"

In answer to that, Josh squeezed her waist and together they headed upstairs. Everyone was exhausted from a long day overseeing the cut cane being hauled in to be milled. In the afternoon, Jasmine and Sam had brought Serafina and Vergil, who were staying with them in town, to a cane party in the sugar house. There they had all sampled the tiny cordial glasses of *cuite*, a thick cane syrup, which the men had followed up with Irish whiskey and the women with anisette. Serafina had danced the fandango to Vergil's guitar. They had helped the children—a total of twelve with Jasmine's five, Serafina's two, Honorée and Clint's son and Zeena's Wood-ko—to string pecans for dipping in the nearly crystallized sugar. Lanie could still smell the sweet odor of the mauling and boiling cane she loved as she and Josh went hand in hand upstairs.

Her peach percale gown with its off-the-shoulder sweep of beige lace swished gently as they peeked in on the children again, then went to Lanie's old room, where they stayed on their yearly visits. Even now, after ten wonderful years with Josh, her garments seemed both too heavy and yet wispily transparent when he smiled at her that way and his eyes caressed her. The heady rush of passion between them had never muted even through three children and their unpopular efforts to free and then pay salaries to black workers here on Magnolia Hill. Their love had only heightened when Josh had been sent to sea. He had finally resigned his commission to begin his own shipping services up and down the New York coast, but still had to spend some nights away. But they were together this night, and the air between them crackled with lightning on the gulf, as dear Serafina used to say.

"It all seems so long ago," she spoke suddenly in the quiet of their room, "and yet only yesterday."

He wrapped his arms around her from behind. "It sure wasn't the game Charlie's made it," he replied. So often Josh sensed exactly what was bothering her or what she would say before she spoke. They sometimes finished each other's thoughts or laughed surprisedly when they both said the same thing at once. "It was serious business then, just as it was the first time you gave yourself to me in the marital act," he went on, his voice barely edged with teasing now. His arms tightened and his tone did, too. "But nothing with you was ever an act, Lanie!"

A smile gilded her lips as she pivoted and they gazed into each other's eyes. He leaned toward her for a kiss and deftly locked the door behind her.

"No accidental visits from would-be pirates for a little while."

"Mmm," she responded, and arched against him at the first addictive, heady taste of his raw desire for her. "I love you, love you, love you!" she murmured as he began to undress her where they stood. Her gown billowed to the floor, followed by her petticoats. She helped him strip off his clothing. They half walked, half waltzed to the bed. He lay her gently on her back as his eyes and hands skimmed her.

She moved perfectly to entice and meet each move he made. He kissed her until she could not think, and she returned the favor. He nibbled, licked, and she did, too. They grasped and held and teased. His face taut with passion, he lifted on one elbow at her side to scan the beauty of her. His eyes and hands moved over her arch of throat, smooth shoulders, her lush, peaked breasts and flat belly hardly changed by the three children she had borne so easily. He skimmed the velvet at the juncture of the thighs she spread so willingly for him as he caressed her sleek skin.

"I declare I cannot even breathe when you do that," she managed, her voice breathless.

"But you're still much, much too dressed," he told her with a deep chuckle as he bent to untie the silk ribbons of her slippers, which she had not noticed she still wore.

"Oh," she murmured and shifted under his hands, unable to hold still even when his eyes and touch were only on her ankles. She sucked in a shaky breath. Her handsome pirate Silver Swords, still marauding her body and her heart, still so devastatingly, captivatingly entrancing.

He bent to kiss the arches of her feet as he untied the slippers, then worked his way slowly, deliberately up. They took turns urging each other on until there was no restraint left. He settled against her, then inside her and rocked the big bed until they shook the world together. They lay warm, still pressed together, breathing in unison in the sweet, heavy night.

"You know," she spoke at last as her thoughts settled, "that day you captured me was really a good thing for me. It changed my life for the best."

"So Jasmine's told me time and again," he responded sleepily. He propped himself up on an elbow to stare at her in the wavering gold of the single candle by the bed. "I've been through some terrible times, too, but *you* saved me, sweetheart. Now everything's the best."

"The very best," she murmured and turned to go to sleep. "No more dashing here and there in the night, no more jumping to someone's orders, no more running—"

Just then, four-year-old Sarah's voice cried out in some childish dream down the hall. They groaned in unison, but both jumped up and grabbed their robes to run to her together.

* * * * *

COMING NEXT MONTH

#29 ROSE RED, ROSE WHITE —Marianne Willman

When Edward IV condemned Lady Morgana's traitorous husband to death and on the very same day betrothed her to bold knight Ranulf the Dane, she was livid. But as they challenged each other relentlessly, the passion of their contempt fast became a love neither strong-willed soul could fight.

#30 MEDICINE WOMAN—Kathleen Eagle

When researcher James Garrett headed west, he was pleasantly surprised that his greatest discovery was not a botanical rarity, but the beautiful, enigmatic Lakota woman, Kezawin. In both their worlds the love they shared was taboo, yet they found no price was too great for their passion.

AVAILABLE NOW:

#27 SILVER SWORDS
Caryn Cameron

#28 WIND RIVER
Elizabeth Lane

 **Harlequin Intrigue**®

High adventure and romance— with three sisters on a search ...

Linsey Deane uses clues left by their father to search the Colorado Rockies for a legendary wagonload of Confederate gold, in #120 *Treasure Hunt* by Leona Karr (August 1989).

Kate Deane picks up the trail in a mad chase to the Deep South and glitzy Las Vegas, with menace and romance at her heels, in #122 *Hide and Seek* by Cassie Miles (September 1989).

Abigail Deane matches wits with a murderer and hunts for the people behind the threat to the Deane family fortune, in #124 *Charades* by Jasmine Crasswell (October 1989).

Don't miss Harlequin Intrigue's three-book series The Deane Trilogy. Available where Harlequin books are sold.

Your favorite stories have a brand-new look!

HARLEQUIN
American Romance®

American Romance is greeting the new decade with a new design, marked by a contemporary, sophisticated cover. As you've come to expect, each American Romance is still a modern love story with real-life characters and believable conflicts. Only now they look more true-to-life than ever before.

Look for American Romance's bold new cover where Harlequin books are sold.

ARNC-1R

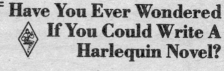

Have You Ever Wondered If You Could Write A Harlequin Novel?

Here's great news—Harlequin is offering a series of cassette tapes to help you do just that. Written by Harlequin editors, these tapes give practical advice on how to make your characters—and your story—come alive. There's a tape for each contemporary romance series Harlequin publishes.

Mail order only

All sales final

Harlequin American Romance®

Gull Cottage

SUMMER.

The sun, the surf, the sand . . .

One relaxing month by the sea was all Zoe, Diana and Gracie ever expected from their four-week stays at Gull Cottage, the luxurious East Hampton mansion. They never thought they'd soon be sharing those long summer days—or hot summer nights—with a special man. They never thought that what they found at the beach would change their lives forever. But as Boris, Gull Cottage's resident mynah bird said: "Beware of summer romances. . . ."

Join Zoe, Diana and Gracie for the summer of their lives. Don't miss the GULL COTTAGE trilogy in American Romance: #301 *Charmed Circle* by Robin Francis (July 1989), #305 *Mother Knows Best* by Barbara Bretton (August 1989) and #309 *Saving Grace* by Anne McAllister (September 1989).

GULL COTTAGE—because a month can be the start of forever . . .
